避疫書信選

從
抱月樓
到
潛學齋

Letters
Written During

the
COVID-19
Pandemic

李保陽、孫康宜——編著

Compiled and edited by
Baoyang Li and Kang-i Sun Chang

序言：奇妙的文字緣

孫康宜

　　這本書的誕生及出版，從頭至尾，見證了一段奇妙的文字緣。可以說，只有「偶然」二字能說明其特殊性。

　　而這個「偶然」也正是我當初向秀威資訊的發行人宋政坤先生（我們一般稱他為「宋總」）提出要出版此書的理由。記得三個多月前（4月19日），我給宋先生的信中寫道：

> 尊敬的宋總：
>
> 　　在這段十分艱苦的疫情期中，我們在美國的人都足不出戶。我目前也正努力於《從北山樓到潛學齋》繁體版（將由貴社出版）和《孫康宜文集》五卷本的簡體版的工作。沒想到就在這樣的情況下，僅僅在一個月不到的時光，有位住在費城附近的傑出年輕學者李保陽博士（大約40歲左右），突然與我開始通信，寫的都是有關閱讀拙作的寶貴心得，每天的電子函一來一去，有時高達數封之多！討論的內容，非常深刻而富啟發性，令我感到驚喜。今天我突然心血來潮，立刻和李保陽博士聯絡，向他建議最好能出版一部書信選……。
>
> 　　……兩人討論之下，果然一拍即合……這本小書可以命名為《避疫書信選：從抱月樓到潛學齋》……這本書可以成為美國……遭遇如此嚴重災難的一個紀念，也可以側面記錄《從北山樓到潛學齋》以及《孫康宜文集》讀者反應的一些花絮，同時還能作為這個時代美國學術界中國研究的一個側影……。

　　且說，當初新冠疫情（COVID-19）剛在美國開始不久，有一天（3月11日）我突然接到一位陌生人的兩封電子函。這兩封信都是深夜寫的，一封寫於午夜之後（即凌晨一點三十六分），另一封於一個小時之內連續發出。這樣的執著引

起了我的注意。我發現這是一個名叫李保陽的年輕人，兩年前才從廣州中山大學中文系取得博士學位，本來獲准留校任教，但後來因發生了一件意外之事，導致他來到了美國，目前他與家人居住在費城郊外的「思故客」（Schuylkill）河畔，他將自己的書齋取名為「抱月樓」。同時，引起我特別關注的是，他在第一封信裡寫到：「前兩天，保陽在先生母校普林斯頓圖書館借到大著《耶魯潛學集》……夜讀先生鴻文，竟引起許多舊事，悵觸百端……。」一提起我的母校普林斯頓，一切有關半世紀前我在普大校園裡的往事，忽然變得歷歷在目。當年的師長大多已經作古多年，而今日的我亦已老邁，自然令我感慨萬分。

李保陽的第二封信也同樣引起我的感動：

孫先生尊鑒：

讀您的《潛學齋隨想錄》，大約是您中年而後之筆，溫潤而透滿生活與生命的智慧。尤其是溢於字理行間的神性，尤其讓人感動！真想讀一讀二十多年後的今天，您對生活，對生命的體悟！

保陽特別喜歡第二十二則馬克吐溫的話。猶記保陽曾在博士論文後記中說過：「人總是會在某一個瞬間，認識到自己的平庸。也總是會在某一瞬間，接受自己的平庸，從而跟這個世界，以及跟這個世界彆扭著的自己達成和解。」保陽覺得這兩句話有比較接近的意思。

《隨想錄》第十四則倒數第二行的「雨窗」誤植作「雨窗」。保陽作過編輯，對錯字比較敏感，請　先生見諒！順頌

教安！

保陽再拜

「人總是會在某一個瞬間，認識到自己的平庸」。啊！那是何等充滿智慧的話！當我讀到那一句時，我立刻意識到這位名叫李保陽的年輕人絕不「平庸」。所以當時我立刻把兩封信打印出來，準備不久之後回覆他。

沒想到後來疫情突然變得十分嚴重，耶魯大學也開始全面改為線上（Zoom）教學。一向對於電腦技術不甚熟練的我，突然為了網上備課而忙得焦頭爛額。所以一直拖到3月29日那天晚上，我才終於能靜下心來，一封一封地回

覆兩個星期來所積壓下來的無數電子函。其中一封就是寫給李保陽的，我當時也順便把臺灣版的拙著《孫康宜文集》五卷本的電子版發給他，心想他可能用得上。

那就開始了我和保陽之間的頻繁通信。他不但集中精力、有系統地閱讀《文集》中的每篇著作，而且還不斷發來讀後感。保陽的「讀後感」還不是一般的讀者反應，他所謂的「感想」大多擴展到他個人對生活、對人生、對世界的聯想。例如，在重讀拙著《情與忠：陳子龍、柳如是詩詞因緣》（李奭學譯）之後，保陽立刻發來一封令人深省的電子郵件：

　　孫先生，
　　　　昨夜讀畢《情與忠：陳子龍柳如是詩詞因緣》，想起二十年前在陝南漢江邊讀此書，情形如昨。如今海外再讀，恍如重逢故人，感慨無端，掩卷不寐，吟成小詩呈教：

　　　　讀《情與忠：陳子龍柳如是詩詞因緣》
　　　　情忠兩字久封塵，
　　　　二十年前已覺親。
　　　　燈下南朝字字血，
　　　　一回掩卷一傷神。

　　　　　　　　　　　　　　　保陽敬上，庚子三月二十三日
　　　　　　　　　　　　　　　（李保陽，2020年4月15日來函）

當時我正在準備「簡體版」的《孫康宜文集》五卷本書稿，為了要給中國大陸的廣西師大出版社北京分社出版，同時我也正在考慮是否要請一位「特約編輯」來幫我校對書稿。保陽既是古典文學出身，又有如此才華和毅力，而且還曾在中國大陸作過編輯，真是最好不過的人選了。所以我立刻聯絡耶魯大學的東亞研究中心（Council on East Asian Studies），說我想聘用李保陽擔任《文集》的「特約編輯」。很遺憾的是，最後卻因為某種外在的技術障礙，此事沒能如願。但保陽仍然繼續為我承擔起proof-reading（校閱）的工作。我的簡體《文集》共

五卷，原稿總字數近一百七十萬字，合計一千九百一十四頁，保陽一共校改條目一千三百二十九處，並為簡體版《文集》撰寫〈校讀後記〉。此外，他接著幫我校對《從北山樓到潛學齋》繁體版的一校稿（已由秀威資訊出版）。這些都是我當初做夢也想不到的事。可以說，這次與保陽的文字緣，也只有「奇妙」兩個字可以形容了。

　　有趣的是，在通信的過程中，由於互相討論的題材愈來愈廣泛，漸漸地我們也把其他有關的友人引進了這個「書信群」——包括陳效蘭（Hsiao-lan Chen Mote）、季進、張宏生、王德威、陳國球、林順夫、林玫儀、黃進興、胡曉真、鄭毓瑜、林香伶、康正果、韓晗、嚴志雄（Chi-hung Lawrence Yim）、王璦玲（Ayling Wang）、錢南秀、凌超、盤隨雲、李若虹、張鳳、劉媛、王文鋒、陸葵菲、孟振華（Michael Meng）、蘇精、張永濤、卞東波、方菲、芳村弘道、萩原正樹、吳清邁、Martin Heijdra（何義壯），Mary Ellen Friends, Haun Saussy（蘇源熙），Jing Tsu（石靜遠），Pauline Lin, Haninah Levine, Jonathan Kaufman, Formosa Deppman, Anne Lu, Isaiah Schrader（史逸軒），Rev.Jenny Peek, Rev. Ian Oliver, František Reismuller, Jeongsoo Shin, Josephine Chiu-Duke （丘慧芬），Austin Woerner（溫侯廷），Stano Kong（江丕賢）等人。

　　眾所皆知，此次「COVID-19已經橫掃美國，感染人數早已接近兩百五十萬，死亡人數超過十二萬，比歷史上的任何一次流行病都要嚴重。我們趁此機會也閱讀了一些有關從前爆發於美國的幾次嚴重傳染病的報導。（保陽在5月1日的來信中，還根據網上的材料，整理出一個統計表）。同時，我們也參考哈佛的李若虹博士所寫的一篇有關一百年前（即1918-1920年）於波士頓城爆發「西班牙流感」（Spanish flu）的文章——題為〈冰天雪地給陳寅恪往醫院送試卷的老先生——藍曼的梵文課與世紀疫情〉。最近，我們又讀到耶魯法學院博士生吳景健所寫的一篇文章——那是關於兩百多年前（即1795年）在美國東海岸所爆發的一場黃熱病（yellow fever）。該文敘述了一個有關耶魯的「若無街墓園」（Grove Street Cemetery）的故事，尤其涉及黃熱病災害如何導致死者數目劇增的情況。以上這兩篇文章很自然地引起了我和保陽（以及其他友人）對這個題目的關注。

　　就在這段期間，即使全球受到疫情的嚴重影響，我的母校東海大學的圖書館（在新館長楊朝棟教授的領導下）仍堅持如期地為我和家父孫保羅辦了一個盛

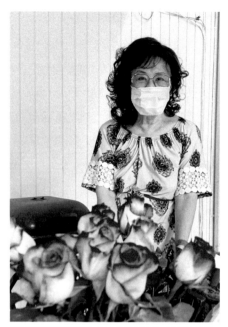

避疫期間的孫康宜（2020年初夏，王郁林攝）

大的著作展和書法展。我要特別感謝王茂駿校長、江丕賢院長、彭懷真教授（即前任圖書館館長）、和張玉生教授的全力支持。尤其是，此次策展人王雅萍館員那種持續努力的精神，令人佩服。她不停地為展覽之事盡力，絲毫不放棄原來的計畫。（在這期間，館內的曾昱嫥小姊也幫了大忙）。難得的是，王雅萍特富想像力，是她把這次展覽的標題定為「陽光穿透的歲月」的。該展覽按計畫於4月13日開始，5月25日結束，從頭到尾辦得十分成功，已成為文化圈人士的一段佳話。我雖然因為疫情的關係而無法「親臨」展覽現場，但在開幕式的當天，東海大學圖書館特別為我和外子C.C.（張欽次）安排了通過視訊連線（Zoom）方式出席開幕式，令我們感到振奮。後來校方還為「孫家人」（包括我的大弟孫康成）安排了一次觀展的機會，並給予熱情的招待。這一切都讓我體會到，即使在疫情蔓延的困難期間，人情還是溫暖的，就如該展覽的題目所示：這是一個「陽光穿透的歲月」。所以這本《避疫書信選》也收了一些有關這方面的信件。

很巧的是，C.C.（張欽次）的母校中原大學，早已定於4月15日那天要舉行一個「贈書典禮」，好讓C.C.能將他今年初剛完成的《文集》（Collected

Works）獻給母校。〔特別感謝李宜涯教授（即前任中原大學張靜愚紀念圖書館館長）的熱心安排〕。可惜後來由於疫情蔓延全球，我們只好取消原訂的臺灣行程。令人感動的是，雖然我們無法親臨「贈書典禮」，但新館長李正文卻在一個行政會議上，代表C.C.將《文集》捐贈給母校典藏。當天張光正校長也特別致辭，並提及C.C.於五十七年前（1963）代表該屆畢業生為母校設計「十字架鐘塔」的貢獻。後來校方還為此作成一段「新聞報導」，登在中原大學的網頁上。這些都令我們特別感到振奮。

　　但令人傷心的是，我的一些親友也在這段新冠疫情（COVID-19）爆發的期間離開了這個世界。（當然他們並不都是死於新冠病毒）。尤其是，我親愛的姑姑孫毓嫻突然於5月7日去世。在那以前，我在臺灣的恩人藍順仕老師已於三月四日過世。又，我所景仰的耶魯傳道人Kate Latimer也在這期間離世。不久前（5月21日）我那一向所最佩服的聖經大師大衛鮑森（David Pawson）也繼之而去。就在最近，我們突然接到一封有關Dr. Jack Chuong（我們最喜愛的醫生之一）已於五月間去世的消息，特別令我們感到痛心。此外，一個月前我還參加了一個學生的母親的線上葬禮。這些特殊的經驗，很自然地引起我對「死亡」意義的深度思考。

　　在躲進「潛學齋」的這些日子裡，我除了埋頭寫作、努力教學之外，還經常在網上聽傳道人的布道。例如，3月22日那天，遠志明牧師所發表的「信心──

最強的免疫力」那次演說，對我特別有啟發。本書「附錄」中所收入的一篇拙作和「對話」，也多少反映了我最近對「信心」這一方面的思考。〔此次特別請Linda Chu（朱雯琪）將其中一篇文章譯成英文，以饗讀者。〕

必須一提的是：本書所選錄的書信來往，既有中文的，也有英文的，也有兩種語言夾雜在一起的。為了存其「真」，我們一律保持信件的原貌，不另行翻譯。凡有刪除之處，我們也一定會加上說明。

有關這部書信選的出版，要特別感謝秀威資訊的發行人宋政坤先生和主任編輯鄭伊庭女士的熱心支持，以及杜國維先生（即副主任編輯）和許乃文女士（責任編輯）的大力幫助。此外，耶魯大學的東亞研究中心（Council on East Asian Studies）慷慨資助了本書的出版，我要特別向Injoong Kim及Amy Greenberg兩位女士獻上感謝，他們在處理「出版補助費」（publication subsidy）一事上，給我們提供了很大的幫助。

孫康宜
寫於康州木橋鄉「潛學齋」
2020年7月21日

目　次

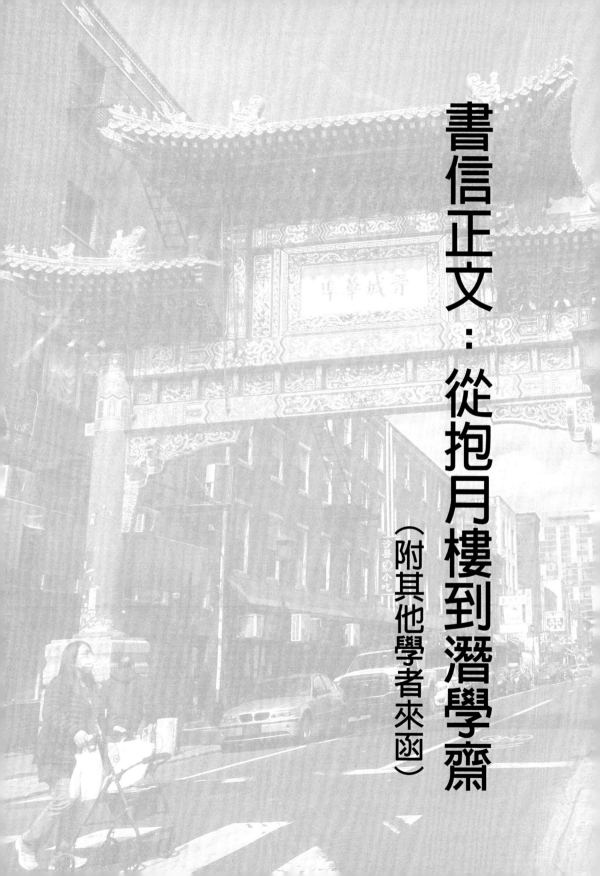

書信正文：從抱月樓到潛學齋（附其他學者來函）

李保陽致孫康宜

孫先生教席，

　　晚生的名字是李保陽。

　　大約二十年前，保陽在漢中讀本科時，拜讀過　先生大作《陳子龍柳如是詩詞情緣》，為書中人事所感動，大學畢業後，保陽去了浙江嘉興的一所中學教書，那裡是柳如是的故鄉。前兩天，保陽在　先生的母校普林斯頓大學東亞圖書館借到大著《耶魯潛學集》，讀到〈詞的嚮往：話說詞家唐圭璋〉一文。保陽在嘉興教書時，和一位當地布衣學人葛渭君先生交往十多年。葛先生一生景仰唐先生人格學問，常常為保陽講起與唐老交往舊事。葛先生立志踵武唐老故事，編纂《詞話補編》、《續編》和《外編》，惜僅成《補編》六冊。2018年元旦，葛先生以八十高齡驟逝。今讀　先生此文，不勝故人今昔之感！

　　夜讀　先生鴻文，竟引起許多舊事，悵觸百端，情難自已。草此短箋，不知可達左右否？耑此，並頌

春祺！

晚關中李保陽百拜

庚子2月18（3月11日）於思故客河上之抱月樓

註：此信有刪節。

李保陽致孫康宜

孫先生尊鑒：

　　讀您的《潛學齋隨想錄》，大約是您中年而後之筆，溫潤而透滿生活與生命的智慧。尤其是溢於字理行間的神性，尤其讓人感動！真想讀一讀二十多年後的今天，您對生活，對生命的體悟！

　　保陽特別喜歡第二十二則馬克吐溫的話。猶記保陽曾在博士論文後記中說

過：「人總是會在某一個瞬間，認識到自己的平庸。也總是會在某一瞬間，接受自己的平庸，從而跟這個世界，以及跟這個世界彆扭著的自己達成和解。」保陽覺得這兩句話有比較接近的意思。

《隨想錄》第十四則倒數第二行的「雨窗」誤植作「兩窗」。保陽作過編輯，對錯字比較敏感，請　先生見諒！順頌

教安！

保陽再拜

3/11/2020

Mary Ellen Friends致孫康宜

Dear Kang-i,

I'm to let you know I have been thinking of you. John and I are out at our lake house in western New York State, keeping up with the news as schools of all types temporarily close or move to online learning. Of course I have heard of Yale's decision. My school, Deerfield Academy, will also move to remote learning.

My goal in this note is to ask if you and C.C. are well and to see how you are faring. I wonder if the change in teaching will present you with unprecedented difficulties or if it will simplify your life. As I speak with educators at different institutions, I am struck by the variety of their responses. As time permits, please let me know how things are in your world.

Please give my best to C.C.,

Mary Ellen

3/13/2020

孫康宜致Mary Ellen Friends

Dear Mary Ellen,

Thank you so much for thinking of us. Sorry for the late reply to your email. But due to the COVIC-19 pandemic, I have been extremely busy setting up various online connections in order to prepare for the days ahead--including "teaching online" at Yale, instacard.com, CVS pharmacy deliveries, etc. You know I'm always afraid of technology, and this has been a very challenging experience for me. However, I am pleased that I have finally made some progress regarding the use of computer, iphone, etc. So, I'm all set now.

So this turns out to be a positive thing for me.

Let's all stay safe during this unusual time!

Best,

Kang-i

3/14/2002

Mary Ellen Friends致孫康宜

Dear Kang-i,

You've been busy! Those of us at Deerfield Academy are also preparing to teach online at least until April 15 and quite possibly until the end of the year. What strange times we live in!

I'm glad to learn that you are pleased with the progress you've made. Our Academic Dean has been wonderful, reminding us that we're not going to move through this new type of teaching and learning without mistakes, and that we're bound to get better at it as we go along. It's another way of reminding us not to let perfect be the enemy of good. You are an amazing teacher, and your students are lucky to have you in their lives (even it if is only virtually).

Happy Day,
Mary Ellen
3/14/2020

Haninah Levine致孫康宜

Dear Professor Chang,

I hope that you and C.C. are well in these frightening times. I don't know whether you are in isolation, but in case you are, I thought I might reach out to send you my best wishes.

Last fall, I began a project that I call my "quatrain of the day" project, even though I don't reliably write a new one each day. Here are a few selected verses, to keep you company.

Much love,

Haninah
3/15/2020

October 16, 2019 (first day of the project)
The Washington Monument's head is lost in the clouds.
Airplanes take off, and their lights soon blink out into the grayness.
The sound reaches me only after they have disappeared from sight –
A babble of metal voices from the white void.

October 29, 2019
Seven fifteen a.m.,

The street like an illuminated set.

One yellow lamp sets off each yellow leaf.

The lamp snaps off, the street snaps to life.

November 10, 2019

Each leaf has turned its own particular color;

Each pigeon wheels at its own particular time.

The day rises in its shifting weathers,

Assembling itself from these atoms of autumn.

November 30, 2019

The birdfeeder spins as the sparrows shift.

The black squirrel circles the tire in the neighbors' yard.

A woodpecker's red flare draws helixes on a telephone pole.

My thoughts circle the quiet moment, but cannot land.

December 29, 2019

Rainy Sunday

A relief of indolence

The bed looms large

In my ambitions

January 2, 2020

Dawn crows

Jet glories on neon ground

And neon glories under jet accents

Flying past

January 8, 2020

Birds' nests: clots of black ink

Lodged in a tree's black veins.

Starlings in flight: one thousand wings

Murmur the same garbled augury.

February 3, 2020

Your feet planted on the tall tree stump,

Your hands in my short hair,

You invite me to enjoy the evening's quiet:

When did you learn to teach me such things?

February 28, 2020

Phlox has flowered in our front yard,

A welcome mat to the world before it.

Do you have no fear of being trampled,

That you set yourself out before the late-winter cold?

March 3, 2020

We walk out the door, and you say:

"So many birds tweeting, and walking around,

And doing stuff!"

And so I know that spring is here.

March 9, 2020

Full moon and stippled clouds,

A sky like beaten silver.

The daffodils stare at their mulched beds,

The magnolias have never flowered so early.

孫康宜致李保陽

Dear Baoyang,

　　Thank you for thinking of me during this terrible time of the COVID pandemic. I no longer go out and just try to stay safe at home.

　　But I'm very sorry for the belated response to your March 11th emails, which I have received with great appreciation. But the last two weeks have been extremely challenging for me, especially because I have to learn how to do online teaching and my daily schedule is full of zoom meetings!

孫康宜在耶魯大學的線上教學（2020年3月）

　　Thank you for letting me know that you have enjoyed reading my works. By the way, I have recently published 《孫康宜文集》五卷本 in Taiwan，which includes many of the things you have read. I am sending you the electronic version of the 《孫康宜文集》五卷本 here, hoping that you would enjoy having it.

　　In this email, I'll send you vols 1-3, and in the next email I'll send you vols. 4-5.

　　Please stay well and safe.

　　In haste,

Kang-i Sun Chang

（孫康宜）

3/29/2020

孫康宜致Haninah Levine

Dear Haninah,

　　Thank you for thinking of us during this terrible time of the COVIC pandemic. We no longer go out and just try to stay safe at home.

　　I have found your "quatrain of the day" project extremely inspiring. First of all, your poem dated 10/29/2019 is especially moving to me:

　　Seven fifteen a.m.,

　　The street like an illuminated set.

　　One yellow lamp sets off each yellow leaf.

　　The lamp snaps off, the street snaps to life.

　　I was surprised when I first read the poem, for coincidentally 10/29/2019 was my late father's 100th birthday!

　　Your poem written on 11/30/2019 is also very interesting to me. (C.C. especially likes the line "The black squirrel circles the tire in the neighbor's yard.) And interestingly, the day before you wrote the poem was C.C.'s 78th birthday. In fact, according to the time zone here in the US, C.C.'s birthday should be 11/30, not 11/29. (11/29 was according to the time zone in Taiwan).

　　Then, another coincidence is your poem written on March 3,2020:

　　We walk out the door, and you say:

"So many birds tweeting, and walking around,

And doing stuff!"

And so I know that spring is here.

It just happens that my teacher Mr. Lan, who helped us survive through the difficult time of the White Terror during the 1950s (see Chapter 5 of my memoir, *Journey through the White Terror*), died on March 4, 2020 . Thus, when I read your poem dated 3/3/2020, I was very comforted!

I just found such coincidences amazing! (And I don't think they are coincidences.) For example, right after receiving the poems from your "quatrain of the day," I received a checklist of the "Kang-i Sun Chang Collection" from National Central Library in Taiwan, in which item #191 is a postcard from you, titled "Visiting National Park in Washington." Then, on the same day, I found C.C.'s Chinese translation of your poem, "Traveling North to Visit Kang-i Chang," which was published in a Chinese journal in 2007.

I can't believe how time flies! It was about 20 years ago that you first took my Man and Nature class. I remember that in November 2001, I attended your choir performance at the Timothy Dwight Church. You are indeed one of the students I'm always proud of!

Anyway, we often thought of you and Emily and Asha.

Best,

Kang-i

3/29/2020

註：此函部分刪節。

李保陽致孫康宜

孫先生尊鑒：

謝謝　先生的回信並惠賜大著！這是保陽來美後，收到的第一位同行前輩的回信，欣喜望外！

近來全國陷入COVID-19蔓延之中，每日目睹罹災人數直線上升，實在讓人揪心不忍！賓州是重災區之一，保陽兩小兒亦在家接受學區安排之Zoom網路授課。值此非常時期，我們只能求助於神，剴切禱告，希望祂能早日將這場災難帶走！

保陽最開心者是《文集》第三卷收錄了先生的《走出白色恐怖》，這本書保陽早就聞知其名，但始終緣慳一面。現在終於可以滿足保陽的孺慕之思了。

另外，先生似乎和浦安迪先生稔熟？保陽二十年前讀先生《陳柳情緣》一書時，也讀了浦安迪先生的《中國敘事學》，對浦安迪先生書中界定之「六大名著」這一概念印象深刻，至今不能忘卻。後來也曾多方嘗試，試圖聯繫浦安迪先生，終因人事倥傯，雜事攪擾，不了了之。

前幾天讀先生《耶魯潛學集》，日記中記了一段讀後感，這裡也分享給先生。等《走出白色恐怖》讀完後，再向先生報告讀後感。

疫情非常時期，先生保重身體是念！專此，並候

諸安！

晚　保陽拜上

3/30/2020

附《耶魯潛學集》讀後感：

位於曼哈頓五大道中央公園旁邊的紐約大都會博物館（New York Metropolitan Museum）二樓，有一處典雅安靜的人造中國園林。2016年我初次訪問大都會時，看到這座懸空於大都會二樓的室內園林的造型之雅緻、明清傳統細節之到位，讓我這個在江南生活了十多年、研究明清詩詞的人，在異域頓生一種時空穿越之熟悉感。前兩天在普林斯頓大學葛思德圖書館借了孫康宜先生所著《耶魯潛學集》，其中有一篇〈在美國聽明朝時代曲——記紐約明軒《金瓶梅》唱曲大

會〉。這篇文章發表在《明報月刊》1981年8月號上。是當年作者與她任職的普林斯頓大學一眾師生，以及美國研究中國詞曲文學的學人，在紐約大都會博物館那座中國園林建成開放前的一次雅集。是次雅集是以耶魯大學傅漢思先生的夫人張充和女士演唱《金瓶梅》中的小曲為中心，參加的人計有：張充和、傅漢思、夏志清、王洞、浦安迪、高友工、江青、孫康宜、芮大衛、陳安娜、康海濤、袁乃瑛、高勝勇等，極一時之樂。從這篇文章中，我才知道這個室內園林是參照蘇州網師園的殿春簃異地仿造，名字叫「明軒」。當時該園尚未完工開放，大都會博物館的何慕文提議讓美東一眾研究中國文化的學人在此雅集。據孫先生的文章介紹，這座園林肇造於1977年，由當時普林斯頓大學教授藝術史的方聞先生，奔走於紐約和蘇州之間協調，最後由蘇州園林管理處派工二十七人建造。「那五十根楠木巨幹是由四川、雲南等僻遠之處直接運來，那些一寸一寸的鋪地磚則全為蘇州『陸墓御窯』的特製精品。此外像那參差錯落的太湖石也輾轉自虎丘附近一廢園搬運來的。」二十年前，我在漢中讀孫先生《陳子龍柳如是詩詞因緣》和浦安迪的《中國敘事學》，尚未想見彼時海外學人曾有如此雅集盛會，而孫先生與浦安迪先生竟同與其會。今日捧讀孫先生之作，始知四十年前，在大都會二樓「明軒」尚未全部完工時，此地還曾有過一次中國文人的雅集，錄此以存一段掌故。

孫康宜致李保陽

Dear BAOYANG,

I'm so glad to hear that you admire Prof Andrew（Andy）Plaks'浦安迪book very much!

I copy Prof Plaks on this email so that you can write to him by email.

(Dear Andy, I hope it's okay that I give your email address to Baoyang!)

Best,
Kang-i Sun Chang
3/30/2020

李保陽致孫康宜

孫先生，

　　今天早上收到先生的回信，又是一個分外的驚喜，這個驚喜是，今天能夠聯繫到二十年前對保陽影響深遠的兩本書的作者！真的感謝主的恩待！

　　上個星期，臺灣一家出版社決定出版保陽的博士論文，保陽這幾天正在向一家組織申請幫助，正好為該組織寫了一段介紹自己的一文字，如果浦安迪先生向您詢問「李保陽為何人？」您可據此向浦先生作個大概的介紹。保陽把那段文字以附件文件的形式附在這封郵件的後面，煩先生查收！

　　疫情洶洶，請先生保重！

保陽　再上
3/30/2020

孫康宜致李保陽

Dear BAOYANG,

　　Thank you for sending me a copy of your bio! I'll definitely share it with Andy Plaks, if he writes to me. However, I should say that I don't know where Andy is now—whether in Israel or in Princeton! Also, after his wife Lily died a few years ago, Andy started to spend more time in Israel! Please do not be disappointed if Andy does not write to you; he does not write emails often.

　　By the way, if you give me your mailing address, I can send you a copy of my book about my father, which was published in 2019. The title is《孫保羅書法：附書信日記》（孫保羅著，孫康宜編注）。Actually I also edited another book by my father, titled 《一粒麥子修訂本》, which came out in 2019 as well.

　　I believe these two books are closely related to my memoir,《走出白色恐怖》. As a Christian, I want to glorify God, and wonder if you would be interested in these two books.

Anyway, please give me your mailing address!

Best,
Kang-i Sun Chang
3/30/2020

李保陽致孫康宜

孫先生，

晚上好！

真的感謝主！保陽初讀您的《隨想錄》時，就隱隱約約感覺到一股神性的悲憫，那層悲憫是不仰望基督的人所沒有的。您剛才的來信，確證了保陽當時的感覺是正確的。感謝神！

非常感謝　先生願意寄贈令尊老先生的大著和另外您主編的書給保陽，相信這兩部書將會加深對大著《走出白色恐怖》的理解。如果不是刻下COVID-19的蔓延，保陽一定親自來紐黑文拜領贈書。保陽對書信和日記，情有獨鍾，因為這些文獻是歷史現場和當事人最真實的紀錄，留存的是一個時代斷面最鮮活的影像。相信令尊的日記和書信，能讓他生活的那個時代立體地展現在讀者面前。保陽除了關注文獻價值之外，對日記書信還有一種超乎學術之外的情結：保陽自小學開始就記日記，至今仍然每晚臨睡前手寫日記，二十多年，極少中輟，積稿數百萬字。前年倉促出奔，將十數年日記、友朋書信，未及帶出，悉數留在了中國大陸。每念及此，輒為腹痛！保陽在中國大陸的時候，喜歡逛舊書攤，並結識了上海一帶許多經營舊書業的朋友，其中有一位朋友在上海的一戶人家處理的廢紙堆裡面，收到一本日記。保陽出國時，將這本日記帶來美國。去年這個時候仔細讀了，原來是當時上海一位女孩子在1947年，到光復後的臺灣路局工作，不幸的是，她到臺北沒幾天，就爆發了「二二八事變」，前後長達月餘的社會動蕩，以及後續的影響，這位女孩子都以她的日記記錄了下來，這應該是關於「二二八事變」最真實的記錄。「二二八事變」是近代臺灣歷史的大事件，所以這本日記的

史料價值，一定不在已知的文獻之下。等過段時間條件允許了，保陽可以和　先生分享這部日記。

　　謝謝　先生贈閱令尊老先生的書信、日記，以及　先生主編的書。也請　先生將郵寄地址賜下，保陽將郵寄一份拙作的抽印本給　先生。那篇文章發表在日本的《立命館文學》雜誌去年冬季號上，上週保陽剛剛收到日本寄來的樣書和抽印本。那篇文章是根據新發現的書信材料，梳理了王鵬運逝後，他的藏書和遺物的流散情況。

　　感謝　主！讓保陽在異國他鄉有機會聯繫到　先生，並可以交流學習。謝謝　神的恩待！

　　疫情嚴重，願　神保守您！

保陽　敬上

3/31/2020

李保陽致孫康宜

孫先生，

　　保陽突然想起近來康州亦是COVID-19重災區，　先生待在家裡會比較安全。贈書如尚未寄出，請　先生暫緩出門，以策安全！

保陽　又上

3/31/2020

孫康宜致李保陽

Dear BAOYANG,

　　No problem at all. All I need to do is putting the priority packages in our mailbox and the postman郵差would pick them up!

Thank you for being thoughtful!

Kang-i

3/31/2020

李保陽致孫康宜

孫先生，

今天和內子一起帶孩子們外出購物，回家後，在Porch上看到郵局送來了您郵寄的兩大包書，真是喜出望外！保陽窮居費城郊外鄉村，周遭三十英里以內，連一張中文紙片都不容易找到，故接到　先生贈書，從中午至晚上，手不釋卷，摩挲細味，欣喜之情，溢於言表。

讀紙本書的感覺就是好！！

這兩天保陽拜讀《走出白色恐怖》一書，無時無刻不被一種強大的情感洪流所籠罩。因為書中所記不管是歷史劇變，還是小人物的瑣屑小事，都讓人那麼的熟悉，那麼的感動！每讀一章，保陽都要數一數，看看還有多少頁就要讀完，不是期望快點讀畢，而是生怕很快就讀完。這是少有的一種閱讀體驗。尤其讀到令堂老夫人攜幼將雛，從林園鄉下輾轉五六次公車、火車、三輪車，才得到新店監獄，和令尊老先生隔著玻璃相對無言十分鐘，竟讀得保陽涕淚滿襟。不由得讓保陽想起了近數年來的自己，輾轉流徙於陝西、浙江、廣東，最後又棲遲於美東的費城郊外（有關那幾年的舊事，保陽曾寫進博士論文的後記中，現在以附件形式隨信附上）。另外，拜讀過程中，保陽也時時札記，待全書讀畢，札記再奉左右。

感謝　先生贈書，若非疫情蔓延，保陽真想親到耶魯，和　先生分享閱讀心得！

時疫橫行，先生及家人保重身體。

願　神用祂大能的手祓除時疫，賜給大家健康和平的生活環境。為您和您的

家人禱告！為美國禱告！為所有不幸遭難的人禱告！

保陽
4/3/2020

黃文吉致李保陽

保陽學弟：

　　來函收悉，經萩原先生之介紹，對你的處境略知一二，今從函中所述，了解你的一連串遭遇，感受更深。雖然彼此從未謀面，但從文字中已一見如故矣！

　　個人研究詞學多年，曾發表一些專書與論文，與國內外的詞學研究者多所交流，華東師大出版的《詞學》從第一輯迄今四十二輯，我都完整擁有。大作發表在三十八輯的〈王鵬運書札四通考釋〉亦曾閱覽，可見你在詞學研究之用心。如今你流落他鄉，仍然不能忘懷學術研究，精神令人感佩！擬申請基金會補助，需要有人推薦，我當然義不容辭。希望我的推薦對你的申請有所助益。

　　近來武漢肺炎肆虐，美國確診人數不斷攀升，你在他鄉的處境相當艱難，一定要多加保重！臺灣因為防範得宜，目前災情還不算嚴重，生活大致沒有太大的影響，只是未來如何則不可知了，希望上天保佑，疫情趕快過去，讓全球蒼生早日脫離苦海！專此，並祝

　　平安

黃文吉覆　4/3/2020

孫康宜致李保陽

保陽，

　　請注意！你的博士論文題目的英譯大有問題！First of all, "Ciological

Literature of Wang Pengyun research and Reproduce Wang Pengyun's Chronicle" has many idiomatic problems（習慣用語的錯誤）in English. 問題是：讓人讀起來不像英文！And the English title should at least read like English!

First of all, "Ciological literature" sounds strange! (Is there such a term "ciological" in English?) Secondly, the word "reproduce" is a verb（動詞）. You can't use it in a title like that!

So please find a good English title for your dissertation博士論文。It has to read at least idiomatically correct in English. I'm sure you daughter can tell you what "idiomatic English" means.

希望你不介意我的批評！

Best,
Kang-i
4/4/2020

李保陽致孫康宜

孫先生，

謝謝　先生指教，不僅英文題目有硬傷（保陽英文水準亦僅限閱讀而已），中文題目也需重新考量。這本論文的問題多多，不僅僅先生所指出者。

保陽因為在圖書館工作過，又聯絡了幾乎所有王氏後裔，故論文優勢在於新文獻資料的發掘利用。但短版也很明顯，即如先生所指出者以及其他面向的不足。因為保陽入學時已三十六歲，時不我予，在三年內寫出三十萬字（中文）的論文草稿，同時還要養家餬口，因之便盡快提交以獲得學位，為謀職作打算，實在沒有仔細修訂的餘裕。這次出版，保陽也明確告訴出版社，至少需一年時間專力修訂，因之才多方尋找各種支持，以便從事修訂工作。

待疫氣稍緩，如　先生方便，保陽打算攜稿來New Haven當面向　先生請教！

保陽
4/4/2020

孫康宜致李保陽

Dear Baoyang,

What you have done is already quite amazing! Please don't worry about the errors in the dissertation. That's why revision is always necessary.

Please don't let my criticism upset you. As a scholar myself, I know how important it is to rewrite and revise.

Best,
Kang-i
4/4/2020

註：此函有部分刪節。

李保陽致孫康宜

孫先生，

謝謝　先生為保陽訪問Yale考慮如此周到的細節。盛情銘感！保陽到訪Yale，主要兩件事情，一是拜訪　先生，二是訪問東亞圖書館。這幾年訪問中外各圖書館的心得，在新近剛剛收到的一篇拙作抽印本的後記中略有表達，茲以附件形式奉上。

不管是社會還是學術的進步，都有賴於不同的批評聲音。　先生的批評不但不會引起保陽的upset，反而是保陽最想聽到的聲音。學術交流中的任何批評意見，都是減少錯舛和不足的有效途徑。保陽非常珍視　先生的批評意見和建議。

保陽　敬上

4/4/2020

孫康宜致李保陽

Dear BAOYANG,

I was so moved by your "ten years journey" article that I must send you the following link for my 2013 interview on the White Terror!

Best,

Kang-i

4/4/2020

孫康宜致李保陽

Dear BAOYANG,

Thank you for sharing with me your wonderful article about your visits to Japan and your comments on American libraries. Your descriptions of your experience with the Japanese scholars are so lively and well written that I simply could not put it down! 太生動了！一般搞文獻學的人寫作十分枯燥，你的文筆唯獨不同，既真實又感人，希望你將來朝這個方向發展！一定貢獻很大！

I had the similar feeling when I read your "10 years journey" piece! I was deeply moved by what you had gone through all these years and was amazed by how you reached where you are today! Yours is a unique story of courage and fortitude! I believe God has been leading your path all along!

I was pleasantly surprised that my good friend Lin Meiyi林玫儀was the person who had helped you become a Christian! Meiyi and I got to know each other very well during the 1990s when we both were close friends with Shi Zhecun施蟄存.（Also, a cousin of mine knows Meiyi and her husband very well）. That's why I have mailed you a copy of my book,《從北山樓到潛學齋》, in which Shi Zhecun mentioned Lin Meiyi in some of his letters to me!

I saw Lin Meiyi in Taipei in spring 2013 when I gave a lecture at the Academia Sinica. But for some reason we lost contact after that. Is she well now? What is her email address?

Anyway, I am pleased that our paths have crossed in so many different ways!

Best,
Kang-i
4/4/2020

孫康宜致李保陽

Dear Baoyang,

Please see attached my translations of Wang Pengyun's *ci* poems. Please note that the introduction to the Wang Pengyun entry was by William Schutz, a scholar whom I knew quite well. But the translations of Wang Pengyun's *ci* poems were done by me.

Best,
Kang-i
4/4/2020

孫康宜致李保陽

Dear Baoyang,

I'm glad you are interested in visiting Yale University Library in the near future. When the time comes, I'll ask the curator Michael Meng to serve as a guide to the East Asian Collections. He can also show some particular items for your interest. Also, Michael Meng has recently published a book on the Yale Chinese rarebook collection（published by中華書局）. An earlier version of my preface to Meng's book also appeard in《孫康宜文集》，卷4，頁483-488.

Best,
Kang-i
4/4/2020

李保陽致孫康宜

孫先生，

謝謝　先生盛情介紹保陽給您的同事。保陽2016年首度訪美，曾專程從紐約趕往New Haven參訪Yale University，去秋也曾和內子帶孩子們再訪New Haven，惜只訪問了法學院圖書館，東亞館兩次皆不得其門而入。保陽近年先後參訪東西岸各東亞館，唯Yale和Cornell兩校東亞館尚未到訪。今春本有訪問Cornell之計畫，因疫氣流行，暫時擱置。若疫氣結束後有機會訪問Yale東亞館，則不勝向往之至。

再次謝謝先生盛情引介！

保陽
4/4/2020

孫康宜致李保陽

Dear Baoyang,

My goodness! Thank you for sharing your January 4th diary entry on our mutual friend Tai-loi Ma（馬泰來）! Ma was a close friend of mine, and both of us had the experience of serving as the Curator（館長）of Princeton's Gest Oriental Library（普林斯頓葛斯德東方圖書館）。

But what telepathy! You and I share so many mutual friends.

Best,
Kang-i
4/4/2020

孫康宜致李保陽

Dear Baoyang,

I am thrilled to see your personal notes on the pages of my father's book,《孫保羅書法：附書信日記》. It's so inspiring to know that you named yourself "Yoke."

Best,
Kang-i
4/4/2020

孫康宜致李保陽

Dear Baoyang,

有關《詠西安》那套書，以及拙作《古色古香：張充和題字選集》（孫康宜

編注）和《曲人鴻爪本事》（孫康宜撰寫），等疫情結束之後，我就會一併郵寄給你。

　　Actually the《詠西安》series has nothing to do with my friend and colleague Kang Zhengguo. The series was given to me by the Academia Sinica（中央研究院）in Taiwan. Somehow they thought I would be interested in the books, and so they kindly shipped the series to me.

　　But at age 76 I have so many projects in front of me that I don't think I would ever do a research on西安。I initially planned to give the set to Kang Zhengguo. But this morning, after reading your moving article about your "ten years journey, " I suddenly changed my mind and thought I should give it to you instead.

　　As to my two books on張充和, I meant to send them to you since a few days ago. But I don't have more priority stamps at home, and so I might have to wait until after the pandemic is over, when I can mail them（along with the《詠西安》series）to you.

Best,
Kang-i
4/4/2020

李保陽致孫康宜

孫先生，

　　玫儀老師已於2014年底從中研院文哲所任上榮休。

　　保陽和林老師初識，是在2008年南京大學的詞學會議上。後來不久的2009年初，林老師到江浙一帶訪書，那時候保陽生活在浙江嘉興數年，對江南一帶的圖書館比較熟悉，作為嚮導，陪林老師在杭州、上海、海寧一帶訪問。有一天拜訪吳熊和先生結束後，林老師在旅館中為保陽講述　神保守她們一家人的見證。尤其林老師父母的故事，竟然和令尊、令堂的故事，有相似之處。那次之後，林老師就經常向保陽傳福音，直至今日仍每天不斷。2010年秋季開始，林老師交代她

在大陸昆山的妹妹琬儀姊給保陽郵寄臺灣的基督教刊物《蒲公英》和《活潑的生命》，這一寄，就是九年，不管我們安家在哪裡，杭州、陝南山中的洋縣、浙北的嘉興、再回杭州，「蒲公英」總是會如期「飄」到我們手中，直到我們一家離開中國大陸來到美國方歇。在生活的艱難中，林老師給我們傳來上帝的愛，給我們以溫暖和希望。2013年，得林老師推薦，保陽在文哲所《中國文哲研究通訊》上發表了一篇兩萬字的長文。2014年，保陽在窮愁困頓中，謀食於杭州天竺山中，年底時有朋友邀保陽往嘉義中正大學參加一個古文獻的學術會議，那次縱貫南北臺灣，並在2014年的最後一天，和林老師一眾　主內姊妹在臺北的士林靈糧堂跨年。那晚，保陽整個被　神的愛所感動和包圍。記得當晚有個節目，就是大家在一個紙條上寫下一段話，並把那段話告訴　神。保陽記得當時所寫的一段話是希望來年能夠離開天竺山，從事自己喜歡的學術工作（記載具體細節的日記滯留大陸，已經記不清了）。沒有想到的是，次年三月，保陽果然考入中山大學中文系，攻讀博士學位。這是保陽一次榮耀　神的見證！

那次是保陽第一次入臺。也是自己的「四九情結」一次大爆發（保陽的「四九情結」，可見諸去年此時稍晚寫的一段文字。那段文字是寫在上海那位女生1947年的日記卷末，那日記前兩天保陽的郵件中有跟您提到過。現在將保陽的文字附件傳送給您）。那次臺灣之行，使遙遠冰冷的歷史，第一次以可感知的溫暖鋪展在保陽面前。當早年接受的教科書上那個中華民國，第一次真切地出現在自己眼前時，保陽在桃園機場竟然兩眼模糊……那些近年來漸漸被理想化的「文化正統」南遷，胡適、傅斯年、梅貽琦等近代紹續中華文化正統的大師們在歷史變局下之抉擇簸遷，以及康樂園中寒柳堂下保陽日日面對的陳寅恪先生四九後的遭際等等等等，加上在臺灣十天的所見所聞，在在都讓保陽有一種朝歷史縱深轉向叩問的感動。最後，那種感動就在2014年的最後一天化作了一首七律：

甲午臺灣度歲
一覺閩嶠歲又添，半簾舊夢落花殘。仙山海外鵑心困，故國門前冷眼酸。
逃去許由千樣好，歸來丁令萬般難。雕欄春水思長駐，玉砌涼飆總覺寒。

這裡的「甲午」實際上「不過是對一種特定的文體的操作」（您《文集》第

四輯頁500），並非中國傳統天干地支紀年的「甲午」，而是指主曆2014與2015
的交替。這個問題，您在回答張宏生老師的採訪時，有一句話的內涵比較相似。
您的這段話保陽有闡發，茲亦以附件奉上。

保陽　再上

4/4/2020

附《傅成家日記跋》：

　　沒想到是在這麼一個「緊迫」的情境下終於錄完這部日記，八萬六千八百餘
字，七十九頁電腦文檔，耗時十八天。本來預計昨天結束，但是因為昨天後半天
忙了一些和日記相關的事情，耽擱了，剩下的那點尾巴文字就拖到了今天。

　　每天沉浸於七十多年前一位上海姑娘相對個人化的世界裡，和她一起從上
海到臺灣，一起經歷心驚肉跳的「二二八」事件，一起看臺灣的山水月光，一起
聽中興輪上的驚濤駭浪，一起在驚濤駭浪裡目送中國這艘巨輪駛向1948——這一
年，這艘巨輪揚帆起錨，開啟了一個空前劇變的時代。它改變了無數中國人的命
運，並在知識人的話語譜系中定格成了一個沉重的歷史象徵——1949！

　　1949對於所有華人——尤其是知識人——來講，不是一個簡單的時間概念和
政治概念。它是一個具有無限張力的巨網。當一系列的敘事映照在它的背景下，
則每個故事都渲染上了一層無法言說的歷史悲愴！這種張力即使過了七十年，無
論是官方的正統敘述，還是民間的叩問追思，以及橫跨這兩者之間的兩岸敘述，
都是如此的色彩異樣，斑斕絢爛。石破驚天的歷史正確總是可以商量的，唯有那
些閃耀著人性光輝和普通生活的智慧是不朽的。當我們以七十年的長視角對一九
四九作遠距離放大時，發現真正導引我們進入這一歷史感動的，絕不是那些勝利
者在大歷史中堆積起來的磚石瓦塊，而是被擠壓在時代巨石下努力留下微弱印跡
的文字。這些文字經過歷史洪流的沖刷後，所攜帶的信息，彌見真實和珍貴。這
也是為什麼蔣介石、國民黨、毛澤東、共產黨最終都成了浮雲，而那些在一九四
九劇變中沉浮於臺海兩岸，花果飄零的知識人在歷史巨變檔口的抉擇，以及這些
不同抉擇給他們個人生命所帶來的影響，對後來文化學術進程所產生的影響，往
往成了後來不斷被反思、被叩問的主題。這種反思和叩問，是基於人類共同群處
生活經驗的一種理性超脫，但往往富含悲劇色彩。

　　七十年過去了，龍應台的《大江大海──一九四九》在臺灣熱賣，在西海岸被查禁，這不能不說是一種悲哀！二十一世紀，人類早已找到了一種較好的群處規則，臺灣人也在努力地將這種規則下移到多階層的社會治理當中，而西海岸的話語權卻仍然緊握在少數肉食者之手，兩岸不斷有文明的衝突，這實在是一種悲哀。如果哪一天，「一九四九」在臺海兩岸間不再是一個複雜的心結和糾結，那就是文明照耀兩岸之時。在文明還不均一的今天，我們仍然需要退回到歷史中去尋找能夠提供文明方向的種子，這雖然不能畢其功於一役，但只要我們努力朝歷史光明、向善的方向去努力，總有一天會將墮落和邪惡驅逐！這也是我所以執著於這本日記的緣故。

　　思故客河上今年的冬天特別漫長，五月中了，人們出門仍要穿棉衣。不知道這在七十個年頭後的2019年，是不是具有某種象徵意義？數日的連陰雨歇止了，傍晚天放晴。走上河橋，放眼望去，滿目新綠，身心俱為舒鬆。不管冬天如何漫長，河邊的草木總會如期發芽，透出新綠，給人以滿滿的希望！

　　　　　　　2019年5月16日，關中李保陽讀畢並識於美東思故客河上。

李保陽致孫康宜

孫先生，

　　保陽的英文速度肯定沒有您的漢語速度快，哈哈～～如果您能使用漢語拼音輸入法，那麼在電腦上寫漢字速度就會快很多。

　　等保陽來Yale拜訪您的時候，可以嘗試下載一款語音輸入漢字系統，這樣寫漢字就比較快了。玫儀老師如果看到您的郵件，應該會很快回覆您。

　　今天和您往復交流，是保陽來美後最為充實的一天！謝謝　先生給保陽這麼一個表達的機會！

　　疫情洶洶，善自珍攝！保陽為您和您的家人禱告！

保陽

4/4/2020

孫康宜致李保陽

Dear Baoyang,

　　No worries! My computer already has語音輸入漢字系統! My computer is very well equipped.

　　However, what I meant is: It's so much faster for me to type in English! It's just easier for me. As you know, I have been in the US for more than 50 years. Hahaha!

Kang-i
4/4/2020

李保陽致孫康宜

孫先生，

　　剛剛讀到這裡，仔細一看，發現下面這張照片正好是六十八年前的今天拍攝的。真的很奇妙啊！您可以回憶一下那時候是怎樣憧憬六十八年後今日的自己。很有意思的。

保陽　敬上
4/4/2020

孫康宜8歲那年兒童節，全校榮譽生與師長合影，高雄林園（1952年4月4日）

Michael Meng（孟振華）致孫康宜

Dear Kang-i,

I hope this message finds you well.

I found the digital copy through HathiTrust. The section of Wang Pengyun included an introduction written by William Schultz. However, I did a quick search on OCLC and some major English journal databases and couldn't find any translation work earlier than yours. I hope the information helps.

Please take care!

Best,

Michael

4/4/2020

註：**Michael Meng（孟振華）**，耶魯大學東亞圖書館館長。

孫康宜致Michael Meng（孟振華）

Dear Michael,

Thank you so much for finding the PDF for me. Also, I appreciate your looking into other major English journal databases for possible earlier translations of Wang Pengyun's works. I'm glad to know that I might be the first translator of Wang Pengyun's *ci*, although I only translated 3 pieces of his *ci* poems. Translation is just not my cup of tea! Hahaha!

I cc Dr. Li Baoyang李保陽on this email, because he is an expert on Wang Pengyun, and his book (originally his Ph.D. dissertation) is going to be published in Taiwan. Once published, please make sure that Yale University Library will get a copy for its collection. Li Baoyang is currently residing in Pennsylvania. I hope that in the near future he will have a chance to visit our Yale Sterling Library. He also knows 吳格, who as you know spent a lot of effort helping us with our rare books 善本書.

With thanks,

Kang-i
4/4/2020

孫康宜致林玫儀

玫儀你好！

　　多年不見，很是想念。去年秋天一直想請樂學書局寄給你剛出版的兩本書——即家父的《孫保羅書信：附書信日記》及《一粒麥子》修訂本（孫保羅著，孫康宜編著）——但因為沒有你的通訊地址，只好作罷。最近有幸與費城的李保陽先生聯絡，由他那兒居然得到你的電子郵箱，很是高興。現在就把兩本書的序言寄給你，請見附件。

　　最高興的是，原來是你首先領李保陽信主的。此事讓我格外感動！

　　現在因為疫情嚴重，我們都不敢出去。以我七十六高齡，目前仍在耶魯任全職（還是本系研究所主任），現在也只能改為線上教學了。

　　希望我們都互相保重，凡事聽從神的帶領。

　　又，請告知你的通訊地址，一旦接你的回覆，我就會請樂學書局寄書給你。我想他們也要等疫情過去了，才會開始寄書，但我還是先通知他們，以免忘記。

康宜匆匆
4/4/2020

李保陽致孫康宜

孫先生尊鑒：

　　避疫在家，捧讀文集，感動應接不暇。本計畫待讀完後將讀後感稍作整比潤色，再奉左右，奈何這幾天焚膏繼晷，讀得口齒生香，此讀後感恐將連綿不絕。遂決定將此草稿先奉上。續有所得，再行呈正！耑此，並候

　　教安！

晚保陽　敬上

4/5/2020

李保陽致孫康宜

孫先生，

　　收到您的來信，非常開心！謝謝　先生的繆賞和信任！

　　保陽以前在圖書館工作，又作過雜誌編輯，所以對文字校對比較敏感。希望保陽傳給　先生的讀後記中沒有太大偏差。

　　保陽非常願意為　先生校對文集書稿。

　　保陽迄今最為遺憾的是，自己系統的教育和學術訓練，皆是在中國大陸接受的。2011年冬，玫儀老師推薦保陽拜讀了臺大齊邦媛老師的《巨流河》，齊老師在這本書的後半部分，比較詳細地敘述了美國進修學習，對她後來學術取徑產生了至關重要的影響。從那時起，保陽即對自己沒有接受過歐美學術訓練深感遺憾。因此自己的學術研究，只能一直在文獻的範疇內徘徊，很難再有新的突破。對西方學術路徑的陌生，在現今的學術研究格局中，是一個要命的缺陷。　先生身為華人，在美國生活、從事學術研究工作逾半個世紀，學貫中西，對西方學術理論，有深入精微的瞭解和運用。如果保陽能系統地仔細地校讀　先生的著作，是一次難得的學習機會，相信對自己目前既有的學術研究格局，會有很大的突破。所以不管有無報酬，保陽都極願擔任　先生書稿的校對工作。

專此奉覆，並請

諸安！

保陽　敬上
4/5/2020

註：此函部分刪節。

李保陽致孫康宜

孫先生，

謝謝　先生的信任，將五卷本《文集》的Word文檔交付保陽！

廣西師範大學出版社是一家很有前瞻性眼光的出版社，最近幾年在業界和讀書界的評價非常不錯。出版海外學人文集是該社的一大傳統，前幾年出版了錢穆、余英時、何炳棣、唐德剛、黃仁宇等一大批海外學者的文集，這是他們分社的一個品牌。桂林分社現主營古籍文獻的影印（保陽的朋友即在桂林負責這一方面的工作），影印了許多海外尤其是哈佛燕京所藏的古籍叢刊。深圳還有一家「理想國」，也屬於該社的一個分支，出版了不少思想深刻的好書。　先生的文集能在該社出版，是個很不錯的選擇。

保陽
4/6/2020

註：此函部分刪節。

李保陽致孫康宜

孫先生，

　　保陽若讀到有問題之處，一定會轉告　先生的。　請放心！這是保陽的職業習慣。

　　上月初，保陽因腳傷在家休息，每天去Gest讀書，美東鄉間初春的林間小徑、清淺可鑑的小溪、散落在路邊的農場、木屋，實在有種故鄉的熟悉感，保陽隨口吟成兩首小詩，茲奉　先生一哂：

> **普林斯頓道中**
>
> 林深水淺草芃芃，野店板橋一路東。三月桃花二月雨，原來已在暖風中。

> **普林斯頓大學東亞圖書館見迎春花盛開**
>
> 一樹黃花乍洩春，滿園細雨密如鱗。階前風信今年早，吹上樓頭最撩人。
>
> 保陽未是草，康宜先生誨正

庚子三月十四日（4/6/2020）

孫康宜致李保陽

Dear Baoyang,

　　Thank you for the most beautiful and inspiring poems! I really appreciate your sharing your poems on Princeton's Gest Library with me. It brings back a lot of fond memories to me.

　　I'll record your two poems in my diary today!

　　By the way, please see my old picture attached below.　The picture was taken in 1980 when I was the Curator（館長）of Gest Library. I was then 36 years old, only two years after I got my Ph.D. degree.

Best,

Kang-i

4/6/2020

時任Princeton大學葛思德
東亞圖書館館長的孫康宜教
授（1980，Princeton）。

孫康宜致李保陽

Baoyang,

I'm sending you the 2017 memorial program which I put together for my adviser Prof. Yu-kung Kao（高友工教授）who died on Oct. 29, 2016. Please see the memorial program attached here.

The Memorial Service追思會took place in the common room（會議室）in Jone Hall, which is near the road you have described in your poem, "普林斯頓道中."

Kang-i（孫康宜）

4/6/2020

高友工教授（Yu-kung Kao，右三）在授課，1973，
Princeton（照片由普林斯頓大學東亞研究系 [East
Asian Studies Department] 提供）。左一為Andrew
Plaks（浦安迪），左二為Richard E. Strassberg
（宣立敦）。

高友工教授退休前，最後一天上完課，與余英時
教授合影（1998年12月18日）。

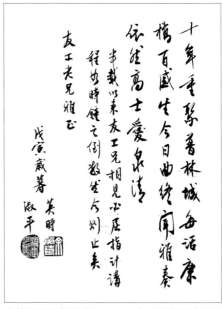

余英時和陳淑平（Monica Yu）夫婦獻給高友工
的贈詩（1998年12月18日）。

李保陽致孫康宜

孫先生，

　　謝謝您的回信，並附來您為紀念恩師高友工先生設計的紀念冊（那時候的安
迪先生好年輕）。讀了那些紀念文字，又讓保陽回到近十年來在中國國內的那種
閱讀體驗當中去了。蓋自從玫儀老師推薦拜讀了齊邦媛先生的《巨流河》之後，
保陽深以沒有機會接受過西方學術訓練為憾，於是連帶著對海外學人之治古典文
史者，多所留心。但高先生的作品似乎在中國大陸並非如黃仁宇、余英時等先生
那麼暢銷，所以保陽對高先生著實所知不多。讀了　先生的紀念冊，則對高先生
瞭解更加深入了。謝謝　先生的贈閱雅誼！

　　先生願將保陽小詩載入日記，真是不勝榮幸。先生的日記，一定是一筆研
究海外學人學術的寶貴文獻。保陽記日記二十餘年，對於有「日記癖」者，倍覺
親切。前年冬和去年春夏間，就將前年出國時帶出來的兩部書藁整理了出來，其

中有一部是傅彥長的妹妹傅成家的日記。傅彥長曾經和您家族好友張我軍先生，一起出席昭和十六年（1941）在東京舉辦的大東亞文學者大會。傅氏日記前兩年在上海圖書館被人發現，整理出來發表。而他妹妹的這部八萬字的日記，則是保陽的一位「鏟地皮」（走街串巷收舊貨古董）的上海朋友，在上海里弄裡收到的。該日記記事起自1947年1月1日，迄於當年12月31日，整整一年，其中有九個月時間，作者是在臺北路局工作。詳細記載了作者入臺後不久爆發的「二二八事變」，是很有史料價值的一部文獻。待疫情結束，保陽可將此日記整理稿拿來New Haven贈送給先生。

下午收到　先生寄來的《走出白色恐怖》和《從北山樓到潛學齋》，感謝萬分。先讀了〈「童化」與「教化」〉，因為那篇您特意用浮簽標註了提到林玫儀老師，第二篇讀了〈施蟄存對付人生災難的態度〉，因為這篇是保陽目前個人所最需的精神食糧。這兩篇中有幾句話保陽覺得特別受用，茲錄如下：

> 「我覺得災難確是一個人生命旅途中的試金石。」（頁161）
> 「即使在絕望的現實中，我們也可以通過想像與信心，把生命的境界無止無盡地提升和擴大。」（頁161）
> 「一個人應當認清自己該做什麼，而一旦選中適當的角色，就必須下決心把它做好。」（頁161）
> 「是一種對生命本身的信心與好奇心使他不斷尋找新的體驗和角色。」（頁162）

以上這些話，是您對施先生自在的生命狀態的解讀，同時也是您在知天命之年，用自己對人生的體悟去感知一位前輩學人的人生。我更寧願把這些智慧的語言，看作是您對人生的一種感悟和總結。這些話和您在《潛學齋隨想錄》裡講到的話，精神面目是如此的相似！保陽在國內教書時，曾經一再和學生講，一個人對未知世界有多大的好奇心，他的世界就有多大。這大概也是一種對生命的好奇心使然，沒想到和先生在二十四年前所說的話暗合。

「一個人在憤怒的時候，最好能藉著音樂來取得心理的平衡。」（頁171）讀到先生這句話，保陽想到了　先父，他是個地地道道的中國西北農夫，但是終

生愛好那些「沒有實用價值」的文學、音樂，他教會了我們兄弟吹笛子，三十年來，每當我心情抑鬱煩悶時，總會找個安靜的地方去吹奏一曲，心情就會好很多。2013年夏，保陽到塞外蘭州拜訪王鵬運後人，在蘭州黃河鐵橋畔的左公柳下，邂逅一位蘇州的賣笛人，買了一枝笛子和簫，前年出奔，亦載之以出。因為它能給保陽偶爾枯燥的生活裡增添亮色。

　　「研究詩歌，若只是套用今日盛行的文學和文化理論，確實是『失其真』了。那種詩歌研究不但不能陶冶自己的心性，也無法感人」（頁171）這句話在保陽的理解是：詩歌（文學）研究，還要帶入個人的經驗。就像嚴迪昌先生寫《清詞史》和《清詩史》，時時有「我」（嚴先生自己）的影子在，就是將他自己的聲音摹寫進文字中。優秀的文學研究著作，確實要能「陶冶自己的心性」，也要「感人」。記得保陽曾經給學生講《項羽本紀》，說了這麼一段話：「『天之亡我，我何渡為！且籍與江東子弟八千人渡江而西，今無一人還，縱江東父兄憐而王我，我何面目見之？縱彼不言，籍獨不愧於心乎？』後人多目項王為粗莽勇魯之人，然其臨終守心、知恥之論，足令多少人汗顏？一個人如果守不住底線，一個社會如果沒有了廉恥感，就是亭林先生所謂『仁義充塞，而至於率獸食人』了。有愧於心，方是英雄本色！項王當日斬會稽郡守首級，僅需叔父項梁一『瞬』，即手起刀落，大功告成。而鴻門一宴，亞父范曾『數目』項王，項王卻猶疑難為所動，前後判若兩人。何也？當日項王與叔父並無尺寸，崛起於隴畝之間，自然無所顧忌，而與劉邦對壘鴻門時，項王已是擁兵四十萬的西楚霸王，他還能像年輕氣盛時那樣輕而易舉地做一個決定嗎？人在做重大決定前，必然經過了與自己的痛苦鬥爭，否則便是輕率，小則貽害身家，大則禍及眾生。把歷史帶進經驗世界裡解讀，我發現：文學的真實，比歷史的真實更受用。因為文學是人學，是學做人。而做人，是這個世界最難的事情，除非一個人慣說假話或者根本就對人生不負責。」還有一次講曹丕，云：「曹丕的名播天下，更多是因為他弟弟曹植那首七步詩。這首詩傳本不一，來自《世說新語》，小說家言。類此故事，尚有曹沖秤象，陳寅恪先生在《寒柳堂集》中已證其偽，難保陳思王此故事不失實。曹丕其人，權謀不及孫氏父子兄弟，虛偽趕不上劉玄德，觀其所作〈燕歌行〉，哀感頑豔，細膩真切，〈論文〉則洋洋灑灑，本色當行，實一皇二代兼富二代文人也，應不至殘忍如傳說所言。又國人有同情弱者心理積習，兼『會哭

的孩子有奶吃」，思王集中多失意廟堂、落拓江湖之作，易引起後來者之同情，故不惜附會牽扯，以為掌故。後之人信而傳播，遂奉為文學經典。」

先生寄來的三聯書店版《走出白色恐怖》，甫一拆開包裹，就被小女搶走。雖然她亦在手機上讀了一些篇章，但我們父女同患愛讀紙本書之癖。猶記剛來美國那會兒，她把我帶在身邊消遣的一冊蔣夢麟《西潮・新潮》翻來顛去讀了數遍，現在每每談到某種類似情形，便張口道「蔣夢麟也⋯⋯」。她喜歡　先生的文字，尤其喜歡令尊老先生的《一粒麥子》。她聞說疫情結束保陽將有New Haven之行，一定要隨行。一笑～

保陽喜歡讀　先生書，讀後喜歡和　先生東拉西扯地談讀後感。這種感覺真好！謝謝　先生給保陽這樣一個美好的讀書機會。感謝主！這個春天真美！

保陽　敬上

4/6/2020

孫康宜致李保陽

Dear Baoyang,

I want to let you know that I have already given most of my diaries（日記）and letters to Yale Divinity School Library耶魯大學神學院圖書館特藏部。Please see my previous email to you (with the subject line: "Paul Yu-kuang Sun Collection & Paul Yu-kuang Sun Family papers).

Apart from the above donation to Yale Divinity School Library, I have also given most of my collections to the following places:（1）北京大學國際漢學家研修基地；（2）臺灣國家圖書館。（3）Connecticut College in New London. As you can see, at age 76 I am trying to give away as many valuable books and manuscripts as possible, so that my personal library does not become a burden to my family in the future. In other words, currently I do not wish to add more manuscripts or art works to my collection. So, please DO NOT give me the 二二八日記 which you mentioned in your email. But thank you for thinking of me anyway.

Regarding my late mentor Prof. Yu-kung Kao（高友工）, I must say that Prof. Kao reminds me of the great Confucius 孔子. This is because Prof. Kao was basically a teacher of 述而不作. He was the greatest teacher one can ever have; both Andy Plaks（浦安迪）and I were his students. (Andy Plaks later became one of my teachers, when I returned to Princeton U to work for my Ph.D. degree--even though Andy is two years younger than me!)

After Prof. Kao died, I asked Andy Plaks to write the obituary（悼詞）for Kao. For the obituary, please see the beginning section of the memorial program (追思會紀念冊)。

When you visit Yale campus in the near future, please bring your flutes 笛和簫 with you. It would be great to listen to your flute music.

I'm so pleased that your daughter Lucy likes my book《走出白色恐佈》and my father's book 《一粒麥子》. I think we share similar interest!

Best,
Kang-i
4/7/2020

孫康宜的「潛學齋文庫」，
是北京大學「漢學家研修基
地圖書館」的一部分。

李保陽致孫康宜

孫先生，

今天收到的《從北山樓到潛學齋》頁153註4第一行的「樂」應該是「欒」，蓋「欒」「樂」形近，易致誤也。

保陽　敬上
4/7/2020

李保陽致孫康宜

孫先生，

謝謝　先生賜閱秀威版序言。以及在序言中補及我的名字。戔戔一言，得先生如此鄭重申明，荒村僻居，感何如之！　先生對後學之提攜，一如三十年前之施　先生！保陽銘感中心！

今天河上春陽正暖，煦風習習，保陽從上午即坐在Porch上拜讀《從北山樓到潛學齋》一書，想今明兩天應可讀完，屆時如有發現可校改處，再呈　先生乙覽。

讀三十年前學人函箚，不勝東京夢華之感，尤其施　先生信中偶爾表露當時生活之拮據，人心世風之澆薄，都使人不勝悵嘆！專此，敬候

撰安！

晚保陽敬上
庚子三月望日於思故客河上抱月樓之Porch上
（4/7/2020）

孫康宜致李保陽

保陽，

　　家父的書法、日記、書信已經存藏在耶魯大學神學院圖書館特藏部！Please see this link for the Yale University finding aid: https://archives.yale.edu/repositories/4/resources/11579

　　Also, many of my diaries and letters were already given to 耶魯大學神學院圖書館特藏部——under "Paul Yu-kuang Sun Family Papers." Please see attached（請見附件）。

Best,
Kang-i
4/7/2020

孫康宜致李保陽

Dear Baoyang,

　　Thank you for pointing out the errors. Currently I am very busy preparing tomorrow's class, so I won't check into these until after my class tomorrow.

　　Thank you again!

Kang-i
4/7/2020

李保陽致孫康宜

孫先生，

　　今天一天集中拜讀《從北山樓到潛學齋》，亦隨著您三十六年前的腳步，一

路走過和施先生交往的十九年。能有機會如此切近地跟隨兩位學人的腳步，把你們之間交往的細節，一一再現，就好似發生在我自己身上一般的親切。因為保陽在江南生活過十多年，像您和施先生交往一樣，保陽也交往過許多江南一帶的布衣學者，雖然他們沒有頭頂施先生那麼閃亮的光環，但是剝去那些耀眼的光環，從上世紀八九十年代到今天，他們的生活環境，是那麼的相似，飛速劇變的時光，在這些傳統的學人身上和生活環境上，似乎沒有留下任何改變的痕跡。其中印象最為深刻的是，施先生一直向您解釋他的經濟狀況不佳。這真是一件叫人無奈和氣短的事情。十幾年前，保陽遊走在江南一帶，去窮鄉僻壤，有時候要轉好幾趟公交車才能找到這些人。那時候，保陽深刻覺得，這些散落在鄉野間的布衣學人，和宋末元初、明末清初、清末民初的那幾代遺民，有某種相似的地方。今天隨著您的腳步，回顧施先生和您交往的十七年，讓保陽很深沉地想起那些朋友！

您的信中提到您的日記已經捐贈給了Yale神學院圖書館特藏部。保陽又回頭查看了您昨天傳送的孫氏家族文獻捐贈Yale的說明。你們家族的捐贈，讓保陽想起了上海圖書館的「熊希齡專藏」，據說熊氏連他們家請客的菜單都詳加保管存檔，以至於今日才有如此序列完整的熊希齡專藏。好像趙元任先生的檔案也是這樣，存藏於西部的某間大學裡。您這種捐贈的意義，是沒有「文獻癖」的人不能理解的。保陽從您提供的神學院圖書館特藏部孫氏家族文獻介紹中知道，您將1979至2019年的三十年日記和書信兩百六十封，都捐贈了出去。這批文獻在秀威版和廣西師大版《文集》中都沒有透露，這部分接下來您有什麼打算嗎？如果保陽造訪神學院圖書館，可以看到那些日記和書信嗎？

保陽對記錄當代學術史文獻非常感興趣，在中國時，曾經採訪過嚴迪昌先生的夫人曹林芳女士。保陽在浙大圖書館工作時，和晚年的吳熊和先生聊天，並記入日記。有關嚴先生的採訪，上次已經在Line中傳送給您了。和吳先生的談話錄，發表在《詞學》第三十二輯，但您既然已經把藏書捐給了北大，保陽把原稿用附件傳送給您。

保陽對藏書史一直很感興趣，您捐贈家族文獻和個人藏書給Yale和北大，其背景和經過，保陽非常感興趣。保陽也擬訂了一些感興趣的話題，想和　先生聊一聊，比如：

（1）捐贈文獻給Yale和捐贈私人藏書給北大的因緣；

（2）翻譯王鵬運詞緣起、經過；

（3）捐贈出去的日記、書信有什麼處理計畫；

（4）談一談您的老師，如高友工、牟復禮以及其他先生們；

（5）您1968年來美之後的奮鬥歷史（這個話題牽扯的內容很多，時間很
　　　長，可以從長計議）

　　以上幾個問題是今天讀書時想到的，如果方便，您可以在郵件中回覆，如果
郵件不方便，我們聊天的時候保陽再作記錄也可以。這個想法完全看　先生的意
願和方便，不必強求。如果　先生覺得有什麼不方便，也可以不談。保陽的初衷
是想留下一些當代海外有關中國研究的學術史料。

　　您轉寄給保陽的高先生紀念冊，填補了保陽的很多認知盲區，感謝。保陽會
帶著笛子和簫來拜訪　先生，這讓保陽想起了四十年前，　先生和張充和女士在
紐約「明軒」的那次雅集！

　　十分期待疫情盡快結束，在四十年後的Yale，又一次弦歌不輟！

　　先生明天上課繁忙，此信不必亟覆！專此，並請

　　萬安！

保陽　敬上
4/7/2020

孫康宜致李保陽

Dear BAOYANG,

　　Thank you so much for your interest in my collections! Your questions are so interesting! However, I cannot give you the answers in simple words! It would take many days to tell you about all the details! 三天三夜也說不完。

　　Let's wait for a future opportunity when we meet in person. Okay!

　　In haste,

Kang-i
4/7/2020

李保陽致孫康宣

孫先生，

　　早上起來，在廚房裡一邊做飯，一邊讀完了〈語訛默固好——簡論施蟄存評唐詩〉。這真是一片融入了人生智慧的好文字，不管是韓愈、施先生，還是您，你們都得了人生的智慧。保陽特別喜歡下面這幾句話：

　　　「他的論點常常呈現出一種非比尋常的創意，一種因生活經驗累積而成的體會，一種灑脫的生活藝術。」（頁155）
　　　「今日的我，由於人生閱歷漸多，初讀到施先生所引的這首韓愈詩，內心產生一種難以形容的感動。」（頁155）
　　　「這首詩表現的是中唐詩人一種從憂患裡漸入清境的心理過程。」（頁156）
　　　「一個老年詩人所創出的另一種自由空間——一種對生命過程的信心，一種把握人生風浪的智慧心靈。人老了……最好安靜下來，憑自己的智慧來思考，使那生命之樹永不枯萎，不斷啟發生命的再思。」（頁157）
　　　「（施先生）以自己的智慧繼續開拓出滿園花開的生命境界。」

　　保陽在前天晚上給您的信中曾提到過，詩應該融入個人的經驗世界來解讀。您以「人生閱歷漸多」而對韓詩產生「感動」，進而以意逆志，聯想到韓愈的這種詩風正是基於人生體悟，成為「以美感取勝」的盛唐，過渡到以「清境」為特色的中唐之表徵。這個看法真是太妙了。如果不是基於對生命進程的感悟和體驗，焉能有如此角度的解讀。由韓愈的〈落齒〉，回想起大約您寫〈語默〉這篇文章那會兒，保陽在鄉間讀李商隱的〈韓碑〉。那時候真的覺得好，尤其是開篇

的「元和天子神武姿，彼何人哉軒與羲」，氣象多麼地華美動人，甚至連後來
「長繩百尺拽碑倒，粗砂大石相磨治」的反覆無常，都覺得是一種歷史和人生共
同起伏的壯觀，那些人竟然都能得到一份與有榮焉的歷史榮光。這完全是少年時
閱讀感受，還體會不到繁華背後的人生感慨和無常。所以那時候也肯定讀不懂
〈落齒〉，讀不懂施先生，更讀不懂您寫人生昇華的那些文字。

刻下的中國大陸學術界言必稱「創新」「理論」，但多隔靴搔癢，不著肯
綮。就本質而言，中國詩歌本身是抒情的，不管是葉嘉瑩先生的「興發感動」
說，還是陳世驤強調中國詩歌「抒情傳統」，以至於您的「消構式批評」（頁
9，因為我還沒有讀完您的《文集》，故不清楚這是不是您在〈北美二十年來詞
學研究〉中提出來的理論，但是從字面理解，這是一種更接近中國詩歌原始狀態
的抒情回歸），都強調中國詩歌的抒情底色。雖然時移世易，人物更替，但是人
類基本的情感是相通一致的，不管是西方還是東土。因之以個人的情感世界和人
生經驗來揆度前人的詩歌境界，也許是更能夠豐滿我們自己的人生體驗，彰顯一
代文學特色的有效途徑。

您由韓詩的感動，不僅關照到詩史的流變動因，還聯想到施先生用生命信
心，創造出自由空間，把握智慧心靈，思考生命，讓生命之樹常青，活出全新
的生命境界。保陽由此聯想到的是，您在十年前六十六歲時，將自己的數千冊
私人藏書捐贈給北大，又將家族文獻捐贈給Yale，誠如您自己所說：「at age 76 I
am trying to give away as many valuable books and manuscripts as possible, so that my
personal library does not become a burden to my family in the future.」我可不可以把
這種與年歲俱增的越來越簡約化的生活方式，理解成昂揚少年的唐詩，向「以意
念造作形象」（您的朋友柯慶明教授語）的宋詩轉變的表徵呢？而越來越簡約化
的這種達觀，表現在將有形的財產捐出，其原因除了表面的「does not become a
burden to my family in the future」，一定還有您「智慧」的「思考」。保陽在江
南生活的時候，也見到過許多枯守滿屋故紙的鄉村老先生，他們往往行為物役，
目光始終聚焦在那些有形的書之愛上，最後反而讓那些「burden」限制了他們對
於生命的想象，形容枯槁，不得享受「滿園花開的生命境界」！以上是今早讀
您的文章所得。一種很美好的享受！謝謝　先生！

保陽　敬上
4/8/2010

李保陽致孫康宜

孫先生：

　　今天讀完了《從北山樓到潛學齋》的後半部分《研究篇》，茲將保陽認為可訂正處錄如左（請先生重點查看第22、第25兩條）：

　　第22條，頁246，第四行「宜都」「建平」為二地名，中間應加頓號「、」（《晉書·地理志五》：「荊州統南郡、武昌、宜都、建平、天門、長沙……。」）同頁第十行括弧後的句號移至括弧前。同頁第十二行「劍芒」當作「劍鋩」。同頁第十四至十七行因「劍鋩」典故而涉及蘇軾、柳宗元詩，並引〈東坡題跋〉為據。「蘇、柳皆貶南方荒蠻之地，而施蟄存也到了同樣的地方。故此兩句既言石林之陡峭遠勝蘇、柳所見，或亦蘊含詩人自己望鄉思家之意。」（頁246倒數第十行至倒數第九行）。元豐八年（1085）三月，蘇軾知登州，〈東坡題跋〉中提到的東武、文登，皆登州地名，在今山東境內。與「南方荒蠻之地」無涉。紹聖四年（1097）二月，蘇軾在貶所惠州，將由嘉佑寺遷入白鶴新居，作〈白鶴峰新居欲成夜過西鄰翟秀才〉二首，其一云：「林行婆家初閉戶，翟夫子舍尚留關。連娟缺月黃昏後，縹緲新居紫翠間。繫悶豈無羅帶水，割愁還有劍鋩山。中原北望無歸日，鄰火村春自往還。」其中「劍芒山」下有註云：「柳子厚云：『海上尖峰若劍鋩，秋來處處割愁腸。』皆嶺南詩也。」陸游《老學庵筆記》卷二：「柳子厚詩云：『海上尖山似劍鋩，愁來處處割斷腸。』東坡用之云：『割愁還有劍鋩山。』或謂可言『割愁腸』，不可但言『割愁』。亡兄仲高云：『晉張望詩曰「愁來不可割」（〈貧士詩〉），此「割愁」二字出處也。』」惠州即今廣東惠州市，古屬嶺南「荒蠻之地」，故此處引〈東坡題跋〉，不如引用〈白鶴峰新居欲成夜過西鄰翟秀才〉為貼切。

　　第25條，頁253，第二段倒數第五行第六字「快」疑為「袂」之訛。同頁第

二段第四行「珍重東坡謫儋耳，隨行猶自有朝雲」，紹聖元年（1094）蘇軾被貶惠州，四年（1097）再貶儋耳（今海南儋州）。王朝雲（1062-1096）是蘇軾貶謫嶺南的隨行侍妾，在紹聖三年已逝於惠州，故無隨行蘇軾到儋耳之可能。施先生此處移花接木，以暗指郁達夫與王映霞情變本事。今人引用時宜加說明，以免誤會。

保陽　敬上

4/8/2020

註：此信有部分刪節。

李保陽致孫康宜

孫先生，

　　今天讀完全書。這是今年開年以來讀完的第七本書，兩天以來，一直沉浸在三十年前的兩位學人的翰札世界裡，何其有幸！誠如編者沈建中先生所云，這本書「可為研究者提供在1980、1990年代中美學者在研究中國古典文學方面的難得的學術案例，具有相當的文獻參考價值。另一方面供應讀者獨特雋永閒適的隨筆式文本，為讀者提供『可讀、樂讀、耐讀』似的閱讀享受。」就保陽的閱讀體驗而言，沈先生的這兩方面的預期，都實現了。

　　明天開始，繼續讀《文集》！專此，並頌

　　文安！

保陽　敬上

4/8/2020

孫康宜致李保陽

Dear BAOYANG,

This is a follow-up email to my message which I sent to you last night! I forgot to mention that I truly appreciate your suggested changes for Item# 22. You have definitely given me a much better reference to Su Shi regarding Jian Mang Mountain.

I'll add a note to my article and will quote your long and thoughtful passage! I don't know how to thank you for this valuable comment.

Kang-i
4/9/2020

李保陽致孫康宜

孫先生，

收到您的來信。謝謝　先生謬讚！

昨晚傳送給您的校記，是保陽憑直覺和以往的工作經驗寫出的。因為手頭參考書的限制，只能就網上找一些材料來印證記憶，沒有查考相關的文獻。希望那些經驗式的校記不會出大錯，也希望　先生不以保陽的直言為忤。

另外，保陽有個想法：目前這樣在秀威版上看到的一些問題，經過校改之後，難保不會在簡體版中再以其他形式出現（作者的Word文檔和出版社的排版系統在轉換時，也會出現差錯）。所以，將來簡體版的校樣如果出來，　先生可否寄給保陽一份作校對？這與您的校對不衝突，將來可以將您和保陽的校對意見一起送交出版社作最後處理。如果　先生覺得不必這樣操作，只在秀威版上作校改即可，那保陽想麻煩　先生，能否給保陽一套紙本書，這樣讀起來更方便、更快。同時可以在書頁上直接記錄，比現在必須依賴電腦或者手機閱讀方便許多（視　先生方便，不必強求）。保陽這段時間在家避疫，正可拜讀　先生大作。同時為　先生校對文字。

　　剛剛看到康州的疫情嚴重程度，似乎僅次於紐約，實在讓人擔心難過。希望您和家人保重身體！

　　阿們！

P.S.昨晚的校記之第22條中有未妥處，茲改訂後奉上：

　　頁246，第四行「宜都」「建平」為二地名，中間應加頓號「、」（《晉書‧地理志五》：「荊州統南郡、武昌、宜都、建平、天門、長沙……。」）同頁第十行括弧後的句號移至括弧前。同頁第十二行「劍芒」當作「劍鋩」。同頁第十四至十七行因「劍鋩」典故而涉及蘇軾、柳宗元詩，並引〈東坡題跋〉為據。「蘇、柳皆貶南方荒蠻之地，而施蟄存也到了同樣的地方。故此兩句既言石林之陡峭遠勝蘇、柳所見，或亦蘊含詩人自己望鄉思家之意。」（頁246倒數第十行至倒數第九行）。元豐八年（1085）三月，蘇軾知登州，〈東坡題跋〉中提到的東武、文登，皆登州地名，在今山東境內，與「南方荒蠻之地」無涉。紹聖四年（1097）二月，蘇軾在貶所惠州，將由嘉佑寺遷入白鶴新居，作〈白鶴峰新居欲成夜過西鄰翟秀才〉二首，其一云：「林行婆家初閉戶，翟夫子舍尚留關。連娟缺月黃昏後，縹緲新居紫翠間。繫悶豈無羅帶水，割愁還有劍鋩山。中原北望無歸日，鄰火村舂自往還。」其中「劍芒山」下有註云：「柳子厚云：『海上尖峰若劍鋩，秋來處處割愁腸。』皆嶺南詩也。」陸游《老學庵筆記》卷二：「柳子厚詩云：『海上尖山似劍鋩，愁來處處割斷腸。』東坡用之云：『割愁還有劍鋩山。』或謂可言『割愁腸』，不可但言『割愁』。亡兄仲高云：『晉張望詩曰「愁來不可割」（〈貧士詩〉），此「割愁」二字出處也。』」惠州即今廣東惠州市，古屬嶺南「荒蠻之地」，故此處引〈東坡題跋〉，不如引用〈白鶴峰新居欲成夜過西鄰翟秀才〉為貼切。

保陽　敬上

4/9/2020

孫康宜致李保陽

Dear BAOYANG,

Thank you for your revised passage, which I'll incorporate into the new edition.

I'll be sure to give you a hard copy of the book, when published! The book will come out in June.

With thanks,

Kang-i

4/9/2020

李保陽致孫康宜

孫先生，

謝謝您轉來東海大學圖書館下週即將舉辦的孫氏家族文獻展覽資訊！

恭喜您！

您在《走出白色恐怖》一書中提到過，東海是您的本科母校。您是東海在海外的傑出校友。今天您到了學術收穫的黃金季節，就像農人的辛勤勞作要得到收穫那樣，這是您應得的一份榮耀。東海是一所教會學校，您的榮耀，也是上帝的榮耀！

保陽雖未嘗親自拜訪東海，但與東海也有一段因緣：2015學年的寒假，保陽應東海大學中文系的林香伶教授之請，與她合作整理校訂《南社詩話》，那部書收錄了幾乎所有能搜集到的南社籍作者撰著的詩話著作，全書收集發表於各處報刊上的詩話著作一百幾十種，字數大概與您的《文集》相當。林香伶老師經常向保陽提及東海美麗的校園裡那座Luce Chapel（就是《走出白色恐怖》英文本頁156您和Prof. Moses拍攝畢業照的那座教堂），是東海的「美中之美」。她一直邀請保陽有機會去東海參觀訪問。希望不久的將來，能有機會實現這個願望。相信當那時保陽走近Luce Chapel時，一定會想起您，想起為教育事業和基督福音鞠

躬盡瘁的Prof. Moses！

再次感謝　先生分享的圖片和信息！

感謝　神，讓保陽見證這份美好！

保陽　敬上
4/10/2020

①東海大學圖書館為孫氏家族舉辦的「陽光穿透的歲月」文獻展覽。
②來自中央研究院副院長黃進興博士的祝賀。
③孫康成和孫觀圻贈送鮮花給東海大學，代表孫氏家族向東海大學致謝。

李保陽致孫康宜

孫先生，

恭喜先生！

沒有想到半個世紀後，　先生竟然找到了自己當初的本科畢業論文，真的是太奇妙了！可見東海大學真的是一所學風嚴謹管理制度完善的學府，無愧臺灣私立大學執牛耳者之美譽！

1990年11月，吳大猷先生重游母校密西根大學，該校為吳先生舉辦了一場名為「The Ta-You Wu Symposium」的研討會，會後校圖書館將吳先生1933年的畢業論文特製了一本，作為禮物送給吳先生作為紀念。保陽想，如果　先生能得到這麼一本自己五十五年前論文的特製本，一定會非常開心的。先生以為如何呢？

專此候覆！

保陽　又上

4/10/2020

孫康宜致李保陽

Baoyang:

    Great, Please give my warm regards to Prof. Lin Hsiang-ling.

Best,

Kang-i

4/10/2020

李保陽致孫康宜

孫先生，

    真沒想到香伶老師和您也是舊識，煞是意外！保陽和香伶老師聯絡比較密切，前兩天保陽還請她為保陽申請紐約的資助撰寫推薦函。

    因為保陽不知道您和香伶老師原來是舊識，所以沒有貿然把展覽的訊息傳給她。不過在給您寫這封郵件前，保陽已把您的郵件轉給香伶老師了，等明天天亮她看到那封郵件，一定會像玫儀老師看到您的郵件一樣開心的。

    最近讀您的《走出白色恐怖》，又知道您捐贈給Yale神學院的文獻是以家族名義捐出，今天又看到您在母校的展覽也是以家族的面貌展出。能看出您是一個非常珍視家庭幸福和家族傳承的人。這一點深深地感動了保陽。保陽有一個幸福的小家庭，也有一個多災多難的大家族。近年保陽也開始關注家族的歷史，雖然也遇到了您所遇到的家族長輩不願提及往事的共同問題，但有您在前面做出的榜

樣，保陽一定會努力去發掘家族背後的那些故事的。謝謝　先生的啟導！

P.S.下面保陽把寫給香伶老師的信也附給您。

香伶老師：

　　這是孫康宜先生剛剛轉給我的一封郵件。內容是下週將在東海圖書館有一個孫氏家族文獻暨孫先生著作展覽，或許您有興趣可以抽空去欣賞一下。孫先生說您曾經在臉書上和她有互動，但現在你們似乎沒有了太多的聯繫。孫先生希望保陽把這個郵件分享給您，並希望保陽能把您的郵件地址分享給她。保陽在未徵得您同意的情況下，已將您的郵件地址分享給了孫先生。您既然與孫先生是舊識，孫先生又是東海校友，想來不會以之為忤吧？

　　疫情變化旦夕，希望您及兩位世任平安！

　　神愛妳！我們也愛妳！

P.S.您上次去醫院候診，不知道最近身體恢復怎樣了？甚念！

保陽　敬上
4/10/2020

孫康宜致Jeongsoo Shin

Dear Jeongsoo,

　　I just forwarded you some previews of the Sun family exhibition at the Tunghai University Library東海大學圖書館！

　　As you can see, it's funny that they picked my recent picture (taken at age 75), and put it next to my father's 1998 picture, taken while he was 78 years old. It creates an illusion that I was about the same age as my father!

　　Also, from one of the pictures of the exhibition, you will see that your translation of my *Six Dynasties Poetry* book is also on display! That's awesome!

Kang-i

4/10/2020

林香伶致李保陽

保陽：

　　謝謝你的來信，並代我問候孫老師。我確實和她在臉書有互動過，也曾送她一本我主編有關東海的書（《借味・越讀──時光・地景・大度山》）。只是我一直忙碌，臉書不常關注他人。

　　我會找時間參觀孫老師及其尊翁在東海的個展，也會幫忙推廣下這活動。請孫老師安心。

　　明天北上開會，依舊忙碌，再敘。祝平安。

香伶

4/10/2020

李保陽致孫康宜

孫先生，

　　今天拜讀《詞與文類研究》過半，得校記如下（所標頁碼以您傳給保陽的Word文本為準）：

　　頁62末行「十歲不到就登基稱帝」，這個說法不合史實。李煜生於西元937年8月，西元961年其父李璟死於南昌，李煜於南京登帝位，其時當是二十五歲（二十四周歲）。

　　頁71註1似可商榷。註中所謂「海門郡」當是指今南通市的海門縣（英語中

的County可譯作中文的「縣」或者「郡」，但是這兩個詞在具體所指上，是不同的兩級行政單位──一個郡往往管轄好幾個縣──故這裡的翻譯應該是「縣」而不是「郡」）。但是海門縣始建於後周顯德五年（958），在劉禹錫（772-842）那個時代尚未有海門縣的建制。這裡的海門不是確指某一個具體的地名，而應該是泛指江河入海處。比如浙江有三門、廣東澳門、崖門、虎門，皆地處江河入海口，遂以為地名。

　　頁72倒數第三行「沉腰」當作「沈腰」。一般而言，「沈」常在詩詞中通「沉」，但作為姓氏的「沈」則不能用「沉」來代替。這裡的沈、潘分別指沈約、潘岳。

　　拜讀之下，總體的感受是：西方學者的中國古典文學研究，側重文本細讀，比如您引用奧爾巴哈（Erich Auerbach）「並列法」（parataxis）和「附屬結構」（hypotaxis）解讀溫庭筠和韋莊的詞、注意到李煜詞中九字句的運用等等，以這種觀念和方法研究中國古典文學，和中國大陸的傳統大異其趣。中國大陸在您撰著《詞與文類研究》那會兒，還熱衷於討論傳統詩詞的人民性、階級性呢。但是近年來，詞學的研究，又拐入另一路徑，即專事乾嘉樸學的考證一路（這主要集中在明清詞的研究領域），或者是作者身世、政治寄託、傳播方式等等文本外圍的研究。不能說以上諸種研究範式孰優孰劣，但現實的遺憾是，西方的這種研究理論和方法，在中國大陸並沒有引起多少反響。如果基於文本細讀來討論，中國的學者做得不夠。

　　保陽喜歡您解讀王國維評後主詞的那一段。王國維謂「詞至李後主而眼界始大，感慨遂深，遂變伶工之詞而為士大夫之詞。」您在這裡指出，溫庭筠的詞幾乎沒有「抒情的個人寫照」，而早前的韋莊詞「多數作品都有『戲劇』色彩」。而「詞之有『戲劇』性的寫法，事實上是在回應早期的演唱本色」究其因，乃是唐人的詞都是寫給歌姬在歌舞宴會場合歌唱的，不方便過多地將詞人的身影展現在作品中。而李煜不一樣的地方在於他的詞「抒情性特強，對詞壇簡直是一場革命」，「他的作品根本就是直接在抒發自己的情感，在敞開心扉深處的個人思緒」，這是「士大夫之詞」的關捩所在。

　　此外，您對唐詞肇興原因的分析，指出唐玄宗的「梨園」設置，功不可沒，而其作用卻並非是皇室本身以詞為娛樂形式的正面催化刺激，乃在於安史之亂

后，梨園子弟星散民間，使得「伎館」在原有基礎上，補充大量高素質的專業樂工與歌伎。這讓保陽想起了杜甫的〈江南逢李龜年〉那首七絕：「岐王宅裡尋常見，崔九堂前幾度聞。正是江南好風景，落花時節又逢君。」李龜年便是當日星散民間的梨園子弟之一。

您說溫庭筠深諳律詩技巧，並以之入詞，熔鑄奇思異想，造就了其獨特的地位。我便想起他的那首〈過陳琳墓〉：「曾於青史見遺文，今日飄蓬過此墳。詞客有靈應識我，霸才無主始憐君。石麟埋沒藏春草，銅雀荒涼對暮雲。莫怪臨風倍惆悵，欲將書劍學從軍。」這和其十二首〈菩薩蠻〉完全是兩種情思和感慨。

保陽　敬上
4/11/2020

註：此信有部分刪節。

孫康宜致李保陽

Dear Baoyang,

　　I'm deeply grateful to you for pointing out so many errors (including numerous type-setting typos) in the Chinese translation of my book on *ci*. As you know, the author is always the worst proof-reader, especially when the book has been translated into a new language!

　　I was surprised when you pointed out the error: 李煜「十歲不到就登基稱帝」！(p. 63, juan 4). I could not believe my eyes! So I quickly looked into my original English book, *The Evolution of Chinese Tz'u Poetry* (Princeton University Press, 1980). On page 67 of my book I wrote: "In his early years (i.e., **before he turned forty**) first as heir apparent and then as a reigning emperor. . .". (Please see attached! 請見附件）。So the correct Chinese translation should be:「四十歲不到就登基稱帝」。

　　My English book was published 40 years ago, and I don't know why I did not say

"In his early years (i.e., **before he turned twenty-five**). . . , "which would have been much more precise! As you have pointed out, Li Yu succeeded his father in 961, after his father Li Jing died. So, at that time Li Yu was 24 years old (by the Western count), a few months short of 25.

So, perhaps to be precise, I should change it to：「二十五周歲不到就登基稱帝」 for the *jianti* edition of my *wenji*.

Anyway, I can't thank you enough for being such an amazing reader! For the last 26 years (ever since the Chinese translation was first published in 1994 in Taiwan), no one (including me) has spotted this error!

Best,

Kang-i
4/11/2020

註：此信有部分刪節。

李保陽致孫康宜

孫先生，

這幾天讀　先生的書，受益匪淺！　先生能用非母語的英語，把詞這麼極其小眾的中國傳統詩歌形式，在四十年前的英語世界裡，講得如此細緻入微。尤其是對文本的分析解讀，即使在今天的中文世界裡，也罕有其儔。因為這不僅需要對詞的本體特徵、詞史、文學史和中國歷史有深湛的研究，還需要對西方文學理論有透徹的了解和嫻熟的運用。所以《詞與文類研究》直到今天，也是詞學研究領域獨樹一幟的佳作。

李奭學先生是一位非常出色的譯者。他的翻譯相當不錯，不管是斟詞酌句、中文慣用語，還是詞學背景的表述，他都翻譯很精確。兩種語言的轉換要不失其準確性，還要直達文化差別的細部，是非常難的。但是李先生的譯筆卻非常到位。

　　像李煜登基年歲問題，這很容易看出來是筆誤，因為不管是作者還是譯者，都不會出現這個錯誤。近代藏書家葉昌熾說過：「校書如几塵落葉，愈掃愈紛。」葉先生說的尚且是校古書。對於作者來說，對自己的書稿早已了熟於胸，任是再校多少遍，顯眼的錯誤也會一掃而過。而初讀者就不一樣，他沒有先在的既定思維定勢影響，只要心細，反而能看出一些問題。

　　保陽能看出來，很多錯誤實際上是筆誤和中英互譯時普遍會產生的一般性誤差，還有一些是電腦打字過程中致誤的同音字、形近字等等，非關作者或者譯者問題。

　　保陽在寫校記的時候，就不一一指出致誤原因了，以免累贅，請　先生不要介懷。

　　疫情洶洶，　先生保重身體

　　P.S.大作《詞與文類研究》普林斯頓版封面是蘇軾的畫像。蘇軾是保陽的超級大偶像。2018年初3月，保陽曾專程從廣州到惠州拜謁西湖孤山上的朝雲墓，記得幾乎是流著淚一步一步登上六如亭的。4月去鶴山，在鶴山城外坡山村，看到一座亭子坐落在村外西江邊上。土人云，蘇軾被貶儋耳，由惠州東江放舟西行，至此，捨船登陸，居停數日離去。村人為紀念蘇軾和隨他貶謫的王朝雲（村人的這個認識和施蟄存先生詩中所寫一致，都是表達了一種對東坡和朝雲不幸遭遇的善良寄託），就在江邊他們登舟處造亭紀念，並名其地為坡山村。並名本地所產一種荔枝為「東坡荔」。保陽在這兩次專程「拜蘇」過程中，分別寫了幾首小詩，現在分享給　先生：

〈惠州拜蘇詞〉

粵西鄒唐蓂題惠州西湖朝雲墓前六如亭聯云：「從南海來時經卷藥爐百尺江樓飛柳絮，自東坡去後夜燈仙塔一亭湖月冷梅花」檃括其辭成絕

夜燈仙塔一湖亭，柳絮藥爐百卷經。一自東坡南海去，江樓月冷梅花亭。

孤山木棉

獨上孤山湖景收，春光正在最梢頭。凌空偏被風姨妬，高處原來不自由。

浣溪沙‧瞻拜惠州西湖朝雲墓

湖上木棉樹樹飛。湖邊春燕啄春泥。誰家花外子規啼。　　亭下六如人去後，重扶藜杖過蘇堤。未乾兩眼淚頻揮。

西湖訪朝雲墓

重踏六橋意未休，此來湖上似曾游。木棉花下覓香骨，情繫西湖到惠州。

泗洲塔

一塔如簪橫臥波，西湖似鏡才新磨。棹歌一曲青山外，子細聽來憶東坡

豐湖書院至聖先師堂趺坐少女背影

誰家嬌女髮真真，至聖像前問此身。何處相思可憐甚，可憐湖水可憐春。

〈鶴山拜蘇詞〉

坡山村東坡朝雲亭

（一）

清歡一晌復向東，料峭春寒正冷風。此去江湖難兩忘，西江一派入長空。

（二）

一笑傾城尚未知，是誰喚醒我情痴。十年熱淚今揮灑，始到坡山花落時。

（三）

西江煙月太無情，誰敢多情任此生。拚卻一身不過死，憐天憐地最憐卿

擬蘇子

春花春水春江行，仙侶高堂天地清。我負卿卿三世債，卿卿還我一生情。無塵無垢無心計，好水好山好江亭。前生本自愛風月，風月多情江上橫。

保陽　敬上
4/11/2020

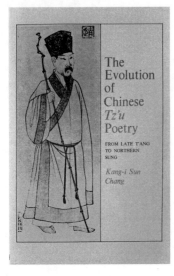

Kang-i Sun Chang（孫康宜）, *The Evolution of Chinese Tz'u Poetry: from Late Tang to Northern Sung*（《晚唐迄北宋詞體演進與詞人風格》），Princeton University Press, 1980.

林香伶致孫康宜

孫老師收信平安：

　　謝謝您提供這麼好的訊息給我，我定會將這麼難得的訊息轉告給系上同事和學生，希望為展覽帶來更多的參訪人數。

　　雖然很遺憾您因疫情之故此次返回東海的計畫未能成行，但我想，此刻，彼此的平安與健康是首要考量。我相信未來一定有機會見面的。幾年前我曾和錢南秀、吳盛青兩位教授一起到歐洲開會，也和她們一同旅遊。從她們口中，我得以聽聞老師的為學與為人；我也常在臉書看到老師的生活分享，心嚮往之。他日若時機到來，也希望能親自拜訪您。值此疫情嚴峻時刻，願上帝保守這個世界，驅散病毒的威脅。敬祝

　　平安

晚　香伶敬

4/11/2020

李保陽致孫康宜

孫先生，

　　剛剛讀完柳永一章，酣暢淋漓，唇齒生香！

　　前天和昨天讀《詞與文類研究》，尚覺苦澀拗口，今天竟漸入佳境。尤其柳永一章的第三節「柳永的慢詞詩學」，更是讀得暢快。這一節前半篇把領字和換頭分析得淋漓盡致，讓人讀之不忍終卷。後半篇以劉若愚的「連續鏡頭」和佛里曼（Ralph Freedman）的「鑑照」為工具，分析〈夜半樂〉和〈戚氏〉，行文真可謂「峰巒疊嶂，翠墨層綿」，層層遞進，如破竹剝筍，讓本來紛繁雜沓的敘述「紛至沓來，幾無止境」，「行文環勾扣結而連場若江河直下」。這些話語雖是您用來評騭柳詞的，但移以表彰這一章行文的綿密酣暢，亦允當也。如無他事攪擾，今天應該可讀畢全書。

保陽　敬上
4/12/2020

註：此信有部分刪節。

孫康宜致李保陽

Dear Baoyang,

　　I don't know how to thank you! You are amazing. I owe you a debt of gratitude.

Best,
Kang-i
4/18/2020

李保陽致孫康宜

孫先生，

　　來信收到，保陽知道您的電腦寫中文不是非常方便，保陽近來閱讀所得之校記，會全部重新改至Word文檔中去，您每次收到的文檔，將是一個保陽修訂過的完整版本。請放心。

保陽　敬上

4/18/2020

孫康宜致李保陽

Dear Baoyang,

　　This is incredible! I am so impressed with what you have pointed out in the Liu Yong chapter!

　　I'll certainly incorporate the changes and corrections soon!

　　By the way, I have just received the NEW 5-vols簡體word files! So please use the NEW 簡體 *jianti* files from now on. In my next email I'm going to send the NEW *jianti* word files to you.（從現在開始，請改用新的簡體word files）. This way, you may be able to spot some possible errors due to the繁簡轉換！

　　But please remember to delete the old files first, before you download the NEW files, so that there would be no confusion.

　　Please wait for my next email to you!

　　With thanks,

Kang-i

4/12/2020

李保陽致孫康宜

孫老師：

　　剛剛拜讀完蘇軾一章，全書的閱讀告結。最大的感受難以用耳目一新和震撼來形容，蓋保陽沒有任何西方的文學經驗，但覺好之一字而已。此種閱讀的酣暢淋漓大約和二十年前拜讀浦安迪先生的《中國敘事學》同一故事。

　　今天開始拜讀第五卷中的兩部專著，希望本週可以讀完。

　　P.S.下面是一點近三數天閱讀體會，也隨信分享給您：

　　作者在本文細讀方面的一個顯著的特徵是，尤其注重詞體的文本特徵，比如「換頭」和「領字」以及「襯字」這些詞體特有的本體特徵。「詞體演變史上最重要的新現象乃「換頭」的形成。」「『換頭』一旦出現，詞的讀法也有新的轉變，較之曩昔體式，可謂角度全非。」（俱見頁44）「慢詞最大的特徵，或許是『領字』這種手法。其功能在為詞句引路，抒情性甚重。柳永提升此一技巧的地位，使之成為詞史的重要分界點……。『領字』是慢詞的獨特技巧，有助於詞句連成一體。」（頁86）「這些詩人詞客（保陽按：指柳永之前少數創作慢詞的唐五代作家）都沒有施展『領字』的手法，而『領字』正是宋人的慢詞所以為慢詞的一種語言技巧。」「柳永首開『領字』風氣，在慢詞裡大量使用，往後的詞人又加以沿用，使之蔚為慢詞的傳統技巧。」（俱見頁92）「『領字』可使句構富於彈性，這是慢詞的另一基本特徵，也是柳永的革新何以在詞史上深具意義之故。」（頁94）外次，作者用襯字來解釋柳永詞集中同調作品沒有一首相同體式的原因，從而對前代詞學家語焉不詳的這一現象，予以讓人信服的解釋：「詞學的另一重要關目是詞律的體式。柳詞讓詞話家深感困惑者，乃為同詞牌的慢詞居然沒有一首是按同樣的詞律填的……。同詞牌而有不同律式，並非因許多詞學家所謂的『體調』變異有以致之，而是由於『襯字』使然。」（頁114）而襯字的熟練使用，乃在柳永高人一等的音樂素養。基於此，作者對歷代墨守成規的詞家大不以為然：「他視自己的每首詞為獨立的個體，即使同詞牌者亦然。這表示他極思解放傳統，不願再受制化結構的捆綁。遺憾的是，後世詞家仍沿襲一脈相傳的『傳統』，以致自縛手腳，發展出『填詞』與『正體』的觀念，以別於所謂『變體』者。他們步步為營，對正統詞家立下的字數與律式的注意，遠超

過於對詞樂的正視。這種發展也為詞樂分家種下難以拔除的根苗。」（頁114）
這一方面凸顯出柳永在詞史上獨特的開創者地位，另一方面也表現出作者力排眾
說，不為前人成說所囿的理論勇氣。這一點在四十年前的海外詞學研究領域中，
尤其難能可貴。該章第三節「柳永的慢詞詩學」前半篇把領字和換頭分析得淋
漓盡致，讓人讀之不忍終卷。後半篇以劉若愚的「連續鏡頭」和佛里曼（Ralph
Freedman）的「鑑照」理論為工具分析〈夜半樂〉和〈戚氏〉，行文真可謂「峰
巒疊嶂，翠墨層綿」，層層遞進，如破竹剝筍，讓意象本來紛繁雜沓的意象「紛
至沓來，幾無止境」，「行文環勾扣結而連場若江河直下」。這些話語雖是作者
用來評騭柳詞的，但移以表彰該章行文的綿密酣暢，亦恰當也。

　　作者對蘇軾在詞史上貢獻的論述，集中在「最卓越的成就則在拓展詞的詩
意」、「蘇軾卻是為詞特撰長序的第一人」、「蘇軾另一詞技是使用史典」這
三個方面的貢獻在二十世紀末出版的中國文學史中，幾乎原封不動地全部予以接
受。作者對蘇軾詞中長序的論述尤其別見手眼。作者稱蘇軾〈江城子〉（夢中了
了醉中醒）一詞的長序是「自我體現的抒情動作的寫實性對應體」，這句讀起來
有點拗口的中文結論，可以看作是作者對詞序這個獨立存在的文體下的定義。
作者對此定義有下面一段解釋：「如果詞本身所體現的抒情經驗是一種『凍結
的』、『非時間』的『美感瞬間』——因為詞的形式本身即象徵這種經驗，那麼
『詞序』所指必然是外在的人生現實，而此一現實又恆在時間的律動裡前進。事
實上，『詞序』亦具『傳記』向度——這是詞本身所難以洩露者，因為詞乃一自
發而且自成一格的結構體，僅可反映出抒情心靈超越時空的部分。詞家尤可藉詞
序與詞的結合，綰絞事實與想像為一和諧有序的整體，使得詩、文合璧，再不分
離。」（頁121-122）這段文字流轉如彈丸，似鹽入水，可以看作是以西方文論
解釋傳統詩詞的範本，為華語世界本土學者提供了一個思考問題的向度。

　　另外，作者將宋詩的傾向於理學哲思的整體風格的形成，與蘇軾開拓詞的
功能聯繫起來，這個觀點亦頗具新意。蓋蘇軾在詞壇的開拓革新，使得早年屬於
「豔科」、「小道」的「末技」，一躍而成具備了與傳統詩歌並駕齊驅的文學體
裁，成為「抒情的最佳工具」，於是宋詩只好別尋蹊徑，開壇張幟：「近體詩在
唐代抬頭，變成抒情詠頌的工具，『詞』在宋代也成為純抒情最佳的媒介。所謂
的『詩』呢？『詩』開始跑野馬，慢慢從純抒情的範疇轉到其他領域去。宋詩和

唐詩有所不同，對哲思慧見興趣較大。宋人又競以理性相標榜，養成唯理是尚的作風。因此，隨著時間的流逝，『詞』反倒成為『抒情的最佳工具』，以別於已經轉向的『詩』。這種轉變誠然有趣，但若無蘇詞推波助瀾，絕不可能在短時間內成就。」（頁123）

保陽　敬上

4/13/2020

李保陽致孫康宜

孫先生，

　　剛剛拜讀完《情與忠：陳子龍、柳如是詩詞因緣》，酣暢淋漓，一如二十年前在漢江邊捧讀時情境。時移世易，當日許多讀之不懂的章節，今日每有會心處。如您以「譬喻」（figura）來綜觀陳子龍前後兩期創作中的「情」與「忠」，實在是一個非常獨特的視角。

　　讀到您在頁265-267（US版Word文檔）中討論〈畫堂春〉中「杏花」這一意象，保陽可提供一點背景材料，或對陳子龍的詩詞政治背景的解讀有助益。明末的僧人智樸和尚曾作《青松紅杏圖》，以紀念在松山、杏山之戰中明軍之敗。後來這個手卷傳至京師的崇效寺，觀者麇集，題跋累累，大家都以此卷為寄託故國之思的載體。據說各家題跋累計長達一百餘尺。王士禎、朱彝尊、曾國藩、梁啟超、王鵬運、陳寅恪、柴德賡等人，都有關涉此畫卷的文字傳世。保陽在網上找到了一些有關的文章，您可以查閱，也許對於陳子龍的〈畫堂春〉中「杏花」這一意象，有他山之石的作用：

　　https://kknews.cc/culture/o2ob9zp.html

　　http://ocean.china.com.cn/2014-05/25/content_32482547.htm

　　頁275第二段第一句「失聲痛哭乃晚明遺子的行為典型」，這裡也可以提供一個外圍的證據，就是清初三大案中的「哭廟案」中江南士子「哭」的意象，這次事件可以參考下面這個連結：

https://new.qq.com/omn/20180816/20180816A09E0K.html

明天讀《抒情與描寫：六朝詩歌概論》。

保陽　敬上

4/14/2020

Jeongsoo Shin致孫康宜

Dear Professor,

They are so proud of you and your father. Thank you for including my translation of your book for the display.

Definitely I will pay a visit to your alma mater for getting some inspiration--next time when I travel to Taiwan.

Everyone knows the Taiwanese are such kind and cultivated people.

Jeongsoo

4/14/2020

李保陽致孫康宜

孫先生，

昨夜讀畢《情與忠：陳子龍、柳如是詩詞因緣》，想起二十年前在陝南漢江邊夜讀此書，情形如昨。如今海外再讀，恍如重逢故人，感慨無端。掩卷不寐，吟成小詩一首呈教：

讀《情與忠：陳子龍、柳如是詩詞因緣》

情忠兩字久封塵，二十年前已覺親。燈下南朝字字血，一回掩卷一傷神。

保陽　敬上

庚子三月廿三日（4/15/2020）

孫康宜致李保陽

Dear BAOYANG,

My goodness! Your poem is truly amazing! I'm going to share this with my Yale students! I'll also record the poem in my diary today!

God has been so kind to put you and me in contact! I'm deeply grateful!

With thanks,

Kang-i

4/15/2020

李保陽致孫康宜

孫先生：

《文集》簡體US版的頁307註2中提到1993年10月23日，施蟄存私函中提到，「日本內閣文庫藏有《吟紅集》原稿。據施蟄存所述，大陸學者一直尋找《吟紅集》未果（私人通信，1993年10月23日）。」保陽覆查了《從北山樓到潛學齋》，發現施先生的這封信寫於1991年10月23（上海書店版，頁85）。為了保險起見，保陽想知道1993年10月23日，施先生是否還另外和您談起過《吟紅集》的事情？因為《從北山樓到潛學齋》中1993年10月23日沒有您和施先生往來信函的任何記載。

保陽　敬上

4/15/2020

孫康宜致李保陽

Dear BAOYANG,

    Only you (a literary detective) can find such discrepancies! I'm deeply impressed with your thoughtfulness and thoroughness!

    Please change 1993 to 1991. 1991 is correct.

Kang-i
4/15/2020

孫康宜致李保陽

Dear BAOYANG,

    I'm a bit confused whenever you said「文集簡體US版的頁307」etc. From now on, would you always specify the volume number of the文集（ie., 文集第幾卷）。

    Thank you for all your help and attention!

Best,
Kang-i
4/15/2020

李保陽致孫康宜

孫先生，

    剛剛讀完《陳柳情緣》後面所附錄的內容，休息了一會，欣賞了您Line中傳給保陽的展覽視訊。雖然在安靜的夜燈下，但是仍然被大家在場的熱烈氣氛感染得笑出聲。

　　保陽覺得很奇怪，您4月6日來信中曾告誡保陽不能輕易「失業」，並且以CC先生往來紐約和紐黑文之間二十四年為例。從那時起，保陽就非常感佩CC先生對於您、對於家庭的那種責任和付出。因為保陽也有類似的經歷，所以尤其能夠感同身受。在視訊中東海江丕賢院長也特意提到這一點。今天保陽第一次看到CC先生，竟然覺得有一種無法言說的親切感。

　　「陽光穿透的歲月」，這個輕柔明光的名字，讓人感到歲月的自在、成熟與安詳。這讓保陽想起保陽母親時常掛在嘴邊的一句俗諺：「能過去的日子都是好日子。」讀了您的《走出白色恐怖》一書，才知道孫家——尤其是令尊孫保羅長老——曾經歷了十年試煉，但是你們一家人最終在　神的帶領下，走出那段不堪回首的歲月，來到美國，在新大陸的陽光下開始新生活。這和摩西帶領以色列人出埃及是何其相似乃爾。而您在視訊裡的笑聲是那麼的健朗，不就是一抹穿透了歲月的陽光嗎？我想這是　神在孫保羅長老身上做的工、也是在您身上做工。你們都用自己的行為榮耀了　神！

　　感謝您的分享！感謝東海人的辛勤工作！感謝主！

　　阿們！

保陽　敬上

4/15/2020

孫康宜致李保陽

Dear BAOYANG,

　　Thank you so much for your comments on the video! I especially appreciate what you have said about my husband C.C., although you have not met him in person yet!

　　It's a miracle that we have become such good friends! Actually the first time I responded to your emails was on March 29, 2020. That was only 17 days ago! And during the past 17 days, we have communicated several times a day! And right now you are helping me do so many things—including proofreading my book.

That's a miracle. No doubt God is behind all these! I believe He has sent you to help me! I give thanks to God everyday!

Best,

Kang-i

4/15/2020

註：此信有部分刪節。

李保陽致孫康宜

孫先生，

謝謝您的回信。從二月底保陽讀了您的《耶魯潛學集》一書，心有所感，然後在Yale的網頁上找到您的郵箱地址，第一次貿然給您寫信。這段時間每天數番郵件往來。讓保陽在這個禁足在家的春天，每天可以靜坐讀書，這真是　神美妙的恩典。這個特殊的春天雖然人間苦難，但是對於保陽來說，卻正在經歷著一次美好的閱讀之旅。感謝　神！

P.S.保陽有下面幾個問題想請教　先生：

（1）您這二十多年中，先後出版過許多不同類別的學術、文化、文學作品的中文專集和選集。2018年由韓晗主編的《文集》是否都把這些發表過的文章整合在一起了？

（2）您對自己的英文論著有什麼樣的整理、出版計畫嗎？

（3）這次在廣西師大出版社重印簡體版，把秀威版沒有收錄的中文文稿都收錄了嗎？

保陽　敬上
4/16/2020

孫康宜致李保陽

Dear Baoyang,

I am going to have a very busy day, so my reply to your 3 questions will be brief:

（1）Yes, for the秀威《孫康宜文集》五卷本，I did try to gather as many (if not all, due to copyright issues) earlier publications as possible. The only publications I could not use were my works included in the two books: 《曲人鴻爪：張充和曲友本事》and 《古色今香：張充和題字選集》. This is because張充和 (who passed away in 2015) and I both served as co-authors for these two books, and I was not able to separate her works from mine.

（2）In today's publishing market in the US, no one is doing "Collected Works" anymore! So, I don't have such a plan at the present time. Instead, I'm planning to write a memoir, tentatively entitled *"Moving Forward: A Half-century Journey in the U.S."*

I have not started to write the book yet, due to my busy schedule as a full-time professor right now. Hopefully after my retirement I can concentrate on the writing of my memoir. For the time being I have declined all the invitations to write Chinese articles! 已經婉拒所有的中文約稿。

（3）Yes, for the簡體edition of my《孫康宜文集》（廣西師大出版社），I have added 9 articles which were not included in the 2018秀威版。So, it should be quite complete now.

In haste,

Kang-i Sun Chang
4/16/2020

Martin Heijdra致李保陽（何義壯）

李保陽，您好！

　　我們已經一個月在家裡工作，並被要求不許返回學校和圖書館。

　　上次您也給我寄Email，但正是我們應該關閉圖書館的時期，我特別忙，沒機會回答，請原諒。我只記得，你對於屈萬里提意見，但是您應該瞭解，屈萬里的書目是以前的書目，我們已經不用這個了，我們也不要別人用，請不要參考它。有效的是網路上的書目。

Martin
4/16/2020

註：此信有部分刪節。

李保陽致Martin Heijdra

Martin館長，

　　您好！

　　收到您的來信，我感到非常的開心！因為上個月我寫了兩封信給您，沒有得到您的回信，我一直懷疑是我寫錯Email地址了。現在我放心了，我沒有寫錯地址。

　　我現在也在家裡一個月了，不能出去工作。希望這場瘟疫盡快結束，大家就可以按部就班地生活、工作了。不過我在這一個月裡，竟然讀了八本書，也是個意外的收穫。

　　是的，您說得很對，屈萬里的書目已經過時了。我讀這本書目不是把它當作實用的館藏指南來讀的，而是當成一部歷史著作來讀。儘管這本書有很多不足之處，但我藉此對葛思德的館藏善本書有了大概的了解。等到這場瘟疫結束了，我會再來葛思德圖書館閱讀新編的善本書目。新舊兩版書目對照閱讀，是一件很有趣的事情。我喜歡閱讀書目類的著作，閱讀書目可以了解不同的圖書館的收藏特

色，還可以從不同的編者那裡學習到更多的版本方面的知識。

不管怎麼樣，我非常感謝您回信給我！讓我感到非常開心。希望將來有機會在普林斯頓和您見面、聊天，那一定是一種非常美好的享受！

病毒流行，希望您和您的家人保重身體！期待下次和您見面！

李保陽　敬上
4/16/2020

李保陽致孫康宜

孫先生，

今天如期讀完《文集》第五卷。凡有更改標記之處，都是保陽改過的（用紅色字體標出）。腳註中也有改動，也用紅色字體標出。

本週拜讀　先生大作已進入語境，尤其喜歡您的文筆，簡淨俐落而富深思。如能有人沿此筆法續寫王粲、曹植、嵇康、阮籍、陸機、左思、蕭統等人，更令人期待。二十年前的暑假，保陽在漢江邊一間出租屋中細讀徐震鍔先生校注的《世說新語》和南開大學羅宗強先生的《魏晉南北朝文學思想史》，至於廢寢忘食，如今避疫新大陸，再讀　先生的《六朝詩歌概論》，大有故人重逢的親切。

先生大著，好處是多參照西方文學批評理論解讀作品，為了弄清那些術語的背景和論述思路，就不得不再重新閱讀所引經典篇章。今天就在拜讀過程中也再次細讀了鮑照的〈蕪城賦〉、范曄的〈獄中與諸甥姪書〉（此文命篇立意絕類司馬遷〈報任安書〉）和庾信的〈哀江南賦〉。尤其是〈哀江南賦〉，您的解讀深得我心，故傍晚重操翰管，將這篇經典之作抄錄了一遍，也分享給　先生。（久疏筆硯，寫字生硬，　先生見笑了！）

您在談到謝朓詩體革新的貢獻時，涉及律詩的形式。保陽近年頗喜歡寫詩，故對　先生的論述，尤有比較身切的體會，作了筆記，茲亦奉上：

作者論述律詩結構的內在邏輯云：「（1）從非平行的、以時間為主導的不完美世界（第一聯），到平行的、沒有時間的完美狀態（第二聯和第三聯）；

（2）從平行而豐滿的世界，回到非平行和不完美的世界（第四聯）。通過這樣一種圓周運動的形式化結構，唐代詩人們或許會感到他們的詩歌從形式和內容兩方面，都抓住了一個自我滿足之宇宙的基本特質。」（卷五，頁121）這正是律詩創作過程中，作者完整的心理和技術過程。律詩的首末兩聯，經常承擔的是一種「附屬結構」的功能，一般是首聯引起將要進入的詩境緣起，尾聯則需有對全詩收束的儀式感。這兩聯都有賴於中間兩聯的豐滿，方始能將全詩「黏」起來，形成一個完整的美學宇宙。中間兩聯要有一種承繼或者平行的關係，又不能犯複，還要講求意蘊和字面對仗，所以是律詩中特別花費心力的部分。因而作者將第二、三兩聯定義為「完美狀態」，洵為的論。而首尾兩聯的不平行和不完美，常常是對讀者的誘惑所在，從作者角度來講，又是支撐中間兩聯「完美」的動力所在。而謝朓何以能在詩歌形式上突破傳統的拘限，作者從謝氏取景與陶淵明筆下景物之異趣得到靈感：「謝朓與陶淵明還是有區別的。謝朓的山水風光附著於窗戶，為窗戶所框定。在謝朓那裡，有某種內向與退縮，這使他炮製出等值於自然的人造物。」「他用八句詩形式寫作的山水詩，可能就是這種欲望——使山水風光附著於結構之框架——的產物。」「他的詩似乎達到不同類別的另一種存在——一個相當於窗戶所框定之風景的自我封閉世界。其中有一種新的節制，一種節約的意識，一種退向形式主義的美學。」（卷五頁130-131）這種細膩入理的文本閱讀和聯想體味，在學理上能自圓其說。有關詩體演變的事實，這是一個角度非常新穎的解釋。

保陽　敬上
4/17/2020

孫康宜致東海大學圖書館各位同仁

Dear all,

I want to thank you again for the most amazing exhibition which you have organized for me and my late father Paul Sun! Also, my husband C. C. Chang（張

欽次）is so moved by your kindness that he has just shipped through UPS Global Express a copy of his recently compiled *Collected Works of C.C. Chang* (2020) to the Tunghai University Library (Attention: Ya-ping Wang). He wants to donate this volume to Tunghai University, because he is proud of being a Tunghai *nuxu*東海女婿。

In fact, he has just recently donated a copy of the *Collected Works of C.C. Chang* (2020) to his alma mater Chung-yuan Christian University. As Stano knows, C.C. has always been very humble and prefers to keep himself in low profile! But I want to send you the following link to the Chung-yuan University website, which describes C.C.'s contribution to the university bell tower when he was only a college senior (in 1963). In the first picture, the one who holds the books is the current President Kuang-Cheng Chang張光正校長 of Chung-yuan Christian University. CC appears in pictures 3 and 4.

https://www1.cycu.edu.tw/news/detail?type=%E7%84%A6%E9%BB%9E%E6 %96%B0%E8%81%9E&id=2300&from=singlemessage&isappinstalled=0

Thank you again for your help and attention.

Best,
Kang-i Sun Chang（孫康宜）
4/17/2020

孫康宜致李保陽

Dear Baoyang,

I always found it most difficult to write the acknowledgments（致謝辭）for my books! But now I have to make some changes and additions for the "廣西師大擴大版 致謝辭". In particular, two years ago I forgot to thank my former student Ling Chao （凌超）for writing the calligraphy for the book cover of the *fanti*秀威edition. Now, again he wrote the calligraphy for the廣西師大 *jianti* version. (See attached). Most important, for all these years he has been extremely helpful to me in many different ways. For example, he was the one who changed the "A4" format to the "US letter size" for me the other day!

Thus, I have added a sentence to thank him this time.

Also, I have made stylistic changes for some other sentences in the acknowledgments. (See attached changes with trackings).

Anyway, please incorporate the changes to vols. 1,2,3,4.（卷1，2，3，4）. I have already made changes to vol. 5, so no worries.

With thanks again,

Kang-i

4/18/2020

李保陽致孫康宜

孫先生：

　　您不用這麼客氣，在這個春天您打算出版《文集》的簡體版，保陽正好做過編輯，我們都出不了門無法正常上班，保陽正好可以藉此段時間把去年荒疏的讀書時間補回來……這些奇妙的事情被　神用　祂那大能的手全部集合在一起了，我們應該感謝　神的恩典才對！

　　在拜讀大作的過程中，保陽的收穫也時時不斷。這會兒正在讀〈北美二十年來詞學研究〉，就中提到了「解構主義」和耶魯學派的關係，這讓保陽手舞足蹈，興奮難耐！早在保陽讀大學的時候，就在外國文學課堂上略聞了「解構主義」這個術語，後來讀了一些相關的書，覺得這個理論非常切合自己的味口，因為這個理論拿來解讀中國古典文學，非常生新。剛剛讀了您的解說，才知道原來解構主義的「大本營」就在耶魯。難怪當年讀您的《陳柳情緣》一書時，覺得那麼的親切，原來您也是此批評理論中心的一員。今早保陽還花了專門的時間了

解了德曼（Paul de Man, 1919.12.6-1983.12.21）、米勒（J. Hillis Miller, 1928.3.5-　）、哈特門（Geoffrey Hartman, 1929.8.11-2016.3.14）及布魯姆（Harold Bloom，1930.6.11-2019.10.14）等四位學者的生平。只可惜Bloom教授在去年秋天故去了。您在《走出白色恐怖》三聯版頁89加入了一張的Bloom教授的照片，這讓保陽可以聊慰孺慕之思。您知道，保陽沒有接受過西方學術訓練，通過拜讀您的〈北美二十年來詞學研究〉，讓保陽和「解構主義」這樣高遠的批評理論的始發之地走得如此之近，實在讓人喜出望外！

　　讀您的作品，因為帶有「校對」的任務，保陽需要不時的查找有關的作家、作品以及版本等信息，這是在中斷近兩年後，讓保陽再次享受到親近學術的感覺，也是在是避疫期間一件很有紀念意義的工作。您在《走出白色恐怖》中坦陳，您是一個有完美主義性格的人（Me too，哈哈～），保陽做任何事情，也是盡可能希望做到最好，盡量減少可以消除的遺憾——尤其是對學術研究——所以保陽願意傾盡全力幫助您減少簡體字版本的舛誤。請您不用客氣！

　　盡管步履維艱，但學習帶給人的快樂永遠是那麼的誘人！

　　您和張先生保障身體！　神保佑你們！

保陽　敬上

4/18/2020

孫康宜致李保陽

Dear Baoyang,

　　My goodness! Your letter made me so inspired! You are truly a thoughtful thinker and scholar, and a genuinely kind person!

　　I have learned so much from your wonderful reader's response.

　　By the way, don't you think it would be interesting if you can gather our email communications together (including our LINE communications) from this COVID-19 Pandemic period and have a book published by秀威？ If you can do this, that would be fantastic. What do you think? The book can be titled: "疫情書信選：從抱月樓到潛學齋"？It can be considered a sequel to 《從北山樓到潛學齋》.

The only problem is this: Some sensitive letters may have to be left out!

Anyway, just a thought!

Kang-i
4/18/2020

李保陽致孫康宜

孫先生，

謝謝先生的這個想法！能有幸紹續當年　先生與施　先生故事，彰顯學術情誼，作為後生的保陽，當然倍感榮幸！謝謝　先生提攜後學的殷殷之忱！

保陽在國內時，曾經有過這麼一個想法：將來要給自己三本書，一本日記、一本友朋書信集，一本藏書目錄。前年倉促出國，藏書散盡，所幸有部分書目還在，去年就整理了出來，給自己留個紀念。日記大部分滯留國內，前途未卜，現在只好在美繼續寫起。書信部分原打算等有空了，把曾經用過的幾個電子信箱整理一下，但是萬萬沒有想到　先生今天有這麼一個提議，讓保陽原來的書信計畫這麼快就會實現一部分，真的感謝　主的恩典！

這本小書可以命名為《避疫書信選：從潛學齋到抱月樓》。這本書可以成為美國獨立二百四十四年來首次遭遇如此嚴重災難的一個紀念，也可以側面記錄簡體版《文集》出版的一些花絮，同時還能作為這個時代美國學術界中國研究的一個側影。我們可以繼續通信，一俟簡體版前期準備工作事竣，即可著手這本小書的編輯。一切編輯工作，由保陽來操辦。

保陽　敬上
4/18/2020

孫康宜致李保陽

Dear Baoyang,

　　You know that I'm a very frank person! I like to speak from my heart. And I truly prefer the sub-title:《從抱月樓到潛學齋》! This is a much more honest and descriptive title for many reasons:

（1）It is true that you wrote to me first! See your first letter dated 3/11/2020 (copied here). So it should be "from Baoyuelou to Qianxuezhai" !

（2）In most cases, because you wrote to me about your "reader's response"（讀者反應）to my works, and I usually wrote as a reply to your response. The most remarkable thing is that you serve as such an active reader, and that's why it is so unusual.

（3）Since most readers for the book would be Chinese 中文讀者, and most of my responses to you are in English, it is not a good idea to start the first page of the《書信選》in English!（我的書信一旦翻譯成中文就不好了，會失其真！）。Thus, I prefer the format of having your Chinese letter on the left hand side, with my English responses on the right hand side. (If agreeable, I would suggest to Showwe 秀威 that they should use the format like the book《深呼吸》, which Showwe just published in 2019, with recommendations from me and Ha Jin哈金. I will send pictures of a few pages from this book《深呼吸》to you by LINE).

（4）The reason my other book was entitled《從北山樓到潛學齋》was not because Shi Zhecun was my senior; nor did I want to show my respect for an older person! No, that's not the reason at all. It's mainly because Mr. Shi wrote to me first (out of the blue)! In 1984 I was totally surprised to receive his first letter. The same surprise I felt about receiving your two emails in a single day—both dated March 11, 2020!

So, the word "從" (from)only means "from one person to another"!

If you feel more comfortable, you could explain the meaning of "從" in your preface to the《疫情書信選》。You can even quote words from me.

I hope you agree with my rationale. I feel so much better with the sub-title《從抱月樓到潛學齋》. Young people should not be afraid of writing to the elders first.

Best,
Kang-i
4/18/2020

李保陽致孫康宜

孫先生，

謝謝您的回信解釋！

保陽之所以將潛學齋放在前面，唯一的原因是you are "my senior", or that I wanted "to show my respect for an older person"（這裡引用您的話，哈哈～）沒有其他考量。現在您用了四個理由來向保陽解釋所以然，保陽欣然接受您的意見。請您不要有任何顧慮。

北山樓為您打開了「四面窗」，潛學齋在二十年前為保陽打開了西方視角解讀中國古典詩詞的一扇窗，將來還會打開什麼樣的一扇窗，真真是讓人期待的……學術的薪火就是這樣在一代代人之間傳遞，她經久不衰的魅力一直是那麼的引人入勝！

保陽　敬上
4/18/2020

李保陽致孫康宜

孫先生，

今天一直沉浸在您的〈二十世紀北美詞學研究〉和〈樂府補題中的象徵與托喻〉這兩篇文章的語境裡，傍晚開始動筆，打算寫一篇像「文章」的文字。因為需要，保陽不得不去查找更多關於Bloom教授的資料，就暫停原計畫，折回頭讀了第一卷中的《布魯姆的文學信念》一文。保陽發現這是一個很可愛的老頭兒，我特別欣賞他那「四次大戰」的精神和勇氣。一個曾經著有《解構和批評》一書的作者，能夠再回過頭去和「解構主義」作戰，這需要的不僅僅是勇氣，還有自我否定、自我更新的學術自信，我特別佩服他這一點！

我非常非常喜歡他的那句「詩歌絕不可被政治化」，我覺得他的那句話簡直就是為我講的（如果我能如此大膽僭越的話，一笑～）。我覺得他能說出這句話，和他對「浪漫主義」的理解和堅持有關。他不僅完全贊同加州大學鵝灣分校Irvine-Wellek演講系列主編Frank Lentricchia所說的「浪漫不僅指一種詩學的方向、一種形上學、一種歷史的理論，也指向一種特殊的生活方式」還進一步引申道：「使人想到了中國古代儒家、道家的生命態度，也令人想到希伯來人的聖經傳統。」這個引申尤其讓我覺得親切。儘管他的學生不同意他的浪漫觀，甚至批評他，但他仍然堅持自己的看法，這讓我對他、對西方學術界的自信和包容，有了更進一步的體會。他尊敬「新批評派」的Empson，但「唯一讓我感到不解的是，他後來居然成了擁毛派，而且還十分欣賞毛主席的詩詞」我讀到他的這句話，差點兒笑出聲來，不僅僅是因為這句話裡透露出來的價值觀的張力統攝了我，還因為一位橫跨兩個世紀的批評大師衝口而出的這句話，讓他的形象就像吳敬梓筆下的白描風景一樣站立在我面前了。

孫先生，憑我今天才第一次間接對Bloom教授一鱗半爪的了解，我可不可以這麼評價一下這位「耶魯學派」的先賢：他是一個幽默率直的、純粹的、堅持文學理想的保守主義學院派學人。

期待您的回覆。

保陽　敬上

4/18/2020

李保陽致孫康宜

孫先生：

您在〈北美二十年來詞學研究〉一文的末尾感慨了一句：「今日我回顧北美詞學研究由萌動到茁壯的這段歷史，益加感到學術自由的可貴。」這句話真是讓人感慨萬端！

中國人近百年來的不自信，根源就在於自由的被限制。自由的被限制和自信之間是成反比的。三四十年前，當中國人來到歐美世界的時候，就像他們的先輩洋務運動的主持者看到西洋的堅船利炮一樣，為炫彩滿目的物質文明所傾倒、驚呆。三四十年後，時至今日，中國的物質文明較之數十年前有了進步，但是夜郎自大的心胸又阻礙了其客觀地看待這個世界，也看不到自己精神文化已經蛻化成一片荒漠。當Bloom們能以一種文學批評理論席捲東西兩方學術界時，中國的錢學森和臺灣的吳大猷兩先生還在仰天叩問：「我們為什麼培養不出大師？」好在臺灣已經從體制上為學術、教育大大地鬆綁了。而對岸是否能夠給華人世界帶來最後的榮光，實在期期以不敢遽論。

保陽　又上
4/18/2020

孫康宜致李保陽

Dear BAOYANG,

Please see the version of my Bloom article which I have just sent to you on line. That particular version was circulated on Wechat right after Harold Bloom died in October! I remember he was still teaching his class on a Friday, and then he suddenly passed away on Sunday! I recited some of his works in my Tuesday class !

I actually added a passage right before the article, but surprisingly the passage is now gone! I don't know what happened?

You are absolutely right in your description of Harold Bloom. He never mixed poetry with politics! Actually he was not a 擁毛派！ He just thought that Mao was a good poet, which had nothing to do with politics! Actually I taught Mao's poetry when I offered a course on modern poetry years ago! And I'm never a 擁毛派, as you know!

Your assessment of Harold Bloom, as you put it at the end of your email, is quite perceptive. Yes, Harold was a pure romanticist, with a bit of a sense of humor. He was also quite conservative as far as gender studies was concerned. He was biased against some feminists such as the authors of the book, *Madwoman in the Attic*!

But I really like Harold, and I miss him a lot.

Best,
Kang-i
4/18/2020

李保陽致孫康宜

孫先生，

謝謝您回信中的肯定，也謝謝您和保陽分享Bloom教授臨終前的細節。保陽對Bloom教授的印象沒有解讀錯，感到很開心。保陽對純粹的人有一種天然的敏感和好感。保陽的父親就是一位非常純粹的人，他純粹到有些「傻」。

表述的自信不來自潮流的喧嘩。就像您論陶淵明：陶淵明並非要在刻下的詩歌傳統裡尋找認同、傾聽肯定的聲音。當一個人足夠自信時，他會以歷史的遠光鏡去審視刻下，挑戰傳統，譬如Bloom教授。這需要勇氣，那種寄望於超現實的勇氣。就這一點來說，我特別佩服愛因斯坦和余英時兩位先生，他們是沒有把自己淹沒在時代洪流裡的勇敢者！

保陽
4/18/2020

註：此信有部分刪節。

李保陽致孫康宜

孫先生，

遵囑將本月初日記書影奉上，祈查收。

保陽
4/18/2020

李保陽致孫康宜

孫先生，

昨晚發給您的日記不知道列印出來會否模糊不清？

今天很慚愧，只讀了〈重讀八大山人詩〉一篇，蓋因昨天一直在醞釀一篇更像「文章」的文字，以致坐在桌前，從8點到1點半，反覆揣摩〈二十世紀北美詞學研究〉和〈《樂府補題》中的象徵與托喻〉兩篇文章，但是很遺憾，只擠出了千把字而已。那一刻，保陽又一次如此鮮明地體會到以往讀書的局限，下筆臨文，無法準確有效地表達自己。主要是對西方文學理論的生疏，這種困擾和焦慮弄得昨晚一直到今天都無法有效地繼續閱讀。

在拜讀《文集》的過程中，保陽時常會先翻作品的文末，看一看發表或者出版的年代，一方面是把作品定位到它撰作的那個年代的語境中，以便隨時提醒自己是在閱讀那個時代的文學批評著作，藉以了解那個時候美國漢學研究的歷史截

面。把眼前的文字推展到歷史的時空距離中閱讀，是一種很有邊際效應的閱讀方法，收穫常常在單純的文本閱讀之外。

您在八、九十年代前後發表三大學術鉅製：《詞與文類研究》1980年在普林斯頓大學出版，十一年後在臺灣出版中文本，又過十一年在北大出版簡體字中文本；《抒情與描寫：六朝詩歌概論》1986年在普林斯頓大學出版，2001年在中國大陸出版簡體字本；《情與忠：陳子龍、柳如是詩詞因緣》1991年耶魯大學出版，1992年在臺灣出版中文本，2012年在北大出版簡體字本。保陽把您這三本書的撰著時間線、內容風格和您1990年撰寫的〈二十世紀北美詞學研究〉一文中的內容對讀，有一個很有意思的發現：您一直是在解構主義批評語境下解讀中國古典文學。您個人的學術路徑選擇，也能大致窺見當時美國的中國文學研究之一代風氣。〈《樂府補題》中的象徵與托喻〉、〈重讀八大山人詩〉等這一時期撰作的文章，更是具體而微地實踐了這一學術理論。直到昨天晚上反復揣摩、細味，才有了這一發現，假如能夠早一點意識到，那麼前幾天讀三大鉅製的時候，理解會更加深刻。有了這一發現，保陽也在閱讀《文集》的過程中，有意識地查閱一些西方批評理論的產生和發展歷史，甚至把一些術語抄出來不時備檢，這樣的收穫真是多面向的。

另外，看到發表的時間，也會聯想起保陽自己的一些體驗和回憶。中文版《走出白色恐怖》出版在2012年4月，那個時候保陽正為第二個孩子的去留和自己在浙大的去留作最艱難的困鬥，常常會坐到杭北三墩鎮的荒郊水邊愁思。《從北山樓到潛學齋》出版在在2014年3月，那會兒保陽正奔走在杭州、上海、揚州和成都之間考博士，後來四月的記憶，就是杭州天竺山中晦暗無邊的夜雨……

保陽　敬上

4/19/2020

李保陽致孫康宜

孫先生，

今天開始讀〈陶潛的經典化與讀者反應〉，感覺很好！

刻下中國本土學者的研究多集中在追求作品中作者的意圖或者還原歷史現場（有點「解構主義」傾向，這個表述是為了方便和「結構主義」進行對比）。這可能和中國的學術傳統──尤其是乾嘉以還的實學風氣──有關，另一個原因是中國學者所處的學術研究環境從來都沒獨立過所致。作為文學研究的一個向度，我覺得把讀者從作品和研究對象中抽離出來，用一種普遍的、經驗性的遠距離眼光來審視，往往可以得到一種意想不到的閱讀感受和結論。比如您說：「有一則提到陶潛不願為五斗米折腰，都是基於一些不牢靠的記載。多數情況下，這樣的逸事只不過是傳聞而已，而沈約──《宋書‧隱逸傳》的作者，拿它們主要用來增強戲劇效果。」五斗米的故事是大家深信不疑的，甚至已經超出了陽春白雪的學術研究領域而進入大眾視野，很少有人懷疑其真實性。我也一直在想，我們努力用正史和歷代的時人筆記去建構自己認為牢靠的文學史，究竟在多大程度上接近了「真實」？學術研究是要「歷史的真實」？還是「文學的真實」？就像您所說：「傳記編者自己更關注陶潛作為隱士的公眾形象」；「陶潛的道德人格及其作為一個隱士的政治角色是這些官修史書的關注焦點」；「陶潛被拿來代表隱士的典型，代表堅貞不渝地拒絕出仕、棄絕世俗價值的典範人物」，這讓我想起顧頡剛先生「層疊的歷史」說，後來的傳記作者，何嘗不是在「層疊」地塑造和經典化他們的寫作對象呢？從司馬遷開始的《屈賈列傳》、《刺客列傳》以及後世史書中分門別類的循吏、酷吏、儒林、文苑、隱逸、高士、列女等等門類化的傳記歸類，歷史人物就開始戴上「面具」出現在公眾的閱讀世界裡。傳主豐富多彩的多面人生不見了，某一方面的特徵誇張地傳播後世，那些戲劇性的故事，尤其能引起讀者的興味，代代相傳，逐漸經典化。這種現象，何嘗不可以視之為對歷史的另一種面向的「解構」？

如果換個角度，用讀者的感受和經驗去理解，又可以在多大的可信度上建立可信的文學史？當這兩個問題都沒有精確答案時──實際上也不可能有精確答案──，那麼站在讀者的立場上構建屬於讀者自己的真實感受，反而能夠更加貼

近文學的初衷。因為不管是古代，還是今天，不管是東方還是西方，人所葆有的感情基本上是一致的，反映在文學中的這種感情也是一致的。中國人的「先得我聲」就是認可這種一致性的明證。所以從讀者的立場出發，我認為並不會導致附會式閱讀（allegoresis）。

〈陶潛的經典化與讀者反應〉中有一句話很有意思：「詩人的名微反映了他在魏晉社會中的地位之無足輕重。」仔細體味這句話，我發現從屈原、陶潛、施耐庵、羅貫中、吳承恩、曹雪芹等等文學巨匠，他們在文學史中的存在，竟然有種前所未有的相似性。龍榆生先生說的「考今之難，不亞於考古」大約也和您那句話的意思比較接近。如果放在今天的經驗世界里衡度，這句話其實也只是一句經驗之談而已。刻下的中國本土的文學研究，把文本太過於經典化了，放棄了讀者經驗的介入，所以呈現出千人一面的尷尬。我覺得用解構主義理論討論中國古典作品，其迷人的地方在於重視讀者的感受，不忘常識的介入。當後人努力去靠近或者發掘作品中的作者所指不靈光時，讓讀者來承擔這一任務，也許反而能柳暗花明，達到同樣的效果。我以前對此不甚了了，現在從閱讀您的作品中，逐漸對此大感興趣。

那麼也許我們現在可以追問一個比較現實的問題：為什麼後來的讀者經常甚至是刻意地去接受那個被經典化了的人物或者作品？即您說近來學者梳理出一個比較接近真實陶潛的見解「始終未能引起關注」。我以為，這可能是後世的讀者一方面囿於對強大傳統的敬畏，另一方面則是不願意去打破那個「面具」，因為「面具」下面隱藏的是每個讀者自己的理想。不是任何人都有表現自己理想的能力和勇氣，他們更多的做法是「借別人酒杯澆自己塊壘」。文學史不斷地在重複著證明這一點：文天祥對陶淵明的解讀、宋明遺民對屈原的解讀、抗戰中聞一多、郭沫若（我不喜歡這個人）對屈原的解讀，他們所以都發生在易代之際，就是讀者們在這些先賢身上看到和寄寓了他們自己的影子。數年前我在編一本詩選的時候，刻意地多選了朱舜水、袁崇煥、史可法的作品，當時也是別有純文學之外的考慮的。

保陽
4/20/2020

孫康宜致李保陽

Dear Baoyang:

請你寫一篇序，我也會寫一篇短序，如何？

Kang-i Sun Chang（孫康宜）
4/20/2020

李保陽致孫康宜

孫先生，

有關《避疫書信選：從抱月樓到潛學齋》的數封郵件保陽均已收悉。現在統一作一回覆：

謝謝先生的熱忱提攜，並且著手為此付出努力。在保陽來說，能和　先生合作，倍感榮幸。如果讓保陽來作序，保陽當然樂意，但是會不會對於　先生來講，有僭越之嫌？中心惶愧，祈賜高見！

另外，我們需要為該書設定一個大致的框架，比如收錄的時限大致截止在什麼時候？（因為我們的通信往來不可能因為這本書的出版而終止）。是否考慮增加附錄？（附錄內容您可以考慮）什麼時候交給出版社初稿？等等。

專此奉覆，並候賜覆！

保陽　敬上
4/20/2020

孫康宜致李保陽

Dear Baoyang,

　　Here are my responses to your questions:

　　I understand your concerns, and my proposed idea is this: My Preface（孫康宜序）will come first（在前）, and then your preface（李保陽序）will follow（在後）. So, no worries about the order of the Prefaces（序）。

　　But please note that the sequence of the editors should be: 李保陽、孫康宜編著。This is appropriate, because it's more honest. I would feel bad if you put my name as the first editor. That would make me look like a senior person who tries to take advantage of a young scholar! That's what I hate to do!

　　By the way, in the title page for the book, please remember to add the English book title and the editors' names in English. This way the American libraries will be able to do the cataloging correctly. I'll make sure that the Showwe Publishing House will print the English words on the book cover as well.

　　Hope I have answered some of your questions.

In haste,
Kang-i
4/20/2020

註：此信有部分刪節。

李保陽致孫康宜

孫老師，

　　昨天收到您的〈儒家經籍的作者問題〉演講影片，當即看過一遍。今早正

好從這篇文章讀起，真是巧合。保陽有兩條線索可供給您參考：（1）您在頁272引用了Martin Kern的"Early Chinese Literature, Beginnings Through Western Han"一文，並贊同他的觀點。Kern教授另外還有一篇文章〈早期中國詩歌與文本研究諸問題——從《蟋蟀》談起〉，發表在《文學評論》2019年第四期（這本雜誌大概剛剛運到Yale的圖書館），這篇文章的第四章標題為〈素材庫、合成文本與作者〉，所談的問題和您的這篇文章論題有關，您或許可以參考一下。這篇文章保陽已分享到您的Line中了；（2）余嘉錫先生的《古書通例》（也可能是《目錄學發微》）中也提到漢以前中國典籍的作者問題，對於大作中關於先秦儒家典籍的作者問題，也許有參考價值。

　　前面的郵件中保陽也向您提到過，在拜讀您的作品時，會特別留意作品的發表時間，以此來作歷史面向的閱讀，以期更多的閱讀收穫。保陽發現，您的幾乎所有學術論著，都有「解構」的影子存在，比如您在1990撰作的〈北美二十年來詞學研究〉中坦陳：「我於1982年轉至耶魯大學服務，無形中耳濡目染，多少受到解構批評的影響，雖然其中有些理論我不能完全瞭解或接受，但僅就作品深具隱喻性這一點來看，則此種『尊崇讀者』的批評理論倒不失為實用的批評法則。」您在這篇文章中還特別對「解構批評」做了幾點詳細的分析，其中有一點是：「作品的真正意義取決於讀者的領會與體認，作者本身並無絕對的權威。」厥後八十年代您的三大學術鉅製，也都沿著這麼一個思路推進研究。1992年您發表了〈《樂府補題》中的象徵與托喻〉一文，您更認為傳統的批評家對《樂府補題》的詮釋「至少在精神上和現代解構主義方法相近，它堅持讀者對於無盡頭的詮釋的發現」。這些解構主義語境中對讀者角色的重視，是不是導致您決定消解作者的Trigger？或者說2016年發表的這篇討論作者問題的文章，是您對解構主義批評理論的一貫堅持所致？如果上面兩方面都不是，那麼是什麼導致您對中國文學中的「作者」問題生發興趣的？

保陽

4/21/2020

孫康宜致李保陽

Dear Baoyang,

Please see attached a picture of the people in San Francisco, when Spanish Flu invaded the city during the pandemic in 1918.

Don't you think history has repeated itself? Now 102 years later we are wearing similar facial masks!

The only lesson we have learned from hsitory is that people never learned from history! People should remember to turn to God for help:

"You have looked deep
into my heart, Lord,
and you know all about me.
You know when I am resting
or when I am working,
And from Heaven
you discover my thoughts.

You notice everthing I do
and everywhere I go.
Before I even speak a word,
you know what I will say,
And with your powerful arm
you protect me
from every side."
（Psalm詩篇139: 1-5.）

Kang-i
4/21/2020

「西班牙流感」（Spanish flu）期間
的舊金山（San Francisco）（1918
年）。

李保陽致孫康宜

孫老師，

　　看到您的「The only lesson we have learned from hsitory is that people never learned from history!」這句話，保陽嚇了一大跳。不是被這句話的意思，因為這句話在中文世界也非常流行。保陽所以被嚇到，是因為它用英文說出來，竟然也是如此的讓人毛骨悚然！這要感謝您。以前保陽讀文章，遇到不得已需要夾雜英文表達的地方，都會慣性地跳過。這段時間，因為要讀您的大作，有很多地方的英文訊息不能跳過，就只好硬著頭皮往下讀，這麼一段時間下來，竟然記住了不少漢學家的名字，以及不少中國古典文學研究術語的英文表達。同時對美國的中國古典文學研究狀況也有了一點點了解。加上要讀您的來信，所以保陽最近感覺英文有很大進步。職此之故，看到您上面那句話，便有錐心刺骨的一種痛感——原來病毒的蔓延也不分語言、國界和種族！

　　自從三月十日以來，保陽每天晚上都會在日記中記錄全國、賓州、費城以及我們當地的感染確診人數。每次記錄那些數字的時候，感覺好像是摩西和他的哥哥亞倫在瘟疫過後數點以色列全會的人數（民26-1-4）。起初一段時間感覺不明顯，但是當三月二十前後，每天的確診人數以五位數激增時，我們全家都感到很難過。因為那一個個數字，都是一條條鮮活的生命，轉瞬間說沒就沒了！小女跟

我建議，我們每天晚上都為那些因病毒逝去的人、為我們阻擋病毒的人和為我們堅守工作職責的人禱告！

月初早櫻盛開那會兒，保陽帶著妻兒專程去了一趟費城。那時候費城地方政府已經建議大家待在家裡盡量減少外出。保陽有「文獻癖」，那天進城，主要是想給這新大陸千年一遇的大災難留點痕跡。結果一上路，發現I-76、US-202上，基本沒有幾輛車，Local上車輛亦屈指可數。回家途徑我們家附近的Valley Forge National Historical Park，看到那裡所有的出入口全部被關閉，聽鄰居說，這是自1893年公園建立以來第一次全園關閉。我們村裡的兒童遊樂場也關閉了。前兩天我寫信給葛思德的朋友，希望能有機會去那裡工作，他的回信說，由於這次疫情的蔓延，導致經濟困難，葛思德已經不再考慮僱傭新的人員，闕員暫時也不考慮遞補；昨天晚上，我的一位朋友，她在紐約大學讀書，下月畢業，本來布魯克林一家機構年前就答應提供工作Offer給她，結果受到病毒蔓延影響，她的那個Offer也被取消了。您今天下午轉來的那封信中說，Yale在這次席捲全球的病毒中，也遭受非常大的影響，實在讓人感到難過。以上這些僅是保陽親見的病毒影響，可見這次對美國的影響真的很大。

在這次疫情蔓延中，保陽觀察到了一個很有意思的現象：美國承平日久，大家在生活中，對災難好像沒有足夠重視的意識。而中國人多數時候生活在水深火熱的不太平中，對災難尤其敏感，所以這次疫情中，華人社區的感染率並不高。一個明顯的例子是，我太太在賓州出現第一例確診時，就把我和孩子關在家裡不讓上班上學了，好在第二週孩子們的學校就關閉了，後來我們公司也奉令關閉。最近我們家附近一家工廠傳聞集體感染，我太太就不再去那附近的Walmart和Costco買東西了，轉而讓我開車載她到二十幾英里外的另一個郡去買，因為那裡闔郡確診才幾百人（我們郡八十多萬人，已確診感染超過三千人）。另外，我們是來自中國大陸那樣一個計畫經濟體的國家，對經濟危機的感覺不明顯。而從最近接觸到的身邊實例觀察，美國社會對經濟危機的敏感度尤高，最直觀的表現就是，現在社區停車場白天停的車比往常多了。蓋美國是一個高度發達的市場經濟體。不知道較之2008年那次危機如何？

庚子多事，新大陸亦然！您和CC先生多多保重，盡量減少外出。

人太渺小了，災難面前，我們只能剴切地禱告，希望　神能盡快把這場災難

帶走！

保陽
4/21/2020

①COVID-19流行期間的費城市區
②COVID-19流行期間的費城唐人街（2020年3月）

孫康宜致李保陽

Dear Baoyang（保陽），

　　I'm taking advantage of a break right now to tell you about the story about a deer! As you can see from the attached pictures, the deer are usually roaming freely around our backyard! We treat them as our family friends, although we must keep them at a distance—due to our concerns of possible tick bites!

　　Just this morning we were so sad to find a dead deer on the road in front of our house, actually right at the entrance to our driveway. The deer was perhaps hit by a car during the night. We have already contacted the Town Hall people to take away the body of the deer.

　　While I was pondering the meaning of this incident, suddenly the verse from *Genesis*（舊約·創世紀》22: 10-14 came to my mind:

He [Abraham] took the knife and got ready to kill his son. But the Lord's angel shouted from heaven, "Abraham? Abraham!"

"Here I am?" he answered.

"Don't hurt the boy [Issac] or harm him in any way!" the angel said. "Now I know that you truly obey God, because you were willing to offer him your son."

Abraham looked up and saw a ram [羊羔]caught by its horns in the bushes. So he took the ram and sacrificed it in place of his son. Abraham named that place "The Lord will Provide"....

So, I suddenly realized that the dead deer might be a sacrifice God has prepared for us. Instead of losing our life during this time of the COVID-19 pandemic, the Lord has let the deer serve as a sacrifice for us. And our house can be called, "The Lord will Provide."

Next time when you visit Princeton University campus again, please go visit the "Abraham and Issac" statue near the University Library (i.e., Firestone Library).

In haste,
Kang-i Sun Chang（孫康宜）
4/21/2020

李保陽致孫康宜

孫老師，

收到您的這封信，心裡難過了好一陣子！

保陽每次上下班，都要橫穿我們家附近的Valley Forge National Historical Park，尤其是去冬以來，每當遠山漸次融入夜色時，在公園的Washington Memorial Chapel附近，總有一個鹿族的家庭在樹下徘徊吃草。保陽幾乎每天下班，都會看到他們一家悠悠安閒的身影。那時候就一邊開車一邊想，那頭帶頭的鹿，和摩西何其相似，帶著他們家族的成員，往那流著奶與蜜之地去求生。現在想來，和您筆下的

天使島上那無數的華人先輩們，也有幾分近似：所求不多，只要一小塊水草豐茂之地安身即可！讓人感慨萬千！不知道此時此刻，那頭倒斃的鹿的同伴，是何等的焦急和淒涼……

　　看了您的信之後，保陽又把《創世紀》二十二章重讀了一遍。記得三十多年前，先父帶著不足十歲的保陽，到附近縣城去撿拾糞肥。有一次，大約是舊曆年的元宵節前，保陽撿了一捆柴，關中舊俗：元宵節次日一入夜，家家戶戶門口要點起火堆，大人小孩在火堆上跳來跳去，俗曰「燎花花」。母親總是捨不得把燒飯的柴用來「燎花花」，於是保陽就告訴　先父，那捆柴是拿回去「燎花花」的。先父不語，遂將那捆柴搭在手推車上，保陽在後面推車。保陽覺得那場景，和亞伯讓他的兩位僕人原地等待，他自己把柴架在兒子背上何其相似！保陽肖羊，以前外婆給取的名字是「寶羊」，和那隻被掛了角的羊大約也有相同處。想起那天您說的「保羅－陽光」，真的覺得自己在幾十年前，就和神有了某種冥冥的聯繫。

　　您說得很對，不管是我們的房子，那隻鹿，先父，還是我們身邊的人，他們都是在替我們作燔祭。所以神一再告訴我們要愛人、愛生命！

　　The Firestone Library附近的那對雕塑原來講述的是亞伯和以撒的故事。我們去年底帶孩子們還專程去那裡參觀了，但是沒有找到解說的文字，只對那截繩子印象很深。等疫情結束再去，一定去仔細瞻仰。

　　Blessings!

保陽　敬上
4/21/2020

孫康宜致李保陽

Dear Baoyang,

　　Please see attached the Abraham & Issac statues at Princeton. As I said, the statues are close to Firestone Library. They are also close to the Princeton University Chapel.

C.C. and I were married at the Princeton University Chapel on August 3, 1968. That was almost 52 years ago!

Best,
Kang-i
4/21/2020

Kang-i Sun Chang and C. C. Chang revisited the Princeton University Chapel in 2017, forty-nine years after they were married at the chapel.

孫康宜致李保陽

Dear Baoyang,

   In my tomorrow's class, I'll talk about the *ci* poetry by Wang Pengyun王鵬運. First of all, thank you for calling my attention to the fact that the correct dates for Wang Pengyun should be 1850-1904, rather than 1849-1904.

   But would you give me the full citation for both Prof. Lin Mei-yi's and your work that refer to Wang's year of birth in 1850? (i.e., including the titles of the works and page numbers that specifically refer to Wang's dates?) For example, 林玫儀，《書名》（城市：出版社，年代），第幾頁。李保陽，〈文章題目〉，《雜誌名稱》第幾期，年代，第幾頁。Also, I could not find the page # in vol. 5 of my *Wenji*文集, where you made the changes of Wang's dates for me. Would you remind me of the page numbers?（第5卷，第幾頁？）This way, I can incorporate the information into the book.

Thank you again for your help and attention!

Best,
Kang-i
4/21/2020

李保陽致孫康宜

孫老師，

　　林老師的文章，保陽用附件分享給您了，看第一頁的註1。這篇文章的修訂本發表在《中國韻文學刊》（2010年），保陽也用附件分享給您了。後者是中國知網上下載的文章，要有專門的閱讀器才可以打開查閱。如果您不能打開的話，請告訴保陽，保陽為您設法解決。

保陽
4/21/2020

孫康宜致李保陽

Dear BAOYANG,

　　Can you tell me in which year Lin Mei-yi's article was published in the 《文哲所集刊》？是哪一年出版的集刊？

　　Unfortunately, I cannot open the file for the 《中國韻文學刊》 version!

Kang-i
4/21/2020

李保陽致孫康宜

孫老師，

　　謝謝您分享的亞伯和以撒的圖片。教堂和圖書館是我們全家出遊的必去之地，所以知道Princeton University Chapel教堂和The Firestone Library在同一個地方，但不知道您和C.C.先生是在那裡結婚的，印象很深的是你們在Gram太太府上舉辦了熱鬧的婚禮招待會。

　　普林斯頓就是一個童話般的存在！2016年秋，保陽第一次從熙熙攘攘的紐約中央車站搭火車到Princeton Junction Station，一下月台，猛吸了一口清涼醒腦的空氣，頓時有種異樣的感覺，就像有一道靈光閃耀般的愛上了這個地方。2017、2018兩年再訪，去年以來更是無數次往返看書。除了喜歡普林斯頓的那份鄉村的寧靜，更喜歡葛思德那百城插架的浩瀚海洋，每每一頭扎進去，就忘乎日月。如果能在葛思德典守書庫一輩子，應該就是最幸福的人生了！

　　您和C.C.先生對普大一定充滿了感情。如果哪天你們故地重遊，一定記得通知保陽，我們一起到普林斯頓訪古探幽！

保陽

4/22/2020

Abraham & Issac statues at Princeton University

李保陽致孫康宜

孫老師，

　　保陽分享給您王鵬運的遺照一幀和手跡，也許對您今天講課有用。這是十多年前保陽在廣西圖書館發現的，後來保陽建議廣西圖書館列入善本保存，於是廣西館就請人重新裝池，並印入廣西圖書館藏善本書圖錄中，讓這張照片化身千百，流傳後世。2013年保陽發表〈王鵬運、龍繼棟唱和詞手稿述略〉，也在文末將此手稿本全部影印作為附錄。

保陽　敬上
4/22/2020

 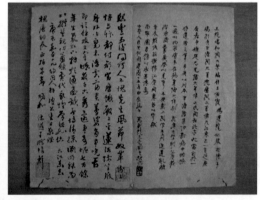

王鵬運（1850-1904）遺像　　王鵬運手跡（左）、龍榆生手跡（右）

李保陽致孫康宜

孫老師，

　　重讀〈一位美國漢學家的中西建築史觀〉，讓人想起了梁思成和林徽音。既覺有味，又感慨無端！

　　去年冬天，保陽在布魯克林大橋靠近布魯克林一端的橋塔外牆上，看到了一

塊紀念碑，紀念一位普通的家庭婦女Emily Warren Roebling。她是十九世紀美國橋樑工程師Washington Roebling的妻子。十九世紀六七十年代，John A. Roebling因勘察設計布魯克林大橋而喪生，他的兒子Washington Roebling子承父業，承擔起設計建造大橋的重任，不幸的是Washington Roebling患上了當時造橋而引起的一種特殊的疾病——減壓症。在大橋設計建造的最後日子裡，Washington Roebling的工作基本是靠著Emily Warren Roebling的支撐完成的。Roebling家族和布魯克林大橋的故事，絕佳地詮釋了牟先生說的那句話：「歐洲自始視建築之輝煌為人生價值之表徵。」中國人重立德立功立言，所以司馬遷父子與《史記》故事，和Roebling家族與布魯克林大橋的故事，真有異曲同工之妙。

費城是北美一座文化古城，費城有數不勝數的各式風格教堂。保陽閒來無事的時候，喜歡到Downtown一帶的那些狹窄、仍葆有殖民地建築風格的街巷間遊走。位於十三街的St. John the Evangelist Roman Catholic Church，上世紀早些時候，這間教堂曾在中國援建過一所學校，四九之後不了了之。記得前不久進城辦事，時間尚早，就溜達到十三街，撫摸著那風蝕雨侵的外立牆，細數著上面的花紋，似乎每一塊石頭裡都滲透著多少歷史和不可磨滅的故事呢。去年秋天，保陽有一段寫費城舊時的文字，也一併分享給您，權作對您〈一位美國漢學家的中西建築史觀〉的回應。

牟先生是一位具有獨特眼光的學者，他是普林斯頓東亞系的創始人，又是您的老師，您應該知道更多他的故事，期待您和保陽分享。

保陽　敬上
4/22/2020

附錄：〈費城的秋天〉

費城的秋天來得要格外早些。涼風一起，總是那麼熟悉，絲毫沒有異國他鄉的生疏，讓人一下回到舊時底色。這時最愜意的事，莫過於搭上公交，漫無目的地到Downtown，然後在某一不知名的車站下來，到那一帶的街巷中閒走閒看。踏著秋風，聽著落葉，它們的存在就是一首歌，一闋詩。

十二街本來就不寬，橫街心還有一條廢棄的鐵軌。鐵路是美國一百多年前經濟發展的保障，尤其是二十世前期，全美鐵路通車里程達到四十萬公里。中國現在的鐵路通車里程才二十萬公里，大家就可以想像一下鐵路在那個時候美國的角色和作用。但是二十年代和三十年代交替那會兒的大蕭條，以及汽車的逐漸普及，鐵路日漸式微，於是有半數的鐵路被廢棄了。作為美國鐵路的發源地，費城人把這些記憶的名片，仍鑲嵌在今日現代繁華的鬧市街心，既不拆除，也不理會。昔日輝煌的見證，今天仍保存著歷史的記憶。這是費城人的聰明，他們對歷史盡可能表達敬意。對歷史的尊重，就是對人記憶的尊重。一棟房子或者一段鐵軌所承載的記憶，往往大過它本身意義無數倍。要拆毀一棟房子或鐵軌輕而易舉，殘滅它們，會讓人與社會的距離更大，最終大家便都一無所有。費城人懂得這個道理，所以才讓費城的街巷至今充滿溫情。

站在City Hall的街心十字，你可以盡情地恣肆在這段被路人的鞋底磨蹭得精光鋥亮的歷史裡：一陣叮叮噹噹的火車鈴聲響起，在Market Street上營生的人們荒忙四散。待一陣水蒸氣瀰漫之後，火車又載著旅客從高樓對峙的狹窄街巷中離去，就像游龍曲折於江河。而身後則依然是拄著拐杖戴著呢帽的紳士，手挽著身穿圓箍長裙頭頂鮮花高髻的入時婦人……

也可以在鬧市擁擠狹窄的街巷邊看到高可參天的大樹，而腳下仍是百數年前的石頭。為其根深，方始葉茂。街邊不時會有藍底金字的標識，告訴路人，旁邊這棟房子曾經是哪位名人的故居，他或她曾經為這個國家在哪段記憶中增添了什麼輝煌的色彩。因為房子和街道的風格、格局都還是兩三百年的老樣子，行走其間，常常讓人生怕，那吱扭一聲輕啟的門扉後，走出來的就是歷史。當日普通如你我的人，也許他們自己都不知道他們在這個國家的記憶裡曾寫下了那麼一筆。默行其中，才真的感覺到原來我們離歷史是如此之近，近到能感受到她的呼吸……。

李保陽致孫康宜

孫老師，

今天重讀了〈介紹耶魯第一部中文古籍目錄〉，有一疑惑請教您：在秀威

版紙本中有如下一段：「最近他又請到北大古文獻中心的楊海崢教授來協助整理耶魯館藏的明清小說善本（但楊教授臨時因緊急事故而無法成行，殊以為憾。盼望她來日能有機會來耶魯大學從事中文善本的整理工作。——孫康宜補註，2018年1月26日）。」覆檢您前後分享給保陽的三種不同Word文檔，這段文字概被刪去。不知道是什麼原因呢？保陽所以對此一節頗感興趣，乃是保陽從中學時代起，即喜歡到鄉間僻肆冷攤收集各種舊印本說部（現在還記得陳端生《再生緣》裡的得勝頭回裡的寄慨詩句：「駿馬卻馱癡漢走，美妻常伴拙夫眠」），剛上大學那一年，把自己手頭收藏的那些「舊本」（主要是一些晚清石印本和排印本）作了一篇提要文字，在學校的學術活動中獲得獎項。本科畢業時，我們系上一位研究明清小說頗有成績的老師計畫讓保陽寫關於《東周列國志》的畢業論文，後來因故中輟，再後來陰差陽錯就研究起詩詞來。但是保陽對明清說部一直興致不減。按照一般經驗，各大館但凡未經整理之書中，往往會有出人意料之大發現。據保陽所知，Yale館藏明清說部珍本中有相當罕見之明遺香樓刻本《三國演義》、明郁郁堂刻李贄評點本《忠義水滸傳》、清初刻本《金瓶梅》（不知是繡像本還是詞話本）、乾隆五十七年程偉元萃文書屋活字擺印本《紅樓夢》等等。這僅僅是已知者，那些未經整理者中，相信一定會有進一步的發現。不知道Yale的這一批未經整理的明清小說現在情形如何？您是否有所瞭解？

亟思拜讀孟先生《美國耶魯大學圖書館中文古籍目錄》，尤其感興趣者，乃這部書目中關於Yale藏書的遞藏源流部分，是瞭解Yale中文古籍藏書史的絕好資料。上月，保陽用了一個星期時間讀了屈萬里先生《普林斯敦大學葛思德東方圖書館中文善本書志》，這部編纂於五十年前的書目著作，比較簡略，但是對於鳥瞰式概覽葛思德舊藏，還是有幫助的。孟先生這部目錄對於瞭解Yale的中文古籍藏書情況，從您的介紹中可知極有助益。孟先生的〈美國耶魯大學圖書館中文古籍收藏史〉一文，尤所跂望拜讀，先生處可有電子文檔？候覆。專此，並候

教安！

保陽　敬上

4/22/2020

孫康宜致Michael Meng（孟振華）

Dear Michael,

Would you respond to Li Baoyang's questions regarding your book?
It's all right to answer him in English.

Best,
Kang-i
4/22/2020

王雅萍致孫康宜

Dear孫院士好，

日安！

近期的展覽陸續收到一些回饋，也謝謝您的學生、親友與師長們的迴響，雅萍也在試著做些紀錄修正與整理。

抱歉答應寄給您的資料請您再稍待……

其中個人簡單的一段感想回應如下：

> 下班時間的辦公室顯得異常安靜，是最適合閱讀、寫作、思考的時光。
>
> 籌辦展覽的日子，因為孫院士的學術成就豐碩，總擔心展出內容會有不足與疏漏的壓力，加上疫情的關係難免有些焦慮。但每每透過閱讀孫院士、孫保羅教授的作品與資料，總能得到一些慰藉。每天也很期待孫院士是否又會發來新的訊息資料，也很感謝每次信中給予的鼓勵。
>
> 某天傍晚望著螢幕前孫院士的信末屬名，Kang-i Sun Chang……，S-U-N不就是太陽嗎？也難怪乎總感到一股無形的溫暖力量。加上這次的孫氏父女聯展是以歷年的著作、書法手稿為主，正是烙印在他們人生歲月的永恆象徵。原先還找不到適合的主標題的狀況下，那天我決定了展覽的

主題——「陽光穿透的歲月」。孫氏父女（Sun family）倆在從黑暗走向光明的這段時空，各自穿透領悟生命與學術的各項課題，並如陽光般散發溫暖的光輝與溫度，深刻而透徹地烙印在人生歲月中。主題決定後，我並沒有直接向孫院士解釋過展覽的構想，遲至開幕當天的視訊連線談話，孫院士提到了。我也很高興這樣的主題初衷正如孫院士的理解感受相同。

　　整個展區的構想，每一個區塊其實也是孫院士的著作書名。「從捕鯨船上一路走來」（著作出版年表區）、「潛學集」（實體專書展示區）、「文學的聲音與光影紀錄……」（多媒體區）、「一粒麥子」（孫保羅年表書法手稿區）等，這些書名和展示的內容又是恰如其意……

謝謝孫院士給予的這次策展機會，雅萍仍有好多要學習的～～再次感謝您！祝好。

雅萍敬上
4/22/2010

註：王雅萍，臺灣東海大學圖書館職員。

孟振華致李保陽

李先生：您好！

　　感謝孫教授將大函轉寄給我。我能完成這部《耶魯大學圖書館中文古籍目錄》，孫教授的鼓勵與鞭策有著決定性的影響。

　　因為拙著仍有諸多版權限制，我只能將導論部分的電子版供您參考，請不吝指正。因為文件太大，請在這一連結下載：https://yale.box.com/s/iny8tdwbb3engs x6a9dxunp9kijl1r65。

　　2018年北京大學的楊海崢教授因故無法來訪，非常可惜。耶魯的孫教授與北大安平秋教授都大力推薦她，當時楊教授是獲得班內基善本與手稿圖書館的特別

邀請與資助來訪。她長期在北大開授海外漢籍研究課程，並對北美和日本等地的中文善本書收藏有著第一手的掌握，兼及理論與實務，實屬難能可貴。不過，今年（2020年）元月底至2月初，在孫教授的支持下，楊教授得以在耶魯大學圖書館和耶魯東亞研究理事會的邀請與資助下，到耶魯訪問一週。這次來訪是為慶祝耶魯大學圖書館中文館藏建立一百七十週年的一系列慶祝活動之一。她在1月30日在耶魯大學東亞圖書館的演講廳，以「漢籍之路」為題，發表了學術演講，頗獲好評https://ceas.yale.edu/events/road-books-culture。

　　有關您提及的幾部明清小說，其中有些是1960年代末，耶魯圖書館購自臺灣藏書家韓鏡塘的《胡天獵隱藏書》。另外，從1936年起，任教於敝校、同時兼任圖書館中文館藏館長的金守拙教授，也曾經捐贈過一批明末清初的珍稀歷史小說刻本。這兩部分的藏書，拙著多有涉及，我就不在此贅述。耶魯收藏有以下清初繡像本《金瓶梅》三種，但確切入藏記錄，付之闕如：

館藏索書號	書名／卷次	著者姓名	刻印年代	行格	冊數	附註
PL2698 H73 C5 1695	第一奇書一百回卷首圖	（明）蘭陵笑笑生撰（清）張竹坡評點	清初（1695-1795）崇經堂刻補修本	框12.7×9.5公分。11行25字，小字雙行同。白口，四周單邊，單黑魚尾。版心上鐫「第一奇書」。	三十二冊	鈐「崇經堂主人印」印。
Fv5758 1384B	皋鶴堂批評第一奇書金瓶梅一百回卷首圖	（明）蘭陵笑笑生撰（清）張竹坡評	清康熙間（1695-1722）刻本	框19.8×13.8公分。10行22字，小字雙行同。白口，四周單邊。上書口鐫「第一奇書」。	十六冊	內封鐫「彭城張竹坡批評金瓶梅／第一奇書／本衙藏板翻刻必究」。康熙乙亥謝頤題於皋鶴堂「序」。
PL2698. H73 C5	四大奇書第四種五十卷一百回卷首圖	（明）蘭陵笑笑生撰（清）張竹坡評點	清乾隆十二年（1747）刻影松軒印本	框21.4×13.7公分。11行24字。白口，四周單邊。版心上鐫「奇書第四種」，中鐫回次。	二十冊	內封鐫「金聖歎批點／彭城張竹坡原本／第一奇書／影松軒藏版」。

這三部書都存藏在耶魯的班內基善本與手稿圖書館。我也將線上書目連結加在館藏索書號內，以利檢索。

您如有其他有關耶魯中文古籍收藏的問題，也請聯繫。順頌

時祺

孟振華　敬上

4/23/2020

李保陽致Michael Meng（孟振華）

孟先生尊鑒：

大函收悉，謝謝您詳為解釋耶魯的古籍整理編目近況，以及諸種珍本小說的檢索信息！您惠賜之尊編耶魯中文古籍書目的前言，對保陽來講，是極為期待拜讀的一篇文字。已經下載轉存到電腦中，待拜讀結束後，再申謝忱。

近年北美中文古籍收藏目錄，一般都是集合中外學者之力編纂，始克告竣。您以一己之力纂錄耶魯中文古籍收藏，其魄力實在不敢想像。蓋中文古籍編目涉及面之廣，每部書情況之複雜，實在非主其事者不能知悉。以故保陽對您的魄力和努力佩服之至！

保陽少年時即對藏書極感興趣，後來在本科母校中文系圖書館做了四年志願者，碩士畢業後在浙大圖書館古籍部工作，負責浙大館藏書史料之徵集與編纂，故對藏書史一直興致不減。職是之故，對尊編目錄中有關藏書源流的考鏡尤感興趣，即孫老師書評中所單獨列出譽之為與別家目錄所異者。中國古籍傳藏悠久，流變複雜，欲梳理其遞藏經過，不比辨章學術考究版本為易。

近日因為COVID-19的影響，禁足在家，保陽通讀了屈萬里先生的《普林斯敦大學葛思德東方圖書館中文善本書志》。觀屈先生此書，以及近年來出版之多數北美東亞館藏中文善本書目、書志著作，皆以某一項目之名義短暫聘請中國或港臺中文學界學者從事斯役，或數月，或一載。凡操觚者，往往格於時限，要完成一定數量之工作，致很多著錄條目，不能深入細查原書。古籍編目，即使同一

版本同一印次的書，也可能因為裝訂失誤、收藏條件等因素導致版本資訊不同，比如我的母校中山大學圖書館藏張祥齡《受經堂詞》和華東師範大學圖書館藏此書，雖是同一版本，但是後者裝訂有漏葉，它們儘管是同一種書，但著錄資訊就有區別。再如叢書的著錄，切不可據一版本來著錄同一書的其他館藏資訊，比如上海圖書館藏清代嘉慶年間王初桐的《古香堂叢書》，收書十三種，嘉興圖書館藏《古香堂叢書》亦收書十三種，但是上海藏本收錄《貓乘》而無《小瑯環館詞話》，嘉興館藏收錄《小瑯環館詞話》而無《貓乘》，蓋古人刊刻叢書，隨得隨刻，隨刻刷印裝訂發行，往往即使同一書，也會有子目的差別，著錄的時候就必須檢查原書，以確定著錄資訊的準確性。

1939年至1947年，美國國會圖書館東方部（今亞洲部）恆慕義主任邀請王重民先生來館鑒定整理館藏中文古籍，編訂《美國國會圖書館藏中國善本書錄》，因為時間和經費限制，他採用節錄原書序跋的方法，盡可能在著錄中提供原書信息，但是這種節錄導致著錄錯誤比比皆是，為學界後來者所病。2005年出版的加州大學柏克萊分校圖書館藏中文善本書目，就因為該館從未徹底清查過藏書，編目人員不得不花了幾個月時間整理清查館藏，後來編目時間非常有限，只得複印了要編目的書影，拿回中國，對比中國國內各館尤其是上海圖書館藏相同版本藏書，編成這本書目。這與上海圖書館的陳先行先生的編目理想尚有距離，但卻是迫不得已的折中之法。版本著錄，一定要檢視所著錄的原書，不可以他館同版次藏書代替著錄。2014年前後，中國全國古籍普查，以運動式作業手段限時完成普查編目工作，保陽親見浙江一圖書館的編目人員，將清代拓本，套用別館的數據，著錄為珂羅版影印，以此趕工省時。碑帖如此，刻本更是不勝枚舉。蓋趕時限也。從事書目編定工作，必須有專人從始至終，躬親力為，這樣才能保證工作的連續性和體例的一致。不會因為趕時限而倉促從事。

這本出自您一人之手的耶魯古籍書目，其體例連貫性、著錄準確性，應該都有保證，這是保陽尤跂望拜讀的原因所在。今既得您惠賜尊編書目序言，可以先快朵頤，紙本書目，容後借來拜讀。專此。並頌

諸安！

李保陽　敬上

4/23/2020

李保陽致孫康宜

孫老師，

今天早上的閱讀很開心。您上次提到希望保陽寫一篇序，保陽為此頗為猶豫了一陣子，不知道從何處著手。今早上研讀（最近已不是「校讀」了）張宏生教授訪談您的那篇文字，便略有了一些思路，寫了千餘字的寫作綱要。現在才讀了《文集》一半的篇幅，相信接下來的閱讀會繼續豐富思路，豐滿內容。

分享一個故事和您：2008年，張宏生教授在南京大學召集了一次兩岸三地的詞學會議，當時保陽在廣西念碩士研究生，專程去旁聽了。大約當年底或者次年初，張教授帶領他的一班弟子大約二十餘人到嘉興、平湖一帶做學術之旅，為他主持的《全清詞》後續諸集訪尋文獻。當時保陽作為「地陪」接待了整個參訪活動。當時張教授贈送保陽的書中就有他增補的胡文楷先生婦女著作目錄一書，這部書在您的研究中不斷被徵引。在平湖葛渭君先生半宋樓（葛先生一生仰慕唐圭璋先生，窮居浙北海邊小鎮乍浦，竟然編出了數百萬字的《詞話叢編補編》，本來有續編、外編之纂，惜前年元旦，老先生意外去世），大家相與欣賞一些詩詞珍本，張教授為保陽此前在嘉興冷攤所得晚清吳中某潘（可能是潘曾瑩，記不清了）的詞稿用毛筆寫了一段題跋。2011年暑假，保陽從嘉興搬家到杭州，匆忙倉促中，不知將此潘氏手稿遺落在哪裡，現在每每思及，遺憾不已。

剛剛看到網上資訊，賓州州長計畫在五月中旬左右逐步恢復本州西北部和中北部地區的社會秩序，費城是此次疫情的風暴中心之一，應該在五月中無望於恢復，也就是說還有一個月時間可以待在家裡讀書。趙翼論元遺山詩云「國家不幸詩家幸」，竟與刻下情形，略有幾分相似。一嘆！您和CC先生保重身體！

保陽　敬上
4/23/2020

李保陽致孫康宜

孫老師，

　　謝謝您轉來張宏生老師的郵件，展讀之下，無限感慨！

　　那次盛會不久，聽說張老師移席香港浸會大學執教，保陽與張老師的聯繫就稀少了。2010年左右，保陽在《中國韻文學刊》曾發表過一篇小文章，文末顯示的責任編輯恰是張老師，那次大概是我們之間最後一次「直接」的交流了。此後因為保陽樸被南北，居無定所，就沒有再聯繫過。沒想到十年之後，因為您，在新大陸看到張老師對保陽的謬讚，真有一種「滄桑」之感！

　　謝謝您！也謝謝張老師的謬讚！

保陽　敬上
4/23/2020

李保陽致孫康宜

孫老師，

　　《文集》第四卷校讀結束，請查看附件。您覺得處理起來比較棘手的校記，保陽已經分別改入正文相應的位置，您直接查看並決定如何定稿即可。尤所引起注意者，乃頁腳註中的錯別字，因為沒有辦法用批註的方式在文檔右邊灰色區域顯示，只得用紅色字體標出，請您注意定稿時更改。

　　卷五保陽已經覆核過了。因為這一卷校讀一開始就是用電子文檔進行，所以所有的校記都在分享給您的電子文檔中呈現了，沒有再行訂正的必要了，請以您的「定稿」為準。

保陽　敬上
4/23/2020

孫康宜致張宏生

Dear Hongsheng,

　　Do you remember this wonderful young scholar 李保陽? Mr. Li (who currently lives in Pennsylvania) and I have become very good friends, although we have not yet met in person.

Kang-i

4/23/2020

張宏生致孫康宜

康宜：

　　李保陽是一個勤奮好學的年輕人，我和他的交往，確實如他信中所寫，雖然十多年沒有聯繫了，但印象仍然深刻。今得知他在賓州，非常高興，想必能夠做出更大成就。他的功底較為扎實，相信你們一定相處愉快。不一一，祝好，

宏生

4/23/2020

孫康宜致李保陽

Dear Baoyang,

　　I want to share with you the following emails, regarding the Tunghai University exhibition for the Sun Family.（東海大學圖書館參觀《陽光穿透的歲月》著作展）.

　　In particular, I was reminding Wang Ya-ping 王雅萍（the organizer of the exhibition）of the important impact my mother had made on my life. As you know, my mother Chen Yu-chen（陳玉真）was the real heroine in my memoir,《走出白色恐怖》。

In haste,
Kang-i
4/24/2020

註：東海大學孫保羅書法暨孫康宜著作展影片網址（此影片由東海大學圖書館授權）：https://m.youtube.com/watch?v=ZoVVH7_RwM0&from=singlemessage&isappinstalled=0

孫康宜致李保陽

Dear Baoyang,

I'm sorry to bother you again. But I really can't help sharing with you what Wang Ya-ping wrote in her reply to my email. I think Wang Ya-ping is not only a brilliant organizer for the exhibition, but she is also a warmhearted person! At age 76, I truly appreciate people who are kindhearted. There are many smart people in this world, but only those who are also kind can really shine.

Best,
Kang-i
4/24/2020

孫康宜致李保陽

Dear Baoyang,

　　I don't remember if I have already shared this letter with you. (Please see below). I'm deeply touched by this email from Wang Ya-ping 王雅萍, who is responsible for organizing the Tunghai exhibition in honor of my father's 100th birthday. (My father was born on Oct. 19, 1919, and if he were alive today he would be a little over 100 years old).

　　It's amazing that Wang Ya-ping first got the exhibition title, 「陽光穿透的歲月」from a reflection on the surname "Sun"（孫）.

　　For some reason, this email from Wang Ya-ping reminds me of what I wrote about in my essay, 「Alta Mesa墓園的故事」. (In Volume Two of the *fanti* edition of my collected works,《孫康宜文集》（卷2，頁415-419）. In particular, on page 418 I talked about the amazing sunshine in the area of my parents' graves near Hillview Drive in the Alta Mesa Memorial Park.

　　It's a pleasure to share this thought with you!

Best,
Kang-i
4/24/2020

李保陽致孫康宜

孫老師，

　　您分享的卷五「定稿」本序言部分已改定。關於王鵬運生年，也將玫儀老師的考證成果作為注釋加了進去。唯玫儀老師的注釋，保陽又在後面加了一段簡短的按語。您看一下並斟酌去留。這段注釋文字在卷五「定稿」本中文較長（四百一十一字），所以在這條注釋以後的內容，可能會被擠壓到次一頁，您在拿保陽

的這個版本對照您自己的文檔時，請特別留意這一點，即這條注釋之後的某一處內容，在保陽的修改本中在298頁，您的文檔可能是在297頁。

保陽　敬上
4/24/2020

孫康宜致李保陽

Dear Baoyang,

I cannot thank you enough for what you have done for me. The preface is beautifully edited. And I'm especially grateful to you for adding the long footnote about Wang Pengyun's 王鵬運 birth year 1850. (Strangely, on my computer this shows on p. 315, rather than p. 298. Is it the case that different computers show different page numbers?)

I'm going to add the following words after the footnote: "（特別感謝李保陽博士提供這個註解的資料）。"

With thanks,
Kang-i
4/24/2020

李保陽致孫康宜

孫老師，

今天開始拜讀《文集》第三卷。

保陽特別喜歡王德威先生寫在《走出白色恐怖》英文版封底的那一段話：

「What moves us most is not only the deep love that her father and mother shared, allowing them to remain mutually faithful for so long, but also the self-respect and determination to overcome hardship that was born in the midst of their great individual solitude.」王先生的文章，在保陽看來，尤具一種穿透瑣碎而展現出來的乾淨與力量，有歷史的深度和當下的硬度，能讀出一股凜凜不倚的學者獨立之氣。尤其他的書評文字，更是如此。猶記他在為齊邦媛老師的《巨流河》寫的那篇長篇導讀，八九年前我在杭州第一次拜讀時，正巧走在錢塘江大橋上，那裡正是在宋詞裡經常出現的「西興浦口」，讀得保陽無限感慨，無限思量！尤其他化用別人的詩句而自鑄偉詞的那三個「如此」的排比句，將歷史變局、個人際遇、生命感喟和文字力量，鎔於這簡練的十二個字中。在當代文壇掀起了一波勢不可擋的巨浪，成為當今文化評論界一個新的典範與模板。一如當年凡有井水處的柳詞。

保陽之所以對王先生不吝溢美之詞，除了王先生文字的魅力而外，還特別感動他那段話裡的love，mutually faithful和self-respect。這三個字，和經上所說的Faith, Hope 和Love（I Corinthians 13:13）有等同力量。當年令堂老夫人就是在這樣一種力量下堅持十年，葆有生命的力量，讓自己的希望沒有凋落，這是一種何其讓人景仰的精神與力量！只有傳統「中國」女人，才有這種「神」性的精神力量。

保陽　敬上
4/24/2020

孫康宜致李保陽

Dear Baoyang,

I was very impressed with your smart questions about David Wang's ideas of "diasporic studies," "imaginary Nostalgic," "Post-loyalism", etc., especially because you are (like me) a scholar of pre-modern Chinese literature. However, after you translated these terms into Chinese and began to express these thoughts in Chinese, I suddenly felt the difficulty of responding to your questions. This is because I'm not very familiar with particular works in modern Chinese literature, and also because I'm really not an expert in David Wang's works!（我是外行，只知道現當代文學的大概情況，並不敢隨便詮釋王德威的具體著作）。

So I quickly wrote to my dear friend Prof. Ji Jin季進教授of Suzhou University （蘇州大學）for help. This is because I want to make sure that you would receive the correct answers from a renowned expert in modern Chinese literature. Prof. Ji Jin is a scholar whom I respect very much, and he came to Yale to give a lecture at the Council on East Asian Studies last fall.

Please see Prof. Ji Jin's answers to your particular questions, as shown below. I'm very grateful to Prof. Ji Jin for his immediate response to my email regarding your questions. I have learned a lot from Prof. Ji Jin's reply too. In fact our 3-party communication reminds me what Tao Yuanming said hundreds of years ago:

奇文共欣賞，
疑義相與析。

Of course, in this case, the 奇文 refers to the works of David Wang（王德威的奇文）.

Best,
Kang-i
4/24/2020

孫康宜致李保陽

Dear Baoyang,

I'm really happy and surprised to receive this wonderful reader's response from you. I'm happy because I always admire David Wang王德威as a scholar and a person.

I'm surprised by your email, because it was only yesterday (April 23, 2020) that he was elected to the American Academy of Arts and Sciences! What a coincidence that you wrote this amazing letter to me regarding David Wang today! It must be a case of telepathy.

In terms of David Wang's scholarship, he is a pioneer figure despite his relatively young age.

Over the past several decades, Professor Wang has established himself as the single most influential critic and theorist in the field of modern and contemporary Chinese literary and cultural studies. He has published extensively in both English and Chinese, and his works have had a revolutionary impact upon the field. Besides his vital contributions as a scholar, Professor Wang is also unique in having shaped the field through his work as editor of numerous book series, which have published major works of scholarship and fiction.

He is a key figure in the shift toward a global conception of Chinese literature and culture. In particular, his scholarly work was pivotal in broadening the conventional view of "diasporic studies" by relating it to the historical study of China and its literature. Such an approach is much needed in modern Chinese literary studies. I can sum up his major intellectual contributions as follows.

（1）He has published several major English-language monographs that have collectively transformed the field of modern Chinese literary studies. These monographs have included discussions of dozens of important texts never before discussed in English-language scholarship, introduced numerous new literary theories (such as "Imaginary Nostalgia" and "Post-Loyalism"), and challenged traditional conceptions of Chinese literary history.

（2）Eschewing the stock characterization of one-sided Orientalism, his scholarly works (and the numerous book series he has edited) restore the historical dynamism of cultural engagement between China and the West, as can be seen in his recent book, *The Lyrical in Epic Time: Modern Chinese*

Intellectuals and Artists through the 1949 Crisis (Columbia University Press, 2014).

（3）In general, Wang offers a more nuanced narrative of strategic alliance and negotiation among the players in the global field of Chinese cultural production over the past four centuries. He consistently produces fresh pictures of interculturality and transcultural practice.

（4）His work does not rely merely on existing Western literary and cultural theories, but instead is grounded in deep archival research in Chinese and other Asian sources to yield fresh interpretations of cultural networks and meanings.

（5）Adept at making arguments that are novel not only for the English-language academy, but also in the context of Chinese-language research, he is well-regarded for discovering unexpected connections among seemingly disparate parameters of place, language, and polity, as can be seen in his Chinese book, *Sinophone Literature: Singaporean Experience* (Singapore: Nanyang Technological University, 2014).

（6）Wang has published an astounding 29 books in Chinese, many of which are regarded as contemporary classics of Chinese literary history, scholarship and theory.

（7）Wang has edited or co-edited 28 other books in both Chinese and English on topics ranging from travel literature, imagining the nation, urban culture, the Great Divide of 1949, to the lyrical tradition, late imperial fiction, and literary history such as his *New Literary History of Modern China* (Harvard University Press, 2017).

（8）Wang has also been responsible for training several generations of graduate students, many of whom are now leading figures in the field of Chinese literary and cultural studies and hold appointments at universities such as Duke, Columbia, University of Washington, Connecticut College, University of Illinois, Urbana-Champaign, UCLA, Hong Kong University

of Science and Technology, The City University of Hong Kong, Harvard
University, etc.

Anyway, what I meant to say is that Wang is a contemporary pioneer who stages
important dialogues between modern Chinese literary studies and world literature.

I really hope that someday you can visit him at Harvard.

Best,
Kang-i
4/24/2020

李保陽致孫康宜

孫老師，

謝謝您的長信！萬分感謝！

保陽讀書的面向不寬，沒有研究過王先生的研究領域，當年讀其文字，只是覺得那股迷人的力量實在不忍釋卷。因為專業方向和語言的隔閡，保陽實在不知道應該用什麼樣恰當的語言來描述王先生文字，所以只能在上兩封信中使用了一些不太精確的模糊語言。讀了您的長信，對王先生的學術路徑有了更多的了解，有些概念也開始逐漸認知。比如您提到的「diasporic studies」、「Imaginary Nostalgia」、「Post-Loyalism」這三個概念，讓保陽對以前比較模糊的碎片化、印象式閱讀，有了比較系統的認識與理解。

「diasporic studies」，大約可以用來解釋中國人的「四九情結」（保陽以前的郵件中曾和您分享過〈傅成家日記跋〉，其中有提到過這個概念）；「Imaginary Nostalgia」，大約就可以用來解釋「民國想像」（前幾天保陽信中曾提到近年來中國大陸的「民國熱」現象）。「Post-Loyalism」比較複雜。近代中國知識人在四九之前，都有感時憂世的家國情懷（比如夏志清先生近年在廣州

出版的一本小書的名字就叫《感時憂國》），這批人在時代劇變的巨流裏挾下，離開中國大陸或者中文世界來到海外，不管他們的現實選擇還是精神苦旅，都充滿了一種複雜的回歸情結。這一點，大約三十幾年前，在港臺、新加坡等華人聚居之地，湧現出了一批前民國題材的影視劇（如新加坡的《絕代雙雄》、《天涯同命鳥》，香港的《萬水千山總是情》、臺灣的《京華煙雲》、《珍珠傳奇》等等），除了當時中國大陸剛剛開放的市場因素之外，那些劇作的好多傳統中國文化因素（如歌詞、配樂等），無不流露出一種比本土還本土的「本色當行」，這應該就是身在海外的文化人在精神上力求回歸與認同的努力，那批人大約還趕上了傳統中國的尾巴，他們努力朝傳統中國的靠近。但那時已是迴光返照，現在早已成為絕響。保陽認為，王先生以上的三個研究向度，實際上最後的指向是一個主題，即近代中國文學、文化的時代特徵。用這三個研究向度去理解他為齊邦媛老師寫的《巨流河》導讀文字、《走出白色恐怖》序，才明白那些文字何以如此精緻！如此深刻！如此感人！

　　這也為今天身在海外而又胸懷傳統的中國人之存在，提供了一個學理層面解釋。

　　王先生的理論結構非常宏大，保陽不知道自己的理解是否準確？是否說了外行話？但是您來信中介紹王先生研究的那三個概念，確實讓保陽對此前的閱讀印象，有了豁然質實的感覺，真是萬分感謝！

　　去年11月中，保陽曾從費城開車七個小時到劍橋，讓孩子們身臨其境地感受了學術殿堂的氛圍。當天晚上和孩子們在學校外面的哈佛書店看書，想到王德威、宇文所安諸先生皆在此教授中國文學，自己也讀過他們的文字，卻沒有機會向他們當面請益，殊為憾事。下次要是有機會去劍橋，一定彌補這個遺憾。那次回程還專門繞道New Haven，帶孩子們參觀了Yale，繞著Beinecke Library轉了一圈，卻不得其門而入，哈哈～

保陽　敬上

4/24/2020

李保陽致孫康宜

孫老師，

　　保陽前段時間讀了您分享的秀威版《走出白色恐怖》，就先快讀了王先生的序言。尤其感動於他的那段英文推薦語。就想起他的《巨流河》前言。還特意在YouTube中欣賞了他力推《巨流河》英譯的影片採訪。去年底保陽曾在普林斯頓藝術博物館見到了這本書，當時沒有想到是《巨流河》的英譯本，直到看了採訪視頻，才從封面判斷得知。今春再去，那本書已經不見了。去學校外面的Labyrinth Books書店尋找，那裡竟然也沒有。

　　保陽很喜歡王先生的那有穿透力的文字風格，挺拔、耐讀！

保陽
4/24/2020

孫康宜致張宏生

Dear Hongsheng,

　　My goodness! Thank you for your quick response! Baoyang has given me a lot of help; he is helping me proofread（and making corrections for）the mainland edition of《孫康宜文集》5卷本（廣西師範大學出版社北京分社）。He has already finished proof-reading the Taiwan edition of another book，《從北山樓到潛學齋》, which is coming out in June.

　　Baoyang and I are currently co-editing a book, entitled《避疫書信選：從抱月樓到潛學齋》（臺北：秀威資訊）. You know what? Out of the blue, Baoyang first wrote to me on March 11, 2020. And I first replied to him on March 29, 2020, only 3 weeks ago. And up to this point, he has already written more than 60 letters to me, all substantial stuff--including the one about you! It's such a miracle. Don't you think?

And all of this is due to the coincidence that this is the time of the COVID-19 Pandemic, during which Baoyang is forced to stay at home to read books! (Otherwise he would have to work all day in a company). That's why the book is called 《避疫書信選》. Don't you think this is an amazing coincidence?

But as you said before, nothing is a "coincidence" in my life!

Fondly,

Kang-i

4/24/2020

孫康宜致李保陽

Dear Baoyang,

I cannot help sharing with you this series of correspondence between Prof. Zhang Hongsheng張宏生教授and me. I think you will be fascinated by the things Prof. Zhang has said in his emails to me. I admire Prof. Zhang Hongsheng very much for his amazing ability to always use the right words to describe things.

This semester I have been using Prof. Zhang Hongsheng's book, 《讀者之心： 詞的解讀》（北京：中華書局，2013），as one of the major reference books for my *ci* class. My students are very impressed with Prof. Zhang's perceptive ideas about *ci* 詞, as well as his beautiful style of writing! I have learned so much from Prof. Zhang Hongsheng over the years!

Best,

Kang-i

4/24/2020

孫康宜致李保陽

Dear Baoyang,

　　This is fascinating! Please see Zhang Hongsheng's email message just now, as a response to my email to you! It's almost like an instant chain reaction 連鎖反應. This is the power of email communication; this is what traditional letter-writing cannot easily accomplish!

　　And the emails are traveling between Hong Kong, Pennsylvania, and Connecticut. How miraculous!

Best,
Kang-i
4/24/2020

李保陽致孫康宜

孫老師，

　　謝謝您轉來和張老師的通信，能夠從你們的字裡行間感受到學者之間的投契。保陽有幸見證了這樣的友誼，真是三生有幸。這讓保陽想起了古人，他們常常在生活的瑣碎中，彼此期待著來自知音的文字。那種瑣碎，就像您對充和先生晚年平靜生活的解讀那樣有味。處於Email時代的我們，一天之中甚至可以享受多次「開拆遠書何事喜」的喜悅，沒有了古人那種漫長的期待，這又是一種何樣的幸福呢？

保陽
4/24/2020

孫康宜致張宏生

Dear Hongsheng,

　　Amazing! The recent correspondence between you and me will also appear in the book,《避疫書信選：從抱月樓到潛學齋》. See my email to Baoyang Li.

　　Is this a coincidence?

Best,
Kang-i
4/24/2020

張宏生致孫康宜

　　是啊，康宜，真是太奇妙了！在康宜身上，確實感覺到了生活中充滿的力量，以一種特定的方式展示出來，所以，以前我曾用了「巧合」這兩個字，其中有著深長的意味。而且，康宜還讓我們不斷見證著這一點。一切都好像是偶然，又好像是必然。誰能想到，這麼短的時間，竟然成就了這麼一件有意義的事情！這真是一段佳話！太令人不可思議了！宏生

4/24/2020

　　謝謝康宜！這真是我們相處歲月的許多美好回憶，奇妙事情的延續！我的書能在萬里之遙和學生們一起分享，也令人感到緣之一字，不可言說。猶記1997年初，康宜邀我到耶魯，在課堂上和同學交流，已經過去了二十多年，而現在我和此刻的學生又以這種方式聯繫到一起了。謝謝康宜精準的翻譯和美妙的講述，我真希望什麼時候也能坐在課堂裡！（當然，我又想起了2018年秋天在康宜課堂的情形）不一一。

宏生
4/24/2020

李保陽致孫康宜

孫老師：

這封信猶豫了好久，不知道以怎樣的語境和方式討論這件事。那天讀了您的信，保陽走到家附近的思故客河邊的樹林中想了很久，終究沒能選擇好表述的姿態，現在還是這樣。但還是回應一下您的那封信。

您說得非常對，學術和我們的情感應該是一碼歸一碼，不可因為我們的情感傾向而忽視或者無視歷史的客觀存在。

保陽　敬上
4/25/2020

註：此信有部分刪節。

孫康宜致李保陽

Dear Baoyang,

Now that you have touched on this interesting topic, I would like to clarify one crucial point about a protocol in the American academic field, which I respect.

In the American academic world, we as literature professors (including Harold Bloom in the Humanities Program and myself in East Asian Literature) must teach ALL representative literary works regardless of our own personal political positions. This is one way to assure that we preserve literary history as it is. It is in this context that Harold Bloom also read Mao's poetry, apart from the works of other English and

American writers.

In my poetry classes at Yale over the last several decades, I taught all sorts of poets from ancient times to the modern and contemporary era--ranging from曹操、曹植、陶淵明、蘇東坡to龔自珍、魯迅、周作人、郁達夫、施蟄存、毛澤東、汪精衛、陳寅恪、余英時, etc. These are just selections of representative works for the students to read, and it's one way to present the literary history as it is.

Okay, I have to stop writing right here. It's time for me to join the Church service now.

In haste,
Kang-i
4/25/2020

註：此信有部分刪節。

李保陽致孫康宜

孫老師，

今早帶孩子們去村裡郵局取回了兩大包書，謝謝！

回到家迫不及待地拆開包裹，赫然看到您送給內子的筆記本，她喜歡得不得了，尤其是封面上貼的那個小紙貼，那是她喜歡的顏色。內子讓保陽轉達她的感謝！謝謝您的盛情！六巨冊《詠西安詩詞曲賦集成》收到，在萬里海疆之外的思故客河畔，能看到來自家鄉地方出版社刊印的鄉土詩詞集，一種熟悉親切之感油然而生。《施蟄存海外書簡》這本書，保陽讀書那會兒在學校圖書館見到過，當時看到封面的書影是寫給「孫康宜」的手跡，那時萬萬沒有想到多年以後，您會在這本書的封面上特意貼一張紙條，告訴保陽那是施先生寫給您的手跡。真是太奇妙了！《曲人鴻爪本事》和《古色今香》兩本書尤其喜歡，一來是因為它們都是關於「最後一位閨秀」張充和的書，二來是保陽一直比較喜歡海外印的紙本書，選紙瑩白硬挺，在平裝書裡，上手很有質感。於是就迫不及待地坐在Porch

的陽光下，讀了一個上午。這些書大部分都是十年以前出版的書，要是在今天的中國大陸，早已歸入舊書一類，但是如今在地球的另一端的山村展讀，真有一種時空倒錯之感！

保陽十多年前的本科畢業論文，寫的是沈從文，那時候知道「合肥四姊妹」，也知道小妹充和遠嫁美國，當時只覺得不過是個傳說中的人物而已。後來在浙江嘉興的崑曲界朋友處，看到過充和先生抄寫的曲譜影本，很喜歡她的字。充和先生的字以隸法入楷，閒逸娟淨，真率秀拙。前者乃其熔鑄諸家，以晉唐人結體出之；後者乃先生積閱歷、書卷、修養後自成一家，所謂觀千劍、操千曲而後所成之境界也。《曲人鴻爪》中之舊時聞人，多已名登鬼籙，而今捧讀，大有江南老杜之嘆。

保陽兒時經常看戲，那時候關中鄉下農閒時節，各村社普遍搭台演戲酬神，劇目多舊時雜劇傳奇所改編。保陽後來喜歡文學，大約和那時聽多了戲文有絕大關係。關中鄉下多唱秦腔，所謂「八百里秦川黃土飛揚，三千萬兒女齊吼秦腔。」。大學畢業後轉往浙江嘉興教書，喜歡看越劇，那是浙江地方戲。江南人文淵藪，故唱詞往往典雅深邃，像詩詞一樣富含深意，因之比較喜歡。後來在廣州讀書三年，課餘兩大嗜好：白天逛舊書攤，晚上看戲。崑曲流行蘇州一帶，雖然嘉興距蘇州只一個鐘頭而已，本地也有崑劇社，但主流還是越劇，故很少看崑劇。秦腔、越劇、粵劇皆屬花部戲曲，所以保陽後來一直不習慣聽所謂「國劇」之的京戲，更喜歡地方戲曲。

今天讀您《曲人鴻爪本事》序言，其中提到充和先生戰後曾在蘇州某次曲會後填了一闋〈鷓鴣天〉。真是巧極，保陽五年前到廣州讀書，第一次去看戲，散場後回學校途中，填了一闋詞，竟與充和先生同調同韻：

鷓鴣天　連日觀劇江南戲院，夜歸馬崗頂，口占一曲為秀珠作
一曲《鵝潭》愁斷腸，雲山珠水照紅妝。誓家妮子芙蓉面，有信江潮薄倖郎。　轉盼倩，又思量。盈盈弄櫂水中央。荔灣一曲清商怨，款款餘音猶繞梁。

註：秀珠為紅豆劇團伍韻飛女士飾演，劇本為廣州越劇院余楚杏先生撰。

　　還有一次，在廣州友誼劇院，當天是粵劇名伶陳韻紅老師的專場，沒想到上海崑劇院的梁谷音（1942-）老師也專程趕去廣州為之捧場，實在讓人意外。梁老師師從沈傳芷、張傳芳、朱傳茗等「傳」字輩梨園前輩。您《曲人鴻爪本事》頁274收錄了一張照片，其中有一位王泰祺，他也是沈傳芷的徒弟。嘉興有一位曲人莊一拂（1907-2001）先生，晚年編有《古典戲曲匯目叢考》三巨冊。他老人家非常欣賞梁谷音，專門為梁老師寫了一篇《梁谷音外傳》，油印傳世。莊先生逝後，遺物星散，保陽在嘉興教書時，曾在舊書攤覓得一冊莊先生簽名鈐印本《梁谷音外傳》。這位莊先生是一位奇人。他民國時期曾師從全福班名藝人陳鳳鳴，與崑曲結緣，與曲家王季烈、劉鳳叔、徐凌雲、管際安、朱堯文等人唱和。著有《鴛湖塚》、《十年記》等傳奇，以及《南溪散曲》等，並與趙景深合編《戲曲》月刊、主編《大成曲刊》等。大約是因其壯年時在政治方面「大節有虧」，最後終老於嘉興城南的白茅庵。保陽的好朋友范笑我與莊先生過從甚密，常常講起莊先生故事。故那晚看完戲，保陽專程到後台與梁谷音老師聊及莊先生舊事，為莊先生晚年為毛澤東詩詞譜曲一事，嘆息不已。觀劇結束，保陽有一詩紀事：

　　　　丙申十月，羊城友誼劇院觀陳韻紅女士《粵韻紅梅》粵劇個人專場，邂逅
　　　　上海崑劇院梁谷音老師，共話禾中莊公一拂舊事。
　　　　舊時風物已成空，嶺外寒梅楚楚紅。粉袖百年舒舊恨，梁音三日繞絲桐。
　　　　憐愁照影顧生媚，巧笑橫波盼驚鴻。一歎盛衰歌場外，梨花落雨趁東風。

　　《曲人鴻爪》第一集中收錄盧前贈充和先生七絕一首。盧前和王鵬運之間有一段故事：清末南京詞壇巨擘端木埰，曾手書《宋詞十九首》冊頁，贈送給王鵬運。王氏逝後，其侄孫婿許頤修得到這本冊頁，以十五元大洋賣給盧前，盧前遍請當時聞人如王瀣、葉恭綽、吳梅、唐圭璋等人，為題卷首，將之影印行世，即現在流傳甚廣的《宋詞十九首》。大約十年前，保陽在廣西南寧讀研究生，成都有一位愛好詞學的老前輩，又據盧前的影印本為底本，影印了若干部，並寄給保陽一冊。前年保陽從廣州倉促出國，將一批詞集贈送給日本立命館大學文學部，其中那冊成都影印本即在焉。

《古色今香》頁241-243收錄充和先生自用本《六也曲譜》，此書題怡庵主人編，分為元、亨、利、貞四輯，三十二開小本，全部二十四冊。初版為上海朝記書莊石印，印成書後，交由上海校經山房成記書局發行。保陽原來藏有這部書，2017年上半年，家中連遭變故，彼時尚在廣州讀書，經濟困難，無奈之下，遂舉以易米。今天看到這部書的書影，引起無限回憶和感慨！

以上拉拉雜雜地講了許多不相干的閒話，謝謝孫老師的耐心。接下來如再讀有心得，再呈請教。

今天去在村裡郵局，看到一向空蕩蕩的大廳，竟然裝上了臨時隔離玻璃，工作人員指示保陽必須戴上口罩，並提醒這是州裡的法律規定。我們是鄉下地方，尚且如此嚴峻，可想這次疫情之嚴重。這麼嚴重的疫情中，麻煩您和CC先生往返郵局，郵寄二十多磅重的兩個大盒子，實在讓保陽於心難安！再次感謝你們！保重身體！

保陽　敬上

4/25/2020

李保陽致孫康宜

孫老師，

接著上封郵件，關於王先生為《走出白色恐怖》寫的英文評論，保陽就這個話題再延伸討論一下。

由王先生的「mutually faithful」，保陽想到了您筆下陳子龍的「Loyalism」。雖然您的主要面向是明清易代之際陳氏的政治立場，但陳氏的忠於國家，又何嘗不是對自己妻子的「不義」呢？任何居於政治、道德層面之上的對人的違拗，都是不義的。所以保陽認為Loyalism沒有mutually faithful可愛。Self-respect是一個人站立於生命高度上的支點。這一點我想也是為什麼令堂老夫人能果決地跳下親戚騙她的汽車，不顧性命之虞來對抗來自外界的玷污。人都有屈服於物質環境而屈就現實的本能，但有時候卻能衝決眼下的利害而奮起一搏，這種力量實來自

self-respect。它是一個人向外在世界定義和展現自己的依據，扎根於此，就可任爾東南西北風而巋然不動。

但弔詭的是，這種精神和力量基本只在女性身上具備，尤其是中國女人身上。中國歷史，虧欠中國女人太多。在中國及其周邊有「溢出效應」的東亞地區，傳統社會道德規範（倫常）中，有許多是專門針對婦女的，如「夫為妻綱」、「未嫁從父、出嫁從夫、夫死從子」等等，這從本質上確定了婦女的從屬性社會地位。歷史上那些「紅顏禍水」、「紅粉骷髏」（femme fatale）們，照鑑的是失敗的男人們無能的推諉。從肉體上摧殘女性，更是他們對自己不自信加上陰暗變態、殘酷扭曲心理的外在表徵。保陽的外祖母那雙小腳刺骨地疼了一輩子，每當念及於此，就禁不住想起孔子那句話「始作俑者，其無後乎」（借用此句話現在一般理解的意思）。這尚且是中國歷史對中國女人的虧欠。即便是到了文明的近代，極具現代公民意識且年過半百的胡適之先生，也在婚後與別的女性有染（參見余英時《從日記看胡適的一生》第五章）。男女之間的事情，從古到今都是最能挑動普通人神經興奮點的事情，也是最能表徵一個人道德（忠）的晴雨表。作為近代知識人標桿的胡適之先生，尚且如此節操有虧，那麼無數中國男人「家裡紅旗不倒，外面彩旗飄飄」的陰暗心理就不難解釋了。這是我們生活的當下，多數中國男人對中國女人的虧欠。以上諸端，大約可以和您二十六年前提到的一個概念「Male ontological anxiety」相對照來解讀。

夫妻之間除了情（Love）之外，必須有義。中國人講情深義重，趙五娘、秦香蓮這些中國女性，對他們的丈夫除了「情」之外，還有「義」（贍養老人，撫育幼雛），但是多數中國男人從來對女人都不義。在帝制時代，他們公然強姦婦女的意志，讓她們對自己的納妾行為「識大體」，自己死後讓女人為他們「守貞潔」，婦女必須把自己圍於沒有自我、沒有自由的窩角裡。一旦婦女有了自我覺醒的意識，那就是潘金蓮、童寄姊之類的「淫婦」、「妒婦」，必須要先「沉潭」「逐出」而後快之。我從來沒有奢望人都像　神一樣的聖潔。法利賽人把那個不潔的女人帶到耶穌跟前，要用石頭打死她時，耶穌問：「你們中間誰是沒有罪的，誰就可以先拿石頭打她。」但是人跟人之間要講「義」，夫妻之間更應如此。令堂老夫人對令尊老先生除了「愛（Love）」之外，還有一層「義」在。職是之故，保陽對令堂老夫人尤其感佩景仰！

保陽
4/25/2020

孫康宜致季進

Dear Ji Jin,

　　This is a correspondence between me and a young scholar Dr. Baoyang Li regarding David Wang's works! Both Dr. Li and myself are scholars in pre-modern Chinese literature古典文學. Please let me know if there are some problems in Dr. Li's interpretation of David Wang's works. I'm not good at reading these ideas in Chinese, and can't tell if there are errors in the Chinese use of terms, etc. So please advise!

Kang-i
4/25/2020

Line訊息

李：這本《曲人鴻爪本事》我會寫一封長長的email給您。因為書裡面的故事，還有我自己知道的故事，都太有趣了，我必須要把它們分享給您。由「曲人鴻爪」突然想起十二年前，保陽在宏生老師的詞學會後，大家一起去揚州，在揚州雕版博物館，保陽突發奇想，就地買了一本空白冊頁，請當時與會的諸位詞學者各為保陽寫一句話，以為「詞人鴻爪」。上圖是宏生老師所寫，他寫的那句話道出了做人治學的一種態度，很好。

孫：Wow, I'll tell Hongsheng about this!

李：謝謝孫老師。等下次來耶魯，我把它帶過來，您也幫我寫一句，是十二年後首次開筆也。

孫：I have already forwarded your messages to 張宏生 by Wechat。

李：中間十二年這本冊子都放在不知道哪裡了。去年冬天整理東西，發現竟然帶來美國了。

孫：Here is Zhang Hongsheng's response to your notes and the picture of his inscription：

> 「已經十二年了，真是彈指一揮間！現代人寫舊體詩，也能出彩，這首詩就是我喜歡的作品之一。『風流莫作高低論，海在江河最下游。』寫出了一種氣度，一種追求，可以做不同層面的理解。大海的位置最低，但卻能包納江河。所以，門第、學歷等等，都不是關鍵因素，主要是看自己有沒有凌雲之志，向上之心。能不能做出成就，或成就大小，外因雖然也重要，但最重要的是內因，是自己。」

季進致孫康宜

親愛的孫老師：

您對王德威的理解與評價實在到位，佩服佩服。雖然您是古典文學教授，但您的點評卻超過了不少現代文學的教授。由此可見，中國文學作為一個整體，從古典到現代，自有同心相通之處。

李保陽先生對三個概念的理解，當然有其合理之處，也看得出作者的好學深思。但從王德威著作來看，這幾個概念都有其特定的意涵與指向。「diasporic studies」，所謂的離散研究，主要是他們所進行的華語語系文學研究，同樣是華語語系文學研究，史書美、石靜遠和王德威並不相同，相對而言，王德威的最為平和理性和包容，希望能把中國大陸、港臺、馬華、北美華文文學等，都作為一個彼此對應的華語語系文學來加以觀察，這對傳統的中國現代文學研究絕對是一個巨大的進步；「Imaginary Nostalgia」、「Post-Loyalism」，想像的鄉愁來自於對沈從文作品的研究，大概是指現代文學史上一批身處城市的作者，對鄉土的回望與書寫，而後遺民寫作，則是借用傳統的「遺民」概念，來討論1949年以後臺灣與海外的一批作家作品，這與夏志清的「感時憂國」是不一樣的概念。夏志清

的「感時憂國」原文是obsession with China，是批評中國作家過於迷戀中國，以至於缺少了世界性的情懷與表現。後遺民寫作，倒是可以與王德威重提「抒情傳統」放在一起來討論。他的《史詩時代的抒情聲音》，關心的是1949年以後抒情何在的問題，旨在說明，即使在革命的史詩的年代，抒情也無所不在，這在在顯示了現代文學的複雜面向。「抒情傳統」應該成為我們考察中國現代文學的重要維度，而不能僅僅是革命的維度、寫實主義的維度。

　　這只是我個人的粗淺理解，沒有好好整理，只是信手寫來，請您批評。

　　請向保陽先生致敬！

季進
4/25/2020

孫康宜致李保陽

Dear Baoyang,

　　I want to share with you what my brother KC (孫康成) said about their forthcoming trip to Tunghai University.

　　I especially treasure what he said: "這趟東海之行對我個人不但重要，簡直可以說就是‘尋根之旅’，感覺上，父親和姊姊將陪著我，在東海的土地上。"

　　I feel you would appreciate what he has said too!

Best,
Kang-i
4/26/2020

李保陽致孫康宜

孫老師，

　　收到您的這封信，保陽也覺得很開心。和您一樣，雖然保陽和您一樣不能到東海的展覽現場去，但是整個展覽的全過程，似乎保陽都在參與其中。不管是雅萍的周至仔細、圖書館的熱情支持，還是您全家的興奮感恩，都洋溢在字裡行間。保陽想，雖然您不能親自與會，借用您研究《樂府補題》的話來說，但這何嘗不是一種「象徵」呢？保陽前年6月畢業典禮當天，正好有美國之行，沒能夠參加。當時頗感遺憾。但是後來漸漸覺得，沒有參加那個學生生涯的最後典禮，何嘗不是表示自己永遠沒有畢業，永遠都是一個走在求學路上的學生呢？對於東海的這次展覽，保陽亦作如是想！

保陽　敬上
4/26/2020

孫康宜致李保陽

Dear Baoyang,

　　Thank you so much for your insightful words, which are so inspiring!

Best,
Kang-i
4/26/2020

李保陽致孫康宜

孫老師，

　　簡體版校讀一過，現在分享給您。

　　當讀到歐保羅教授1965年在東海痛失兩子，和您1969年的故事，讓人兩度落淚！感謝　神的保守，給保羅教授力量和信心，讓他擁有了更大的家庭。

　　每一個人心靈的最深處，都有一塊最柔軟的地方。保陽分享一個自己的故事：2012年3月，當小兒來到我們跟前時，我太太問保陽是保孩子還是保工作，保陽當時的第一反應是：我們的第一個孩子又來投奔我們了！所以幾乎沒有猶豫就選擇了孩子。因為當時的環境，周圍很多人都選擇了悄悄去醫院拿掉孩子。保陽後來三年的「低位運行」，就是違逆了　神的意旨，　神給保陽機會去彌補那個過失。

　　後來玫儀老師介紹我們認識了　神，她說凡事要靠　神，就不會張皇失措。我們才漸漸地意識到，我們那時候沒有認識　神，凡事總相信和倚靠自己的判斷與力量，結果不是顧此失彼，就是捉襟見肘。當我們認識　神之後，慢慢地學習當面臨選擇的艱難時，把自己不能抉擇的部分交給　神，我們自己去做能做的事情。這樣往往「壞事」就變成了「好事」，就像您說的那樣。我想這樣的見證，也是在榮耀　神！

　　就像您上次說的那樣，希望您能繼續寫出普林斯頓的故事，保陽相信，它也會像東海的故事一樣感人！

保陽　敬上

4/26/2020

註：這裡的「簡體版」指的是〈言猶未盡：且從「陽光穿透的歲月」書展說起〉
　　的簡化漢字Word版。

李保陽致孫康宜

孫老師，

　　在《文集》第三卷看到一篇〈許宏泉聽雪集〉，看題目還以為是您某位同名的友人。急急翻到正文一看，果然是和州許宏泉。這位許先生和保陽在嘉興的兩位好朋友范笑我、吳香洲是很好的朋友，他們是同屬繪畫藝術圈的好朋友。大約十一年前，保陽還在讀研究生，許先生請保陽到上海圖書館翻拍了鮑源深《補竹軒詩文集》。許先生是安徽和州（今和縣）人，鮑源深是和州鄉賢，那時候許先生打算編一套《和州文獻叢書》。保陽還在2010年春天應請把那部文集標點了出來，但是後來沒有了下文。許先生曾經寄過一套他主編的《管領風騷三百年》給保陽。前年出國之前散書，不知道給誰拿去了。

保陽　敬上
4/26/2020

孫康宜致李保陽

Dear Baoyang,

　　I'm so glad that you knew Xu Hongquan in person! Thank you for telling me the context of your mutual friends, etc.

　　I have never met Mr. Xu in person. But he did two paintings for me, and I still have them in my home. (See attached picture).

　　I should also mention that I was lucky to inherit the first volume（初集）of《管領風騷三百年》from余英時, and the second volume（貳集）of the collection from張充和! Both Prof. Yu Ying-shih and Chang Ch'ung-ho gave（轉送）their copies to me! See attached pictures below.

Best,

Kang-i
4/26/2020

李保陽致孫康宜

孫老師，

謝謝您分享的許先生畫作和余、張兩先生送您的《管領》前後二集。這封信真可以當作一段學界掌故來細細品味。

說到余英時先生，大家都知道他是目前華人學界的巨峰。但是他的作品更富吸引力，保陽每讀余先生的書，筆就停不下來地在書上畫線做筆記。2017年春，保陽買齊了幾乎所有余先生的著作（那時余先生的書在大陸已經被禁了），並詳細拜讀，當時作了很多筆記，打算在當年秋赴美向余先生請教，進行一次「問道賢者」之旅。但是很不巧，僅僅在普大轉了一圈拜訪了朋友而已。回國後，保陽專門去杭州拜訪了曾經主編北大版《余英時作品系列》的彭國翔教授，和他談了一個下午。彭教授那時在浙大哲學系教書，地點在杭州城北的紫金港校區，那裡是保陽曾經工作過的地方，也是「低位運行」的起點，〈十年蹤跡〉一文中已做詳述了。

今年保陽在家休息那幾天，給余先生寫了封信，卻不知道怎麼寄給余先生，普大東亞系的Martin Kern教授告訴保陽，信可以讓東亞系轉交。二月底，保陽專程駕車到普大去送信，也是從那時起，在葛思德開始了今年的閱讀計畫。但是很可惜，只看了兩周書，就因為普大有人感染COVID-19，圖書館不再接待校外讀者，後來乾脆學校都關閉了。只得作罷！

保陽三年前此時讀余先生書，記下了不少想請教的問題，現在分享一些給您，請見附圖（其中〈學術何以必須自由〉篇末的那段跋語，正好寫於三年前的今天這會兒，真是太奇妙了～）。

保陽　敬上
4/26/2020

李保陽致孫康宜

孫老師，

　　保陽完全理解您的提議。喜歡一個人就是替他著想。我們不應這個時候去打擾余先生。能和您討論余先生，就是一種幸福。

　　余先生的學問和文字，有跨時空的魅力，尤其是他對中國文化和中國知識人的論述，此前保陽還沒有看到過有如此冷靜、如此犀利、如此高度的人。余先生八九之後不入中原，九七之後不涉香江，更是踐行了他筆下的「士」的高行節操。僅此一點，即可標榜史冊，傲立儒林了！

　　保陽對余先生的道德文章之傾慕景仰，即便是隔著一條特拉華河，也能感到和余先生生活在同一時空的榮幸！

保陽　敬上

4/26/2020

李保陽致孫康宜

孫老師，

　　胡曉真所長的信收到了。相信胡老師的讀後感，是所有讀過您這篇文章的人的同感。

　　保陽相信，正是在陽光還未普照的那段艱困歲月裡的持守，您和您的家庭在無所依傍的暗夜裡踽踽獨行，相互取暖，才使得您對家人相互扶持、相互依靠的感情才那麼的強烈，對今天東海岸邊的那一縷陽光的感受，才較之他人更有「穿透」的體會。這大概就是人們常說的「沒有在暗夜長哭者，不足以言人生」吧。您和您的家庭經歷了那麼多的磨難、堅守，最後一步步在　神的帶領下，穿透濃雲霧障，走出一片新天地，賦予了生命全新的意義，使生命飽滿，榮耀　神！

　　保陽能體會到您的那份陽光下的感慨和愛！

李保陽致季進

季老師，

　　您好，今早收到您的長信，讀過之後，非常感謝，也非常感動您加入我們的討論。

　　保陽和孫老師都覺得，當我們的討論涉及到一些非常專業的學術問題時，就請這方面的專家來加入討論。因為我們每個人的學術專長都是有限的，如果保陽和孫老師的這個討論能夠搭建一個討論的平台，讓大家的思路相互碰撞，從而對參與討論的人有所激發，這是我們最希望看到的事情。

　　最近因為讀孫老師的書，保陽也在思考下面這個問題：在近幾十年，西方文學研究中的一些方法論，比如耶魯學派、王德威先生的一些視角等等，為什麼會在東西兩造學術界掀起一股熱潮？我想這應該不是從學者或者學術本身能找出原因的。學術也是思想，思想史的追溯，絕對不能離開其所處的刻下環境。所以保陽在想，中國目前為什麼在文學研究領域，很難有振臂一呼應者雲集的研究成果或者理論，癥結可能出在非學術因素上。因為學術思想史並非保陽的專長，討論起來難免隔靴搔癢說外行話，所以沒法深入探究。因為保陽是在中國大陸接受的系統教育，讀孫老師的書之後，所以有此一問，希望能引起大家的討論。

　　感謝季老師參與討論，期待您更多的新見！專此，並頌

　　教安！

孫康宜致李保陽

Dear Baoyang,

　　This is a letter from my former student Qian Nanxiu錢南秀，who is now a professor at Rice University in Texas! Nanxiu came to Yale to study in 1987, and she is among my many students during the last several decades. As you know, I have been teaching at Yale since 1982.

　　Nanxiu and her family suffered a lot during the Cultural Revolution in China, and that's why she talked about the "Red Terror" in her email.

Best,
Kang-i
4/26/2020

孫康宜致李保陽

Dear Baoyang,

　　This is Prof. Cheng Yu-yu's（鄭毓瑜院士）feedback on the Tunghai exhibition video,「陽光穿透的歲月」視訊：

　　　「我看完了，真是充滿陽光的一場視訊。老師笑容可掬，氣色妝扮都很亮眼，對東海大學有深深的愛，尤其與父親遭遇身心艱困相連的歲月裡，東海真是明亮的所在。東海也很用心安排，江院長的致詞特別表揚CC，而最後CC談的Cheese rolls，真是神來一筆，有趣又真摯！」

　　　「在我印象中，東海一直是很有深度、很美麗的大學，是我故鄉臺中的驕傲！」

　　　「王校長很努力校務，東海除獲教育部計畫補助，也獲得科技部『人文創新與社會實踐』計畫，前年曾來科技部報告，很看重大學的社會責

任。」

　　Just to let you know that Prof. Cheng Yu-yu sent the above comments to me by LINE.

　　By the way, Prof. Cheng Yu-yu's is someone whose scholarship I admire very much! In 2015 she came to teach at Princeton University, as Visiting Professor of Chinese Literature. Amazingly, the day I invited her to give a talk at Yale was also the day when I heard the good news that I was elected to the American Academy of Arts of Sciences! What a surprise!

Best,
Kang-i Sun Chang（孫康宜）
4/26/2020

孫康宜致李保陽

Dear Baoyang,

　　We should definitely include this email from胡曉真! As you know, Hu Siao-chen is the Director of the 文哲所 at Academia Sinica. She was the person who introduced me for my lecture in 2018. Remember the video you watched recently?

　　Dr. Hu is going to visit Princeton University for a semester during the fall of 2021.

Best,
Kang-i
4/26/2020

註：此信有部分刪節。

孫康宜致李保陽

Dear Baoyang,

I like this letter from Prof. Ji Jin very much! He is a true humanist and I respect him for that. But I don't think my article is only addressed to Christians. My purpose is to share my memories with more people.

I am so glad that I have reached out to Prof. Ji Jin, exactly because he is not a Christian.

Best,
Kang-i
4/26/2020

芳村弘道致李保陽

李保陽先生台鑑：

久疏音問，實深歉仄，尚祈鑒諒。

前月退職紀念論集印行，撥冗撰寫高作〈王鵬運藏書及遺物散佚鉤沉〉，增光篇幅，不勝榮幸之至。尊論博尋王氏後人所留存之貴重資料，詳細闡發四印齋所藏古籍、稿本、書畫之鳳毛麟角及散逸過程，令人感慨文物聚散無常，甚為欽佩。

拜讀附記，兩次晤談，歷歷浮現在眼中。文中言及王亮老兄未克訪到曾祖王國維故居之一事，實是傳聞之譌。2015年11月28日，王兄參加敝系召開之國際檢討會，次日與會人們一起清遊嵐山，下午赴吉田山訪過王國維故居，主人特地慨允進門，暫時參觀庭園。鄙人漢語甚差，想必當日先生聽錯吾談舊。（又有兩處錯字，頁434上段第3行「焯」當作「文焯」，同頁下段第15行「政法大學」當作「法政大學」）。

鄙人已退專任教授，四月之後，以特任教授繼續任教，負擔如舊。又承乏東

洋文字文化研究所所長，責任重大。

　　據悉貴國新冠疫情尚未穩定，敝國失政，疫禍深刻，全國學校已久停課，敝學五月以後開始網上課業。疫情未盡，惟冀攝衛。專鳴謝忱，順頌

　　康泰

芳村弘道　敬上

4/26/2020

註：芳村弘道，日本立命館大學文學研究科教授。

李保陽致芳村弘道

芳村先生尊鑒：

　　今天收到　先生的來信，既意外又高興！謝謝先生信中指出的兩處失誤：王亮兄的故事，肯定是保陽記錯了，您當日應該沒有講錯；兩處文字問題，是當日校對時的疏失，實在抱歉。保陽非常敬佩　先生對學問一絲不苟的認真嚴謹態度，讓保陽慚愧難當！其實還有一處錯誤：703頁上欄倒數第8行第6個字「雲」當作「運」。

　　很高興聽到　先生仍在上課，以您的學術成就和聲譽，如果完全不從事學術工作，那非常可惜。立命館大學的這個安排，是非常明智的。萩原老師2018年秋天的時候就告訴保陽，將為您編印紀念文集，去年往復聯絡，修訂校對，今年三月分印出來後就寄來美國。萩原老師的工作非常認真，讓人感動。紀念文集印製非常精美，保陽把它放在書架最顯眼處，不時摩挲，就會想起和您在京都訪書的情景。那是何等美妙的一段記憶！！將來保陽會再來京都拜訪您，屆時我們再續往游，以慰孺慕之思。

　　網傳日本疫情也持續嚴重，希望您和家人都注意安全，保重身體！希望和先生保持聯絡。謝謝！專此，並頌

　　教安！

晚　保陽　敬上

2020年4月26日星期日於費城思故客河上

錢南秀致孫康宜

Dear Kang-i,

　　Many thanks for sharing this touching article! It helps me see the origin of you strength. The sunshine you received from those who enlightened you later also beamed into our lives. Now when I think about it, my Yale education not only exposed me to the knowledge previously unknown to me, but also, more importantly, guided me to incorporate this new knowledge into my moral judgement. Your teaching led me through this difficult process precisely because I could, from your life experience in Taiwan under the white terror, make sense of my life experience under the red terror. You have helped me understand how I could cultivate good, healthy values from past sufferings. For this I am utterly grateful to you!

Love, Nanxiu

4/26/2020

胡曉真致孫康宜

孫老師：

　　我讀了您的文章，真是太感動了，在捷運上，眼淚也止不住流下來（還好戴著口罩可以遮掩）。您在歐保羅夫婦身上學到的功課，多麼深刻啊！您生命中奇異的恩典這麼多，這黑暗走向光明的歷程，真的要讓很多人讀到，在這世界的至暗時刻有信心。Amazing Grace！

曉真
4/26/2020

張宏生致孫康宜

康宜：

讀了〈言猶未盡〉，心裡久久不能平靜，生活中，磨難和希望並存，讓人感到前面永遠有引路的光。康宜從東海一路走來，是一段令人感動的經歷。順便提到，Sun在廣東話中，對應的字是「新」，似乎也可以為這個題目增添一點意味。不一一。

宏生
4/26/2020

季進致孫康宜、李保陽

親愛的孫老師、保陽：

很高興為你們的學術討論貢獻一點粗淺想法，承蒙不棄和肯定，備受鼓舞。

孫老師充分肯定了「抒情傳統」作為連結「傳統與現代」之橋的重要性，我也深為贊同。事實上，晚清以來的中國現代文學始終是在古今中西之間折衝發展的，既深受西方文學的影響（1949年以後的相當長時期，大陸文學又深受蘇聯文學的影響），又與傳統密不可分。雖然五四文學以反傳統為號召，但文學革命並沒有能割裂傳統文學與新文學千絲萬縷的聯繫。王德威《被壓抑的現代性》一書，著力挖掘晚清文學中被壓抑的現代性，解構五四文學的神聖性，闡明五四新文學的現代性並不是憑空而來，早在晚清文學甚至更早的文學中，即已蘊育生長。因此，借用王德威兩篇文章的標題，我們可以說，「沒有晚清，何來五

四？」同樣：「沒有五四，何來晚清？」晚清與五四，從來就是彼此依存的文學整體。王德威提出「抒情傳統」也是基於這樣的思考，著力挖掘1949年以後被遮蔽、被壓抑的傳統的聲音。

保陽關於魯迅與沈從文的閱讀體驗，應該是比較有共性的，沈從文小說的抒情性，尤其是作品中人性的憂傷、鄉土的力量、湘西世界的蠻荒等等，的確都很容易吸引讀者，我自己也非常喜歡沈的作品。他1949年以後放棄寫作，轉向文物研究，也自有其迷人之處。我曾經還寫過一篇〈論沈從文的物質文化研究〉。魯迅的作品，年輕時讀了也就讀了，並不能真正理解，隨著年歲漸長，不斷重讀魯迅作品，尤其是他的一些雜文，那真是不得不佩服魯迅的深刻與偉大。且不論《吶喊》、《彷徨》中的短篇小說常讀常新，特別是他的雜文中對中國國民性的反思、對現實社會的批判、對世道人心的諷刺，其深刻與尖銳，無與倫比。很多的論述，放在混亂、撕裂、顛倒的當代社會語境中，一點都不過時，總是讓我們時時警醒，如芒在背。因此，放眼整個二十世紀中國文學，魯迅是當之無愧的思想家、文學家，無人能及。當然，這只是我個人的體驗，供保陽參考。

我的專業是中國現當代文學，以後若有相關的問題，請隨時來信。你們的討論讓我受益匪淺，謝謝你們。

祝安好！

季進
4/26/2020

孫康宜致李保陽

Dear Baoyang（保陽），

While you are editing vol. 3（卷3）and vol. 4（卷4）of my *jianti* edition of《孫康宜文集》, I wish to call your attention to an important sinologist（漢學家）Paul Ropp（羅溥洛）, who unfortunately died a year ago in 2019. Paul Ropp was a great mutual friend of Zhang Hongsheng（張宏生）, Kang Zhengguo（康正果）, and myself. As you can see, in vol. 4 of my *wenji,* I have discussed Paul Ropp's scholarship on the woman poet Shuangqing. (In the article,《中國文學作者原論》). Also, in vol. 3 of my *wenji*, I have quoted Kang Zhengguo's poem on Paul Ropp, which reads "前世莫非史震林……"。[In item #62, under 康正果,《浪吟草》, in the section called〈張充和的「古色金香」本事〉本事（選錄）].

Ever since Paul Ropp passed away last year, I miss him very much! And just this morning, I was suddenly preoccupied with memories of his wonderful trip to Jintan, China, with Zhang Hongsheng and our other mutual friend Du Fangqin 杜芳琴.

Then, I was surprised to receive an email from my History Department colleague Prof. Denise Ho. She attached an article by Paul Ropp which is entitled, "My Serendipitous Chinese Journey." (See PDF attached here). Prof. Ho writes:" I was corresponding with Vivian Ling and she sent me this essay by Paul Ropp. I imagine you have seen it, but I thought I would send it to you just in case. "(Email dated today, April 27, 2020, at 9:14 a.m.) The article is from the book edited by Vivian Ling, entitled *The Field of Chinese Language Education in the U.S.: A Retrospective of the 20th Century* (UK: Taylor & Francis Book, 2018).

I started to read Paul Ropp's essay and found his recollection of the Jintan trip on pages 359-360. He mentioned Zhang Hongsheng, Kang Zhengguo, Du Fangqin, and me in his narrative. And of course, reading his essay brings me so many fond memories from the past.

Thus, before today passes, I want to send you this email along with Paul Ropp's essay. I copy both Zhang Hongsheng and Kang Zhengguo here, so that they also know about this!

Best,
Kang-i
4/27/2020

註：Paul Ropp（羅溥洛，1944.3.25-2019.4.14），生前為克拉克大學（Clark

University）歷史學教授，1974年畢業於密西根大學，獲得東亞和中國歷史的碩士學位和博士學位。先後任教於阿肯色州立大學（State College of Arkansas）、麥吉爾大學（McGill University）、孟菲斯大學（University of Memphis）以及Clark University。其研究主要涉及十七和十八世紀的中國社會、文化和歷史，開設課程和研究包括中國儒釋道家思想，現代亞洲、中國、日本文明，中國婦女文學和社會研究，以及中華人民共和國史。著有*Dissent in Early Modern China: "Ju-lin wai-shih" and Ch'ing Social Criticism*（1981），*Bannished Immortal: Searching for Shuangqing, China's Peasant Woman Poet*（2001）等。

李保陽致孫康宜

孫老師，

　　謝謝您分享這篇文章給保陽。在校讀第四卷中您新添加的那篇〈中國文學作者原論〉時，保陽有意細讀過羅溥洛和張、杜兩人在金壇做田野調查的故事。因為這樣研究清代文學的方法比較少見，且三人中有熟悉的張宏生老師，所以當時特別留意了。沒有想到今天能讀到羅先生的自述文章，太謝謝您了。保陽很喜歡讀前輩學人的自述文字，那是他們一生治學和人生智慧的總結，文字間總流淌著有趣的故事和靈性的光輝。羅先生這篇文章保陽先收藏起來，容後細讀。

　　謝謝您的分享！

保陽　敬上
4/27/2020

Line訊息

孫：Actually I was going to incorporate the article (taken from《曲人鴻爪本事》) into卷3 of文集！But for some reason, I could not find my original word file. Now someone is creating a new word file for me! So I'll add it to卷3, after you return the edited version to me.

李：好的。充和先生的書法老師沈尹默先生是湖州人，但他出生在陝西漢中，保陽在那裡讀了四年本科。保陽很喜歡沈先生的書法，二王的一路風格，溫潤中和，富有文人氣。

孫：The following feedback comes from my cousin黃麗秋：「視訊當天就覺得小紅姊的意猶未盡，讀了這篇文章，果然見證了生命中就是有這麼多的無常與無奈。很感動小紅姊總是能在艱苦中，一步步地攀越山峰，克服萬難平安度過。點點滴滴盡是血淚，走過來了就是溫暖的印記。」黃麗秋是我的表妹，很有藝術天才，她的書法得過日本藝術獎，我把其中一幅捐給臺灣的國家圖書館。

These are the important feedbacks from Lu DANQI（陸丹琦）, the leader of an important students' group from China! They visited America in August 2019, and they interviewed me at Yale in front of my Davenport portrait.

「Great to see you and your husband in this video!我也特別喜歡這個展覽的題目——陽光穿透的歲月，彷彿一種清麗、明媚而古雅的精神長存。往後聽，竟然還與Sun family、與您父親孫保羅教授super natural miracle相照應，真的非常奇妙了～～在COVID-19的現況之下，還有這樣溫暖的分享與Exibition，真好。還有，您與張欽次教授的故事真的特別可愛！螢幕那邊的我聽著，真的很羨慕這份相攜相伴的幸福。『當從心裡彼此切實相愛』，真愛也是像陽光一樣，有感染力、能穿透歲月的，還能浸潤為對生活的愛意。打開video的時候，我這裡還是早晨，相信這一天都能暖暖的了～～讀下來鼻子酸酸的。您的文字也揪著我們讀者的心，兩段過去激起我們強烈的共情。您在落筆的時候一定是克制著隱痛的，讀著都好疼。但文字是一種抒懷，更能通過分享帶給更多人力量。在現下這樣的特殊時期，尤其需要這樣的『信』。」

季進致李保陽

保陽：

　　你好！

　　很高興加入你們的討論，不同專業不同背景的相互交流，一定可以激發出更多思想的火花，讓我受益匪淺。

　　你提出了一個很有意思也很重要的問題，就是為什麼西方學界的成果可以產生普遍性的影響，而中國大陸學界卻少見原創性的應者雲集的著述或理論。最近十多年，我一直關注海外的中國文學研究，主要是海外的中國現代文學研究，出版了《英語世界中國現代文學研究綜論》等成果，深感以孫老師、宇文所安、李歐梵、王德威等為代表的海外中國文學研究學者，在問題意識、研究方法、理論視角、立場取向等諸方面，都與中國大陸學界有著極大的不同，不斷給中國大陸學界帶來刺激和啟發，甚至引發諸多的爭論。比如夏志清的《中國現代小說史》就直接影響了1990年代以後大陸學界的中國現代文學史的重寫；李歐梵的《上海摩登》推動了中國大陸學界的都市文化研究；王德威的《史詩時代的抒情聲音》引發了海內外關於抒情傳統問題的重新反思。孫老師和宇文所安主編的《劍橋中國文學史》也給中國文學史的書寫帶來了嶄新的可能。類似的例證，不勝枚舉。當然，海外學者的著作不可避免地有著大可商榷之處，甚至帶有理論霸權的味道，但是，正如你所說，我們必須要問一句，為什麼會從者如雲，引發熱潮？

　　我想至少有三個方面是值得我們本土學者思考的，一是海外學者兼通中西的知識結構，他們往往既有較好的中國文學的基礎，又在西方接受過系統的學術訓練，形成了較為完善的知識結構。二是海外學者的理論修養，各種西方理論的此起彼伏，也多少影響到了中國文學研究，尤其是在中國現代文學研究方面，「理論化」是相當突出的。理論往往成為照亮文本、闡釋文本的利器，給中國文學研究帶來了新異的面貌。比如這些年印刷文化研究、文學生產研究、視覺文化研究等等，就直接影響了海外的中國文學研究。三是海外學者跨文化的國際視野，他們從來不是僅僅局限於中國文學領域，而往往從跨文化的世界性視野，來觀照和研究中國文學，往往能道人所未道。比如夏志清之所以能在六十年前識英雄於風塵草澤之中，獨標張愛玲、沈從文、錢鍾書等大家，原因正在於他是將中國現代

文學的文本置於世界文學背景下加以比較品評，從而得出了不一樣的結論，這與他的世界文學研究的背景直接相關，他在耶魯讀博士時，研究的就是西方文學。

當然，說到中國大陸學界較少產生廣泛影響的成果，原因可能也很複雜。比如中國大陸每年的成果汗牛充棟，要想成為熱點，殊為不易。由於從業人數眾多，不同專業、不同領域、甚至不同課題，都可能自然形成各自為陣的圈子，也許圈內很熱鬧，是熱點，但對於圈外來說，就不甚了了。除非是像葛兆光等少數大牌學者，一般學者的成果，確實很難突出圈子，成為廣為人知的熱點。當然，也必須承認，當下社會的各種非學術的因素，確實制約了更多有創見的成果的產生。這個話題比較敏感，無法深入闡述，但我想大家都能理解。

拉雜寫來，只是一些隨感，不知你們以為如何？

祝安好！

季進

4/27/2020

季進致孫康宜

親愛的孫老師：

剛剛拜讀完大作，寫得真好！「陽光穿透的歲月」，上帝之光引領你們走過了種種磨難，終成大器。感恩！現在很多人就是缺少敬畏之心、感恩之心，才讓這個社會亂象頻生。雖然我不是基督徒，但相信如果更多一些感恩、向上、敬畏之心，這個社會一定會更好。

好可惜沒有機會前往東海大學現場觀摩您的大著和您父親手稿的聯展。也許以後你們可以考慮印行你父親的手跡？

祝安好！

季進 上

4/27/2020

王璦玲（Ayling Wang）致孫康宜Line

I was deeply touched and greatly inspired by your article! Thank you so much for sharing with me such precious memories. I am so lucky to be your student. Love you as always,

Ayling.
4/27/2020

李保陽致孫康宜

孫老師，

　　保陽在讀《文集》卷三〈何謂「男女雙性」？──試論明清文人與女性詩人的關係〉、〈末代才女的亂離詩〉等篇章時，發現這些篇什與卷四中明清女性文學研究的主題比較接近，反而與卷三的大多數文章風格不類。比如卷三中有大量九十年代的影評，以及對時事的批評（比如P.C.問題等等）。當時秀威版做如此分卷（冊），不知出於什麼考慮？廣西師大版還是沿襲這個分卷（冊）辦法嗎？

　　保陽建議不再做那種「磚頭書」，重新分冊，每冊文章主題比較集中，這樣主題分明。對於讀者來講也更加便攜。不知您意下如何？

保陽　敬上
4/28/2020

153.Line訊息

李：孫老師，保陽已回信給您了。沒有問題，羅先生應該包括在我們的書中的。

孫：Yes! I just read your email! We are truly a great team!

李： 是的。您和其他學者交往的故事應該也很有趣吧。比如夏志清先生。他的《中國現代小說史》，很迷人的一本書，保陽曾經「跨界」在課堂上給學生介紹過。

孫： Yes! You should read 夏志清日記，季進編！Also, Did you read my article about CT HSIA? Please see 卷2。

李： （圖略）這是夏先生小說史的香港「友聯」版，是前年帶出來的。今年初讀余英時先生自傳，才得知是友聯版。原來不知道是哪裡出版的，因為沒有版權頁。

孫： Amazing! The real expert of 夏志清 is 季進！

李： 好的，那可以向季老師請教。

孫： This is a message from 張宏生 in response to my email regarding Paul Ropp:

> 「康宜，這可真是太奇妙了，奇妙得不可思議！這個世界上真的是有神祕的力量存在！看了這封信，我也想起了1997年康宜、正果和我的烏斯特之行，想起不久之後的金壇之行⋯⋯。」

> Whenever I thought of Dostoevsky (1821-1881), the hardship we have gone through seems so insignificant!

孫： Please see my email to you just now, regarding Vols 3 and 4.

李： 孫老師，您的email保陽看過了，明白了。這兩天在抓緊時間校讀書稿。請放心。

孫： Thank you! Again, you and I are a perfect team! As soon as I finish some school deadlines, I'll reply to your earlier emails one by one!

李： 不急不急，您保重身體！

李： 這幾天讀的文章，收穫了不少歐美學術史方面的知識。實在要感謝您。

孫： But I should thank you too!

李： 保陽覺得這段時間讀您的文章、直接向您請教，就好像坐在您的課堂上受教一樣，甚至收穫還要更多。因為文字的表達更加集中，思想更加準確。

李保陽致孫康宜

孫老師，

　　剛剛讀了《兩個美國女人的故事》，很感動。1998年前後，最能挑動全球人神經的克林頓總統緋聞，就連當時讀高中的我，在中國偏遠的西北鄉下地方都知道。後來我也曾經想過：那時候的克林頓先生的太太怎麼熬過那段時光？讀了您的文章，才瞭解了喜萊莉夫人，對她也更加敬佩。保陽對「soldier on」、「endurance」和「tolerence」三個字印象特深。深深地感到，每一個人都不是那麼的平面，他們的經歷和背後的思考，在很大程度上是他們所以成為他／她本人的動力。很喜歡這篇文章裡的三句話：您說的「寬恕有時要比仇恨或報復來得有意義。」喜萊莉夫人說的「You live your own life. You make the choices that are right for you.」Eleanor Roosevelt夫人說的：「A woman is like a teabag..., You never know how strong she is until she's in hot water.」智慧的人總是能把對人生的感悟輕描淡寫地表達出來，給人以啟示。但是這背後卻不知是他們多麼辛苦地付出呢。

　　今天是您的好朋友Jim逝世九週年！他在您生命裡意義非常。

保陽　敬上
4/29/2020

李保陽致孫康宜

孫老師，

　　讀了〈道德女子典範姜允中〉一文，很有意思。沒有想到王先生的母親還有這麼一段傳奇的經歷。

　　今天讀的文章大部份都是有關女性研究的主題，有好些句子，感觸特深，一時也說不清是什麼樣的感慨，茲錄如下：

　　　　「許多海外的中國人也與李彤一樣，他們忘不了過去的中國，在異鄉

翻過一山又一山，仍然發現自己憶戀深處最深的還是中國。」（頁283）

「最美麗的人生經驗莫過於愛情所帶來的幸福感，知道生命中除了瑣屑的家常以外，還充滿了美麗的夢境與希望。」「所謂愛就是無限的慈悲與包容，它使人凡事為周圍的人著想。」（頁288）

「愛情有其根本缺陷，但也因為有了缺陷才更令人看到其中的神祕價值。」「是否擁有對方已經不是問題，問題是如何忍受永恆的回憶與思念。這也是真正的愛所付出的代價。」（頁289）

「當人們對自己的罪惡已完全麻木而無動於衷，而且還一味地企圖從無辜人身上的血得到贖罪時，那麼世界就必然要毀滅了。」（頁296）

「如果強烈的欲望最終不求解脫，一定會產生災難。」「女人一旦為愛而受苦，而犧牲，內心的世界也就變得特別豐富。」「欲望真是危險啊，它使人忘了如何適可而止。」（頁299）

「她雖然不再扮演妻子的角色，她卻成為更加德高望重的母親，可以充分發揮許多從未想過的倫理熱情，從而積極地證實自我價值。」（頁311）

「一個人只有在孤獨中才能面對自己，進而自覺地從事創作。」（頁316）

「傳統中國的環境中，當女性很少有其他權力的管道時，她們經常藉著她們的道德精神獲得某種權威意識。」（頁319）

「一個女子若能在她人生的有限性中，用感人的文字寫下她心靈的崇高，那麼她所獲得的更是一種不朽的文學和道德的力量。」（頁325）

〈寡婦詩人的文學「聲音」〉讓我想起了我的姨媽——一個傳統的關中鄉下女人——她如果在世已經九十多歲了。在我的印象裡，我的這位姨媽就像方以智的兩位孀居的姑母方維儀、方維則一樣，一直住在她的娘家——我舅家。我的這位姨媽很早很早以前就嫁到了渭河邊一個小村莊——草灘寺——據說那裡是唐玄奘去西天取經經過的第一個借宿寺院，寺院早就蕩然無存，但地名仍在。我姨媽生了三個孩子以後，我那姨夫就害了一種「癆病」——家族裡的傳說是餓死鬼附身——因為他在死前吃盡了家裡甚至屋頂的房樑。現在想來，是我們關中鄉下人

特好面子，也許是我那短命的姨夫沒有什麼錢，為了治病，連房頂的樑柱都賣了去換治病的錢，向外就說成是吃光的。這種兒時在鄉間聽過的因為面子而打死人命者，比比皆是。後來我的大表兄終於娶了媳婦，我姨媽總算熬出頭了，可是婆媳之間的關係糟糕得一塌糊塗。從我記事起，我姨媽就一直住在我舅家。因為這樣的生活經歷，讓我姨媽成為一個性格怪僻的人，我小時候特別怕她，除了我那位獨身一生的表姪女，我們姊弟表兄妹都很怕她。今天讀您的文章，我才深覺，我這姨媽守寡五十年，又不識字，她除了井臼灑掃，哪來排遣寂寞孤苦的渠道？內心的壓抑，自然外在地表現出一種異常的怪脾氣。無奈的是，我的大表兄和表嫂恩愛融洽，處在母親和妻子之間，只得選擇了村人認為「不孝」的一條路。我姨媽後來住到我舅家去，我想她也許是為了成全她的兒子。後來熬了三十年，終於臥病，但那時她似乎已經回不去她那草灘寺的家了。她是一位可憐的女人，為了丈夫、為了兒子，把自己苦了一輩子，不為人所理解，甚至遭到子姪輩的誤解和疏遠。我姨媽是個心底善良的好人，要不是她，我父親在我出世之前幾個月就離開這個世界了。

　　我的那位大表兄有個小女兒，比我還大七、八歲，生得端莊清秀，一直在鄉間唸書，希望藉讀書之路走出窮苦鄉村，進城去吃「國家飯」。高中畢業後，沒有考上大學，又沒有門路複習再考，就在各種學校做「兼課老師」，只要是一個「公家單位」，她就不挑剔，並且矢志不嫁，努力複習應考。她的想去念書，絕非是求知的欲望使然，而純粹是為了改變自己的生活處境。但是很不幸，她始終無法通過考試。後來年齡漸漸大了，除了我姨媽，親族都認為她腦子有問題，便以「不正常」人視之。但她仍日復一日地懷揣著她的讀書夢。我姨媽臥病，她主動擔起陪侍病床的重任。姨媽逝後，聽說她用自己的腦袋死命地撞我姨媽的棺材，血流滿地，她說要追隨我姨媽一起到地下去。我那時在已在外省工作，聽了這事，直覺得她就像大觀園裡賈老夫人逝後的鴛鴦。未久，我的表嫂臥病，也是她親侍湯藥。表嫂逝後次年，我的表兄臥病，她侍奉我表兄下世後大約四十來天，也一同物化。親戚中沒有人為之難過，甚至大家都有一種如釋重負的慶幸，說她終於完成了她的「任務」，解脫了。我一直覺得，我這位比我還大幾歲的表姪女，和我姨媽是心靈相通的。她們都在各自的生活環境裡「不得志」，迫不得已壓抑自己。她們的生活環境又是那麼的粗糙，她們攪纏在生活的無奈與壓力

中，又沒有抒發排解的管道，以至於成為「不正常」的人。我那表姪女，她不滿於待在她所處的那個同層面，希望改變，就這一點來說，她就和她的同儕不一樣，算是有「才」的一類人，但是他們被現實攪絆得無暇照顧自己的心靈。也許到了後來，那樣屢敗屢戰的複習功課，便成了她一種儀式感般的排遣，因為只有在那裡，她覺得自己還有希望，還有動力，還有存在的意識。環境的力量太強大了，制度的殘酷（比如中國大陸當時的高考制度等等）讓她無法按照自己的理想追尋想要的哪怕是卑微的東西。讀您的文章，尤其是每每讀到您引用胡文楷先生的書，說到明清之際，有三千九百多位女性作者，我就想：那些不知名的人去了哪裡？有人關心過她們的生死處境嗎？還有傳統方志裡面那厚厚的《列女傳》、《烈婦傳》，連名字都沒有。我就想起我的姨媽和她的孫女——我那位比我大了好幾歲的表姪女，心裡好生一股悲涼！

保陽　敬上
4/29/2020

孫康宜致李保陽

Dear BAOYANG,

　　Just to let you know that Kang Zhengguo has translated the English article (which I shared with you earlier) into beautiful Chinese. I think you would enjoy reading his translation. See attached!

Kang-i
4/29/2020

Line訊息

李：謝謝孫老師分享，康正果老師的翻譯非常棒。沒有想到聖經故事他也能翻譯得這麼好！

孫：He is not a Christian though!

李：是的啊。所以我驚歎他能把基督教的故事翻譯得這麼準確，確實厲害。

孫：Yes! He has a sense of objectivity, which is so rare!

李：康老師身上有我們關中人的那種「直」。昨天讀到您和《霸王別姬》編劇蘆葦的談話錄。孫老師和西安人很有緣分。

孫：Yes, I like people from陝西!

李：哈哈～諺云「十陝九不通」，意思是說陝西人耿直執拗，認準的理十頭牛都拉不回來。

孫：I also know陳忠實。

李：陳先生的《白鹿原》寫得真好。那就是我小時候從父親嘴裡聽到的一個真實的關中。但是他的小說是抒情的。很巧的是，我第一次讀《白鹿原》就是在昨晚給您的信中提到的我那姨媽家附近。1993年，二十七年了。

孫：Oh, that's great! By the way, Chen Zhongshu 陳忠實 came to visit me at Yale in 1995. He accompanied me all the way to 乾陵 and other places during my trip to 陝西 in 1996.

李：是嗎？您去乾陵那一年保陽正好初中畢業。第二年暑假，保陽一個人獨自騎腳踏車從家裡去參觀乾陵，往返一整天。當時父母不知道，等我回到家，我母親讓我找我父親去道歉，因為他擔心了我一整天，晚上仍不見人影。我就往田邊他一手搭建起來的瓜棚邊找他，他一見到我，哇地一聲就哭了。那是我平生第一次見他流眼淚。他是一個沉默寡言的人，但是很剛強。多年以後，當我有了孩子以後，尤其能理解他那一刻的心情……您那麼早就去過陝西啊！真是不可思議。很巧的是陳先生也是4月29日過世的，就昨天，2016年。陳先生是一個很耿直的人，他過世那天，我正帶著孩子在嘉興的南湖邊，當新聞裡報道他過世的消息之後，我當時望著湖面，心裡默默地重複了他《白鹿原》裡的那句話「白鹿原上最好的先生走了……」

孫：Wow, my goodness! That's a mysterious coincidence! I was especially interested in Qianling! I could never forget the 無字碑! I teach 武則天's poetry every year in my Women and Literature course. I should send you a course syllabus so that you would know more about the American academic system!

李：好啊。謝謝孫老師！我們陝西沒有啥特產，就是皇帝陵墓特多，漢唐兩代帝王陵墓，都在陝西，還有北朝為數眾多的皇帝陵墓。所謂「江南才子山東將，陝西黃土埋皇上。」楊貴妃和漢武帝劉徹的陵墓，一西一東，離我們家只有幾英里路程。所以陝西人就連形容一個人笨，都說那人是個「墓疙瘩」，哈哈～

孫：陳忠實 also accompanied me to the tombs of 楊貴妃 and 皇帝! No kidding, you lived near the tomb of 楊貴妃？

李：是的。我們家距離楊貴妃的墳墓大概就十來分鐘車程。

孫：That's amazing! I wish I had known you back in 1996!

李：哈哈，我那時候還是個什麼都不懂的孩子而已。我們鄉間有很多關於楊貴妃的傳說。我們去乾陵，楊貴妃墓是必經之地。

孫：Yes, I know! How time flies!

李：因為楊貴妃長得美，她死後，傳說她墳頭的土用來洗臉，可以變得更美白，所以鄉間婦女每每成群結隊前往。管理墳園的人就奇怪，為什麼楊貴妃的墳頭越來越小，後來才發現凡來參觀的婦女都會拿一小撮土回去，於是那個園吏就把墳頭用磚頭包起來，以免麻煩。這就是您當日看到楊貴妃墓為什麼是磚頭包起來的原因。在我們鄉下，墳頭是不用磚頭包的。

孫：I see! This is a funny story about the reception of 楊貴妃！

李：而且楊貴妃的墳墓裡傳說是沒有埋葬她的屍體的。這個傳說很血腥：傳說當時六軍在玄宗處死楊妃後，陳玄禮要求驗屍，驗屍完畢，譁變的士兵為了洩憤，就千軍萬馬從那可憐的女人身上踏過，屍身竟然一絲不留，都黏在馬蹄上了。

孫：That's what I was told too!

李：另一個傳說是：當時高力士不忍殺死楊妃，就找了個宮女做替身，悄悄放了楊妃，讓她隱名埋姓，終了一生。楊妃就流轉到了日本。所以今天的日本有

很多楊貴妃墓，就是循著這個傳說來的。

孫：Yes, that's what I heard too!

李：不過我猜測，可能是那個時候的日本人太傾慕唐文化了，希望代表唐人高雅文化的楊貴妃能魂歸扶桑。就像今天的明星崇拜一樣吧。因為那個時代的交通條件，以一介弱女人，很難有可能翻山跨海到達日本。

孫：I totally agree with you! It's like the reception of stars today, on the part of the fans! 粉絲！

李：小女和我開玩笑，說楊妃是我們的太太太太太太太奶奶，哈哈～～

孫：That's funny!

李：我們興平還埋葬了一位薄命的女人，近代以來才被人知道。就是隋朝的董美人。她的墓誌嘉慶年間出土於我們家附近。上海陸君慶在我們興平做官時所得到此石，旋歸上海徐渭仁，徐氏當時也在關中做官。徐氏十分珍愛這塊墓石，從關中把它攜至上海，自號其齋曰「隋軒」。咸豐年間，上海小刀會農民暴動期間，亂民放火燒了徐氏宅園，原石毀佚。徐氏拓本流傳甚少，吳湖帆曾得到一部初拓本，為了紀念此一盛事，他遍請當時海內聞人為之題詠。保陽一直以來想編一本書，就是收集自此石出土以來的文獻資料、詩詞歌詠等等，以保存鄉邦文獻。

孫：I see! This is incredibly interesting. Thank you for sharing this!

李：孫老師，分享一首小詩給您。這幾天讀您的散文，思緒湧動。就想起了以前教書的地方：廣州北部山區的從化，那裡的山水，經常讓我感動到心疼。「從化／南芳湖畔／枝頭春睡的小鳥／走進夢裡／流溪河的波光裡／是九連山的花木／無邊的春光／揉碎了時光隧道／在烏土村的肩頭／我／守望千年」。南芳湖是校園裡的一面湖泊，和學校一樣在群山環繞中。以前課餘經常在湖邊散步、寫詩。時光隧道是學校建造的時候劈山開鑿出來的一條汽車路，學生們給它命名為「時光隧道」。烏土村是學校後門外的一個村子，淹沒在無邊無際的荔枝林裡。

孫：My goodness! This is incredibly moving and inspiring! Your poem is so meaningful! And you are truly blessed by God for having such literary talent and poetic sensibilities! Also, the 〈時光隧道〉reminds me of Tunghai's exhibition for me and my father: 陽光穿透的歲月。By the way, please include our conversation in the《避疫》book! Including the lovely pictures!

李保陽致孫康宜

孫老師，

剛剛讀到了《文集》中的〈斯坦福大學圖書館〉，從《古色今香》摘錄出來的一篇，其中提到趙復三先生介紹朋友往也盧拜會充和先生，並請其為斯坦福大學東亞圖書館題字。猶記2016年秋，保陽來美訪書，朋友向保陽分享了趙復三先生2015年去世時他撰寫的哀啟，保陽讀後，深為感動，並賦詩一首為報。沒想到時隔兩年，那首詩竟成保陽自己的寫照，錄此以呈左右：

> 〈趙復三先生哀啟〉書後
> 國家多事挺書生，風雨淒淒去海瀛。
> 寵辱誰關天下計，斯文我在一燈擎。
> 夷齊重出神州陷，赤縣又遭大廈傾。
> 感念河清圖出日，長埋息壤伴容閎。

趙復三先生逝後，葬於康州首府Hartford郊外之Cedar Hill Cemetery，與晚清赴美留學幼童監督容閎在同一墓園。容、趙兩先生在二十世紀首尾，皆以反對專制政府而流亡新大陸，又同葬一地，殆遇合之數耶？

保陽　敬上
4/30/2020

李保陽致孫康宜

孫老師，

　　今天很開心，比預計提前了一天，在四月分最後一天把《文集》卷三書稿校讀結束，多爭取了一天時間。

　　今天費城郊外大風雨，讀完第三卷書稿，猛然抬頭，發現窗外的那株橡樹的葉子，已經有巴掌那麼大了。窗玻璃上飛滿了雨水，想起古人的雪夜閉戶讀書的故事。此刻風雨山居，閉戶讀書，真人間賞心樂事也！專此奉上，並請

　　教安！

保陽　敬上4/30/2020

註：此信有部分刪節。

孫康宜致李保陽

Dear Baoyang,

　　I just came out of the zoom meeting and was thrilled to get this wonderful email from you!

　　Thank you so much for completing vol. 3 so fast! I'm so grateful to you for all your help!

　　Currently we are in the midst of "the-end-of-the-semester madness" and I'm still swamped with administrative works related to the students' funding, etc. As soon as I have more free time, I'll start catching up with my replies to your emails.

　　With a million thanks to you again!

Kang-i
4/30/2020

李保陽致孫康宜

孫老師，

　　剛剛讀到卷二〈耶魯在中國〉。猶記2016年10月初，在哥大圖書館訪書時，認識了一位北京的朋友，他當時在耶魯法學院作為期三個月的交流。我們當天一起遊了中央公園，他並邀請保陽去耶魯參觀。那時第一次去耶魯，在夜色中看到「雅禮協會」的牌子豎在一棟房子的花壇中。讀了您的文章，始對「雅禮協會」的來龍去脈有了大概的瞭解。

　　中國人把傳教士當成「文化侵略」，至今猶然。教科書都是這麼寫的。這也是今天上午您在談到眾人的信仰問題時，我特別覺得失望的原因。因為中國的統治者一直在刻意地阻止民眾接受外面的訊息。保陽的母校中山大學現在的廣州南校區是原嶺南大學，這所學校是十九世紀紐約的長老會支持籌辦的教會大學，從建校一直到上世紀五十年代初，不計其數的教職人員源源不斷地從美國遠赴廣州，到嶺大教書，有許多人是放棄了在美國原本優渥的環境，在嶺大一待就是一輩子。他們逝後，埋在校園一角的墓園裡。四九之後，嶺大解散，嶺大的牌坊被推倒，掩埋在荒煙蔓草間。另外在珠江邊原嶺大牌坊原址，豎起原來中大在廣州城裡的牌坊複製品。從此，中國境內沒有一所教會大學了。傳教士們長眠在校園一角的那個墓園，沒有學生知道其來龍去脈，因為官方主宰的學校當局從不宣傳這些，他們一直刻意淡化甚至迴避校園原來的宗教色彩。

　　對西方的敵視，讓他們健忘、不知感恩！想來真是讓人替那些長眠於康樂園的人心寒！

保陽　敬上

4/30/2020

孫康宜致李保陽

Dear Baoyang,

　　As promised, I'm sending you a copy of my course syllabus for my "Women and Literature" class. Hope you will find it interesting.

Best,
Kang-i
4/30/2020

註：指孫康宜教授在耶魯大學2019年秋季學期開設的Women and Literature in Traditional China課程講義。

李保陽致孫康宜

孫老師，

　　謝謝您分享的syllabus，太感激了！

　　自從四月分以來校讀書稿，焚膏繼晷，似乎又回到了久違的校園生活。收到您的syllabus，那種在教室上課的感覺又回來了。待剩下的兩卷書稿讀畢，再細細學習您的syllabus。五月底疫情若有好轉，就得返回公司上班。所以五月分的時間非常緊張，得優先推進手頭的幾項工作。

　　三月分讀了屈萬里先生普大中文善本書志、《文集》卷三、卷四、卷五、您和施先生的通信集等，總算沒有虛度光陰，很是欣慰。今年預計可以把去年沒認真讀書的缺憾補回來。

　　感謝主！在這個舉國疾疫橫行的艱困時日裡，讓保陽可以在小樓安放一張書桌，不管窗外風和雨，潛心靜氣地讀書寫字。感恩！！

　　再次感謝孫老師分享的syllabus！專此，並頌

　　文祺！

保陽　敬上
4/30/2020

Line訊息

李：〈梅邊壓笛留鴻爪，曲苑舊事人間春——張充和與她的《曲人鴻爪》〉。孫
　　老師，卷三新加的那篇《曲人鴻爪》的前言，這個題目您覺得如何？

孫：Great title! Thank you!

李：不客氣。今天讀了幾首充和先生的詩，真是好詩。不墜合肥張氏家風。

孫：Yes！

李：〈小園〉第二首寫枝頭松鼠，實在惟妙惟肖。保陽今天在廚房洗碗，正好望
　　見後院籬笆上的松鼠來回跳躍，就想起充和先生的這首詩。第九首「一徑堅
　　冰手自除，郵人好送故人書。」極富生活細節之美。

孫：Great! My husband also loves squirrels!

李：孫老師，現在讀到三年前的本月《南方週末》記者朱又可採訪您的文字：
　　「我寫的撰著，頂多五十個人看。」很榮幸，保陽就是那五十個人之一，
　　哈哈

孫：Hahaha!

李：孫老師，卷三已經分享到您的Email了，請您查收。

孫：Yes I already replied to you by email! A million thanks to you again!

李：孫老師，收到您的Email了，能為您工作，保陽感到很榮幸。現在讀到第二
　　卷了，關乎耶魯的歷史和故事，越讀越有意思了。「耶魯最光榮的一面，乃
　　在於它對書的尊重：學校自始至終建立在書的基礎上；書比錢還要重要。」
　　這句話最好，也最能體現大學精神。您在《書的演出》中，對耶魯圖書館和
　　書以及捐贈書籍的讚美，讀來真讓人嚮往、感動……待機緣合適，保陽也會
　　捐贈一批書給耶魯。

孫：Thank you! I know you would like those pieces about Yale!

李保陽致孫康宜

孫老師，

讀您的〈墓園詩情〉，真喜歡您考證那座墓園的歷史。

美國的每一座城鎮，甚至每一棟建築，都有她們深邃迷人的歷史。記得去年有一陣子，保陽就特別喜歡留意我們住的附近一帶城鎮的歷史，比如我們常去買東西的Pottstown，是因為當年給駐紮在Valley Forge的大陸軍供給麵粉而興盛，那家磨坊現在還在，已經成為一個歷史景點。另外一個小鎮Phoenixville，別稱Steel City，是因為那裡有鐵礦，南北戰爭的時候，他們為北方軍鑄造過一千四百門鐵炮；另外一個村子Audubon，除了紀念Audubon本人以外，還因為歷史上這裡曾住過一個家族，他們養豬很有成就，故別稱Pigtown，我把它翻譯成「豬鄉」，每次開車經過，孩子們總要用這個中文翻譯來戲謔一番。

我們村子，是在1879年，由一對德裔的Roy兄弟在思故客河畔建造的，比保陽整整年長一百歲。他們紮營後第一件事情，就是在全村最高處建造教堂，十年後，教堂建成，就是我們家後面Church St.上的衛斯理公會教堂，我們全家都是其成員。去年秋天，我們教堂的Jim牧師從Downtown的St George Church（那是北美第一座衛斯理公會教堂，我們一家人也去那裡敬拜）借來了當年John Wesley送給Preacher Francis Asbury的一本古老的《聖經》，在我們教堂展示。Asbury是Wesley的好朋友，後來他成為獨立後的美國衛斯理教會首任會督。我們教堂就有一間「Asbury Room」，那裡是唱詩小組彩排的地方。在那樣一種既有歷史的厚重感，又有神性的莊嚴聖潔氣氛中敬拜，有一種震撼人心靈的感動。

早上還幹了一件很無聊的事情：您在〈墓園詩情〉提到和這個墓園創建有關的一件事情，即十八世紀末爆發於New England地區的黃熱病。我沒有找到相關的詳細資料，但在網上找到一篇署名丁見民的〈外來傳染病與美國歷史早期印第安人人口的削減〉，這篇文章比較詳細地引述了北美新大陸自歐洲人殖民以來的流行病歷史，可以和目前正在美國肆虐的COVID-19相比，於是我把它們摘錄了出來：

費城Saint Peter's Church墓園　　費城Saint Peter's Church墓園簡介

　　1793年，黃熱病（Yellow Fever Epidemic）襲擊美國首都費城。費城Saint Peter's Church墓園埋葬了一百四十三位因疫情而喪生者；有八位部落首領代表團成員亦葬於此，他們死於當時流行的天花。他們應華盛頓總統之邀，來費城參加解決西北邊界糾紛的和平會議。圖一為位於費城市區Society Hill 的 Saint Peter's Church 教堂墓園，圖二為墓園簡介。

（1）1585-1587年，英國人湯瑪斯・哈利奧特（Thomas Harriot）記載，在羅阿諾克島的一百名英國人，至少經歷了兩場傳染性疾病。

（2）1616-1619年北美新英格蘭地區的鼠疫暴發。根據現代一位學者的保守估算，這場流行病中土著人口損失比例高達百分之七十五。

（3）1633年，康乃狄克總督布拉德福德報告稱，在康乃狄克河谷，天花和鼠疫導致九百／一千多人死亡，土著患者的死亡率高達百分之九十以上。

（4）1634年1月，麻塞諸塞總督溫斯羅普（John Winthrop）說，傳染病導致納拉甘西特地區死亡七百人。

（5）1638年，約翰・喬斯林（John Josselyn）記載，在航行的第八天，一位乘客的僕人患上天花；到第十九天，天花在乘客中流行起來；到

第六十九天該船抵達波士頓，船上的最後一位天花患者去世。

（6）1667年，一名感染天花的水手，使一度強大的波瓦坦聯盟（Powhatan）遭到災難性打擊。幾乎所有部落都落入死神之手。

（6）1688-1691年的威廉王之戰中天花傳播，英國被迫中止軍事行動。

（7）1696年，天花由維吉尼亞傳播到卡羅來納，導致當地半數土著死亡。

（8）1698年4月，維吉尼亞總督和參事會在一封信中說，天花導致其中一個土著部落幾乎完全被摧毀。

（9）1701年，旅行家約翰・勞森在卡羅來納遊歷時發現，天花「將一個個土著村落一掃而光。」

（10）亨利・多賓斯（Henry F.Dobyns）記載，十七世紀北美至少暴發了十二次天花、四次麻疹、三次流感、二次白喉、一次斑疹傷寒、一次淋巴腺鼠疫和一次猩紅熱。

（11）1738年，南卡羅來納爆發天花。

（12）1757年，英國軍隊向法國軍隊投降。法國人所屬軍團接觸到英國士兵的屍體而被感染。

（13）1780年春，切羅基人（Cherokee）俘獲一艘裝載二十八人並向西遷移的移民船，一位叫斯圖亞特的乘客一家人感染了天花。結果，天花就像閃電一樣在各個佈道站傳播。同年，天花襲擊密蘇裡河流域。據估計，土著人口因此致死一萬三千人，死亡率為百分之六十八。

（14）1801-1802年，天花沿密蘇裡河向北傳播到各個部落，向南橫掃整個大平原以及路易斯安那，向西越過洛基山甚至到達太平洋沿岸。

（15）1837-1838年，天花大暴發。有旅行者估算西部邊疆六萬名土著死亡。

（16）1848年開始的淘金熱時期，當時正在大平原地區的斯勞特（T. J. Slaughter）寫道：「霍亂正在大規模肆虐。」

（17）根據多賓斯的研究，從十六世紀初到二十世紀初，北美土著中暴發了九十三次傳染性疾病。各種傳染性疾病「在1520至1900年間，平均每四年兩個半月就暴發一次」。

截止今天，COVID-19已經橫掃美國，感染人數突破一百一十萬，死亡人數

接近六點四萬，比歷史上的任何一次流行病都嚴重。真真切切的是一場前所未有的災難！祈禱上帝，只有　祂才有能力結束這場災難！

保陽　敬上

5/1/2020

孫康宜致李保陽

Baoyang,

Here is some information about Rev. Kate Latimer! See the link below!

By the way, Rev. Kate Latimer and Chaplain Rev. Harry Adams baptized our daughter Edie in 1986, when Edie was 6 months old!

Kang-i

5/1/2020

孫康宜致Rev. Jenny Peek

Dear Jenny,

I know Rev. Kate Latimer recently passed away. Does Battell Chapel have some information about her? Would you send it to me if you happen to have it?

Several years ago I published a Chinese article about Kate, and now one of the readers wants to know more about her.

Any help from you would be appreciated. I can also try to see if there is any internet information about Kate.

With thanks,

Kang-i

5/1/2020

註：**Rev. Jenny Peek, Associate Paster of the University Church in Yale.**
Katherine Millham Latimer (1942-2020), Former Associate Pastor of the Battell
Chapel at Yale.

Kate Latimer and Kang-i Sun Chang at
Battell Chapel, Yale University, 2015.

李保陽致孫康宜

孫老師，

　　白天收到您的這封信，保陽難過了好一陣子。這是保陽聽到的第一個和保陽
有關聯的人，因COVID-19去世。我們為Charles和他的家人祈禱！保陽每晚都在
日記中記錄當天全國感染和死亡人數，那一個個冰冷的數字後面，是一個個鮮活
的生命和原本幸福的家庭！那種痛感，尚是第一次體味到。也第一次體會到生命
的脆弱，真的好難過！！

保陽

5/1/2020

Line訊息

孫： Thank you for sending such an amazing email, in response to my essay on the Grove Street Cemetery! I'm deeply grateful!

李： 現在拜讀的卷二，講了很多很多耶魯的歷史，和耶魯現在的社區文化，真是開了眼界，非常享受的一種閱讀體驗。謝謝孫老師！https://drive.google.com/file/d/1JYsCkPUzAP5AJc1Sw6-ielIemjtepfbs/view?ts=5eac178b這是我們每天都從教堂收到的音樂連結。是我們教堂的一位叫Tom的弟兄彈奏的。他的鋼琴彈得非常非常棒！

孫： Wow thank you for sharing this beautiful music! Tom is great!

李： 是的。我們教會在疫情期間，每天給大家分享屬靈的「聖餐」，讓大家即使在家裡，也可以緊緊地連結在一起，得享　神的恩典！「為被囚禁和被折磨的人，為各處的受壓迫者，為那些改過自新的壓迫者，為通過非暴力革命取得的人類和解，為爭取和平、正義和自由的全球運動，為那些最需要的和為上帝嘉許的改革者、先知、布道者和詩人，為一切我們的智慧尚難以解答的事物，我們一起祈禱。」這是您在〈耶魯大學女校牧的故事〉中引述的副校牧凱特姊妹的禱告詞，感動得讓人熱淚盈眶……

孫： Thank you! You are an amazing reader! Would you include this message of yours (including the quote) in our book! By the way, Rev. Kate Latimer just died during this COVID 19 season and I miss her very much! (I don't know if she died of the corona virus or not, but she died during this period of the pandemic).

李： 孫老師，〈墨西哥詩人帕斯與耶魯的一段因緣〉中涉及到《陳柳情緣》一書的寫作，當時您的行文中稱之為《明末詩人陳子龍》，保陽給這個書名後面加了一個頁腳註：「此書後來以"The Late-Ming Poet Ch'en Tzu-lung: Crises of Love and Loyalism"為書名，於1990年在耶魯大學出版社出版。1991年，由李奭學先生翻譯成中文，以《情與忠：陳子龍、柳如是詩詞因緣》為書名，由臺灣的允晨文化實業股份有限公司發行。2012年，簡體中文本由北京大學出版社出版（孫康宜補注，2020年5月1日）。」您看合適否？

孫： 1991年的臺灣版書名是「情緣」！不是「因緣」。2012年簡體版才改成「因

緣」。

李：我剛剛讀了〈情感的遺跡〉，起初我懷疑帶您去王維的終南山，在中途休息
　　去古寺的人是陳忠實老師，後來您寫到1976年他二十三歲，那麼1953年出生
　　的，應該就不是陳老師了。

孫：You are right! He is not陳忠實！

李：好的。等到維基百科一百年後來解密，哈哈～作文學的「偵探」，就像您說
　　的那樣，能得到很多樂趣。

Rev. Ian Oliver致孫康宜

Prof Chang，

Thanks for this reference to Kate's obituary. I knew Kate and Walter before they moved to California. I know she was beloved by many at Battell.

We received word today that Charles Krigbaum, former Battell organist died yesterday of Covid-19.

Ian

5/1/2020

註：Rev. Ian Oliver, Paster of the University Church in Yale.

李保陽致孫康宜

孫老師，

　　早安！

　　這會兒正在拜讀〈人權的維護者：戴維斯和他的西方奴隸史〉、〈尋找隱喻
——普羅恩和他的器物文化觀〉。在耶魯校園裡，只要有某一方面的興趣，總能

找到可以聊天的人，甚至某個人的研究領域都能觸發人的探究熱情，這樣的環境真令人嚮往！

　　保陽對第二篇文章尤其心有戚戚焉。猶記保陽還在十四、五歲的時候，不知什麼原因，突然有一段時間很想找些東西來印證書本中的話，好在我們關中一帶是個遍地古史遺留的地方，我就到田間去挖，希望能挖到我要的東西，但是只弄到了一些碎陶片。後來上高中了，有一陣子對古瓷器很感興趣，但那時根本不知道向哪裡去弄到這些東西，就去鄉間的廟裡，在神像前的香案上仔細看那些香爐的造型、質地、銘文。後來這些興趣都因為沒有條件培養，就漸次消退了，唯有對書興致不減，蓋書在我們那裡還是可以得到的東西。所以從一開始，我對書的興趣，除了它本身的內容外，更關心它的作者、版本、紙張、油墨、裝訂這些書作為一個非知識載體的「東西」的存在。記得那時候在鄉間能得到的最好的「古書」，也就是一些晚清民國石印或者排印的唱本、說部、醫案等。這大概是保陽關注「器物」的開始，並且後來一直維持著對古書版本的興趣，至今未泯。

　　由此我想，一個人的早期，有好多發展的可能，後來因為所處環境的限制，大多數可能就漸漸消失了。教育的功能就在於發現並維持那些可能。記得您在〈經營的頭腦：耶魯校長雷文和他的治學與治校〉中稱讚雷文校長重視通識教育，並引用他的話：「通才教育並不教我們去思考什麼（what to think），而是教我們如何去思考（how to think）。」您在他的話後面加了一句：「這是因為他認為每個人都必須獨立地尋找自己、面對自己，才真正能發揮通才教育的效用。」這話說得多好！我覺得，理想的教育就是小心翼翼地維護受教育者的那種多面向的興趣，讓他們其中的一項興趣可以謀生，其他的興趣可以用來豐富自己的人生經驗，讓生命飽滿而充實。作為受教育者要做的，就是堅持自己的興趣所在，不移不易，終有所成。您在〈人文教育還有希望嗎？〉一文裡，重點從老師和課程設置方面檢討了如何維持和振興人文傳統。實際上，從戴維斯教授的身上，印證了一個更重要的因素——興趣！他小時候在科羅拉多州的家鄉，一直聽故事，家庭又有寫作的氛圍，以至於後來他終身從事文史研究工作，這與他小時候生長的環境關係極大。環境激發和維持了他歷史方面的興趣，成年以後選擇從事的專業時，也就順理成章。這樣背景故事下成長起來的人文學者，不勝枚舉。保陽之所以選擇中國古典文學專業，其淵源也是兒時在鄉間的月亮地裡聽多了各

種歷史故事。

　　保陽不太同意今天人文教育衰落這個說法。在保陽看來，人文教育從來就沒有繁榮過。即使繁榮，也是不正常的曇花一現。比如中國八十年代各種文藝現象的洄瀾，那是在紅色恐怖統治了三十年後的一種過火的反彈，後來沒多久便消停了。蓋人文精神本來就是一種貴族精神，不慍不火，即便是在大學象牙塔裡，它也是象牙塔尖尖的尖尖那一小部分。就像中國的毛時代，要不識字的農民一夜寫詩三百首，那是不可能的。詩歌是高雅的陽春白雪，它永遠普及不到普羅大眾中間去。現在的大學教育世俗化、普及化、功利化，是大勢所趨，慨歎大學人文教育的失落、衰退，乃是以今日功利教育的眼光來審視這顆「鑽戒上的紅寶石」。我這麼說不是說大學就不要人文教育了，而是說這顆「寶石」不必追求它會像理工醫農學科那樣廣被關注、報考、研究，這不現實。人文精神自古就是曲高和寡的東西，它就像鹽和光，只要一點點，就有味，就能照亮世界。

　　不知您怎麼看這個問題？

保陽　敬上

5/2/2020

李保陽致孫康宜

孫老師，

　　普羅恩教授的「器物文化」，就是把許多不同的思維方式交叉結合在一起的一門課程，也是多元化的興趣和邏輯、視角重疊的一個研究領域。我非常欣賞這種沒有思維限制的自由狀態，能激發起很多創作的靈感和學術上的新發現。這也是我一直深覺遺憾，沒能接受西方的教育訓練之所在。

保陽　再上

5/2/2020

孫康宜致李保陽

Dear Baoyang（保陽），

I'm sure you have read my article，〈於梨華筆下的性騷擾〉，in vol. 3 of my *Collected Work*（《孫康宜文集》，卷3）. I just want to call your attention that the 88 year old writer Yu Li-hua於梨華just passed away yesterday in Washington, D.C. due to COVID-19（新冠肺炎）.

Yu Li-hua was a very popular writer in Taiwan, known for her novels such as 《又見棕櫚、又見棕櫚》. Prof. Fan Ming-ju（范銘如教授），one of my good friends in Taiwan, includes a discussion of Yu Li-hua in her book，《眾裡尋她──臺灣女性小說綜論》（臺北：麥田，2001）。

https://zh.wikipedia.org/wiki/於梨華

I still remember it was in the fall of 1994 that both Fan Ming-ju and I met Yu Li-hua at a conference in the University of Maryland. How time flies. That was 26 years ago!

I cc Prof. Fan Ming-ju on this email.

Best,
Kang-i
5/2/2020

李保陽致孫康宜

孫老師，

傍晚一覺醒來，讀到您的來信，吃驚了半天！

保陽雖然沒有和於梨華女士直接聯繫過，但是前兩天在讀《文集》卷三中

〈於梨華筆下的性騷擾〉時，發現原稿中有好幾處把「於」誤排成「于」字。為了避免自己弄錯，那天還專門在網上查閱了於梨華女士的資料。

保陽之所以對「於梨華」這個名字印象深刻，乃二十年前在漢中母校圖書館借您的《陳子龍柳如是詩詞情緣》時，這本書的旁邊就是黃嫣梨的《蔣春林評傳》和於梨華的一本什麼書（記不清了）。雖然沒有借閱她們的書，但是對她們的名字印象太深了，因為她們名字裡都有個「梨」字，中國大陸人取名字很少用這麼質實而生活化的字眼，尤其那個「嫣」字和生僻的姓氏「於」，保陽直到今天都沒有見到過第二人。所以對於梨華女士那種陌生的新奇感印象深刻。沒想到今天竟然收到於女士因COVID-19在華府過世的消息，真是讓人難過。冥冥之中這種巧合也算是一種「相識」，故有一種「故人」逝去之嘆！

薄暮中讀您的來信，突然有一種莫名的古今之感！《後漢書》云：「建安二十二年，大疫。」這次大疫，文學史上著名的「建安七子」，有四位死於這場大瘟疫。曹丕給他的好朋友吳質寫信說：「昔年疾疫，親故多離其災，徐、陳、應、劉，一時俱逝，痛可言邪。」曹植也在他的〈說疫氣〉中記載了這次大瘟疫：「建安二十二年，疫氣流行，家家有僵屍之痛，室室有號泣之哀。或闔門而殪，或舉族而喪。或以為疫者鬼神所作。人罹此者，悉被褐茹藿之子，荊室蓬戶之人耳。若夫殿處鼎食之家，重貂累蓐之門，若是者鮮焉。此乃陰陽失位，寒暑錯時，是故生疫。而愚民懸符厭之，亦可笑也。」

這兩天，社區裡一有救護車的警笛聲呼嘯而過，內子就愁容滿面地感歎、禱告！上面這兩段中國古書的記載，和今天大洋對岸的新大陸之情形，竟是如此之雷同！病毒對古今中外的人威懾是一樣的。希望這次大瘟疫，能驚醒世人，敬畏上帝，尊重生命，知道感恩，不要起無謂的紛爭，活在當下才是最真實的！

保陽　敬上
5/2/2020

孫康宜致李保陽

Dear Baoyang,

I'm really sorry that, due to my crazy schedule during the last two weeks, I could not find time to answer all your emails. Now, I'm trying to do my best to catch up!

First of all, I'm so grateful to you for reading through vol. 4 of my collected works 《孫康宜文集》 and giving me such inspiring reader's response! I have learned a lot from your feedback, and I want to express my sincere thanks!

In particular, I want to thank you for calling my attention to a problem of translation in the Chapter on Su Shi. As you have correctly pointed out: "作者稱蘇軾〈江城子〉（夢中了了醉中醒）一詞的長序是「自我體現的抒情動作的寫實性對應體」，這句讀起來有點拗口……。" Actually in my original book in English, *The Evolution of Chinese Tz'u Poetry* (Princeton: Princeton University Press, 1980, p. 167), the passage reads:

"Evidently this preface serves as a realistic counterpart to the poem's lyric act of self-realization. And the poem in turn represents a lyrical version of the external reality."

I have therefore re-translated the passage into Chinese. Please see the new translation as follows:

顯而易見，此一「詞序」很寫實地表達出詞本身所富有的自我抒情性。同時，我們也可以說，那首詞的本身也同時以抒情的意境來呼應現實的真相。

I hope this re-translation works.

Thank you again for all your help and attention!

Best,
Kang-i Sun Chang
5/2/2020

註：此函回覆李保陽4月13日來信。

孫康宜致李若虹

Dear Dr. Ruohong Li（李若虹博士），

　　Please forgive me for writing to you out of the blue. But just recently I have read your Chinese article, 〈冰天雪地裡給陳寅恪往醫院送試卷的老先生——藍曼的梵文課與世紀疫情〉, with the greatest interest and admiration! I'm intrigued by the fact that Charles Rockwell Lanman (1850-1941) was originally educated at Yale, under the direction of the renowned scholar William D. Whitney (1827-1894).

　　Also, as you said, it was during the terrible Spanish Flu epidemic (during 1918-1920) that Chen Yinke 陳寅恪 happened to be in Lanman's Sanskrit class at Harvard! What a coincidence; that was exactly 100 years ago! And now we are right in the middle of the COVID-19 Pandemic!

　　Right now I just have a quick question to confirm with you, and it's related to Chen Yinke's name in English. From Lanman's handwritten envelope addressed to Chen Yinke, it seems that Chen's whole name in English was Yinkoh Tschan. This is the first time that I saw Chen's English name spelt out like this!

　　And it leads me to an interesting discovery. Scholars in Chinese studies, especially those in mainland China, often insisted that Chen's name should be read as "Chen Yinque." In fact, many years ago when I pronounced Chen's name as "Chen Yinke," I was told by Chinese scholars that the correct pronunciation of恪should be "que." But from Lanman's handwritten envelope, Chen obviously called himself "Yinke," rather than "Yinque."

　　Do you agree that Chen should be called Chen Yinko? In fact, Library of Congress, as well as other major libraries in the US, catalogued Chen's works under Chen Yinko.

　　I cc Dr. Li Baoyang (a Chinese scholar who currently resides in Pennsylvania) on this email, because he was the person who first called my attention to your amazing article.

With thanks,
Kang-i Sun Chang（孫康宜）

5/2/2020

孫康宜致Rev. Ian Oliver

Dear Ian,

I just realized that charles Krigbaum was on the Emeritus faculty, so he was not a young man as I said in my previous email!

Somehow I forgot that Charles was also aging over the decades, as we all are!

Kang-i

5/2/2020

Line訊息

孫：I think I want to include my short article, 言猶未盡 (both the Chinese and the English versions) in the Appendix of our避疫book. This is because it's an important article to me, which I wrote during the COVIC 19 pandemic.

李：這個想法很好。孫老師，如果您有空閒。也把您打算寫的普林斯頓的憶舊文章寫出來，一併收入《避疫》中。因為我那天是借好書要離開Gest了，一眼瞥見您的《耶魯潛學集》，順手抽下來借了出來，後來讀了，給您寫信，於是才有了後來我們交往的故事，很有趣的一個紀念，一個見證。

孫：Thank you! But I really don't have time to write Chinese articles about Princeton! Writing in Chinese is very difficult for me; I just don't have the time and energy to do that now! I have a lot to catch up with my English writings, and I'm under a lot of pressure! Thank you anyway! I think I'll mention Princeton in my short preface to the《避疫》book！Actually I don't know why Princeton is the hardest topic for me!

李：好啊，很期待拜讀孫老師來美之後的回憶文字。剛剛讀到〈永恆的緣份——
　　記耶魯同事McClellan〉，文末寫到1987年余英時先生移席普林斯頓時，曾親
　　筆書贈McClellan教授一首張繼的〈楓橋夜泊〉。後來輾轉由您收藏。猶記
　　Gest一進門左手邊的閱覽室牆上，就掛著一幅俞樾書〈楓橋夜泊〉的拓片。

方菲致孫康宜

親愛的康宜大姊：

　　收信平安！

　　我終於找時間去東海的圖書館看了展覽，但我更想跟您分享的是：

　　我好喜歡看孫伯伯的書法和信件，從他的字裡行間，真的體會到他對神、對
人的愛。我也很感佩您的用心，將這些整理出來成書，讓更多人有機會獲益！

　　家父上個月急診住院，在那段時間裡他說他的命是撿回來的，後來我們向他
傳福音，他終於在九十三歲時願意禱告接受主。因為他也喜歡寫書法練字，所以
我就訂購了您這次的兩本書送給他，當作信主受洗的禮物。

　　謝謝您和大家分享您與家人的這些典範、珍藏！我也期勉自己能成為這樣的
長輩，能對後輩有屬靈上的幫助！

　　敬祈

　　闔府安康喜樂！

方菲　敬上

5/2/2020

註：方菲女士，東海大學王茂駿校長夫人。

李保陽致孫康宜

孫老師，

今天讀了卷二中大量關於美國當代生活和文化的隨筆、散文。因為有同樣的文化背景，面對的是同樣一個全新環境的新大陸，您這種過來人的敘述，對於保陽來講，真的又像回到了三十年前，開始打開蒙昧狀態，一步一步地探頭瞭解這個文明世界那樣，開始瞭解美國。這是一塊我將要生活於斯、老死於斯的土地，但我卻對她沒有足夠的瞭解。前陣子就以影視作品和文學作品（比如《Turn》等）、當地博物館和維基百科中那些數不勝數的小城鎮的歷史為據點，慢慢瞭解這片土地，這個國家。

現在從您的文章中，從另一個層面和視角瞻仰、解讀這片土地，那種收穫的愉悅，是如此的真切！如此的感動！尤其是透過您的文字，給那些物化的東西都賦予了一層人文精神的溫情，一下子把那些冷峻的距離柔化了。它們不再是另一個種族的陌生，不再是另一片土地的遙遠，而是刻下真真切切的生活。這種可觸摸的感知，每當我帶著孩子們在一塊遠望的山水間，或者一間荒僻的博物館生鏽的犁鋤上，都能真真切切地感受到。雖然它們穿越了時空和語言，但是中間散發出的一種莫名親切的氣息，倒是從來都沒有改變過似的熟悉。那種感動，常常使人熱淚盈眶。我覺得這正是文學魅力所在。

李保陽敬上
5/3/2020

孫康宜致李保陽

Dear Baoyang,

I feel compelled to share with you this dialogue between me and Ms. Fang Fei, who is the wife of President Wang Mao-jiun at Tunghai University（東海大學）.

As you can see, I'm very grateful to my alma mater Tunghai University for making the Sun family exhibition possible, even during this difficult time of the COVID-19 pandemic!

　　Also, this is a good demonstration of how a Christian university like Tunghai University grows and flourishes under the leadership of an exemplary couple like President Wang and his wife Fang Fei.

Best,

Kang-i

5/3/2020

孫康宜致李保陽

Dear Baoyang,

　　I know that very soon you are going to read my article, 〈我被掛在耶魯的牆上〉, in vol. 2 of my Collected Works. So I hasten to send you these pictures (see below) to give you some contexts for the article. In April 2018, when the Davenport portraits were finally revealed, I felt extremely honored and humbled! I think this group portrait might be the greatest recognition that I have ever received from Yale. This means I might be remembered in Yale history for a long time! (Please see pictures attached here).

　　When you come to visit the Yale campus in the near future, I'll definitely take you to Davenport College (one of the 14 residential colleges at Yale) to see the portrait.

　　By the way, I want to share with you an extremely interesting experience I had today, which had something to do with Brenda Zlamany, the painter of the Davenport portraits. First of all, Brenda Zlamamy invited me to participate in an international Film Festival online at 2:00 p.m. today, during which I saw a video showing how she (as a uniquely talented painter) painted 100 portraits for the celebration of the 100th anniversary of the Hebrew Senior Center in New York. Then, I discovered to my surprise that today's International Film Festival happened to take place in my daughter

Edith's alma mater, the Roger Williams University in Bristol, Rhode Island! What an interesting coincidence! It's all meant to be, and It's indeed a small world .

In my next email, I'll forward you my note to the painter Brenda Zlamany, thanking her for getting me involved in today's 100/100 event online. I'm sure you would be interested in knowing about the general environment of senior people in the US.

Best,

Kang-i

5/3/2020

①孫康宜的畫像被掛在耶魯大學戴文坡學院牆
　上（2018年4月）
②孫康宜畫像的作者Brenda Zlamany

孫康宜致李保陽

Dear Baoyang,

I just want to call your attention to this famous painting, featuring 7 Yale female Ph.D. at the end of the 19th century. This painting was also done by Brenda Zlamany. It's now hung on the wall of the Yale University Library!

I'll definitely show you this painting too when you visit Yale. It was due to the success of this 7-women Ph.D. painting that Davenport College decided to appoint Brenda Zlamany to do the group portrait! It was a total surprise to me when I was told in 2017 that I would be included in the Davenport group portrait!

Kang-i

5/3/2020

孫康宜與耶魯歷史上最早的七位女性博士的
畫像合影（畫像作者Brenda Zlamany）

李保陽致孫康宜

孫老師，

　　一覺醒來連續收到您三封來信，太開心了！如果不久的將來能在戴文坡學院您的畫像下面和耶魯三百年來第一位女性華裔系主任，在她的油畫下合影，那將是一件多麼讓人不可思議的事情！上帝的預備真是妙不可言！這讓保陽感到十二萬分的榮幸！

　　Brenda Zlamany真是個天才的畫家，她怎麼會有這麼了不起的創意呢！這讓保陽想起了六年前在杭州的時候，曾經去一個浙西山中的藝術學校，那家學校校長是一個非常有創意的人，他發動攝影專業的學生們，在附近一帶山裡，為超過一百歲的老人拍攝生活紀錄照片，最後恰好找到了一百位老人，學校就出資印了一本攝影集，名字就叫《百人萬歲》（剛才網上查了一下，這本書2015年在杭州的一家出版社正式出版了，見附圖）。多麼有創意的名字啊！這和Brenda Zlamany為紐約100位老人畫像，是不是不謀而合呢？如果Brenda Zlamany要出版她的這本畫集，就可以命名為「100 people, 100th Anniversary of the Senior Center。」

保陽　敬上
5/3/2020

孫康宜致畫家Brenda Zlamany

Dear Brenda,

So happy to participate in your 100/100 screening today! I'm always proud of you. You are just amazing! I miss you !

Best,

Kang-i Sun Chang

5/3/2020

孫康宜致李保陽

Dear Baoyang,

I feel I must forward you the following series of correspondence I had with Wang Ya-ping 王雅萍, who accidentally discovered my B.A. thesis on *Moby Dick* which I wrote 55 years ago (1965-66) at Tunghai University東海大學. (Please see the series of emails below, as well as the attached files for my senior thesis)**.**

But first of all I want to share with you an interesting interaction I had this last week with Dean Kathryn Lofton, Dean of the Humanities at Yale University, regarding my B.A. thesis. On April 29, Dean Lofton had a chance to watch my zoom video for the opening ceremony of the Tunghai exhibition. She noticed that during my zoom interview, I mentioned Herman Melville's *Moby Dick*（《白鯨記》）, the topic of my senior essay. So she asked me afterwards: "What did you argue in your senior thesis about *Moby Dick*?"

I found it rather difficult to reply to Dean Lofton but managed to send her an email anyway. In my email I wrote:

"As for my senior thesis on Moby Dick, it was titled 'The Importance of Herman

Melville to Chinese Students, With a Comparison Between the Ideas of Melville and Prominent Chinese Thinkers.' But actually . . . I feel extremely embarrassed now that the thesis is on display at the Tunghai exhibition! When I was first struggling to do my B.A. thesis in 1965, my written English was still not very good. . . .''

But, then, she wrote back right away, saying:

"Kang-i, don't be embarrassed. Allow yourself to imagine the students walking through the Tunghai exhibition, imagining a future where what you do is what they do. Don't be hard on your work. It's clarity of purpose that will help other students see themselves, clearly. With congratulations and admiration—Katie.''

I was deeply touched by Dean Lofton's words of encouragement. What she meant is that as long as we have a "clarity of purpose," we are bound to exercise influence on people of the future generation.

I am very impressed with Dean Lofton. She is only 41 years old, and yet she is always full of wisdom and vision.

Best,
Kang-i
5/3/2020

李保陽致孫康宜

孫老師，

　　剛剛讀了您的信，Kathryn Lofton的下面這句話我覺得很有道理："Don't be hard on your work. It's clarity of purpose that will help other students see themselves, clearly。"

Kathryn Lofton是個非常有智慧的人！

她的話讓我想到了王羲之的「後之視今，亦猶今之視昔」。您的論文主要是給今天的莘莘學子看的，給予他們一個可能的人生高度預期，而非讓今日學貫中西的您去評價論文的學術質量。

您有沒有想過重刊這本論文呢？

保陽
5/3/2020

孫康宜致李保陽

Dear Baoyang,

As you can see, I'm sending the programs of the Tunghai Exhibition (see attached) to Chris Anderson, Head of the Special Collections Department at the Yale Divinity School Library. This is because Yale's Divinity Library has established the "Paul Yu-kuang Sun Collection" in 2018, and the collection of "Sun Family Papers" in 2019. As I have told you before, Yale Divinity Library will be the permanent house for our Sun family papers.

Best,
Kang-i
5/3/2020

孫康宜、張欽次致方菲

方菲你好！

很高興知道，令尊終於以九十三高齡接受主，真是大好消息。你還特地訂購

了家父的兩本書《孫保羅書法：附書信日記》和《一粒麥子》送給令尊，作為信主受洗的禮物，真讓我們感激不盡。我記得，令尊和你母親從前都是臺大醫學系的教授，令人無限景仰。你曾在「新手上路」那篇文章裡（《鎏金歲月風華：東海婦女會六十年會史，1957-2017》），提到你的父母親給你們的開明教育！一直給我很深刻的印象！

這次承蒙王校長的強力支持，能有如此盛大的「陽光穿透的歲月」書法展和書展，真是孫家的一大榮幸。特別令我們感恩的是，即使受全球疫情（COVID-19）的嚴重影響，你們仍堅持如期進行辦展之事！

我一直記得，當年你和王校長的婚禮是在路思義教堂舉行的。你們真是上帝祝福的一對模範夫妻。果然在王校長的努力領導之下，東海大學終於成為世界上一流的大學，頗令人驚嘆！我相信這就是神帶給大家最大的禮物了。

祝你們平安喜樂！

孫康宜（和張欽次）同賀

5/3/2020

Line訊息

李：「美國可以說是世界上最能容忍和接受diversity的國家了」。孫老師，這句話是〈一個外科醫生的人文精神〉這篇文章中您的朋友Gary Price說的。我特別喜歡這句話。這句話正是我當初為什麼選擇來美國的原因！

孫：Yes, diversity is very important! That's what I always said to my students in my classes!

李：「今天很多人已經忘記syringe一詞本來出自希臘古代一個女神的名字Syrinx。這其中牽涉到一個十分動人的故事。原來，Syrinx是Arcadia河畔的一個仙女（nymph）。有一天，牧羊神Pan偶然在路上遇見Syrinx，很被她的美貌所吸引，於是就瘋狂地追過去。問題是，牧羊神Pan長得實在很醜，他的下半身如同公羊，而且頭上有角。據說Pan的母親剛生下他時，就被他的醜相

嚇得立刻逃走了。而且Pan有時還會發出可怕的嚎叫聲，讓人陷入一陣驚惶（panic）。所以Syrinx一見有這麼個怪物在後頭追趕她，她就死命向前奔跑。最後跑到了Ladon河的河邊，眼見Pan就要追上她了，她一時情急，就請求河神把她變成了一束蘆葦。Pan看見美麗的仙女已經化為蘆葦，而且混在河邊無數的蘆葦之間，已無法辨識。Pan一時傷心欲絕，只好採下幾根蘆葦做成笙，從此以吹笙的方式來紀念Syrinx。雖然在現實中，男神Pan無法擁有美麗的Syrinx，但他卻能透過笙樂的想像來懷念她。後來管樂器『panpipe』（牧神笙）一詞就出自Pan的名字。」Price醫生講的這個故事真美。原來英文世界的文字訓詁學也是如此的博大精深。

孫：Wow, 李若虹 just replied to me and she copied you on the email! She even mentioned your name in her reply! We must include this episode in our book, especially because it touches on陳寅恪！

李：孫老師，剛剛讀完您轉來的李若虹博士的郵件，這是一條很有力的旁證，說明陳寅恪確實應該讀作「Chen Yinke」。記得剛剛入學那會兒，保陽在康樂園曾經聽老師說，他一直讀作「ke」，當時未深究他的研究過程，現在看來老師是對的。謝謝您！謝謝李若虹博士！您和方菲女士的通信，可以收入我們的書中，很有紀念意義的一份文獻。

孫：Good！（孫老師分享疫情期間美國最流行的社交軟體Zoom創始人袁征的故事）

李：一個優秀的華裔。和我剛剛讀完的〈在休士頓「遊」太空〉一文中的張元樵博士一樣。

孫：Too bad, 張元樵already died! I met him in 1999. I just received your email regarding Brenda Zlamany! Please correct an error; it should read: "三百年來第一位女性華裔系主任"！The media keeps making the same mistake! It is女性華裔，not華裔！（張光直在我之前，已是人類學系系主任）. 張光直later went to Harvard after 1977.

李：「對天國的嚮往不貴在達到終極目標（事實上人不可能完全達到完美，否則人的意義也就喪失了），而貴在『切切地渴想』五個字。有渴想才有進步，而且要『切切地』，不斷地努力，才使人生有意義了。」孫老師，您的這句

話說得真好！！出自您的〈論張曉風《武陵人》與布萊克精神〉。

孫：Thank you!

李：很多話，只有到了一定的年齡階段了，才能讀得懂。這段時間讀您的文章，
　　這個感覺特別明顯。不斷的感動，來自於對生活的閱歷和認識。

孫：But you are still so young! You are amazing! I'm sorry I gave you the wrong
　　interpretation for 100/100. It should be 100 portraits done at the 100th anniversary
　　of the Hebrew Senior Home（老人院一百周年紀念）．

李：您的這篇文章，對保陽的感觸是多面向的。一個人只有不斷超越舒適區，才
　　能進步。所以「武陵人」黃道真最後選擇離開桃花源，回歸武陵，和布萊克
　　放棄無邪選擇經驗，兩者翻譯過來就是：在面對選擇的時候，選那個難一點
　　的，才可能進步和有意義。但是世人大多會趨易避難。保陽的父親六十多年
　　前去新疆修鐵路，後來退回陝南山中，再後來更退回關中鄉下，終老鄉曲。
　　多少年來，這種「退一步」一直是保陽引以為戒的警鐘。故〈十年蹤跡〉一
　　文中表達的那種對自己「向上」的苛刻，在外人看來是一種求上進。實際
　　上只是對選擇時「退一步」的恐懼的刻意迴避而已。所謂「開弓沒有回頭
　　箭」，有時是一種無奈，但更多是一種主動的選擇。

孫：That's why I think you are so special! It needs courage and faith to leave the
　　comfort zone!

李：孫老師，我剛剛讀完您的〈論張曉風《武陵人》與布萊克精神〉，這篇文章
　　竟然寫於1973年！我的天，那時候您才二十九歲啊！那麼年輕就對人生有如
　　此寬廣深厚的體驗，並把它帶入到對作品的解讀中，實在太了不起了！萬分
　　期待您筆下1968年之後的經歷，那應該是更加厚重的一筆人生閱歷的財富。

孫：I'm glad a friend found this old article accidentally! This article is not included in
　　the 秀威版！

李：這篇文章讓目前還「年輕」的保陽覺得，人生還是需要不斷學習和突破的。
　　更重要的是，這篇文章讓保陽在「理論」上為自己找到了一個支點──保
　　陽一直認為2018年到美國來，是生命的一個轉折，也是上帝對保陽的一個試
　　煉。但這些認識都略顯高遠和形而上。如今讀了您的這篇文章，能從可感觸
　　的身邊人的文字裡汲取同一生命感悟，則對自己刻下的處境更加有信心了。

　　謝謝您！

孫：Great!

李若虹致孫康宜

Dear Prof. Sun,

　　I am so very delighted to receive your email. I have known about your great scholarship through our scholars in Chinese literature, but I regret that I haven't had a chance to meet you here at Harvard. Needless to say, I am truly thrilled to learn that you enjoyed my piece recently published in《文匯學人》.Thank you so much for your interest and kind words. Many thanks, Dr. Li Baoyang, for sharing this with Prof. Sun.

　　Right, how to pronounce "恪" has been a long debated issue among scholars of Chinese studies. I myself had used the two different pronounciations in the past. However, as I read more through archives about Chen Yinke's experience living abroad, I now believe that "ke" should be the standard way to go. Chen's student records at Harvard show that **Tschen Yin Koh** was the official spelling of his name on transcripts. This was also the case while Chen studied in Germany and England. As we can tell from Lanman's archives, Tschen Yin Koh was also used in their correspondence and other documents on their contact.

　　Shared below are some additional information that you may find interesting to read. The first piece is an article reviewing the debates on "ke" and "que"; and the second is the citation of an article Chen Yinke published in *Harvard Journal of Asiatic Studies*, and Tschen Yinkoh was the way he spelt his name for scholarly publication. Hope these two pieces help to support our view.

　　（1）https://www.douban.com/note/310693018/

　　（2）Han Yü and The T'ang Novel Tschen Yinkoh *Harvard Journal of Asiatic Studies* Vol. 1, No. 1 (Apr., 1936), pp. 39-43

Once again, thank you so much for writing to me. I greatly appreciate your taking time to read my piece and contact me to share your view. I am so honored and hope to write more on similar topics.

Take care and stay healthy in these uncertain and trying times.

All best,
Ruohong
5/3/2020

Michael Meng（孟振華）致孫康宜

Dear Kang-i,

Attached please see the article. I hope you, C.C. and your family are staying well and healthy.

Best,
Michael
5/3/2020

註：信中提到的article是耶魯大學東亞圖書館長Michael Meng（孟振華）先生分享給孫康宜的陳寅恪〈韓愈與唐傳奇〉（發表在《哈佛亞洲學刊》第1卷第1號，1936年4月哈佛燕京學社出版）書影。

Brenda Zlamany致孫康宜

Dear Kang-i,

So nice to hear from you!

It means a lot to me that you got to see the film. Thanks so much for the kind words! Hopefully Oona and I will be able to visit you in New Haven in the near future. Wishing you health and happiness!

Much love,
Brenda
5/3/2020

孫康宜致李保陽

Dear Baoyang,

It's interesting that I have just received a letter from an Italian student concerning Shi Zhecun's poem-series, 〈浮生雜詠〉.

I have done my best to answer the student's questions. Please see my email exchanges with Silvia De Biase.

Best,
Kang-i
5/4/2020

Silvia De Biase致孫康宜

Dear Dr. Kang-i Sun Chang,

I am writing in reference to 施蟄存〈浮生雜詠〉80首. I'm De Biase Silvia, an Italian student in Rome. I'm working on my master thesis about Shi Zhecun's modernist poetic and I would like to translate into Italian some of the 80 poems of his miscellany.

The website of the Graduate Institute of Taiwanese Literature wrote about a special conference held by you on April 19, 2013 "On modern classical style poetry: Shi Zhecun as an example"（〈現代人的舊體詩：以施蟄存為例〉）. On the same website I found a document in original language "施蟄存〈浮生雜詠〉80首.pdf".

For being located under particular quarantine Covid-19 circumstances, a proper bibliography research could be difficult and problematic. I would respectfully ask for your support with this email. On your availability, could you please kindly let me know if it's possible to obtain the original source of 施蟄存〈浮生雜詠〉80首？I would like to cite it correctly in my analysis.

Thank you in advance for any help you might be able to provide and for your precious time.

Sincerely,

Best regards

Silvia De Biase

5/4/2020

孫康宜致Silvia De Biase

Dear Silvia De Biase,

The proper bibliographic citation should be:

Shi Zhecun 施蟄存. *Fusheng zayong* 浮生雜詠, in *Beishan lou shi*《北山樓詩》. Shanghai: Huadong shifan daxue chubanshe 華東師範大學出版社, 2000. pp. 125-183.

You can also consult my article for further information:

Kang-i Sun Chang, "Poetry as Memoir: Shi Zhecun's Miscellaneous Poems of a Floating Life," Journal of Chinese Literature and Culture, Duke University Press, Vol. 3, Issue 2 (2017): 289-311.

Just in case you can't find my published article on line, please see attached an earlier version of my article.

In haste,
Kang-i Sun Chang
5/4/2020

李保陽致孫康宜

孫老師，

　　剛剛讀完了〈沈從文的禮物〉，這篇文章是以馬悅然教授刊登在《明報月刊》上一篇評論高行健的文字引首的。保陽讀本科時，非常喜歡沈先生的文章，尤其是他的那兩本散文集《湘行散記》、《湘行書簡》，實在美得不可方物。四年級實習的時候，保陽在學校的實習簡報上仿沈先生那種「鄉土筆調」，寫過兩篇陝南山水的文字，沒想到竟然因此獲得優秀實習生獎。次年並以沈先生為畢業論文論題。職是之故，保陽對您寫沈先生的文字尤覺親切。沈先生的文字乾淨淳樸，深為馬先生所賞，後者曾經力促瑞典文學院將諾貝爾文學獎頒給沈先生，惜後來未果。沈、馬兩先生是您的好朋友，所以保陽很想聽一聽您分享他們的故事。

保陽
5/4/2020

李保陽致孫康宜

孫老師，

　　剛剛讀完了〈讀其詩，想見其為人——悼念余國藩教授〉，很是驚嘆余先生那些精美的舊體詩詞創作。舊體詩詞在中國大陸的中文系課程中已經早成絕響，所以現在的學生幾乎都不識平仄，遑論作詩。但是沒想到余先生身居海外，竟然能寫一手好詩，實在意外。猶記好多年前，保陽在浙江嘉興的舊書攤，淘到過一冊詩詞集手稿影印本，序言的落款是某年某月某日作於美國某地。當時也頗為驚異，感歎身居異域的中國人，仍不忘以傳統的文體來抒發情感，想來應該是一位受過傳統教育的長者。（當時沒有想到自己有朝一日也會如此，真是冥冥之中說不清的事情！）

　　保陽想知道，余先生的詩詞集有結集出版嗎？真希望多多搜集一些這樣的旅美學人舊體詩詞讀一讀。您知道在美國的其他學者，誰還作舊體詩嗎？

保陽　敬上
5/4/2020

5月4日Line訊息

李：孫老師，讀到您回憶高先生在課堂上給你們講王維「行到水窮處，坐看雲起時」。他說：「如果有一天你走到窮途末路時（dead-end），千萬不要喪氣，你要從容地坐看雲起，這樣就會絕處逢生。」保陽記得自己在博士論文後記中，提到杭州山中那段艱困歲月時，也引用了這句話。無限的感慨油然而生。詩歌總有這種穿越時空的魅力，讓異代人之間心靈震撼，情感相通！

孫：Yes, would you include this in the book? I suddenly received an email from an Italian student! Please see my email reply! I think this is a perfect case of transnational scholarly contact during the COVID 19 season!

李：這封信太有趣了。您手頭要是沒有施先生原作可以提供給這位義大利的學

生。保陽可以幫忙。保陽有好朋友在華東師範大學出版社工作，找這本書應該不難。

孫：No, actually that's not what she wants! What she wants is the proper citation for her Bibliography, which I already gave to her! (Didn't you see that?) In other words, she wants the proper information for 注釋 documentation! This is a special requirement for all Western publications. 我想，這一方面的西洋教育，是你尚未學過的。將來見面時，我可以教你！

李：哦，好的。謝謝孫老師！

孫：Just to let you that I'm going to add this piece to 卷3.（指《曲人鴻爪》中胡適的那篇）Can you come up with a good title for the article?

李：您能把word文件發給保陽嗎？孫老師，剛剛保陽沒有正確理解您的意思。現在明白了，這個標題容保陽想一想再回覆您。

孫：I am currently asking a person to type the article into a word file! Unfortunately I don't have the word file for the《曲人鴻爪》！

李：不用了，我來打字，很快，要不了半個小時即可。我可以用手機軟體輸入，更快，幾分鐘即可解決。

孫：No，她已經快打完字了！I should have said: my typist is about to finish typing! But I would rather let you focus on reading the《文集》and preparing the《避疫》work!

李：哦，那好。以後您要是有需要請人打字，把文檔給保陽。我的手機軟體輸入既快又準確。

孫：Please remember to give me a title for the article on Hu Shi's calligraphy for〈清江引〉。I'm about to incorporate that article and pictures into the 卷3 text。As for the title, How about: 胡適與貫酸齋的〈清江引〉？

李：〈胡適題張充和《曲人鴻爪》背後的故事〉、〈胡適題張充和《曲人鴻爪》本事發覆〉。您覺得上面兩個題目哪個比較合適？

孫：The first title ...〈背後的故事〉is better! Let's use it! Before the title, there will be the main title:選錄三〔It's under張充和的《曲人鴻爪本事》（選錄）〕。

李：好的。那保陽就將它加到卷三中去了。

孫：No, you don't need to do that! I'll send you an updated version for all the 卷, when the final version is done! I have made some changes (including adding pictures) to every volume!

李：好的。其實這篇文章中提到的古董商作偽的例子，保陽在江南十多年，遇到太多了。有一回還買了一份吳湖帆的「手跡」。我知道是贋品，純粹好玩而已。中國古董作偽，由來已久。去年底，保陽帶孩子們去普大藝術館，看到南宋楊皇后書七言絕句，我認為這幅作品有問題，很可能是晚清古董商的偽作。上面分享給您的那段文字（指普林斯頓大學藝術博物館藏楊妹子手書七絕考證文字），是保陽參觀普大藝術館之後，抽空寫的。本來還打算去曼哈頓的大都會博物館，和那裡收藏的幾件楊皇后的同一形制的作品進行比較，沒想到疫情爆發，紐約之行只得推後了。

孫：I see! This is interesting! Actually someone once faked my手跡and was selling the piece on the market! Mr.吳永勝bought it and later showed it to me! I told him that was definitely not my handwriting!

李：哈哈，太有趣了～

李：孫老師，《從北山樓到潛學齋》中的〈重新發掘施蟄存的世紀人生——《施蟄存先生編年事錄》序言〉這篇文章中，有一處錯字，當時保陽沒有看出來。剛剛讀《文集》卷二才發現。就是「我發現施先生1937年那段充滿曲折故障的逃命旅程……」這句，這裡的「障」字宜改作「事」才比較通順。不知道現在告訴秀威的編輯還來得及否？

孫：Thank you! I'll tell the Showwe editor! Can you tell me the page number!

李：上海書店版頁181倒數第3行最後一個字。文集卷二頁393倒數第7行第7個字。

孫：Thank you!

李：正讀您〈序蘇煒《走進耶魯》〉，蘇先生對中國的批評，尤其對中國男人的批評，一語中的，真是快哉！快哉！在有關鄭振鐸的那篇文章裡（〈夜讀西諦〉），蘇煒曾這麼說道：「雖然中國歷史悠長，當代中國歷史、中國政治包括中國男人中最欠缺的，恰恰就是這個……歷史感。」

孫：Yes!

吳清邁致孫康宜和張欽次

Dear CC and Kang-i:

Chao-chen (Jan) and I visited Tunghai yesterday and made a point of stopping by the Library to see your exhibit.

There was quite a collection of books authored by Kang-i on display, all part of the Tunghai Library collection. We spent a bit of time browsing them. Chao-chen was particularly interested in the one about women in Chinese literature. I enjoyed browsing one of your several 散文集，and took a look at the first article on耶魯，哈佛. The thick Cambridge Anthology of Chinese Literature is too challenging, particularly since literature is a subject of which I am quite illiterate.

Keep well and with regards,

Ching-mai

5/4/2020

註：吳清邁博士（Dr. Ching-Mai Wu）是東海大學董事會董事長，前東海大學校長吳德耀之子；Chair of the Board of Trustee & CEO of Ecolifestyle , Taiwan（新綠節能股份有限公司）

孫康宜受邀於1999年4月28日回母校東海大學，為「吳德耀人文講座」作演講。

李保陽致孫康宜

孫老師，

　　按計畫將《文集》卷二校讀結束，現在呈給您。因為上週四晚上制定的閱讀計畫有點緊張，所以這兩天幾乎沒有下樓趕讀。今天下午準備放鬆一下，開車帶家人到附近山裡玩半天，為明天開工的卷一校讀工作積蓄力量。所以您的郵件留待晚上回來再處理。

保陽　敬上
5/5/2020

孫康宜致李保陽

Dear Baoyang,

　　Thank you for being thoughtful and for adding an important footnote (Note 13) to 卷2. I'm sorry I should have told you the exact title of the Taiwan edition for my Chen Zilong book: 《陳子龍柳如是詩詞情緣》. In other words, There is no "情與忠" in the book title for the Taiwan edition. Thus, I have already made the correction as follows.

> 此書後來以《*The Late-Ming Poet Ch'en Tzu-lung: Crises of Love and Loyalism*》為書名，於1991年在耶魯大學出版社出版。1992年，由李奭學先生翻譯成中文，以《陳子龍柳如是詩詞情緣》為書名，由臺灣的允晨文化實業股份有限公司發行。2012年12月，簡體中文本更名為《情與忠：陳子龍、柳如是詩詞因緣》，由北京大學出版社出版。（孫康宜補註，2020年5月1日。）

　　It has just occurred to me that I have never shown you the Taiwan edition of the book. So please see the attached picture of the book cover.

Kang-i

5/5/2020

孫康宜原著、李奭學翻譯《陳
子龍柳如是詩詞情緣》，臺灣
允晨中譯本，1992

5月5日Line訊息

李：謝謝孫老師分享。讀您發來的文章（保陽按：指張隆溪〈追憶馬悅然先
　　生〉），向您請教，感覺自己又回到了小學生時代。這種「重生」的感覺真
　　好！謝謝！

孫：Thank you! I'm so impressed that you used the term重生to describe your reader's
　　response!

李：「在研究學問的旅程中，我發現自己一直是個尋求新知的『學生』，一直在
　　努力尋找、努力學習，也一直在試驗中。」孫老師，這句話是保陽剛剛讀到
　　的。您說的不就和保陽那句差不多一個意思嘛～

孫：You are so impressive! I'm glad that I have got to know you!

李：保陽很小的時候就有知識崇拜的傾向，這幾天集中拜讀您的大作，不斷的有
　　新的收穫。謝謝！

孫：Thank you！You are the only reader in the world who reads every single piece
　　from my Collected Works! What a great honor!

李：是的啊。這種閱讀的幸福感不時湧上心頭來。

孫：Great！

李：今天十二點之前可以把卷二書稿交給您。

孫：My goodness! You are amazing! Thank you!

李：孫老師，《文集》卷二已分享給您，請查看Email。

孫：Yes, thank you! I have got it! Hope you and your family have a good outing for the rest of the day! I think you must read the following article by 李廣平！I have sent Li Guangping's music video to your wechat account! This is because I could not forward it to LINE! The music is called《神州聖經路》! You will like it!

孫：卷2，頁63，這句話不太通順, can you improve it?頁63:「基本上，伊蒂絲・華頓深信人類無法超越社會的道德得到自由的時候，也同時會意識到社會的牽制。」

李：「基本上，伊蒂絲・華頓深信，當人類無法超越社會道德的束縛而得到自由時，就會意識到社會的牽制。但也只有極富想像力的第一等人，才會在自己陷入感情自由的危險時，領悟到道德之可不抗拒。」可以作如是改，語意就比較流暢了。

孫：Great! This is perfect! Thank you!

李：您分享的《神州聖經路》，這個創意真好。去年在西部的豐收華夏教會，舉辦了一次紀念和合本聖經一百週年紀念，那次展覽中，有一個展品，是一位弟兄用毛筆手鈔了全部聖經，好是震撼的說。

孫：Wow, that's amazing! Actually I was very honored to participate in the 100周年和合本抄經project! I myself copied the《彼得前書》. My two brothers, as well as my Yale friends Li Rongzhen and Ling Chao, all participated in this event!

李：保陽下次來可以欣賞一下～

孫：I can send you an electronic copy!

李：孫老師，卷二中保陽改了不少文字和語句，都是出於中國大陸讀者的閱讀習慣，您在訂正的時候，如果覺得不妥，可以不理這些校記。另外，卷二後面有很多頁腳註沒有轉為簡體字，保陽已將之轉過來了，您特別留意一下。頁腳註您要特別注意，因為那裡沒法批註顯示，只能用紅色字體標出。

孫：Thank you for converting some footnotes to *jianti*!

陸葵菲致孫康宜

尊敬的孫康宜教授：

您好！

現將訪談提綱發送給您，敬請過目。若有冒昧，誠望海涵。

順祝

安康！

陸葵菲（方舟）頓首

5/5/2020

註：陸葵菲女士目前正在準備完成哥倫比亞大學神學院的文學碩士的網上課程，一方面也在負責「三啟學會」的一些事工，其中「基督徒訪談系列」由她負責。（「三啟學會」就是2019年發起「紀念和合本《聖經》一百週年抄經計畫」的學會）。

孫康宜致李保陽

Dear Baoyang,

I must share with you this information about Dr. František Reismuller, the translator for the Czech edition（捷克版）of my book, *Journey through the White Terror*（《走出白色恐怖》）。

Please see my email correspondence with František on Feb. 11 and Feb. 12, 2020. Don't you think it's amazing that he completed the book of translation right before COVID-19 was going to arrive in Europe?

That's another coincidence that I observed during this pandemic season! It seems that a lot of things have happened to me during this unprecedented period of the pandemic.

Well, I can't help sharing this information with you!

Best,
Kang-i
5/6/2020

註：由František Reismuller博士翻譯的《走出白色恐怖》捷克文版將由布拉格（Prague）的Charles University, Faculty of Arts出版。

孫康宜致李保陽

Dear Baoyang,

I thought I already sent you this short report about C.C.　C.C. was the one who designed the Chung-yuan bell tower, for which I'm very proud of.

https://www1.cycu.edu.tw/news/detail?type=%E7%84%A6%E9%BB%9E%E6%96%B0%E8%81%9E&id=2300

Now, I suddenly found this old picture of myself, which was taken in the fall of 1966 when I visited Chung-yuan Christian University for the first time. (Please see attached picture). At that time CC was already a Ph.D. student at Princeton University.

Where were you in 1966?

Best,
Kang-i
5/6/2020

1966年孫康宜第一次參觀中原大學，其身後的大鐘樓為張欽次先生設計。

孫康宜致李保陽

Dear Baoyang,

I want to send this picture to you, because the picture was taken at a very meaningful occasion last November, when we were celebrating the 170-year anniversary of the East Asian Collection at the Yale University Library (the so-called Sterling Memorial Library).

As you can see, in this picture C.C. and I, and Michael Meng (Head of the East Asian Library), were standing next to the statue of 容閎 (Yung Wing). From Michael Meng's work about the Chinese rare books, you can see how Yung Wing（容閎）was an important contributor to the Yale collection. In fact, in 1854 Yung Wing donated a rare copy of the 1853 edition of the《創世紀》to the Yale library.

When you come to visit Yale, I'll be sure to take you and your family to meet Yung Wing (i.e., his statue).

Best,

Kang-i

5/6/2020

耶魯大學圖書館慶祝中文典藏170週年，孫康宜夫婦與耶魯大學東亞圖書館孟振華館長和容閎銅像合影（Sterling Memorial Library，2019年11月）。

孫康宜致陸葵菲

Dear Lu Kuifei（陸葵菲），

Thank you so much for sending along the interview questions to me! But this is the busiest time of the semester at Yale. At age 76 I'm still teaching full time as you know, so there may be some delays for my reply to your questions!

Thank you for your understanding!

Best,

Kang-i Sun Chang

5/6/2020

吳清邁致孫康宜

康宜學姊：

　　謝謝告知。我就說，沒CC張先生相關資訊！

　　張光正我熟，他父親曾是東海董事長呢。小時父親們在高雄見面時我就跟光正見過。他在臺灣教育界以辦學理念與績效聞名！也是虔誠基督徒。

　　祝。平安健康

清邁

5/6/2020

李保陽致孫康宜

孫老師，

　　昨天您分享中原大學鐘樓前照片、與孟先生在容閎雕像前的照片，以及今早

您發來的余英時先生墨跡照片俱已拜領，這些照片都有非同一般的文獻價值，將來收入書中化身千百，意義深遠。謝謝您的分享！

剛剛讀到〈一九四九年以來的海外崑曲〉，大有夢回陶唐東京夢華之感，所述勝代流風雅韻，著實令人嚮往。趙珩先生對「文人」的界說更是準確而感人：「文人的概念絕非我們今天所說的知識分子，也不同於西方的貴族和上流社會……。這個群體具有深厚的文化積澱，有綜合文化與藝術的修養和造詣，有超然物外的獨立精神，也兼有絕塵脫俗的人格魅力和不可逾越的道德操守。文人可以任何身分和職業立世，但無論順達或坎坷，富貴或清貧，畢竟是精神的貴族。」

頁84腳註中提到周素子女士，引起保陽一段回憶：「2014年4月，吳格先生講學杭垣，彼時保陽正棲遲於天竺山寺。先生瞭解到保陽的處境，特意把一冊託人買的周素子《晦儂往事》贈予保陽。保陽將讀後感寫得滿紙都是。8月，吳先生夫婦重遊郎當嶺下之寬兄片雲齋，招飲左近小樓，詢以周女士此書如何。保陽彼時正落拓湖山，年輕氣盛，對於同樣強項的周女士豈肯頷首，也是藉由略舒怨忿，遂逕以爾爾為對。其時吳先生應是不高興的。人在某些時候，並非刻意執拗地將自己置於一種難堪的境地之下，哪怕這份執拗引起了身邊人的不適。這時候他實際上是在和另一個「我」在較勁。人的那份執拗，也許才是成就我之為我的根由。最近一次見吳先生，是前年冬初在廣州的事了，那晚我和漆園老哥在珠江畔的淒淒冷風中聊天到大半夜……」

上面這段文字是兩年前的「九一一」那天寫的，距保陽離開中國，只有一個多月時間，因與周素子女士有關，分享給您做個紀念。剛剛讀到有關周素子女士一節，特別感慨，遂略做改潤以奉。周女士後來與其丈夫還曾刊印其丈夫叔叔的詩詞於海外，當日在浙江嘉興，友人浮碧詞客曾贈給保陽一冊，前年倉促出國，已不知所蹤矣！

保陽　敬上

5/7/2020

孫康宜致李保陽

Dear BAOYANG,

Thank you for telling me your personal experience with Mr. Wu Ge 吳格 , and for your reader's response to the works by Zhou Suzi 周素子.

It's really fascinating to hear your own stories of the past in connection with these amazing people!

I know Wu Ge in person, because a few years ago he spent several months working on our Chinese rare books at the Yale University Library! I really admire his solid knowledge in Chinese rare books.

Best,
Kang-i
5/7/2020

孫康宜致李保陽

Dear Baoyang,

As I may have told you before, I have already donated my collection of the original handwritings of Prof. Yu Ying-shih 余英時 to Taiwan's National Central Library 國家圖書館. They are mostly letters from Yu Ying-shih during the 1980s and 1990s, as well as his scroll to me and C.C. in 1987. (See a picture of the scroll below).

However, just today I have discovered some of Yu's letters sent to me by fax. They were dated in 2001,2004, and 2008, respectively.

I'm now sending you pictures of Yu's faxed letters, just for your information.

Also, I did not give away Yu's calligraphy originally written for my late colleague McClellan, before Yu left Yale for Princeton in 1987. I did not donate this item to Taiwan's National Central Library simply because I could not bring myself to break the beautiful frame which McClellan had spent so much effort and money to have it done by the famous art shop called Merwin.

Best,

Kang-i

5/7/2020

①余英時先生給孫康宜夫婦
的贈詩及書法（1987年4
月）。
②余英時教授為日本文學教
授Edwin McClellan所寫
的書法（1987年，現藏於
「潛學齋」）。

註：此信有部分刪節。

孫康宜致李保陽

Dear Baoyang,

Oh I just found this memorable picture of C.T. Hsia, his wife Della（王洞）, and myself. The picture was taken during the retirement conference for C. T. Hsia at Columbia University in the fall of 2005.

As you know, I talked about this conference in my article,〈「快人」夏志清〉。 It was after that conference that I got the inspiration to write the article.

I was just thinking that C.T. Hsia would have found "social-distancing" intolerable if he were still living today!

Best,

Kang-i

5/7/2020

孫康宜教授與夏志清夫婦在紐約
哥倫比亞大學（2005年秋）。

孫康宜致李保陽

Dear Baoyang,

You asked me about some pictures of Prof. F. Mote牟復禮before. Just now I have found these valuable pictures regarding Mote.

（1）Picture #1 was taken when Fritz Mote and Hsiao-Lan had "just married" in the U.S. Embassy, Nanking, 1950.

（2）Picture #2 is a picture of Prof. Mote's old house in Princeton.

（3）Picture #3 is a picture of Prof. Mote and Andy Plaks（浦安迪）, when Plaks visited Mote's house in Colorado! The date is unknown.

（4）Picture #4 is a picture of Mrs. Mote and my husband C. C. Chang, taken in 2006, when CC visited Mrs. Mote in Colorado (about one year after Prof. Mote's death). C.C. was responsible for compiling an album for a memorial service（追思會）in commemoration of Prof. Mote, which would take place in Taiwan later during that year.

Hope you like these pictures.

Kang-i
5/7/2020

①牟復禮、陳效蘭夫婦（南京，1950年）
②牟復禮在他的Princeton寓所前留影（約
　1980年前後）

孫康宜致李保陽

Dear Baoyang,

These are the Bible chapters which my two brothers and I personally copied by hand last year, as part of the celebration of the 100th anniversary of the Chinese Union Bible（和合本百週年紀念）.

As you can see, I copied the *Book of 1 Peter*（《彼得前書》）, my brother K.C.（孫康成）copied the *Book of Jude*（《猶大書》）, and my other brother Mike（孫觀圻）copied the *Book of Zechariah*（《撒迦利亞書》）.

Because the *Book of Zechariah* is very long, I am only sending you the first quarter of the book which Mike has copied.

Anyway, I thought you might be interested in taking a look at these hand-written copies by the Sun family members.

Best,
Kang-i
5/7/2020

①孫康宜手鈔和合本《彼得前書》（2019年）
②孫康成手鈔和合本《猶大書》（2019年）
③孫觀圻手鈔和合本《撒迦利亞書》（2019年）

孫康宜致李保陽

Dear Baoyang,

Since last Sunday on May 3rd, I have been wanting to share with you this prayer of mine which I wrote during the virtual Sunday service at Yale's Battell Chapel!

As you know, last Sunday was the Good Shepherd Day. And the main Biblical passage we read during the service was the famous Psalm 23, "The Lord is my shepherd. . .".

I was extremely inspired by the sermon by Rev. Ian Oliver, which emphasized the importance of our holding on to Christ (ie, our shepherd). We need to learn how to be led by the Lord! Under some circumstances, we should let go of our own plan, because it's not working anymore!

Anyway, I just want to share with you the context of my prayer. Please see my prayer attached.

Best,

Kang-i

5/7/2020

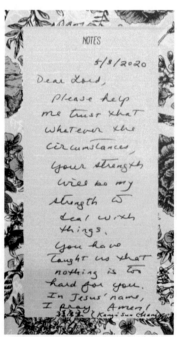

孫康宜在耶魯Battell教堂線上禮拜時
寫的禱告詞

孫康宜致李保陽

Dear BAOYANG,

　　I meant to share with you these pictures which were taken during my online class two weeks ago. Thanks to your help with valuable first hand sources on Wang Penguin 王鵬運, my class on late Qing *ci* went quite well. As you can see from the pictures, I used an old fashioned way of showing my notes and pictures, etc. Please don't laugh at me! But my students loved what I did!

Best,
Kang-i
5/7/2020

李保陽致孫康宜

孫老師，

　　您和夏先生伉儷的合照收到了。很珍貴的文獻！謝謝！

　　剛剛讀完〈好花原有四時香：讀《獨陪明月看荷花：葉嘉瑩詩詞選譯》有感〉，想起一些和葉先生有關的故事，和您分享如下：

　　2008年10月，張宏生老師在南京大學召集兩岸三地詞學會議，開幕式主題演講嘉賓是葉先生，記得葉先生一開場就指著會場那幅背景荷花圖，娓娓講述起她的小名與荷花的故事。那天的演講原定半小時左右，而葉先生竟然講了兩個多小時。她那天還講起她早年在臺灣的遭遇。那是保陽第一次見葉先生。後來在浙江嘉興和半宋樓葛渭君先生交往，葛先生與葉先生早年也有交往，葉先生送過一些書給葛先生，葛先生把其中的幾本轉送給了保陽，前年去國，不知道散佚到哪裡去了。那幾本書扉頁還有葉先生的簽名，思之可惜！

　　專此，並祝

　　教安！

保陽　敬上
5/7/2020

註：此信有部分刪節。

李保陽致孫康宜

孫老師，

晚上好！

季老師信收到多日了。因為這幾天一直在按計畫趕讀《文集》，所以沒有倉促回覆季老師。實在抱歉！下周一（5月11日）回覆季老師。

保陽計畫在5月10日左右將文集最後一卷讀完交給您，並在本月之內將《避疫》書稿編輯完成、將序言寫好、附錄及圖片插入交給出版社。因為六月分公司可能要復工，屆時保陽將要去上班，時間和精力勢必會分散，所以最近將其他事情概行推後。

有關於夏先生的話題，保陽很感興趣，不能倉促回應季老師，所以等《文集》最後一稿交您後再向季老師請教。

（此信保陽亦抄送一份給季老師了，勿念！）

保陽敬上
5/7/2020

孫康宜致季進

Dear Ji Jin,

Thank you so much for reaching out to me just now! Actually I did read your reply to

Baoyang's questions regarding why Western criticism and sinology have overshadowed the works of Chinese scholars on the mainland. I thought your answers are extremely interesting. But for some reason I thought I had already responded to you. I must be dreaming!

First of all, your explanation about the interdisciplinary and comparative approaches used by Westerns sinologists is very well taken. Basically those of us who teach Chinese literature in the US are comparatists, for we often belong not only to the department of East Asian Languages and Literatures, but also to the Department of Comparative Literature. When I taught Tang Xianzu湯顯祖 in the past, for example, I also talked about Shakespeare.

Secondly, the theoretical approach has become the norm of literary studies in the West for the last several decades, a phenomenon that was especially found in the Yale School of Deconstruction.

Honestly, I myself don't understand why the Western approach would be so attractive to the Chinese readers! Actually I was really surprised that Chinese publishers were competing against each other for the translation rights of the *Cambridge History of Chinese Literature* several years ago! The Cambridge UP people were surprised too. Perhaps only Chinese readers would be so eager to read about the Western approaches that had been adopted by the *Cambridge History of Chinese Literature.* In fact, both Stephen Owen and I did not want to have the *Cambridge History* published into Chinese at first, because we were afraid that the Chinese readers might be disappointed.

So instead of describing such a trend as "理論霸權," I think it is more appropriate to say that it is all due to the Chinese problem of "worshipping things foreign "崇洋"！ What do you think? I myself always respect the scholarship done by Chinese scholars! That's why Yale has invited you all the way from China to give a lecture on Qian Zhongshu 錢鍾書last year. After your talk, faculty and students alike all said in Chinese: "季進真了不起呀！"

Best,

Kang-i

5/7/2020

李保陽致孫康宜

孫老師，

　　晚上好！

　　季老師的回信認真拜讀了，說得真好！今早讀了您給季老師的回信，也對您的看法——尤其是「崇洋」一說——深有感觸。誠如您所言，中國的一些學者和學術，是您一直以來所尊敬的，這一點保陽也有同感。比如前陣子我們共同談到的嚴迪昌先生，諸如這樣的學者中國大陸有不少，但這樣的學者經常囿於這樣那樣的環境限制，終不能人盡其才。這個問題一旦討論起來，常常會涉及到學術之外的因素，遺憾的是，今日中國大陸學術一旦涉及到學術之外，討論各方就很難淡定地坐而論道了。最好就是像季老師那樣，實實在在地做一些具體的事情，反而是推動學術前進的不二之選。

　　今天集中讀卷一的明代文學研究諸篇，收穫很大，感觸亦深。因為時時作筆記（見附錄圖片），查資料，所以進度比較慢（保陽閱讀速度比較慢，讀學術性比較強的文字，一天可推進四十頁左右，散文可以達到八十頁左右），今天想趕一點進度，加到五十頁，以為後面的工作騰時間。所以這會兒還有幾頁的任務需要完成。不贅。

保陽　敬上

5/8/2020

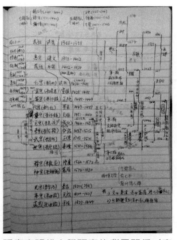

孫康宜明代文學研究的背景關係（李保陽整理）

孫康宜致李保陽

Dear Baoyang,

Thank you for sharing me with your notes! They are really impressive.

What a hard-working scholar you are. No wonder you are so solid in your scholarship.

Kang-i

5/8/2020

孫康宜致李保陽

Dear Boyang,

Please look over this article quickly for me! It might be needed for the web funeral for my aunt.

In haste,

Kang-i

5/8/2020

李保陽致孫康宜

孫老師，

遵囑將您剛剛傳來的〈我的姑姑〉拜讀一遍，只改了幾處錯別字和衍文，調整了一下排版格式。其餘一仍其舊。請放心傳給您的表弟。

天下事真是巧合者多遇。沒想到5月7、8、9號三天，在您生命中有如此重要的紀念意義。明天5月10日，是屬於全天下所有母親的節日。

我們會為您的姑母禱告！

也祝令嬡Edie生日快樂！

保陽　敬上
5/8/2020

李保陽致孫康宜

孫老師，

您的姑姑和於梨華女士該不會住在同一家敬老院罷？！如果是這樣的話，那就不好了！因為那是一個老人聚集之地，老人們對COVID-19的抵抗力是最弱的。如果確是如此，就需要趕快轉移分散這些老人。

保陽
5/8/2020

孫康宜致李保陽

Dear Baoyang，

You are right! They are trying to do something about it.

But it's really difficult at the nursing homes. Actually my gugu was tested negative at the nursing home first, but later at the hospital she was tested positive.

Best,
Kang-i
5/8/2020

孫康宜致季進

Dear Ji Jin,

　　I really like what you have said in your email: "確實，面對海外著作的大量湧入，良莠不分，一概擁抱，正是一種典型的崇洋心態，也使得這些海外著作產生了理論霸權之效。隨著海內外學術交流日益密切，我們應該有所鑒別，有所選擇..."．

　　Actually I wish American sinologists would pay more attention to new research done by scholars in China. There is no reason why the American sinological/comparative approach should be "superior"! In fact, I'm worried about the decline of the quality of American sinology, which looks more and more like a narrow field!

Best,
Kang-i
5/8/2020

張宏生致孫康宜

康宜，

　　這篇文章寫得動情，原來也是和新冠肺炎有關，不禁一聲浩歎！令姑真的是有孫家人的特點，自尊、自信、自強、自立，在風雨如磐的歲月裡，頑強地生存，培養出優秀的兒子，晚年生活幸福。她的一生，令人敬重！

宏生
5/8/2020

孫康宜致張宏生

Dear Hongsheng（宏生），

　　Thank you so much for summing up my aunt's life is such an inspiring way. You have used only a few words to say so much.

　　With thanks and admiration,

Kang-i

5/8/2020

孫康宜致Jing Tsu（石靜遠）

Dear Jing,

　　I thought you might be interested in reading my article,〈我的姑姑〉. My aunt just died of COVID-19 last night!

Best,

Kang-i

5/8/2020

Jing Tsu（石靜遠）致孫康宜

Dear Kang-i，

　　What an amazing tribute, Kang-i--thank you for sharing it with me. How fascinating to know that their son worked at the Kennedy Space Center. That was certainly a different era and history of Chinese in America. I'm just rediscovering these Chinese-American scientists at M.I.T. in the 1960s whose contributions have been largely forgotten...

　　We have lost many of our elders during this pandemic... Yu Lihua died a few days ago... sad times, but at least we can take solace in remembering what extraordinary lives they led.

Best,

jt

5/8/2020

註：**Jing Tsu（石靜遠），John M. Schiff Professor of East Asian Languages and Literatures & Comparative Literature, as well as Chair of the Council on East Asian Studies, at Yale.** 此信原無抬頭，系編者所加。

孫康宜致Jing Tsu（石靜遠）

Dear Jing,

　　Thank you for such wonderful feedback! I'll definitely let my cousin Jeremy Lee（李志明）know about your kind words.

　　Yes, I was very sad about the passing of Yu Li-hua a few days ago. I think the problem is the nursing home, where so many elders live together. It's very easy for the virus to transmit from one person to another.

Best,

Kang-i

5/8/2020

Line訊息

孫：我的姑姑剛去世！這麼突然！She was tested positive for COVID-19! And she died of heart failure!

李：啊！太突然了！請您節哀。

孫：She was my father's younger sister! The last one to pass among my father's siblings!

李：好的。您可以仔細醞釀一下思緒，在這個特殊的時期用這種特殊的方法來紀念您的姑姑！

孫：I was very close to my Gugu! I think I'll write an article in remembrance of her!（孫老師發來她與姑姑的照片）The photo was taken exactly a year ago in Maryland!

李：那個時候老人看起來精神還不錯啊！這個想法很好！您可以寫一篇比較長的文章來紀念您的姑姑，收入我們的書中。

孫：Yes! They will have a church web funeral. And I will be invited.

李：好啊。這個非常時期，網上葬禮是一個特殊的紀念儀式。

孫：Urgent! Please see my email! Please look over my article quickly. It may be needed for the web funeral! I told my cousin I'll send it to him by the end of today!

李：孫老師，修訂稿已Email分享您了。請查收。

Jonathan Kaufman致孫康宜

Dear Prof. Kang-i,

I hope you're doing well and are staying healthy and safe in these crazy times! My wife Clare and I are self-quarantining in Ghana, West Africa, where we've been living for the past few years. (I think I mentioned to you in my last E-mail that I started a human rights non-profit here in Accra.) Also, we have a baby now - a sweet, fun-and food-loving little girl.

I wanted to pick your brain again on a Chinese cultural question. You may remember that the last time I wrote, I asked for advice on a Chinese poem for a couple whose marriage I was about to officiate.

Now that couple has just had their first baby yesterday, and they've asked us to try and choose a Chinese name. The bride's mother, the only person of actual Chinese origin in the family, keeps proposing very authoritarian and traditional names that she doesn't like.

The family name is德, and they are looking for names for their baby girl that will evoke independence and strength of character, but also a spirit full of peace and love. Does anything appealing come to mind?

Thanks so much, and sending love to you and the family (and, restrained Papa that I am, just a few photos of Sora), Jonathan (and Clare)

P.S.- In case you were wondering why we ended up choosing a modern poem called 致橡樹 by Shu Ting for our friends' wedding ceremony... it's a good poem for lovers and environmentalists!

5/8/2020

註：此信有刪節。

季進致孫康宜

親愛的孫老師：

剛剛拜讀了您的新作〈我的姑姑〉，情真意切，又不假華麗詞藻，非常感人。原來就是《走出白色恐怖》中的上海姑姑，願姑姑安息。

海外學者的著作在中國大陸大受推崇已是不爭的事實，其原因可能就是我上封信分析的幾個方面。現在您的現身說法，再次印證了我的分析。跨學科的、比較的視野與方法，對於您來說，只是再正常不過的取向。您要向國外學生講解中國文學，最好能為學生提供他們熟悉的西方文學的背景，以便他們能更好地進入

中國文學，理解中國文學。將湯顯祖與莎士比亞捉置一處，將哈代與沈從文相提並論，於你們而言都是自然而然的選擇，而於中國大陸學者來說，則是相對陌生的比較文學的視野。

至於理論取向，我相信對於你們而言可能也不是有意為之，畢竟如您所說，過去幾十年，這已成為西方文學研究的常態。而理論也確實照亮了很多傳統的文本，補充、修正甚至解構了一些文本的傳統闡釋，比如高友工、梅祖麟的《唐詩的魅力》、葉嘉瑩先生的《杜甫秋興八首集釋》等都有煥然一新之效。而我說的「理論霸權」原來是想指那些過於依賴理論、甚至犧牲文本，讓文本成為理論的試驗場的做法，這主要體現於中國現代文學研究界少數年輕學者的著作。讓文本臣服於理論，由此構成了理論霸權，這其實是對文本對審美的傷害，完全不可取。

您又提供了新的思路，將理論霸權與崇洋心態相聯，我也完全同意。確實，面對海外著作的大量湧入，良莠不分，一概擁抱，正是一種典型的崇洋心態，也使得這些海外著作產生了理論霸權之效。隨著海內外學術交流日益密切，我們應該有所鑒別，有所選擇，應該更多地引進像《劍橋中國文學史》、《新編中國現代文學史》（王德威主編）這樣的著作，更多地引進海外中國文學研究的一些經典著作。我曾經主編過一套《海外中國現代文學研究譯叢》，譯介了一些海外中國現代文學研究方面的重要著作，其實海外中國古典文學研究方面，還有大量的重要著作沒有中譯本，非常值得譯介，可惜限於專業和水準，我只能寄希望於古典文學專業的學者來促成此事。只有更多的重要著作的譯介，才有可能與中國大陸學界展開更為廣泛的對話，甚至在未來有可能形成不分中外的中國文學研究的學術共同體。

這是一個美好的未來，可能需要幾代人的努力，也許也只是一種學術烏托邦，哈哈哈。

祝安好！

季進 上
5/9/2020

註：季進教授地處東半球，在回信孫康宜教授時，西半球仍是8號，故繫於此。

李保陽致孫康宜

孫老師，

　　昨天和今天集中讀完了七篇關於明代的文章，酣暢淋漓，收穫不少。同時，保陽認為這七篇文章的內在脈絡非常清晰，既有縱向宏觀的歷時概述，也有相對應的個案研究分析。比如明初文學（以瞿佑為個案）、明中期文學（以楊慎為個案）、明中晚期之際文學、晚明文學（以吳梅村與錢謙益為個案）。這幾篇文章之間的邏輯關係，竟然和《晚唐迄北宋詞體演進與詞人風格》、《抒情與描寫：六朝詩歌概論》，有著驚人的相似。如果把這七篇文章整合在一起，就是一部獨立的《明朝文學研究》。

　　嚴迪昌先生在《清詩史》後記中有一句話：「決意為三千靈鬼傳存他們駐於紙上的心魂……。」十多年前，保陽讀到這句話時，真有一種「靈魂為之一驚」的震撼。下午讀到〈錢謙益及其歷史定位〉這一篇，其中引述錢謙益那句「使一代詩人精魂留得紙上」，那種熟悉感，讓保陽深信，嚴先生一定是受到錢氏這句話的啟發而說出那句話的。蓋嚴先生一生生活、工作在環太湖流域，他有許多單篇論文著重討論明清環太湖流域詩史。加之他四九之後的個人遭際（嚴先生的生平可參見保陽分享給您的那篇採訪嚴夫人的文字），一定使他對牧齋產生過異代共鳴的知己之感。故其援用牧齋這句話，應無疑義。

　　今天下午您的一條短信說：「I always want to put myself into their shoes!」嚴先生說他「積斷續三十年間的悟解，並促動我甘願耗大心力，決意為三千靈鬼傳存他們駐於紙上的心魂，是因為我深深體驗及曾經生存在愛新覺羅氏王朝二百七十年間的這一代代文士所承受的心靈壓抑和創痛是史程空前的。尤其是神魂的羈縛、扭曲之慘酷以及他們即使是放浪形骸或野逸自得形態下的掙扎、奔突、驚悚、迷茫和苦楚，時時震撼著我。」嚴先生和牧齋有異代知己之感，下午讀您的那句話又和嚴先生的話有共通之處，這種超越了時空的精神聯繫，真是讓人感到魅力無窮。學術研究——尤其是文學研究——只有這種身心的了解、體悟、玩味，才能達到一種靈魂上的震撼，文字才會有精神和靈氣！

　　這幾天保陽讀您的文章，其實眼睛最為一亮之處，往往就是在邏輯敘述和史事考證間隙，不時宕開的一兩句意味深長之筆，就像今天下午分享給您的：

「一個優秀的讀者理應學會全面公允地考察事物，他應該不拘成見，獨具慧眼，從歷史的罅隙中探幽索微，切忌抓住一點不及其餘，以偏頗的根據作出全域性的結論。」「對於那些出處行藏困身歷史棋局的古人，如果其所犯過錯並非出自本心，乃迫於事勢所使然，今人持論，既有後瞻之優勢（the advantage of hind sight），還應設身處地，心平詞恕，不可以脫離特定的歷史情境而求之過苛，責之過峻。」這些文字，經常讓人神為之王！

保陽　敬上

5/9/2020

黃進興致孫康宜

康宜，

　　親人離去，總是令人傷心不已！節哀順變只是老話，人實在很渺小，能活得發光發熱，也真不容易。佩服您的姑姑一生的故事。感謝您的分享！

　　祝健康平安！

進興上

5/9/2020

孫康宜致黃進興

Dear Chin-shing,

　　Thank you so much for your kind words regarding my gugu! My gugu was a very special person in my life!

　　Amazingly, today (5/9) is the 13th anniversary of my father's passing. And tomorrow (5/10) is Mother's Day during which I'll think of my mother who passed 23 years ago. Surely my cousin Jeremy will think of his mother too.

Suddenly all these consecutive dates, 5/7, 5/8, 5/9/ , 5/10 , have become so meaningful to me! So amazing!

Kang-i
5/9/2020

孫康宜致Jonathan Kaufman

Dear Jonathan,

What a lovely girl Sora is! Thank you for sending along such beautiful pictures.

As for a Chinese name for the couple's new baby, can you tell me what the baby's gender is? Also, what is the baby's English name?

By the way, please see my other email to you. It's about an article I have just written today: 〈我的姑姑〉。

Kang-i
5/9/2020

Line訊息

李：我們這個年齡及以上的大部分中國農村人的生日都存在這個問題。所以這是個有趣的歷史現象，也許以後會有人作為一個題目來寫一篇文章，哈哈。

孫：Yes! The Chinese are so funny! They don't take "what's truth" seriously! They are 差不多先生！The Chinese are not 嚴謹 enough! That's why I appreciate the concept of 約 in the contexts of 舊約、新約！God likes to make people 守約！He himself also 守約！

李：是的。中國的廚藝和醫藥這樣需要嚴謹科學的東西，都是建立在經驗的基礎上的，更別提歷史、文學、藝術等其他學科，更是模糊的、經驗的。中國人的思維是歸納式的，不夠精確，常常會出現偏差。歐美人是發散式思維，推演出可逆的理論後，用實證來證明其正確，就可放諸四海而皆準了。但是到了現代文明語境裡，中國人那一套已經吃不開了。所以近代文明，尤其是關乎今日實際生活中的技術發明，基本上都來自歐美。因為中國人的那一套方法太虛，沒法驗證。這種不精確的傳統，給現代文明大背景下的中國人自己，已經造成了很大的困擾。一百多年前的五四先賢們之所以大聲疾呼，要革新中國文化，大概也和這方面的考慮有關。

孫：Yes, you are absolutely right! Yes, precision is the key to success in the US too! Write with precision, think with precision, and talk with precision! By the way, I think the best model of English writing is the Contemporary English Version of the Holy Bible. But in terms of speaking in English, the best model would be David Pawson's lecture series on the Bible!

李：謝謝孫老師，*the Holy Bible: Contemporary English Version* 前天已經在網上訂購到了，這幾天應該可以收到。謝謝您分享的這個視頻，我現在正在聽。

孫：If you imitate how David Pawson speaks in English, you should be fine! The key to success in the US is : write well , speak well with clarity and precision, and listen well with respect for others! 表示對別人的尊重！切記切記！

李：謝謝孫老師金玉良言！您是過來人。謝謝您的諄諄教導！保陽一定謹記您的教誨!!

孫：Thank you! I'm very sympathetic to Qian Qianyi! I'm glad you like my comments!

李：是的。任何人處在歷史的當下，都不容易，能出於同情之理解，得要有仁厚的同情心，共情感才行！您是仁厚之人！

孫：I always want to put myself into their shoes! 如果我是他，遇到同樣的遭遇，我會如何做？

李：是的。推己及人，言之不難，行之非易！

孫：Yes！

Stano Kong（江丕賢）致孫康宜

Dear Kang-i,

My heartfelt condolences to the loss of your aunt. From your tribute to her, I could tell she was a great woman. She was ahead of her time and wasn't afraid to right the wrongs. You must be very proud of her.

Also, Happy Birthday to Edie. I wish I were still 34. Haha.

Stano

5/9/2020

註：Stanor Kong（江丕賢），東海大學文學院院長

張永濤致孫康宜

謝謝孫老師，

讀完您的文章，真感人，真感慨！文中的場景竟如電影畫面一般在腦中閃過，其間北京的潞河中學，我多年前差點兒去那兒當老師了……真是花開花落，物是人非，斯人已去，親情長存。

永濤

5/9/2020

孫康宜致李保陽

Dear Baoyang,

I just want to share this with you. As you can see from the attached picture, my daughter Edie had to drop off her Mother's Day gift for me on our front porch--merely because of the social distancing during this COVID-19 pandemic!

But at least I did have a chance to throw a kiss（飛吻）to her and to my son-in-law and the two kids from a distance!

What an interesting way of "social distancing" between the loved ones.

Best,
Kang-i
5/10/2020

孫康宜致李保陽

Dear Baoyang,

I must share with you these interesting interactions today (i.e., May 10th, Sunday) regarding my aunt Sun Yuxian 孫毓嫻, who just died last Thursday in Maryland.

First of all, I heard that during the zoom meeting this morning hosted by Yale University Church, the participants prayed for my aunt. (Actually earlier I had joined the zoom meeting at first, but for some reason my zoom video suddenly stopped working and I was not able to get back to the meeting, so I missed the prayer session.)

Then around 3:20 p.m. this afternoon, I got two wechat messages from my Yale colleague Peisong Xu, who was in today's church zoom meeting:

> "Prof Chang, We prayed for you and your family at the Zoom meeting of the Yale University Church! Your aunt is a respectable and admirable person. I am moved by her touching story. I like your article very much!"
>
> "She will live in our hearts forever!"

①孫康宜與她的姑姑（2019年3月，馬里蘭）
②孫康宜的姑姑中學照片
③左起：孫康宜的父親孫保羅，孫毓嫻（姑
　姑），李志明。（1997年9月，攝於加州，
　當時孫康宜母親去世不久）
④孫康宜的姑姑與丈夫李兆強（1979年孫康
　宜攝於上海）

I immediately responded to her with the following message:"Thank you! I'll share your words with my cousin Jeremy! He will be comforted that members of the Yale Church prayed for his mom! And today is Mother's Day!"

And less than one minute after I forwarded Peisong Xu's messages to my cousin Jeremy, I got the following response from him:

"My mother was destined to the US ivy league school after潞河。Finally she made it...! "

What Jeremy meant is this: While attending the Luhe High School in Beijing (which was funded by American missionaries) many decades ago, his mother (i.e., my aunt) was expected to go to one of the Ivy Leagues in America after graduation. But of course all her dreams of attending American Ivy Leagues were later destroyed by the political circumstances in China. Now, finally my aunt had reached her goal, as she was remembered in the prayers by people at Yale, one of the US Ivy Leagues. That's why

Jeremy said: "Finally she made it. . . ."

In order to celebrate this special day in commemoration of my aunt, my husband C.C. suddenly got a great idea! He went out to gather some fallen cherry petals from our front yard and put them into a bowl. (Please see picture attached). Indeed, this bowl of cherry blossom is the best gift for my aunt on this Mother's Day.

Best,
Kang-i
5/10/2020

李保陽致孫康宜

孫老師，

　　看到CC先生的那隻櫻花碗了，真是一個了不起的創意，我想您的姑姑在天堂看到，一定會欣然一笑的。

　　這兩天讀到您轉來的許多朋友對您姑姑的懷念文字，其中保陽印象最深的是剛才您發來的劉嫄女士的話「孫媽媽話語不多，但看得出仍有大家閨秀的韻致和老一輩知識人的風骨。」那句話，讓保陽想起您在《走出白色恐怖》裡描寫的令堂。都是有一樣堅韌性格的女人。還有，您的表弟說在紅色恐怖年代，您的姑姑收聽短波電台裡面的福音，那個場景是如此的逼真。透過這些親友們的碎片式回憶，保陽大概能想像出一個有風骨、有信仰的中國女性形象。正是因為她有知識人的清醒和遠見，才早在1982年就將兒子送到文明世界，進而割捨一己私情，囑咐兒子不要回頭向那埃及地。她的信仰，讓她在領導的壓力下，敢於拒絕簽那不義的字。所以您的姑姑，應該就是蘇州詩人金天翮所理想的那種獨立了的中國女性。

　　不管怎麼說，　神還是恩待您的姑姑的，讓她晚年能和家人在新大陸重聚。回到天家，您的姑姑應該看到了她的父親、哥哥、嫂嫂等親人，她又開始了一段新的人生！

保陽　敬上
5/10/2020

孫康宜致李保陽

Dear Baoyang,

You won't believe this! I just received this wechat message which my Harvard friend Chang Phong（張鳳）had forwarded to me. It's a response to my article in remembrance of my aunt. And the reader's response was from Liu Yuan 劉嫄, the granddaughter of the famous Liu Dabai 劉大白.

But what is amazing is that after reading my article, Liu Yuan realized that her mother (i.e. the daughter of Liu Dabai)happened to stay in the same nursing home as my aunt, and that the two elders were actually neighbors at the nursing home！Liu Yuan's mother just died last month, and Liu Yuan was very sad to read about my aunt's passing a few days ago. That's why Liu Yuan wanted Chang Phong to forward her letter to me.

Anyway, here is Liu Yuan's letter in Chinese:

張鳳老師，

在您的微信朋友圈裡看到孫康宜教授的悼念文字，黯然神傷。

先母劉緣子今年二月不慎跌跤住院後，也入住了同一座老人康復中心，與孫媽媽比鄰而居。與其子李先生聊起來，才知道兩家的先人可能在昆明和天津都有一些共同相知的故舊。

孫媽媽話語不多，但看得出仍有大家閨秀的韻致和老一輩知識人的風骨。

不幸兩位母親先後都駕鶴西去了（先母是在4月9日走的），希望她們在天堂裡仍能比鄰而居。

能否麻煩妳將此轉給孫康宜教授，也請轉告她我一向很喜歡讀她的文字。

劉嫄敬上

Also, here is a link to the article which Liu Yuan wrote in commemoration of her mother last month:

https://mp.weixin.qq.com/s/Ldwbt8V_EEM1ykKdgL72XQ

It turns out that Liu Yuan's mother lived to 101 years old. What an amazing woman.

Best,
Kang-i
5/10/2020

孫康宜致李保陽

Dear Baoyang,

I just got this follow-up information from my cousin Jeremy regarding Liu Yuan's mother, whom Jeremy referred to as Liu Laotaitai（劉老太太）.

Jeremy said that he was very impressed with Liu Laotaitai, who at age 101 was still extremely alert and energetic.

Liu Laotaitai told Jeremy that, while pursuing her undergraduate education at the 西南聯大, her Chinese teacher during her freshman year（大一國文老師）was Shen Congwen（沈從文）！

Best,
Kang-i
5/10/2020

孫康宜致吳清邁

Dear Ching-Mai,

What telepathy! I was about to email you the following link to my new article ,我的姑姑, when I received this wonderful email from you!

https://mp.weixin.qq.com/s/Xbd4nr3997gnk6ScC7a7EA

This new article can serve as a sequel to my book, 《走出白色恐怖》！

Anyway, I was deeply moved by your feedback on my memoir! Yes, I'm a person who lost my mother tongue 母語 due to political trauma! Thank you for going back to my zoom interview last month to testify that! Whenever my friends listened to my father's lectures, they could not believe that my spoken Chinese could be so different from my father's' ! (I will send you one of my father's YouTube's, and I'm sure you will be amazed too).

I'm so glad that you like CC's recollection of the cheese rolls about your father 吳德耀校長 . Every time CC and I ate cheese rolls, we always talked about your father. Actually I remember very fondly of your mother too! She was always very kind to me. I even had a picture taken with her in front of Luce Chapel at my graduation in 1966. I'll see if I can find the old picture for you!

Our warmest regards to your lovely wife Jan.

Best,
Kang-i
5/10/2020

註：此信有部分刪節。

孫康宜致Linda Chu（朱雯琪）

Dear Linda,

I'm sure my cousin Jeremy is very grateful to you for translating my article into English!

As you can see, my aunt and my uncle were lucky to move to the US in 1993. Before 1993 they thought they would never see their son again, if the political situation continued to be difficult.

I was so relieved when they were reunited in the US in 1993. Jeremy is very grateful to the US and has been working extremely hard for American government all these years! I'm especially impressed that Jeremy also joined the US Navy.

Brest,

Kang-i

5/10/2020

Line訊息

孫：Also, due to social distancing, my daughter had to drop off her Mother's Day gift on our front porch!

李：謝謝孫老師分享。令嬡送給您的禮物看起來真漂亮。

孫：I think the following exchanges between Ji Jin and me are important! See below:

　　李進：孫老師好，《孫保羅書法》收到啦，印得好漂亮啊，謝謝謝謝，我好好學習和珍藏！

　　孫：Great! I'm glad you have a copy of the book now! If someone asks me what's the most important book I have done so far, I would definitely say it's《孫保羅書法：附書信日記》！

李進：太棒了，剛剛已經欣賞了書法部分，回頭來細讀書信部分。您的工作太有意義了，不僅僅是女兒的私事，它傳遞的還是更廣大的福音與愛。

孫：Also, you will be amazed by the Wechat communications I just had with my cousin Jeremy Lee !......

李：天啊！這太巧合了吧！！竟然在美國碰到了劉大白的後人，真是不可思議之極！

孫：Oh my goodness! It's such a small world!

李：關於龔自珍的那篇文章中，引用了下面這篇文章。但是保陽在五卷文集中並沒有看到這篇文章。

孫：Right! I do not want to include that old article! Also the newer article which is included in the《文集》is much better!

李：明白。謝謝孫老師的解釋。剛剛讀到您說：「我一向把求學的經驗視為生命的主要內容……。離開了『學』，便無所謂人生的樂趣。」讓保陽又想到嚴迪昌先生的話：「學術即生命，吾輩捨此，豈有他哉！」這兩句話說的是一個意思。

孫：Yes !

李：浦安迪先生比您還小一歲呢！

孫：I think Andy Plaks is 2 years younger than me!

李：您不打算把〈我的姑姑〉收入《文集》嗎？

孫：I already did. I already added it to vol.2.

李：好的。

李：孫老師，剛剛讀完了您二十一年前參觀了加州月谷傑克倫敦公園後寫的〈酒鄉月谷憶倫敦〉，您對「狼宅」（Wolf House）的感慨，竟然和保陽是如此巧合。蓋這個週二，保陽將《文集》卷二讀完交給您之後，帶孩子們入山遊玩，在山澗中看到了一座已然廢棄多年的老房子，當時帶領孩子們湊近了憑弔了一番。竟然和您對「狼宅」（Wolf House）的感慨非常巧合。（分享Pickering河谷的照片）後面幾張照片是在日記中寫到的那座廢棄的日式庭園

中拍的。那座山谷中的橋建於1918年11月14日。2000年11月14日是我和我太太在一起談戀愛的日子，剛好在這座橋建成後八十二週年那一天。

孫：Wow that's wonderful! You were destined to visit this meaningful site!

李：是的。我覺得是　神用祂的手帶我們那天下午去了那裡，並發現了那座橋。以後每個我們的紀念日，都會去那裡慶祝。那裡是一個山水清嘉的地方，離我們家只有半個小時車程。

孫：Perfect!

孫：Please also see my email: follow-up! 沈從文was mentioned!

李：孫老師，太奇妙了，那位去世的劉老太太竟然是沈從文先生的學生。

孫：Yes amazing!

李：這個世界太小了！

Rev. Jenny Peek致孫康宜

Dear Professor Chang,

I am so sorry to hear of the passing of your aunt. What hard news in this already difficult time. I will keep you and all those she touched and who loved her in my prayers.

Once it is translated I would love to read it. I am sure you honored her life and put words to her life than many will appreciate reading.

I hope you are feeling well on this beautiful day—and hopefully we will see you at 11:15.

Warmly,

Jenny

5/10/2020

王德威致孫康宜

Dear Kang-i,

Thanks so much for sharing this essay with me. It is most touching. I remember the way you described your reunion with your aunt in your memoir, and I can (almost) understand how your aunt went through those tough years as my aunt (my mother's sister who is now turning 93 now) had a similar experience after 1949.

Your family was tough to have withstood so many trials. It is lucky for your parents and your aunt's family to have finally settled down in the States.

May your aunt rest in peace in Heaven, together with your parents.

Best wishes,

David
5/10/2020

王璦玲致孫康宜Line

Thank you so much for sharing with me your article about your aunt. My deep condolences to you and your family. The wonderful coincidences of dates and ages among your family are really miraculous! My heart goes out to you~

Ayling

Linda Chu（朱雯琪）致孫康宜

Dear Professor Kang-i,

I would be honored to translate this article about your aunt. I read this touching article this morning and was going to write to you to give you my sincerest condolences on her passing. I can feel her strength through your words, which I found immensely moving, especially at the end when you wrote that your aunt and your father在天堂團圓. And the timing is indeed special and奇妙.

Warmly,
Linda
5/10/2020

吳清邁致孫康宜

Dear CC and Kang-i學姊：

From the photos I see Spring is upon you. Hope your lock-down ends well so you can once again be out and about, like we so fortunately enjoy in Taiwan. I just had a game of golf with the Tunghai Alumni Taipei golf team which meets monthly. Lots of other people on the golf course, with those who work in China stuck here in Taiwan.

康宜學姊，I read your book, 走出白色恐怖，and met the side of 孫康宜 I am sure I would never otherwise meet. The writing so vividly expresses your feelings at the time, and of the people who helped the family, including Aunties on your Mother's side. I particularly enjoyed reading the chapter "在語言夾縫中", and re-listened to the Youtube recording to see if your speech carried any hint of 臺灣國語! And, I was dismayed to see you write that you have forgotten all your 臺灣話!

Finally, CC, I laughed at your joke about cheese rolls and my lad Dad. What a wonderful memory, in Princeton no less. I used to be impressed that my Mom and Dad would recall the names of quite a few early alumni when they met them, either in Taiwan or in the US.

We early Tunghai alumni all benefited from the extraordinary liberal arts education received at Tunghai, which at the time was so different from the other higher education institutions in Taiwan. Nowadays, unfortunately, all universities basically look alike.

Will let you know when I receive the book you so kindly will be mailing to me. By the way, I have purchased the e-book collection of your writings. It is on my iPhone!

With kind regards,

Ching-mai
5/10/2020

註：此信有部分刪節。

李保陽致孫康宜

孫老師，

《文集》最後一卷校讀結束，茲將校讀稿奉上。

全部文集五卷，總字數一百六十八萬七千五百字，合計一千九百一十四頁，校改條目一千三百二十九處。4月5日接到您第一次發送來秀威版Word文檔，中間經過簡體字版、美國頁碼調整版等改換，從4月10日起，保陽正式以簡體美國頁碼版Word《文集》為校讀本，到今晚結束工作，歷時總計三十二天。每天有效工作時間十二小時左右，每小時大約推進五頁。這是保陽第一次校讀如此大規模的書稿，也是第一次測算出自己校讀書稿的速度，是一個意外的收穫。感謝主，在這段時間沒有讓任何意外的事情打擾校讀工作！

校讀中間還摘錄筆記約二點七萬字，為撰寫《避疫書信選》前言做準備。又隨讀隨將文集中所有英文單詞及中文釋義摘出，約一點八萬字，這個附帶的工作是保陽想藉此熟悉西方漢學研究界的一些術語表達，也可以當作《文集》的英文索引來檢索。

本月接下來的二十天，大約十天時間用來撰寫《避疫書信選》前言（以拜讀《文集》之感想為主，篇幅稍長一點），十天時間用來統編全書初稿。如果沒有意外情況打擾，六月初當可以交稿給出版社。

這是來美之後最為集中和愉悅的一次閱讀體驗，每日之收穫，以自己能感覺

到的速度在增加！最明顯的收穫是，從您百六十萬言的文章精粹中，對您的學術研究特色有了宏觀的認識，對某些微觀細部的批評理論有了直觀的了解，對西方中國文學研究近四十多年的學術史有了感性的認識。另外，也從您的文字中讀到了生命的質感和人生的智慧！！

　　感謝主的帶領！感謝孫老師給保陽的這個學習機會！！

保陽　敬上

5/11/2020

孫康宜致李保陽

Dear Baoyang,

　　This is such a special letter from you, summing up your experience of reading (and editing) my collected works, 《孫康宜文集》5 卷本。I did not realize that my collected works in Chinese contain as many as 1,687,500 words! That's such a daunting number.

　　The fact that you have finished reading through the 5 volumes (total 1,914 pages) --including taking tons of notes for yourself--in only a short period of 32 days is truly impressive. You are no doubt the first person to do such a thorough scrutiny of my works, and I have learned a lot from your questions along the way!　This is an awesome experience for me too.

　　I don't know how to thank you, and hope that our friendship will continue to grow in the future.

Best,

Kang-i

5/11/2020

孫康宜致李保陽、季進

Dear Baoyang and Ji Jin,

I have good news to report! My student Anne Lu has just been awarded the prestigious Biancamaria Finzi-Contini Calabresi Prize in Comparative Literature for her senior thesis, which is about the French woman writer Louise Labe and Liu Rushi （柳如是）. The title of the thesis is" "Singing for Herself." Louise Labe lived around 1555, and Liu Rushi 柳如是 was of course from 1618-1664. I especially appreciate my student Anne's argument that both women poets were "so fluent in the poetic discourse of their male counterparts" that they were able to define a voice for themselves.

Anyway, I think this thesis is a good example that shows why American Sinologists teaching in the US usually adopt a comparative approach. First of all, that's how our students think when they study Chinese literary texts. Also, it's much more effective to relate the Chinese authors to Western authors whom they were already familiar.

Best,
Kang-i
5/11/2020

陳國球致孫康宜

Dear Kang-i Laoshi:

I hope this message find you safe and healthy. In this pandemic time, we have to be alert and stay calm.

Attached please find an article on Professor Kao Yu-Kung whom I respect so much. It takes me a lot of effort in the past months to write it. Yet I feel so guilty that I cannot do my job better.

Please skim it through when you have some spare minutes. Your comments, of course, will be very much welcome.

　　Best,

Guoqiu
5/11/2020

孫康宜致陳國球

Dear Guoqiu （國球），

　　As I said via LINE, I have read your article with the greatest enjoyment and admiration! You not only talked about Prof Kao's scholarship but also his family history. That's awesome! The parts about Prof Kao's elder brother Gao Ergong（高而公）are especially interesting! I also appreciate your making references to Prof Kao's PhD dissertation on 宋代方臘之亂!

　　What a fantastic article in remembrance of my mentor Prof Kao.

　　Also, thank you for mentioning my name on page one of the article!

Best，
Kang-i
5/11/2020

孫康宜與陳國球合影，
攝於潛學齋，2005年
11月13日。

Line訊息

孫：But you are wrong! You again reversed the order of the editors! Didn't we agree that the order should be 李保陽、孫康宜，and 抱月樓、潛學齋，respectively? I always like to take an honest approach, especially because you are the one who actually put all the letters together.

李：謝謝孫老師，您說的非常正確。

李保陽致孫康宜

孫老師，

　　要感謝您的信任，在和保陽初識一個禮拜之內，尚未謀面，就將一百數十萬言的作品Word文件傾囊相授，這種信任，讓保陽倍感珍惜和榮幸！這份信任，讓保陽決定，無論如何，一定要盡全力幫您校讀《文集》。

　　《文集》近一百七十萬字，是您從事學術研究工作半個世紀以來的結晶，保陽相信，只要認真拜讀，任何讀者都能從您的文字中汲取不同的滋養。保陽何其有幸，成為汲取滋養的第一人！

　　感謝那萬主之主的　神，讓保陽在這時候認識您，拜讀您的文章，拓展自己的世界！

　　希望疫情盡快結束，我們可以在耶魯見面！

保陽　敬上

5/12/2020

孫康宜致李保陽

Dear Baoyang,

　　I just noticed that in vol. 1（on my article about 吳偉業）, your editorial note recommends that the word "衫？" in the parenthesis be deleted.

> 青山（衫？）憔悴卿憐我，紅粉飄零我憶卿

　　But I think it's important that I add a word "衫？" in parenthesis there, because I believe that "山" is a typo in the original printed text from which I cited the passage. I think it should read "青衫" here, because it was a term to describe young scholars in traditional China. Am I not right?

Best,
Kang-i
5/12/2020

李保陽致孫康宜

孫老師，

　　如果原始引文是「青山」，您不用特別註解。「山」為「衫」。您知道的，這個典故出自白居易的〈琵琶行〉中「座中泣下誰最多，江州司馬青衫濕」。納蘭性德有自度曲〈青衫濕遍〉悼其妻盧氏。但前人好古、好生僻，常將「青衫」諧音成「青山」，有一詞多義的指涉，來加強這個詞的表現力。如王鵬運〈中年聽雨詞〉就寫作「青山濕遍」。因此，在詩詞語境中，「青山」的語意指涉，往往無須那麼截然分明。這裡不用特別交代「山」是「衫」。

　　當然您註出來，把「山」字的意向所指挑明，也沒有問題，但在《文集》的上下文語境中，可能會給讀者造成一個誤解：即這個「山」是引文底本訛字？還

是衍文？或者作者吃不準？與其可能產生這樣的歧義，保陽以為倒不如刪掉比較省事。在這個語境裡，讀者自然能準確把握「青山」的意思。

　　不知您意下如何？

保陽　敬上

5/12/2020

孫康宜致李保陽

Dear Baoyang,

　　I meant to share with you my student Isaiah Schrader's reader's response to my article on my gugu. On May 9th I received this lovely message from Isaiah via LINE:

> "Dear Prof.Chang,
>
> 　　I am so, so sorry to hear about your aunt. Thank you for letting me read your beautifully written and very moving essay; it was incredibly touching. In Judaism, we say, "May her memory be a blessing." And I'll be sure to pray for her.
> Isaiah"

　　I should add that this Isaiah is the same Isaiah whom I mentioned in my preface to the Showwe *fanti* edition of the forthcoming book,《從北山樓到潛學齋》："最近我的耶魯學生 Isaiah Schrader（史逸軒）就針對施老的〈浮生雜詠〉詩歌做了一次非常精彩的演講。"

Best,
Kang-i
5/12/2020

孫康宜致李保陽

Dear Baoyang,

　　You know what? Early this morning I suddenly received from Han Han（韓晗）the following wechat message, as well as very good news about my Nanjing friend Prof. Yang Yi 楊苡教授 (who is now 101 years old). It's quite surprising that Han Han also forwarded to me a very valuable old picture taken during a gathering in honor of me back in July 1979. I remember that the hosts were Prof. Yang Yi and her husband Prof. Zhao Ruihong 趙瑞蕻；the couple were both teaching at Nanjing University then.

　　Here is Han Han's message to me this morning:

　　康宜師雅鑒：復旦陳引馳教授囑我轉呈楊先生早年與您的合影。特此呈上。陳教授說，這是吳新雷老師保留的照片，太珍貴了。韓晗。

　　Please see the attachments below for more information about the context of the 1979 gathering.

　　What is most interesting is that this story of my old 1979 picture apparently went viral on wechat today. First of all, around noon time Prof. Zhang Hongsheng 張宏生 sent me the picture via wechat, with a comment: "今天看到南京大學同事發的……。" And just now Chang Phong 張鳳 forwarded some messages to me, which she had received from her friend on wechat:

　　這是南京大學文學院黨委書記劉重喜昨夜發的照片。有關孫康宜先生。
　　北京作家，老家伊犁的安鴻毅先生傳來的。

　　What an amazing day I had today!

Best,
Kang-i

5/12/2020

右起：張月超、孫康宜、楊苡、趙瑞蕻、吳新雷（1979年，南京）

李保陽致孫康宜

孫老師，

　　謝謝您分享這些珍貴的舊照片，保陽能夠感受到您那種故人相逢般的欣喜。就連保陽看到這張照片都有些感慨，因為您照相那會兒，保陽還是個未滿月的小嬰兒呢，哈哈～

　　在您的交往中，像張充和、楊苡這樣老一輩的才女學人，讓我們這樣的後輩，就是遙想，都覺得是一種時代際會的恩賜。剛剛讀了您的來信，保陽還特別在網上又找到一篇寫楊先生的文章，分享給您如下：https://posts.careerengine.us/p/5d798c4855cd0d7b1f397580

保陽　敬上

5/12/2020

孫康宜致李保陽

Dear Baoyang,

　　I want to call your attention to my correspondence with Prof. Chen Guoqiu 陳國球教授, who is a scholar whom I respect very much. He has just sent me the following long article about my mentor Prof. Yu-kung Kao 高友工教授. I have just sent my response to Chen Guoqiu about the article. Please see my email below.

　　You may like to take a look at Chen's piece about Prof. Kao too, since you have talked about Prof.Kao before.

Best,

Kang-i

5/12/2020

李保陽致孫康宜

孫老師，

　　謝謝您轉來陳國球教授的新作，對於了解高先生學行，真是再好不過的一篇文章。

　　粗讀一過，印象比較深的竟然是陳先生對高先生研究特色的這麼一句總括：「高友工留下的著作不算多，但新創或重新定義的術語和觀念頗多，思路和演繹方式既細密、多向又迂迴，予人難讀難明，拒人於千里之外的感覺。」這引起了保陽細讀高先生的興趣，待疫情結束，就去Gest借閱高先生的書。另一個印象比較深的是高先生的兄長高而立，萬萬沒有想到的是，我們從小就在教科書中耳熟能詳的「小英雄劉胡蘭」，就是出自高而立先生之手。「劉胡蘭」是四九之後在中國大陸婦孺皆知的眾多「人造英雄」之一，如果以西方分析理論來研究這個形象，一定會得出很多匪夷所思的有趣成果。陳先生文中提到高而立先生喜歡的左翼文學，讀來竟讓保陽感到極為熟悉，因為我們讀的文學史教材，基本上都是這

麼一個敘述套路和立場選擇。但是讓人感歎的是，這樣教科書教出來的學生，將來卻不得不在海外花十倍百倍的精力來「解構」以前所學，在非中文世界裡去了解另一面的中國歷史！

陳國球先生是前中國社科院文學研究所張暉兄的博士研究生導師（更有趣的是，張暉兄後來在中研院的博士後合作導師就是您的高足嚴志雄先生）。張暉兄本來在南京大學追隨張宏生老師讀書，本科三年級就撰成〈龍榆生先生年譜〉，其中最鮮明的特色是大量的田野調查，採用了龍氏後人及龍氏舊交收藏的大量第一手文獻。張暉兄後來到香港跟隨陳先生讀書，最初到香港的一段時間，他長於文獻的治學路徑和陳先生的理論研究風格，一時很難適應，但是後來接受了陳先生的影響，學風丕變。以至於後來的學術文字中，那種深沉的憂思和情懷，遠遠超出我們這一輩人之上。就像陳先生對其評價：張暉不是成就某一門學問的專家，而是將來成就大學問的大家。保陽對張暉兄初隨陳先生讀書的那段學術轉型的痛苦，有切身的感受（因為保陽也是「入」於文獻，而不知如何「出」之以理論）。但後來張暉兄在陳先生門下能脫胎換骨，完成治學方式的轉型，在學術文字中沉潛出一股骨重神寒的憂思，想來除了他本人的天賦外，就要歸功於陳先生的教授有方。職是之故，保陽對陳先生有深刻的印象。陳先生以前撰文論述過高先生的抒情美學思想，今天這篇從高先生的「學思旅程中的境遇」切入，雖是一種知人論世的傳統視角，但對於深入了解高先生其人，卻不失為一個研究視角的創新，因為中文世界或者說學術界對於高先生的了解，實在太模糊了。這種多樣化的研究思路，讓保陽隱約能體會到張暉兄十多年前為什麼跟隨陳先生讀書時，會有一段痛苦的轉型，因為陳先生對傳統既有一份由衷的尊重，又時時保持其研究向度和方法、理論的多元化，這可能是當年張暉兄覺得壓力山大的原因。

P.S.陳先生大作頁8第2段第3行「中國語文扎記」中的「扎記」當作「札記」。煩您轉告陳先生訂正。

保陽　敬上

5/12/2020

Line訊息

李：孫老師，《文集》第一卷剛剛分享到您的Email中了，今天收到您的郵件，明天再回覆您！實在抱歉！您推薦的書今天也收到了。謝謝！

孫：I am thrilled to know that you have received this fantastic Contemporary English Version of the Holy Bible! You will love it, and your written English will improve dramatically if you read it everyday , and from cover to cover! God bless you!

李：謝謝孫老師的推薦！昨天收到以後，拿在手上，封面的手感特別好。保陽打算每天晚上寫完日記，專門騰出一個小時，一邊朗讀一邊抄寫，這樣大概三年左右時間就可以讀完。

孫：Yes! Reading aloud is the best way to improve English proficiency!

李：謝謝孫老師指教!!

孫：Dear BAOYANG, I cannot open your word file 修訂版授權書! Please see below! I think something is wrong with my computer!

孫：Please ignore my message above. My computer is fixed now!

李：孫老師，文件可以打開了嗎？

孫：Yes！

嚴志雄致孫康宜

Dear Kang-i,

I miss you so very much too. I just recently started using this WeChat and got your contact from our common friend 卞東波 from Nanking Univ. It is easier for me to talk to you through this now. I hope you and your family are doing well during this difficult time because of the Covid-19. (I am sorry to learn of the passing away of your aunt because of this).

Chi-hung

5/12/2020

孫康宜致李保陽

Dear Baoyang,

  （1）Please look over the REVISED list of my publication on the last few pages of vol. 5.

  （2）Please see the REVISED 簡體修訂版自序, where my acknowledgment of your help（給你的謝詞）has been rewritten. You will also note that the preface is now dated May 12, 2020.

  Please make stylistic changes, when needed.

With thanks,

Kang-i

5/13/2020

李保陽致孫康宜

孫老師，

  《文集》第五卷末尾的那三部論著的處理方式非常好，這樣既強調了那三部論著的重要性，也不會和廣西師大版《文集》的出版時間發生前面所講到的矛盾。

  序言部分保陽做了一處增補（請見附件）。因為保陽的數字是根據Word文檔統計出來的，按照大陸出版社的統計習慣和方法，將來廣西師大的版權頁統計字數，應該在兩百萬左右。所以特別加了「原稿」二字。

  謝謝孫老師對保陽校讀工作的肯定，《文集》出版，是您半個世紀以來學術研究生涯的標誌性工程，保陽能躬逢其盛，並貢獻綿力，深感榮幸！保陽的校讀工作只是整個《文集》出版複雜工作中小小的一部分，其他人的工作比保陽更加重要和關鍵。但孫老師仍願意不吝筆墨特別給予感謝，讓保陽深覺榮幸，又慚愧不已！謝謝！

李保陽致孫康宜

孫老師，

　　謝謝您轉來臺中社會局懷真局長的長信，這是一封很有意思的來信！

　　五年前，保陽曾從南到北訪問臺灣，歷時九天，那是第一次切身地接觸臺灣社會，對臺灣的社會、人文、地理有了直觀的印象。懷真局長的長信，真真切切地把臺灣民主社會的治理日常，近乎瑣碎地呈現在面前，讓保陽有一種細讀歷史文獻的興奮和新鮮感！懷真局長細緻入微的日常描述，比看新聞報道更加具有現場感。他以一位民主社會地方官員的視角，客觀詳細地再現了臺灣社會治理的運作機制和制度細節，讓人感動。保陽來美之前，也曾參加過一些政府部門的會議和活動，兩相比較之後，才明白了五年前何以能感受到那麼一個淳樸、自在臺灣社會，原來那份從容和友善，是好的制度和規則養成的。

　　臺灣為全世界最大的華人民主社群，臺灣人經過幾十年的努力經營，建立起華人民主政治制度的樣板。雖然社會上不乏一些論調，從中國傳統文化及其養成下的民族性出發，論證華人不適合西式民主，但是臺灣的成功模板，讓那些言論不攻自破。大家都認為政治是黑暗骯髒的代名詞，但是人類群處至今，民主制度仍是社會發展和進步不可或缺的選擇，它是一種群處的規則。好的規則可以涵養人與人之間的友善，糟糕的規則可以製造人與人之間的對立甚至仇恨。真為臺灣人慶幸，希望他們能夠繼續涵養這個制度，為華人世界樹立典範。

　　感謝懷真局長分享的這段記載，也感謝您的分享！對於我們華人來講，這真是一份值得保存的歷史文獻，它尤其記錄了COVID-19這個艱困時刻，臺灣民主社會治理的一個靜態的斷面。

保陽　敬上
5/13/2020

孫康宜致李保陽

Dear Baoyang,

I have revised the vol. 5 preface again. Please see attached.

Mainly I have made some changes, with special references that would distinguish the *jianti* edition from the earlier *fanti* version.

Please make sure that the changes read well. If not, please help me improve them.

Thank you.

Kang-i

5/13/2020

註：此信有部分刪節。

李保陽致孫康宜

孫老師，

保陽剛剛將您的〈簡體增訂本前言〉讀了一遍。很完美，沒有發現什麼地方需要增補。如果接下來還有什麼地方需要補充或者修改，我們再行商討。目前的這個版本已經很完美了。

保陽

5/13/2020

李保陽致孫康宜

孫老師，

　　剛剛拜讀了雅萍有關孫氏家族參觀展覽的文字紀錄，雅萍是一個非常細心、也非常有關懷的人，所以她的文字讀起溫暖、圓潤。保陽也要特別感謝雅萍，是她擬訂的這次策展題目，激發了您的靈感，賦予了「保陽」以「保羅＋陽光」的嶄新內涵。這可能是　神特意在這個時候讓保陽與大家相遇，在跟隨　神的道路上，給自己的名字賦予一層「新我」的意義！

　　感謝雅萍！感謝孫老師！感謝主！

保陽　敬上
5/13/2020

孫康宜致陳國球

Dear Guoqiu,

　　I hope you don't mind that I have shared your essay on Prof. Kao with a young scholar Dr. Li Baoyang李保陽who lives near Philadelphia (Mr. Li is 41 years old) . In the following I will be quoting from Mr. Li's preliminary response to your essay: ......（原信略，見5月12日李保陽致孫康宜信）。

　　Just to give you some background information: I came to know Dr. Li Baoyang when he began to write to me regarding my Princeton associates, including Prof. Andrew (Andy) Plaks, Prof. F.W. Mote, and Prof. Yu-kung Kao. He was a frequent user of the Princeton Gest Libray, where I used to serve as Curator decades ago. So he was thrilled to read your essay on Prof. Kao.

　　I cc Baoyang here on this email so that he knows about what I have written to you.

Best,

Kang-i

5/13/2020

孫康宜致張宏生

Dear Hongsheng,

　　Indeed, you are absolutely right about the power of popular media（大眾傳媒）！Actually only a few hours after I forwarded you my email to Li Baoyang regarding my 1979 picture, I received this wechat message from my former student Chi-hung Lawrence Yim（嚴志雄）: "By the way, I saw this posting and pictures from 劉重喜 at Nanking Univ. and thought you might want to know."

　　Thus, all day yesterday I could hardly cope with such a volley!（真是應接不暇！）

　　By the way, it's interesting that you mentioned the fact that 41 years ago in 1979, when I visited Nanjing University (still called Nanking University then), you had not gone to Nanda yet! But I also want to mention that during that time, our mutual friend Li Baoyang was only a one month old baby! Please see his email to me yesterday, which is copied below.

Best,

Kang-i

5/13/2020

孫康宜致彭懷真

Dear Huai-chen懷真，

　　Knowing how busy you have been in your current position as the 臺中市政府社

會局局長 (!), I was quite surprised to see you in the pictures of my relatives' visit to the Tunghai exhibition on May 12th! I cannot thank you enough for going out of your way to meet with my brother KC and other members of my dear ones!

As you know, without your initial plan and all your help for the preparation, there would be no exhibition for the Sun family. I still remember how, on a hot July day in 2019, we enjoyed a wonderful visit from you and your family--including you wife Grace（許惠仙）, your son Rio, your daughter-in-law Judith, your daughter Anne, and your three lovely grand kids Max ,Ashley, and Christina! You then carried many of my father's works (including his calligraphy, notes, etc.) all the way back to Taiwan during such a warm summer day! The plane to Taiwan was long delayed. And then, you were all trapped in Hong Kong airport for more than 48 hours! Whenever I recall your special visit last summer, I couldn't help feeling grateful for what you have done for me and the Sun family. So I want to give you my special thanks again. And, of course, thank you also for hiring Wang Ya-ping 王雅萍, who is so gifted and organized!

I'm so pleased that you have read my article on my aunt, 〈我的姑姑〉. It's such a coincidence that the date of your mother's passing was also on May 7th, the same as my gugu.

Thank you for sharing your notes with me about the meetings you had chaired and attended these days!   I'm amazed how you could manage so well in such a high-profile administrative position! I don't think I could have survived under such demanding circumstances.

I'm especially interested in what you have said about your management of "social distancing" due to the COVID-19: "與過去最大不同的是空間因為疫情而有的調整，第一天調整為半數局處長要在官員席，半數業務為幕僚性質的官員休息室，社會局是議題眾多的，雖不至於算爐主，也常被質問。所以當然在官員席，在執行兩天之後，議員要求所有首長都得列席。因為疫情，在各席位都設置了隔板，因此特別熱。市長坐在面對議長席的右側，社會局等局處長則坐在左側。右側因為有市長比較受矚目，左側被問到的機會少一些，某些議員開玩笑說是搖滾區，其實包括我左側的環保、衛生，右邊的勞工，都常被問，輕鬆不得。"

Anyway, it is such a delight to hear from you!

Best,
Kang-i
5/13/2020

李保陽致萩原正樹

萩原先生尊鑒：

　　好久沒有寫信給您，不知道日本最近疫氣流行的情況如何。希望　先生和家人一切平安！

　　保陽最近為耶魯大學的孫康宜教授校讀其《孫康宜文集》書稿，其中有一篇〈日本文學懷古〉，那篇文章記錄了孫教授三十八年前，在東京——尤其是京都、大阪——一帶的文學訪古之行。如大津江戶時代著名詩人芭蕉（1644-1694）的墳墓，大阪的通天閣，《萬葉集》故地、也是大和文化發源地的飛鳥，奈良的東大寺，和《源氏物語》有密切關係的宇治等日本文學聖地。孫教授優美的文筆和文學典故，一再把保陽拉回2017年和2018年的兩次關西之行的情境中。

　　保陽的兩次日本之行，先後得您引介，參觀了立命館文學部中國文學專攻的圖書典藏，以及參加中國文學專攻的讀書會，一起步行過等持院等等，都得到了一種豐盛的文學享受。文學常因其發生的地方而具真實感，固定的地方則因文學的發生地而充滿靈性和歷史感。這就是中國人所謂的「讀萬卷書，行萬里路」的魅力所在。保陽而今流寓美國，對周遭城鎮的歷史和人文，依舊充滿一種考古的熱情，和孫教授的日本文學訪古之旅是同樣一種感受。京都、大阪和奈良，是保陽兩次日本之行都曾走過的地方，讀了孫教授的文章，保陽很想再到關西，細細品味京阪一帶文學和地理的幽古之美。

　　疫氣橫行，希望　先生及家人一切平安！

　　隨信附上孫教授〈日本文學懷古〉一文，聊供　先生清賞。

　　專此，並候

夏安！

保陽　敬上
2020年5月13日

Line訊息

李：孫老師，保陽剛剛把《文集》卷五翻閱了一遍，建議您將最後一頁的〈將要發表和出版的作品〉刪除，因為當廣西師大版《文集》出版時，這三部作品已經發表了。

孫：But how do I call the reader's attention to these works? Especially regarding the捷克翻譯版 of《走出白色恐怖》？

李：這部分資訊可以合併進該卷的「附錄四」〈作者治學、創作年表〉中。廣西師大版最早應該也得2021年才會出版，在這之前的學術活動和成果發表資訊，都可以加進「附錄四」中。

孫：But I think it's best to say that the 捷克版 and my review of Owen's book are scheduled to be published in 2020. Then, later during the editorial process at the publishing house, I can confirm with the press editors whether these are indeed published in 2020. I really don't want to delete these two important items from the book. Actually I'm planning to add《從北山樓到潛學齋》（繁體版）and《避疫書信選》（李保陽、孫康宜編撰）to the 2020 publication list for that matter!

李：我明白您的意思了。但是一定要確定這三部論著是在廣西師大版出版之後發表。如果這三部論著發表在廣西師大版《文集》出版之前，就要調整這部分內容的表述語言，以免出現關公戰秦瓊的尷尬。

陳國球致孫康宜

Dear Kang-i Laoshi,

　　Glad to know about the response from a capable reader trained in the Mainland. I lack the knowledge which would be tremendously helpful for writing this paper. I am sure I would learn even more if Dr Li would kindly consider to comment and criticize the paper further in the near future.

　　I also feel guilty to pass you the raw draft with many typos, grammatical mistakes, gaps and holes, etc. I will try to amend all these in due course.

　　The paper on Professor Kao is one of the toughest that I have ever written. I would choose the word 'ordeal' to describe my writing process. Yet I enjoy the nights and days of dialoging with a scholar I respect.

　　It is my pleasure to know that our correspondences will be included in your new book. I am looking forward to reading the book.

Best,
Guoqiu
5/13/2020

張宏生致孫康宜

康宜：

　　大眾傳媒的效果真是驚人，這麼短時間，大家不約而同，將這個資訊傳遞出去，都覺得是一個重要的文化瞬間。四十一年前，我還沒有到南大，康宜已經在那裡見了這麼多的同事，對我來說，也感到非常奇妙！不一一。

宏生
5/13/2020

張宏生致孫康宜

康宜，

　　這真是奇妙，這麼集中的一段時間裡，這麼多人關注同一個資訊源，而且，又在差不多在同一天，集中通向四十一年前的當事人。這種事情，以前似乎很難發生，但在這個時代，發生了！

　　保陽和我同樣想到了自己的四十一年前，也是奇妙的事。

　　不一一。

　　宏生

5/13/2020

孫康宜致林玫儀

Dear Mei-yi，

　　Thank you for your thoughtful email! I hope your skin infection is completely cured now. I'm so excited to know that you are going to visit the Sun Family exhibition at Tunghai tomorrow! It means a lot to me that you will do that.

　　Thank you for your kind words regarding my zoom interview for the Tunghai exhibition, the Chung-yuan report on CC's design of the bell tower in 1963, and my article 《言猶未盡》which I recently wrote.

　　By the way, I want to let you know that my aunt (i.e.,my gugu, the younger sister of my father) suddenly died a few days ago on May 7th, due to heart failure directly caused by COVID-19. I have written an article in remembrance of my gugu. Here is the link to the article:

　　　　https://mp.weixin.qq.com/s/Xbd4nr3997gnk6ScC7a7EA

Please pray for my gugu. She was a person I'm very proud of. And with her passing, my father's generation in my family is now gone. (My uncle Sun Yuheng, my father's younger brother, died in Nanjing just a few years ago.)

Please send me pictures after your visit to the exhibition.

Best,
Kang-i
5/14/2020

Line訊息

孫：Actually I admire Qian Zhongshu too! Usually people in the Comparative Literature Department (such as張隆溪) would like Qian Zhongshu! Qian Zhongshu's insight into comparative literature is most admirable! I have got a lot of inspiration from Qian's knowledge in European literature! It's awesome! There is a reason why many readers respect Qian Zhongshu! Also, the term大師is a relative term! It's not an absolute term! By the way, I just cc you on my email to 王文鋒! Prof Wang is the leader of三啟學會that sponsored the 紀念和合本聖經百周年抄經 project!

李：我在現實世界中，更多地喜歡文獻研究，就像乾嘉諸老一樣，盡量少一些傾向性的表述。這就是我前陣子說過的，中國的知識人從來就沒有獨立於政治之外過，中國的學術也從來沒有獨立於意識形態之外過。我自己也是這樣。這是教育方式的問題，中國人很少接觸到純學術的訓練！！我覺得這也是中西學術交流經常流於皮相的原因。柯馬丁（Martin Kern）在一篇採訪中也有這樣的看法，他最後說需要中西兩方面的學者要繼續努力云云，但我能感覺到他其實是很悲觀的。

林玫儀致孫康宜

康宜姊：

　　謝謝妳的來信。在此先向妳道歉，我前一陣子在趕一篇審查報告，之後可能因為太累，免疫力下降，竟得了帶狀皰疹，很不舒服，所以有好多天都沒有上網收信，今天下午因為要與東海預約看展，去翻查妳上次寄來的信，才發現妳給了我好幾封信，我居然都沒看沒回，真是不好意思。

　　妳在東海展覽開幕式的發言，瑛妙當時就用Line傳給我了，我立即收看，一方面為妳的發言激賞不已，一方面也因多年不見，能透過螢幕見到妳，感到十分開心。你一點都沒有變，真是得天獨厚啊，怎麼經過這麼多年，仍然能那麼年輕漂亮呢？

　　真高興看到張先生贈書母校的專輯相片，我沒想到張先生在大學時代就能為中原大學設計鐘塔，府上真是一門俊彥。

　　拜讀大作〈言猶未盡：且從「陽光穿透的歲月」書展說起〉，久久未能回神，真是太感動了。是的，基督徒的人生就是和普通人不一樣，上帝並沒有應許天色常藍，但是祂會賜下力量，帶領我們度過一個一個難關。歐保羅教授夫婦和伯父母能由痛苦中走出來，都是因著神的愛，他們的所作所為，正是「一粒麥子」的真諦，你藉著撰述及幫助伯父整理著作，也是在發揚這種愛，我相信透過這次展覽，必然能對世道人心，有極大的提振作用。

　　我明天下午一點半左右就會到達東海展場，真的很期待。夜深了，就此擱筆，順祝平安喜樂。

玫儀

5/14/2020

李保陽致孫康宜

孫老師，

　　今早在編輯書稿時，保陽想起我們討論毛澤東詩詞和蔣寅論錢鍾書文章的事。以前保陽以為，中西學術研究的不同，最明顯的是對知識的理解和研究方法、理論的異趣，通過和您聊這兩個主題，保陽覺得，東西學術的差異，更重要的是訓練方法的不同。歐美學者盡量客觀地面對文本，細讀文本，深入解讀。往往就文本發展出不同的解讀方法，不大涉及其他非學術的因素。中國學者多留意——甚至專事於作者考訂、版本流傳等等非文本研究。中國學者有知人論世的傳統，但這個傳統的界線很難把握：不足，會被譏為隔靴搔癢；過之，難免脫離文本。價值判斷附著在學術研究之中，這是中國學者的學術研究一個非常明顯的特徵，這從行文表述中言必稱「××先生」可窺一斑。雖然有時只是一種慣例的尊重，但卻是一種情感傾向的下意識表達，這樣就很難做到對研究對象的客觀中立。

　　保陽這個看法不知道您怎麼看？

保陽　敬上
5/15/2020

孫康宜致李保陽

Dear Baoyang,

　　I really like this email from you, in which you have pointed out very perceptively the crucial differences between the Western and the Chinese methodology in studying literature. I'm especially pleased that your ideas are very much to the point（一針見血）!

　　As you said, the Western methodology (or we may say the "American" methodology) tends to emphasize close reading of the text, apart from our research on the author's personal background, political issues, etc. It does not mean that the

Western approach neglects the "personal" aspects of the author; it simply means that we should go BEYOND（超越）our biases in the process of doing literary analysis. For example, when we study Mao's works and his political impact (good or bad) on the Chinese people, we are expected to keep a distance and take a more or less objective view, so that readers would be convinced by our conclusion. And it's up to the readers to make their own judgment.（讓讀者自己決定他們個人的看法）。

For example, in 1972, before we knew anything about the terrible Cultural Revolution in China, there was a kind of hero-worship（英雄崇拜）of Mao in the US. And in my MA thesis, entitled "Carlyle's Literature of Heroism and Its Contemporary Model-Mao," I compared the 19th century British writer Thomas Carlyle's concept of "hero-worship" with the "hero-worship of Mao" in China. Nobody would think that I was a Maoist, simply because I chose this topic for my thesis. And the university which I attended then (namely South Dakota State University) approved of my MA thesis with the following words:

"This thesis is approved as a credible and independent investigation by a candidate for the degree, Master of Arts, and it is acceptable as meeting the thesis requirements for the degree, but without implying that the conclusions reached by the candidate are necessarily the conclusions of the major requirement."

Later Princeton University faculty loved my thesis and unanimously recommended me for the admission to the Ph.D. program at Princeton in 1973! What they liked about the thesis is the methodology I used to research the topic (the thesis was as long as 168 pages!), and in particular they appreciated the detailed close-readings I had done in my thesis. In general they approved the way I wrote in English, and the way I made a convincing argument throughout the thesis.

Of course, back in 1973 we did not yet know the many awful things Mao had done to the Chinese people. At that time I did not know that my grandfather had committed suicide due to the political pressure as early as 1953, and that my uncle and my aunt's family all suffered tremendous torture during the Cultural Revolution. Otherwise I would have got more materials to work with and might have reached a different conclusion. But at the time my MA thesis was viewed as an exceptional work, considering the fact that only limited materials were available then. The point is: nobody would call me a Maoist, just because of my MA thesis!

What I have tried to say is that the Western approach basically emphasizes an objective approach, which does not usually mix up the "person" with the person's "literary work." Although Mao might be an " evil" person, he was capable of writing good poetry at the same time. And we as literary critics should not ignore this reality.

Best,
Kang-i
5/15/2020

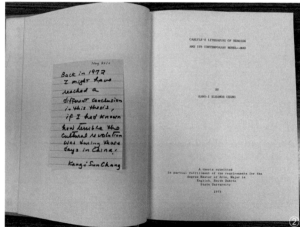

①孫康宜在南達科達州立大學獲得英國文學碩士（1972年，南達科他）
②孫康宜英國文學碩士學位論文（1972年）

孫康宜致張宏生、李保陽

Dear Hongsheng and Baoyang,

Ah, this chain of大眾傳媒 is really non-stop! As soon as I woke up this morning, I saw this wechat message from my Nanjing friend Tong Ling 童嶺regarding my 1979 picture with Prof. Yang Yi（楊苡）and others:

「哇喔！我保存下來，上大學時有機緣拜訪過楊先生……」

By the way, along with the 1979 picture, Tong Ling also sent me a picture of the book cover of Prof. Yang's legendary book of translation:《呼嘯山莊》. (See attached picture). That's of course a translation of the English classic novel, *Wuthering Heights,* written by Emily Bronte (1818-1848). Originally *Wuthering Heights* was published in 1847, under the pseudonym of Ellis Bell.

What is most amazing is that this book cover of《呼嘯山莊》suddenly brings back so many fond memories of my visit to the house of Yang Yi 楊苡 and Zhao Ruihong 趙瑞蕻 on that hot summer day in July, 1979. At this moment I can still recall that I was discussing the novel *Wuthering Heights* with Prof. Yang Yi 41 years ago, including questions regarding Emily Bronte's pseudonym Ellis Bell. For example, I asked Yang Yi: Why did the 19th century English woman writer Emily Bronte had to assume a male name for the publication of her novel, while Li Qingzhao李清照 (1084-ca. 1155) did not have to do that when she published her collections of poems as early as the 12th century? And of course, there were other topics we also discussed that day, including questions regarding kunqu 崑曲。I particularly remember how beautiful Prof. Wu Xinlei's 吳新雷 flute performance of kunqu was during that wonderful gathering.

Anyway, the popular media 大眾傳媒 is so incredibly powerful. It brings back my vivid memories of events more than 40 years ago!

Best,

Kang-i

5/15/2020

Line訊息

孫：As you can see, 林玫儀 just visited the Tunghai exhibition。

李：好親切。謝謝孫老師分享。現在初稿已經編輯了大約全部百分之二十的工作量。草稿先編出來，然後再刪潤二稿。二稿結束就可以呈您過目了。

孫：You are just amazing! I'm so impressed with you! I'll write a preface, and you will write a preface too!

李：是的。

孫：I can't believe it! I have already known you so well. But I have never met you in person, and you only started to write to me (as a stranger) in mid-March! And I did not respond to you until March 29. That was only one and a half months ago. And all of this happened during the time of the COVID 19 pandemic!

李：一切都是　神的帶領！感謝主！

孫：I have a question about 卷2. On page 397, you raised a question about this sentence: 設詎鋪主人設正欲走避郊. Actually I did double check the *Complete Works of Shi Zhecun*（《施蟄存全集》），and I can confirm that his diary《西行日記》 also contained the same problematic sentence. What should we do?

林玫儀致孫康宜

　　展覽很棒，除了展出的材料本身是無價寶，主辦單位的用心也隨處可見，他們將伯父和你的大事年表及著作製成看板，提綱挈領，配合桌上陳列的著作，讓觀眾很容易就能進入情境，了解每本書寫作的背景及大致的內容（你的著作量太

驚人了吧！）又製作了幾個音像檔，掃描以後，可以回去慢慢欣賞品味。展出伯父的墨寶時，又特別輯出他的印譜，此外，還把古早時代圖書館卡片中登錄你的大學論文那一張連同卡片櫃一起展出，令人回味無窮。（哈哈，年輕人恐怕看不懂吧！）總之，規模雖然不是很大，卻很有深度，真的很難得。

今天是收穫豐碩而又美好的一天，很謝謝王小姊熱忱接待，細心招呼導覽，幫我照相，還帶我去看你當年沉浸在書堆中的舊圖書館。他們的組長也來致意，主辦單位真的很熱心，只是太麻煩他們了，讓我很不好意思。（我本來想悄悄的去，靜靜看完就走，誰知防疫時期，不透過他們還進不去，終歸還是給他們添麻煩了。）

張宏生致孫康宜

康宜：

這個由一張照片引發的微信傳遞潮，至今餘波不息，不斷有新鮮的內容，令人感到奇妙之餘，也不免懸想，在這個傳播鏈上，還會帶來什麼驚喜。事實上，有意無意之間，一些記憶深處的情思已經被觸發出來，四十一年前的現場也更加清晰。這些在相同的時間、不同的空間所彙聚到一起的資訊，一起通向當事人的同時，也創造了新的想像。期待康宜能夠寫出一篇散文，記下這件發生在2020年5月的有趣的事情。不一一。

宏生
5/15/2020

陳國球致孫康宜

Dear Kang-i Laoshi,

Attached is a slightly revised version. Thanks for your comments and reminding me of the errors.

Professor Ji Jin comes to me for the draft. I sent this new version to him just now. I would expect him to offer me criticism and advice.

I am glad to have friends helping me to better the essay. As I have said, the writing process is indeed tough, though I find the ordeal rewarding.

Best,

Guoqiu
5/16/2020

孫康宜致陳國球

Dear Guoqiu,

Thank you for sending along this revised version of your article about Prof Kao Yu-kung 高友工! I copy Li Baoyang on this email so that he will also have an updated version of your piece.

I also cc my dear friend Prof Lin Shuen-Fu 林順夫 here. I know he will be very happy to read this article by you! Shuen-fu, whom you have mentioned on page 1 of your essay, was the first PhD student mentored by Prof Kao.

Kang-i
5/16/2020

Line訊息

李：孫老師，現在書稿編到牟復禮先生的部分了。5月7日您寫給保陽了好幾封信，關於余英時、夏志清、牟復禮等先生的內容。還有許多珍貴的歷史照片。這部分內容記錄了美國漢學研究的一段輝煌的歷史！

孫：Yes! For 卷1，p. 82, I have just added the English name of 宣立敦: Richard Strassberg. 他也是高友工教授的學生，是我的先後同學！

李：宣立敦會唱崑曲，藝事多能，是個了不起的學者。

孫：Yes!

李：他現在哪裡教書呢？

孫：He taught at UCLA and has already retired. 加州大學洛杉磯分校！已退休！

李：好厲害的一個人。我去過加州大學的鵝灣分校，那裡圖書館的中文藏書也很豐富。

孫：Yes!

李：孫老師，保陽晚上讀孟振華先生的耶魯古籍書目序，在了解裘開明中文編目法時，看到下面這本書（圖略，指張鳳《哈佛問學》），這位作者應該就是您的朋友張鳳了？

孫：Yes.

李：晚上讀孟先生的書目序言，對耶魯的中文古籍藏書歷史有了粗略的了解。

孫：Great!

李：保陽三月分通讀了Gest善本書志，獲益良多，相信讀了孟先生的書目全文，一定也會學到不少知識。

孫：Yes!

李：耶魯圖書館有系統收藏家族文獻資料的傳統。所以您捐贈的令尊和您的文獻，也是在紹述這一傳統。

孫：Absolutely! Please see my email! I just sent you a revised version of my article, 〈我的姑姑〉！

李：保陽十年前在浙江大學圖書館古籍部工作，當時建議部門主管向館長建議，專門徵集、收藏、展覽、借閱本校退休尤其是過世教授的藏書，但沒有下文。2012年吳熊和教授過世，藏書星散，很可惜。這是一部吳先生的舊藏（圖略，指吳熊和批註本《文心雕龍》）。吳師母在吳先生故去後，把這套書送給了保陽。前年去國，帶著來到了美國。那些批註大約作於上世紀六十年代。

孫：Amazing!

李保陽致孫康宜

孫老師，

接讀此詞，心實不忍！

目睹中美兩國疫情先後席捲，普通黎庶，無辜遭尤，實在不忍心以遊戲心態表而出之！此刻對普通人的同情和悲憫，勝過一切！

保陽每載內子去幾十里外採購食物，看到停車場上、商場內外的普通人，一律戴口罩自保，心裡有種說不出的難過。這是一個幾百年來生性自由的民族，現在卻不得不為了保命而把自己遮藏起來，放棄自由，禁足在家！

年初當中國疫情流行的時候，看到網上有人「喪事喜辦」，為了營造所謂「和諧」氣氛，氣得我不知道說什麼好！後來風向一轉，舉國封城、封村，甚至網上流傳有照片：村民手執紅纓槍，嚴格盤查出入村民，檢查所謂「健康碼」，不禁讓人想起八十年前中日戰爭期間的「良民證」。是本該可以避免的大災難，最後都落在了普通民眾頭上。當時亦有兩詩紀事云：

庚子神州不太平，今年處處變孤城。
豬瘟未遠豬頭在，華夏當真病不輕。

神州再現紅櫻槍，八十年前舊武裝。
舉國封城又封口，人人都是待烹羊。

當時這兩首詩中滿含了義憤。而今目擊新大陸民眾心驚膽戰的日常，則全然是悲憫和難過!!竟無一字能出之筆下!!!

保陽

5/17/202

註：此信乃就網路流傳之一首謔詞而發。其詞云：「新冠肺炎何時了。患者知多少。小城昨夜又被封。京城不堪回首月明中。口罩酒精應猶在。只是不好買。問君還有幾多愁。最怕發燒確診被扣留。」

孫康宜致李保陽

Dear Baoyang,

　　Thank you for your thoughts on the COVID-19 issue, as a response to the Chinese poem which I forwarded to you earlier today.

　　Actually I meant to share with you Rev. Ian Oliver's commencement Sunday sermon at Yale this morning:

> https://m.youtube.com/watch?v=NgVpIzmwwJQ&from=singlemessage&feature=youtu.be&isappinstalled=0

　　Rev. Ian Oliver's point is that the COVID-19 crisis should not be treated as a disaster; instead he has noticed the great strength shown by the American people during this difficult time. Thus, he calls the graduating class of 2020 the "overcoming class," the class which overcame all sorts of difficulties. In other words, the 2020 class is one which "turns disaster into possibilities."

　　Rev.Ian Oliver also reminds us that as Christians we should bear in mind that we are not going through this all by ourselves. Jesus has promised us that, with the help from the Holy Spirit, we are never alone!

　　Hope you will enjoy Rev. Ian Oliver's sermon!

Best,
Kang-i Sun Chang（孫康宜）
5/17/2020

孫康宜致李保陽

Dear Baoyang,

I'm sorry that due to my full-time teaching responsibilities at Yale, especially during this very difficult time of the COVID-19 pandemic, it has taken me such a long time to reply to several of your earlier emails.

Here is my reply to your May 4th email (with the subject line: 保陽：關於余國藩）. One of the questions you have raised in your email is: Did Anthony (Tony) Yu ever publish his classical-style Chinese poems in a collection?（余先生的詩詞有結集出版嗎？）

First of all, I don't think Tony Yu had his Chinese poems published in any collections. Writing Chinese poetry in the classical form was just his hobby, and he loved to share his poems with friends in a casual way. To this day, I still keep many of his spontaneous poems, which he sent to me via his emails. For example, I am sending you a *ci* poem, "Zhe gu tian 鷓鴣天, " which Tony wrote in July 2011, after he had finished the revised version of his complete translation of the Chinese novel *Xi you ji*（《西遊記》）. Please see attached.（請見附件）。

I thought you would be interested in seeing his autograph（簽名題字）for me and CC in his 4-volume set of *The Journey to the West*. The set came out from the University of Chicago Press in 2012, and he kindly gave us a copy in 2013. (Please see attached picture). Tony passed away in Spring 2015 due to heart failure, and needless to say we have missed him very much.

The other question raised in your 5/4 letter is: Who else in America are also writing classical-style Chinese poetry?（您知道在美國的其他學者，誰還作舊體詩嗎？）

Of course there are numerous other scholars in the US who are still writing class-style Chinese poetry. The ones who shared their poems with me include people like Yu Ying-shih 余英時 and Chow Tse-tsung 周策蹤（who passed away several years ago）. And among the younger writers, there are also my Yale colleagues Kang Zhengguo 康正果 and Su Wei 蘇煒.

I hope this email clarifies things for you.

Best,
Kang-i
5/17/2020

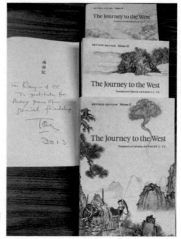

余國藩教授贈送給孫康宜夫婦的
《西遊記》英譯本（2013年）

Line訊息

孫：Amazing, a Chinese American graduating senior Joy Qiu represents the Yale class of 2020! I'm so proud of her! Sorry ! I meant she was one of the representatives of the graduating class of 2020. She talked about COVID 19.

The following is Lin Meiyi's林玫儀response to Rev Ian Oliver's Commencement sermon：「這一屆畢業生受到史無前例的衝擊，這麼特殊的畢業儀式，勢必會讓他們終身難忘。疫情中的畢業禮拜好溫馨喔，相信這麼懇切的勉勵教導和誠摯的禱告，必會深深觸動這些年輕學子的心，在他們踏上人生另一段旅程時，成為重要的指引。」

李：是的。百年一遇的艱困時期，對這一屆學子來講，真是終身難忘。保陽今年也有一屆學生畢業。前幾天學生論文答辯，保陽為賦詩一首鼓勵之。

嶺南鳳凰花開，學子答辯季也。今年疫情蔓延，諸生只能網路答辯，亦四年大學生涯之尤可紀念者。吟此一首，為諸生明日答辯壯色。

流溪四載曾同窗，五月南芳歲月長。

同學少年方意氣，鳳凰花下論文章。

　　保陽教書的地方附近有一條河叫流溪，珠江支流之一。南芳湖，校內一湖泊。嶺南鳳凰花五六月開，畢業季也。讓人想起古人的「槐花黃，舉子忙」。

孫：Wow, wonderful poems!

孫：I have a question to ask you! Is that on Nassau street in Princeton? Please see my email!

李：是的。是Nassau St.

孫：You see? I remember everything!

李：孫老師記憶力超人，哈哈~我們一家每次去普大都必去那家書店的。

孫：I think that bookstore is new! But I remember the street!

李：應該是您離開普大以後開的，已經快四十年了。

孫：Yes!

林順夫致孫康宜

Dear Kang-i,

　　Thank you so much for sending me a cc of your communication with Professor Chen Guoqiu and Dr. Li Baoyang, with Professor Chen's article on our beloved teacher attached. I enjoyed reading (and learned a lot from) Professor Chen's excellent article. I have caught several typos and added a brief "comment" (on the three sons of Mr. Kao Hsi-ping). I used "Tracking Changes" to correct the typos and add the comment. You and Professor Chen should be able to locate the changes and comment without difficulty. Once the article appears in print, would Professor Chen be so kind as to send me a PDF of it?

　　Please stay well and keep healthy!

Shuen-fu
5/17/2020

林順夫致陳國球

Dear Professor Chen,

Thank you so much for letting me know where your article will be published, and for your willingness to send me a PDF copy when it appears in print. I greatly appreciate (and admire) your effort in going over all the important sources of Kao Yu-kung's (and Mei Tsu-lin's) scholarly works. I cannot think of many people who are equipped to do this onerous task. Most of the information in your article about Kao Yu-kung's family is new to me too. I look forward to having it later in the year.

With best regards,

Shuen-fu
5/17/2020

陳國球致林順夫

Dear Lin Laoshi,

Many thanks for your comments and correcting my (many) errors. The information you provided is indeed very helpful. The paper has been amended accordingly.

It is a contribution to a book collection which will, hopefully, be published in Taiwan later this year.

For sure I will send a pdf copy to you and all the friends whom I owe a debt of gratitude.

Warm regards,

Guoqiu
5/17/2020

孫康宜致李保陽

Dear Baoyang,

My belated reply to your 4/22 letter which I have read with the greatest enjoyment! It means a lot to me that you are also very familiar with Princeton, a place which C.C. and I started our life as immigrants to the US more than half a century ago.

To answer you question regarding the exact place of our wedding（"但不知道您和CC先生是在那裡結婚的"）, I'm sending you two memorable pictures here. (Please see pictures attached). The first picture was taken on August 3, 1968, only a few minutes after CC and I had our wedding ceremony at the Princeton University Chapel. In those days people were not allowed to take pictures inside the chapel (not even for weddings!). That's why our wedding pictures were taken outside the chapel. As you can see from the picture, C. C. and I were standing between Princeton University Chapel and Firestone Library.

The second picture was taken at Princeton University Chapel on March 11, 2017. I remember that on that day visitors were not permitted to visit the chapel. But after we explained to the gate-keeper that "we were married at the Princeton University Chapel 49 years ago," he gave us a special permission to go in. He even took a picture of us inside the chapel.

I should mention that it was also on that particular day--i.e., March 11, 2017-- that we attended my mentor Prof. Kao Yu-kung's memorial service（高友工教授追思會）at Jones Hall, which is the headquarter of the East Asian Studies Department. As you may remember, I have already sent you a copy of the Memorial service program, which I designed for the occasion.

Anyway, your 4/22 email has brought back so many fond memories of Princeton.

Kang-i

5/18/2020

孫康宜致李保陽

Dear Baoyang,

I was very happy to find a copy of this letter addressed to Prof. Mote back in January 1992. That was 28 years ago.

The background for this letter is quite interesting: Apparently Prof. Mote had solicited an English article from me for the *Gest Library Journal*（《葛斯德圖書館雜誌》）, and in this letter I was reporting to him about the progress of my paper. I later submitted the paper to Prof. Mote on time, and it was entitled: "Ming and Qing Anthologies of Women's Poetry and Their Selection Strategies," which appeared in the *Gest Library Journal,* 5, no. 2 (1992), pages 119-160.

Later a Chinese translation of the article was done by Mr Ma Yao-ming, and it appeared in 《中外文學》，1994年，7月號。

As you can see, the Chinese translation can now be found in 《孫康宜文集》，卷5，附錄2：《明清女士人選集及其採輯策略》。"

Hope you will find this background information helpful.

Best,
Kang-i
5/18/2020

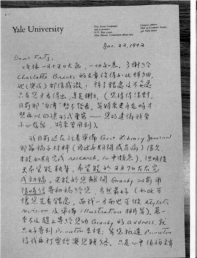
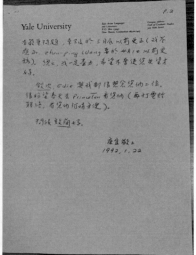

孫康宜致牟復禮信（1992年1月）

李保陽致孫康宜

孫老師，

　　這種憶舊類的文字非常好。碎片往往真實，碎片聯綴起來就是歷史了！我
們多收集，把它們印出來，就是文獻！就是歷史！一份海外學術史、華人史的紀
錄。我們能做多少就做多少！勝過讓其湮滅於荒煙蔓草間！

　　謝謝您！謝謝林教授！

保陽

5/18/2020

李保陽致孫康宜

孫老師，

　　您分享的1992年初寫給牟先生的信和關於該信的背景，十分的有意思。像這
樣有趣的故事，有圖有文有背景，就是最好的談論內容。希望我們的書中能夠多
多包括這樣的內容最好了。

　　您每天晚睡早起，這樣不利於牙齒恢復。希望您保重身體。並問CC先生
好！

保陽　敬上

5/18/2020

孫康宜致李保陽

Dear BAOYANG,

　　I'm so glad that you like the background information which I have provided for my 1992 letter addressed to Prof Mote.

　　By the way, as to Prof Mote's letters for me, there were quite a few of them! But I have already donated them to National Central Library 國家圖書館 in Taipei.

　　The Yale curator Michael Meng 孟振華 was the one who presented all my donations to the National Central Library on November 22, 2019.

Best,
Kang-i
5/18/2020

C. C. Chang（張欽次）致李保陽

Dear Baoyang,

　　This is C.C., Kang-i's better half.

　　I noticed you had sent to Kang-i a picture taken from Nassau Street in Princeton showing the Princeton University Store. Actually Princeton University rented this place since several years ago. The location of the store used to be the Woolworth Departmental Store while I was a student there more than 50 years ago. So, I would like to share with you the Woolworth link here, as it shows the icon of the store in the old days.

C.C.
5/18/2020

李保陽致C. C. Chang（張欽次）

欽次先生，

　　您好！

　　很高興收到您的來信，謝謝您詳細介紹Nassau street上Labyrinth Bookstore前世今生的故事。保陽相信，四十多年後，再次看到您和孫老師的母校街景，你們一定會有種熟悉的感覺。我們家離Princeton兩個小時不到，週末的時候我們經常帶孩子去那裡看書，我們全家都喜歡Princeton的安靜和書卷氣息。在美國，有很多小城鎮，教堂，甚至一棟房子，都有它們迷人的歷史和故事，相信Princeton更不會例外。你們是「老普林斯頓」。如果你們方便，保陽希望能聽到你們講更多有關Princeton的故事。專此，並候

　　夏安！

晚　保陽　敬上

5/18/2020

Line訊息

孫：我這兒有點忙不過來，正在給研究生打分數，日夜趕工，怕忙出病來！By the way, another main topic is about Princeton 普林斯頓, even if some emails about the topic are not scholarly! This is because our initial correspondence starts with information about Gest Library, Andy Plaks, etc! Even things like our 1968 Wedding at the Princeton chapel, Nassau Street, the Abraham statue, etc. would be fun! What do you think?

李：孫老師，請您保重身體，不要太過於勞累。您的這個建議太好了。您和欽次先生是「老普林斯頓」，如果談起普林斯頓的掌故來，一定更有趣。可以增加這本書的可讀性。您如果忙，可以讓欽次先生回信。保陽剛剛讀完欽次先生有關Nassau street書店的歷史，非常有趣，保陽正在給欽次先生寫回信。

孫：Wow that's great!

李：孫老師，看到保陽同學發來的信息。他睹物思人，想起十多年前我們的讀書、買書舊事。讀書愛書，至今不倦！

孫：It's true! It's rare to find young people who still love books like you do!

李：保陽的藏書在2017年達到峰值，浙江、漢中、西安三處，有一萬多冊。2017年初，內子和保陽岳母先後因病住院，那時候保陽正在廣州讀書，經濟困難，賣掉了一些。2017年暑假，把三處聚合到浙江，委託鐵路公司運輸，裝了三個鐵殼集裝箱。

孫：Wow, incredible!

李：所以您當時捐贈八千冊書給北大，海運往北京，保陽完全能想見到那個規模和場景。

孫：Actually there were more than 8,500 volumes!

李：剛剛瀏覽了您的捐贈目錄，確實是一筆寶貴的文獻資料。學者的藏書能夠保存在一處，其本身就是一種學術思想的傳承與彰顯。中國歷史上那些希望「子孫永寶」者，最後都煙消雲散了，就連傳承規矩嚴格的天一閣都不能倖免，所以還是集中捐贈給學術機構，是最妥善的辦法。

林順夫致孫康宜

Dear Kang-i,

I did meet Professor Kao's parents, but not in Taichung, and only once and very briefly. I know that they immigrated to the US in 1973, but they visited their son in Princeton sometime in 1969 or 1970. I don't remember the exact year and month they visited Princeton. I do remember, however, one day I was reading at a desk in Gest Library (which was still in Firestone Library then), when Professor Kao introduced his parents to me. His parents were very amiable and said to me "Yu-kung had spoken well about you to us!" They must have just visited Professor Mote in his office which was also located in Gest.

All the best,

Shuen-fu

5/18/2020

註：此信有部分刪節。

萩原正樹致李保陽

李保陽先生：

　　道鑒

　　非常感謝你的來信和孫康宜先生的文章。孫康宜先生是《劍橋中國文學史》的作者吧？我從來不知道她來過日本京都、奈良等地方。她的文章飽含對日本文學的感情和瞭解，真的讓我很感動。非常感謝你特意把孫康宜先生的文章寄給我。

　　以前你寄給我的兩篇玉稿之一〈康樂園讀詞箚記（一）〉，日本一般的讀者不太習慣這樣箚記形式的論文，我覺得，在日本發表比較困難吧。還有一篇關於梁啟超的玉稿，我會推薦給其他日本學術雜誌上發表，請你等一下為幸。

　　你有沒有FaceBook的ID？有的話，一定方便於聯絡，請分享給我為幸。謝謝。

　　日本最近新型冠狀肺炎很厲害，我們大學已採用了網路授課的方式。但是這個方式太麻煩，我因為網路上課而痛苦呢。哈！

5/18/2020

弟　萩原正樹　敬上

孫康宜致李保陽

Dear BAOYANG,

This is a special report about my brother KC Sun 孫康成 and my other relatives' visit to the Tunghai exhibition! It's most amazing that Tunghai University would spend this extra effort to glorify the Sun family in publishing this announcement! I'm deeply grateful to Wang Ya-ping 王雅萍 for everything she has done for the Sun Family. Indeed, this is about 陽光穿透的歲月！

Best,

Kang-i

5/19/2020

①孫氏家族參觀東海大學「陽光穿透的歲月」書展（2020年，臺中）
②孫康成在「陽光穿透的歲月」書展上演講（2020年，臺中）
③孫康宜送給東海大學的禮物，感謝母校在COVID-19期間籌辦「陽光穿透的歲月」書展（2020年，臺中）

孫康宜致李保陽

Dear BAOYANG,

Have you ever come across a place in China called 望娘灘?

Please see email exchanges below!

Kang-i

5/19/2020

李保陽致孫康宜

孫老師，

保陽沒有關注過「望娘灘」的傳說。剛才在網上搜索了一下，那些資訊 Denise可以在網上搜尋得到。保陽可以向四川籍的朋友請教一下，如果他們有回覆，保陽會聯繫您。

保陽　敬上

5/19/2020

孫康宜致嚴志雄

Dear Chi-hung（志雄）：

First of all, I'm so happy to be reconnected with you recently via wechat! Thank you for telling me the good news that a Japanese edition of your award-winning book, 《錢謙益〈病榻消寒雜詠〉論釋》, will be published soon in Japan! I'm so proud of you!

In fact, our EALL website posted a congratulation note on your book, 《錢謙益

〈病榻消寒雜詠〉論釋》, when your book first won an award: "*Qian Qianyi "Bingta xiaohan zayong" Lunxi* (A Study of Qian Qianyi's "Forty-six Miscellaneous Poems to Dispel Cold on My Sickbed"), by Dr. Lawrence Yim, is a study of the last poem series, 'The Sickbed Poems',of the great scholar-poet Qian Qianyi (1582-1664) of the Ming-Qing dynastic transition. It breaks new ground in Qian Qianyi studies and Qing poetry studies. The book is based on meticulous research, attention to detail, and careful close-readings of the related poems and texts, therefore the discussions are well-grounded, balanced, and comprehensive. 'The Sickbed Poems' by Qian are of great literary and biographical value, and this is the first book to offer a comprehensive and exhaustive interpretation of the poem series."

Thank you also for letting me know that you have assigned my chapter on Tao Qian 陶潛 to your class, and I'm very grateful to you for your kind words: "By the way, my class on 陶潛 is just finished this year. I asked all of my students to do presentations on Shizu's 師祖（i.e., your）六朝詩 book in relation to 陶公. They learned so much from your book and this will change them forever!"

What you have said means a lot to me.

By the way, just in case your students are interested, I attach here a copy of my other article on Tao Qian, which is entitled, "Unmasking of Tao Qian and the Indeterminacy of Interpretation." This article is from the book, *Chinese Aesthetics* (2004), edited by Prof. Cai Zongqi（蔡宗齊教授）. As you know, Prof. Cai Zongqi was also a student of Prof. Kao Yu-kung高友工教授（my mentor）.

Best,
Kang-i
5/19/2020

註：此信略有刪節及訂正。

李保陽致萩原正樹

萩原先生教席，

　　謝謝　先生的回信。現在日本疫情也在擴散中，希望您和家人注意安全，保重身體！

　　這位孫康宜教授，正是《劍橋中國文學史》的主編者。保陽最近在和孫教授合編一本有趣的書：《避疫書信選：從抱月樓到潛學齋》。這本書選擇了一部分我們最近的通信，內容大多數是討論學術的，也包括一些學者朋友的來信。我們出版這本書，為海外漢學研究和這個特殊艱困的時期，留一點紀念。孫教授2014年曾經出版過一本《從北山樓到潛學齋》的書，收錄了她和施蟄存先生的通信。我們這本新書，也有繼承和紀念施先生的意思。

　　謝謝　先生一直以來對保陽的鼓勵和提攜。　先生在年初介紹保陽加入貴國詞曲學會，這是保陽今年在美國學術工作的一個良好的開端，謝謝！前呈拙作，　先生方便的時候推薦給合適的刊物即可，不必刻意為此事煩惱。

　　今年的疫情席捲全球，給所有人都帶來了工作和生活上的不方便。全美國現在的學校都已經關閉，採用網路授課的方式。保陽的孩子們也都在家裡接受學校提供的網路教學。孫康宜教授在耶魯大學開始使用網路授課的時候，也倍感麻煩和不便，不過她很快就適應了這種新的教學方式，相信您很快也能適應這種授課新方式。

　　疫情洶洶，請多多保重！專此，並頌
　　諸安！

保陽　敬上

5/19/2020

Line訊息

孫：Wow, we talked for more than one hour on the phone!

李：謝謝孫老師。所說五件事情保陽都記下了，請放心。您把秀威的《從北山樓
　　到潛學齋》的文件先給保陽。

孫：But I already forwarded the 秀威一校稿 to you early this morning! Have you
　　received it? The subject heading of my email is: 保陽，請幫忙，謝謝！Maybe I
　　should send it again to you!

孫康宜致李保陽

Dear Baoyang,

　　Luke Yang is a Canadian Chinese and is currently a PhD candidate at Stanford
University. He was one of my M.A. students at Yale before going to Stanford University
for his doctorate.

　　He is one of the numerous students of mine who sent greetings to me during this
period of the COVID-19 pandemic.

Kang-i

5/20/2020

李保陽致孫康宜

孫老師，

　　看到您的高足寄給您的賀卡和口罩了，值此艱困之時，真是一個特別的紀
念。收到學生不遠萬里寄來的禮物，作為老師，您應該倍覺溫暖和欣慰。真替您
高興。謝謝您分享這份溫暖和喜悅給保陽！

　　猶記2017年秋，保陽造訪史丹佛大學，在其東亞館書庫的書架之間蹲了一整
天，發現了不少有趣的書，其中有一冊清代後期滿洲人的詩稿，當是藁本。一直
想寫一篇文章，奈何2017年從美國回去，就獲得了一個意外的兼任教職，就一邊

教書，一邊緊張地撰寫畢業論文。次年更是教書、準備上半年畢業，下半年又出乎意外來美。一直到今天，從史丹佛發現的那本書還躺在電腦裡，每一想起，有種對不住史丹佛東亞館讓保陽單獨在書庫蹲了一整天的優待。希望不久的將來能有機會寫出來。

保陽　敬上
5/20/2020

孫康宜致李保陽

Dear Baoyang,

I wish to let you know that my former student Haun Saussy also took courses from Yu Ying-shih（余英時）during the 1980s when Prof. Yu was still teaching at Yale. It was probably during the years 1985-1986.

So this is just a footnote to both Haun Saussy and Yu Ying-shih.

Kang-i
5/20/2020

孫康宜致李保陽

Dear Baoyang,

Please see attached a piece of calligraphy by Chi-hung Yim's嚴志雄former teacher Prof. Chang Zonghao常宗豪. It was presented to me as a gift during the 1990s.

Please see also Chi-hung's note for the background information.

Earlier this semester I did share with my *ci* class this beautiful piece of "集句" written by Prof. Chang Zonghao . As you know, the line "更能消幾番風雨" has come

from the poet Xin Qiji's 辛棄疾 ci poem, "Mo yu er" 摸魚兒. And the line "樹猶如此"
is drawn from Xin Qiji's other ci poem, "Shui long yin" 水龍吟. My students love the
ci songs by Xin Qiji very much.

By the way, I have already donated this item to the National Central Library（國
家圖書館）in Taiwan. I hope that more people will have the chance to enjoy Prof.
Chang Zonghao's calligraphy in the future.

Best,
Kang-i
5/20/2020

常宗豪贈送孫康宜的書法作品

孫康宜致李保陽

Dear Baoyang,

This is my correspondence with my former student Qian Nanxiu, who is now
Professor of Chinese Literature in the School of Humanities at Rice University. She
came to study in our Ph.D. program in 1987, and after she got her Ph.D. from Yale, she
directly went to Rice University to teach. Nanxiu's dissertation was on Shishuo Xinyu
《世說新語》 and its reception.

Nanxiu was one of the lucky students from mainland China in those years. She
graduated from Nanjing University before coming to the States as a Visiting Scholar,

and before applying to Yale.

Nanxiu's younger brother is the famous painter Qian Dajing 錢大經, who had his gallery in New York City for many years before returning to China. As you may remember, a few days ago I already sent you a picture of my portrait done by Qian Dajing. It's amazing that back in 2001 Qian Dajing did my portrait merely based on a picture of mine! He did not meet me in person until a few years later.

Best,
Kang-i
5/20/2020

錢大經為孫康宜創作的油畫肖像（2001年）

孫康宜致李保陽

Dear Baoyang,

I'm forwarding my correspondence between my former student Mary Ellen Friends and myself during this COVID-19 period.

First of all, I want to let you know that Mary Ellen Friends, who has been teaching at the History Department of the famous Deerfield High School, first became my graduate student during the early 1990s. She passed her Ph.D. qualifying exam as early as 1993, and she accepted a teaching position at Deerfield right after the exam.

Over the past two decades Mary Ellen was busy building up her busy career as well as raising a family, and so she did not officially receive her Ph.D. degree from Yale University until May 2019. (I think I have already sent you a copy of her graduation picture with me.) Her dissertation topic was about the myth of the Double Seventh（七夕）.

You will be interested to know that Mary Ellen appears quite often in the book,《從北山樓到潛學齋》，but she used her maiden name Kivlen in those days. She also communicated with Shi Zhecun 施蟄存 from time to time during the 1990s.

After Mary Ellen got married, she changed her last name to Friends, following her husband's family name.

Best,
Kang-i
5/20/2020

李保陽致孫康宜

孫老師，

剛剛讀《北山樓》到施先生1992年5月20日、7月16日寫給您的兩封信，信中因提到紀曉蘭女士，應該就是這位Mary Ellen。施先生因為Mary Ellen翻譯自己《唐詩百話》，進而談到「中國詩的各個名詞，必須有一個統一的譯名」。保陽當日就是讀到這一句，才一個閃念，開始著手編製《文集》的英文索引。當時是為了自己能了解西方批評術語的英文表達，沒有考慮到我看到的中文，已是經過各位不同譯者的轉述了，未必建立在您原來基礎上之意義了。這樣一來，具體英文術語特定的上下文意義不易判斷；另一方面，這樣的翻譯，未必代表您的觀點。保陽以為，這些西方名詞術語，還是經您親自認可之後，較為穩妥。所以您今天下午談到的「索引」處理方式，保陽覺得很好。我們並無建立一套中西批評術語標準的雄心，但是如能藉這個索引，讓有興趣的讀者，對西方批評理論表達語言有一個粗略的認識，這就是簡體本在中文世界的一個獨特貢獻了。

孫康宜致陳國球、林順夫

Dear Guoqiu and Shuen-fu,

　　Many thanks to Shuen-fu for contributing so much valuable information about Prof. Kao. I did not realize that Shuen-fu had actually met Kao's parents in person.

　　I think I should also use this opportunity to provide more information about Prof. Kao:

（1）First of all, on October 17, 2018, Prof. Kao's ashes were buried in the Oakwood Cemetery at University of Syracuse. (In a shared plot with his mother, Chung-Huang Tang Kao)

（2）In the fall of 2018, I helped the Kao family (actually Kao's sister Chun-juan Kao Wang's family) to donate Prof. Kao's last collection of books (roughly 300 copies of books) to Wesleyan University in Connecticut. At that time I had a special ink stamp made (with the inscription, "Memory of Prof. Kao Yu-kung"), and my Yale student Ling Chao 凌超 helped me put the stamp on each book before the 300 books were shipped to Weslyan University.

（3）On Nov. 16, 2016, soon after Prof. Kao died, Princeton University displayed a half-mast flag in honor of Prof. Kao's contribution to the university. (I attach a picture of the half-mast flag here for your reference).

（4）Please see attached a most memorable picture of the Kao family taken in Shenyang 瀋陽 way back in 1932.

（5）I feel that somewhere in his article, Guoqiu should mention Kao's sister Chun-juan Kao Wang. It was Chun's son and her two daughters who took care of the burial of Prof. Kao and managed to deal with the legal side of Prof. Kao's belongings. I'm sure Shuen-fu still remembers meeting Chun and her family at Prof. Kao's memorial Service in Princeton in March 2017.

Hope the information is useful!

Kang-i

5/20/2020

①左一：高友工的姊姊高筠若（Chun
-juan Kao Wang），右二：高友工
（三歲）。（照片由Andrew Wang
提供）

②普林斯頓大學為高友工逝世降半旗
（2016年11月，普林斯頓）

③張欽次（C.C. Chang）與高友工教
授在紐約街頭合影（2008年，孫康
宜攝）

孫康宜致Luke Yang

Dear Luke,

What a wonderful card & note you have just sent me! I am also very grateful to you for sending me such a wonderful box of facial masks. You are always so thoughtful!

Your note is extremely inspiring to me especially during this difficult time of the COVID-19 pandemic: "The battle against COVID-19 has turned into a new normal, which has changed and will continue to reshape our lives in the years to come. . . ."

I'm also very impressed with your Japanese! I really look forward to your visit to Yale campus again soon!

I like your term, "a new normal," a lot. Yes, I have been trying to adjust myself to this "new normal." At age 76 I'm surprised how smooth this transition is for me.

Thank you again, and let's all stay safe.

Best,
Kang-i
5/20/2020

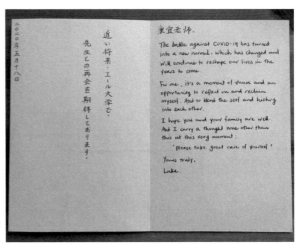

美國疫情最嚴重的時候，學生Luke Yang
寄給孫康宜的卡片（2020年5月）

陳國球致孫康宜

Dear Kang-i Laoshi,

Very glad to know more about Prof Kao Yu-kung and see the picture of the Kao Brothers and family.

Before I wrote the essay, I know nearly nothing about the Kao family, although I started reading Prof Kao's critical works for more than 40 years, ever since I was an undergrad student at the University of Hong Kong.

To write this essay, I have to gather every piece of information and try my best to make sense of it (that means I did a lot of wild speculation). I am so happy to confirm/correct a great part of the speculation with the help from Lin Laoshi and you.

I will try to add a note about Professor Kao's sister in the essay, but I would like to know the Chinese name of hers.

Thank you once again,

Guoqiu

5/20/2020

註：此信有部分刪節。

陳國球致孫康宜

Dear Kang-i Laoshi,

Thanks for sending me your Tao Yuanming article and news of Yim's Japanese edition of his book. I feel also honored because I was one of the reviewers of his manuscript for its first publication by Academia Sinica.

I enjoy very much in reading your refreshing article on Tao Yuanming, and I am going to share it to my friends and students if allowed.

Best,

Guoqiu

(p.s. I attached a very small piece of writing about the debate between Zhu Guangqian and Lu Xun on Tao, which is also mentioned at the end of your paper.)

5/21/2020

孫康宜致陳國球

Dear Guoqiu,

　　Thank you for letting me know that you have found my article on Tao Yuanming interesting.

　　Actually some years ago I already read your 導論 to the book, 《抒情之現代性：「抒情傳統」論述與中國文學研究》, with the greatest enjoyment and admiration. Indeed I was very interested in what you said about the debates between Zhu Guangqian and Lu Xun.

　　You probably forgot that you did send me a copy of this amazing book, 《抒情之現代性：「抒情傳統」論述與中國文學研究》, as a new year's gift in January 2015. Your inscription reads: "康宜老師誨正，晚國球敬奉，壹伍年元旦".

　　Anyway, you have been so kind to me all these years!

Best,

Kang-i

5/21/2020

František Reismuller致孫康宜

Dear professor,

I am doing some last editing in the text of the translation and there is one thing unclear to me. In Chapter 14 (Victioms on both shores) you write that "Grandfather wanted my dad to take the Boxer Indemnity scholarship exam. Dad placed first in the exam and then went to study abroad in Japan."（in Chinese edition:爺爺要我爸爸去考庚款留學，爸爸考取第一名，就留學日本去了）.

This is a little unclear to me, since the Boxer Indemnity Scholarship, as far as I know, was meant for studying in the U.S. (and actually targeted against the influx of Chinese students to Japan).

Could You please clarify?

Thanks a lot!

František

P.S.I am putting together a list of important people / historical figures in your book as an annex to the translation that will include more names than the ones in the English edition. I might also come back to you for some clarifications there, if that's ok.

5/21/2020

孫康宜致František

Dear František,

Actually I recently found out that it's not true that Boxer Indemnity Scholarship was always meant for studying in the U.S.! Here is a witness report from Prof. Tang Ling-wu's on how he and my father both got the Boxer Indemnity scholarship to Japan in 1939. (My father won the first prize among students in North China, and Prof. Tang won the first prize in South China. Here is a quote from my preface to my recently published book about my father—《孫保羅書法：附書信日記》. As you can see, I have quoted form Dr. Tang at length:

> 有關父親的「前半生」與」後半生」，他的老同學兼摯友湯麟武先生（1922-2012），即著名的臺灣海岸工程之父，臺灣成功大學教授），在他的《有人要我寫回憶錄》（2003）一書中寫得最為中肯：

> ……說明了上述的時代背景後，我與孫保羅（1919-）結識之事即不必多費唇舌。戰爭中日本與中華民國既未斷交，主管庚款留學費用的「外務省文化事業部」運作如常。1939年，他們委託北京的「中華民國臨時政府」、南京的「中華民國維新政府」招考庚款留日學生，當年我們身陷淪陷區，大部分的學校已隨國民黨政府西撤，我與他分別在南北考上後，1939年九月先後到東京，在補習日文的時期住在一個宿舍...

I noticed that most people do not know about this, so I particularly called the reader's attention to this.

Hope this clarifies things.

Kang-i
5/21/2020

Line訊息

李：謝謝孫老師分享的耶魯二〇二〇畢業典禮內容。這幾天太忙了，想在明天把《北山樓》看完給您，再處理《文集》，還沒有時間觀看耶魯校長的演講。等今晚看了再回覆您。

孫：No problem! I want to send it to you so that I don't forget. That's all.

李：孫老師，本週日之前保陽要集中精力校讀《北山樓》和處理《文集》收尾工作，所以暫時不回應您的Email，您儘管寫Email給保陽，下週保陽會集中時間處理的。

錢南秀致孫康宜

Dear Kang-i,

　　It's just a small event that Professor Zhang Jian organized at CUHK, to continue on their academic activities under the current circumstances. Zhang Longxi opened the series last week, with Ge Zhaoguang serving as his commentator. Mine is going to follow, and Ge's wife Dai Yan will be my commentator. So you can see it is really something arranged among friends, not worth your attention. I am happy though if it makes you happy! Thanks to Ling Chao for mentioning this to Sun laoshi. Please keep doing well!

　　Love,

Nanxiu

5/21/2020

註：此信指的是錢南秀於5月23日在香港中文大學主持的線上講座之事，可參見5月23日附錄凌超致孫康宜函。

孫康宜致李保陽

Dear Baoyang,

　　In the near future, I am going to send you a memorable copy of Prof. Kao Yu-kung's 高友工book, which comes from Prof Kao's last collection of 300 books. (Please see attached pictures). Let me tell you the story behind this.

First of all, In the fall of 2018, before I had Prof. Kao's 300 books shipped to Wesleyan University, I specifically reserved a copy of Prof. Kao's book,《美典：中國文學研究論集》（北京三聯）, for Lin Shuen-fu林順夫. And this copy contains the special inscription, "Memory of Prof. Kao Yu-kung."

But for some reason I forgot to mail this book to Lin Shuen-fu in 2018, and just yesterday I found the book still sitting on my bookshelf all this time! So I quickly wrote an email to Shuen-fu to let him know that I would mail the book to him after the COVID-19 pandemic is over.

But Shuen-fu just realized this morning that he already got a copy of the book with Prof. Kao's personal autograph, and so he suggested that I give this extra copy to someone like you who would treasure a copy of Prof. Kao's book. This is what Shuen-fu wrote in his email to me today.

Best,
Kang-i
5/22/2020

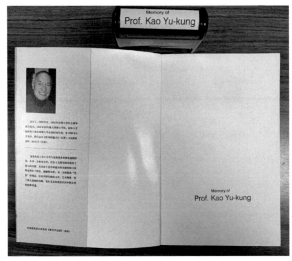

高友工教授著《美典：中國文學研究論集》，中國大陸版由北京的生活・讀書・新知三聯書店於2008年出版。

林順夫致孫康宜

Dear Kang-i,

　　After I got up this morning, I suddenly remembered that the copy of Professor Kao's book that I possess was sent to me with his autograph soon after it had been published by Sanlian. I just double-checked and found out that this is indeed the case. Seeing Professor Kao's autograph done in his distinctive handwriting brought back to me a lot of fond memories of him! Thus there is no need for me to "own" another copy of it. Please give that extra copy to somebody else who is likely to read it and benefit from it. A good choice might be your friend Li Baoyang who appeared to have not read but wished to read Professor Kao's book. Or perhaps one of your graduate students who would appreciate having the book.

　　Thank you kindly all the same, however, for thinking of me when you discovered that you had extra copies of this great book!

　　With best regards,

Shuen-fu
5/22/2020

孫康宜致林順夫

Dear Shuen-fu,

　　Thank you! Your email makes a lot of sense!

　　I'll give that memorable copy of Prof Kao's book to Li Baoyang then! I'm sure he will be grateful!

　　Best,

Kang-i
5/22/2020

Line訊息

李：孫老師，施先生〈浮生雜詠〉第七十八首：

> 橫河橋畔女黌宮，蘦圃風流指顧中。
> 罷講閒居無個事，茗邊坐賞玉玲瓏。

這首詩中的「園」字我懷疑是「圃」字，您幫我核對一下。

孫：You are right! It's 圃！

李：謝謝孫老師。因為我讀到這裡，感覺平仄不對，所以懷疑這是個錯字

孫：The name of the garden is 蘦圃！

李：而龔鼎孳的蘦圃很少會有人寫成「蘦園」。「園」字在此也出律，所以生疑。

孫：You are amazing! Thank you!

李：不客氣。晚清的鄭文焯把這種遵循聲律校勘的法則命名為「律校」，這是區別於對校、理校的一種校勘方法，在校詩詞時，這套方法很有用。朱祖謀也用這套方法來校詞。保陽校王鵬運詞的時候也用這套方法，比較管用。

江青致孫康宜

康宜你好，

高筠若是她的名字。

我仍然在瑞典，一時也動不了，寫寫文章。

希望大家平平安安

祝福

江青

5/22/2020

孫康宜致李保陽

Dear Baoyang,

I just heard the news that Rev. David Pawson 大衛・鮑森, to whom many of us owe so much for his "Unlocking the Bible" lecture series, passed away two days ago on May 21, 2020. He was 90 years old.

As I said to you via Line, during the COVID-19 lockdown I have been listening to Pawson's lectures on the Bible almost every single day.　In fact ever since August, 2018, I have been doing this. And every time after I listened to his lecture, I felt I had learned immensely from his teaching.

Please see attached a quote from my March 1st diary, in which I mentioned what I had learned from Pawson's lecture on the *Book of Jeremiah*.

Recently I listened to Pawson's lectures on the *Book of Jonah*（《約拿書》） and the *Book of Nahum*（《那鴻書》）, the two books in the *Old Testaments*（舊約·聖經）that are often ignored in today's Protestant church. I was especially inspired by Pawson's interpretation of God's mercy and God's justice. According to Pawson, in the *Book of Jonah*, God exercises mercy（施憐憫）because of the people's repentance. But in the *Book of Nahum* God exercises justice（對不義的譴責）, for "the sheer inhumanity" found in the city of Nineveh:

> Woe to the city of blood,
> full of lies,
> full of plunder,
> never without victims. . .
> (*Nahum*, 3:1)

> 禍哉！這流人血的城，
> 充滿詭詐
> 充滿強暴，

搶奪的事總不止息

（《那鴻書‧3:1》）。

So, repentance（懺悔）is the key. As the *Book of Jonah* (3:10) writes: "When God saw what they did and how they turned from their evil ways, he had compassion and did not bring upon them the destruction he had threatened."

I feel we have a lot to learn from the lessons as taught in the *Book of Jonah*, as well as the *Book of Nahum.*

Today as I moan the death of Rev. David Pawson, I especially give thanks to him for his brilliant interpretations of the Bible.

Best,

Kang-i

5/23/2020

Line訊息

李：（我分享洛桑寫張充和的文章給孫老師）下篇的「鄭孝胥」被作者寫成了
「鄭考胥」。

孫：I see! Thank you for sharing! By the way, If you change 昆曲 to 崑曲，I think the press editor will change it back to昆曲again! Just look at my《曲人鴻爪》book
（the 廣西師大 edition）!

李：孫老師，保陽後來想了，不做改變。因為現在的簡體字，已經「昆」「崑」
不辨了，所以還是把「崑」統一成「昆」才合乎現在中國大陸的規範。

李：我們在學校讀了二十多年書，魯迅一直是個非常正面的形象，用來灌輸給學
生。魯迅冷峻地揭穿和批判中國文化、中國人的劣根性。魯迅的這種風格在
「革命」的語境下，讓人有一時之快，甚至在面對日漸窶頹的現世際遇時，
會發出「讀懂魯迅已中年」的感嘆。但是反過來想想，魯迅這種「一個都不

饒恕」的刻薄、極端，實在讓人感慨。尤其是當走出「革命」語境之後，從另一個面向去認識人事，更覺得魯迅的這種姿態，既是他自己性格使然，也是一個時代無法選擇個人發言姿態的悲哀。如果不能超脫那個環境，想來很多人還是和自己一如既往地纏鬥於那種悲哀裡！從我個人角度來講，對魯迅的那種「不饒恕」有某種認同，但最終還是覺得施先生的恬淡，才是人生應該選擇的一種態度。以及施先生的那份基督徒般的寬恕。

孫：Yes! I totally agree! I like Mr Shi's attitude toward life!

李：孫老師，秀威所有的圖版都已經核對清楚了。保陽現在要出去一下，晚上會寫一封比較詳細的信給您，說明秀威新版的和上海舊版的不同。這對讀者瞭解兩個版本的不同有幫助。

孫：Should we include your remarks as the 附錄三？

李：好的啊，謝謝孫老師。終於按計畫完成了此書的校讀。

孫：Oh, BAOYANG! During the COVID-19 period I have been listening to Rev David Pawson's lectures almost everyday! (Actually I have been doing that ever since August 2018). Oh, I have benefitted so much from his series of lectures on the Bible! 感恩不盡！From my March 1 diary! See below!

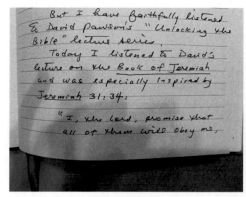
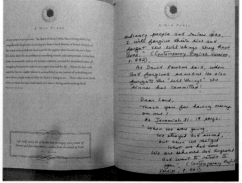

Linda Chu（朱雯琪）致孫康宜

Dear Professor Kang-i,

Please find an updated version of your article attached. Besides adding in our names, I also proofread one more time with fresh eyes. In the process, I made a few minor edits that I have highlighted in yellow for your consideration.

All the revisions are very slight ones for clarity or style. For instance, I replaced "left this world" with "went to Heaven" as I think it paints a more vivid image and goes better with "prayed to God." (Full sentence now reads: Later I learned that my aunt went to Heaven as I prayed to God last night.)

Warmly as always,

Linda

5/23/2020

凌超致孫康宜

Dear Prof. Chang,

Prof. Qian's talk about the worthy ladies is very successful today—more than three hundred audiences around the globe joined. I particularly enjoyed her erudition about the ramification of this pre-modern Chinese stereotype in the entire East Asian cultures and its influence on the May Fourth Movement. Prof. Qian's comments about the two discursive models as 賢媛 and 列女 and the underlying nuanced ideologies are also very insightful.

I attach a photo of the title page of her talk, and you can see her there.

Best,

Chao

5/23/2020

李保陽致孫康宜

孫老師，

現將《從北山樓到潛學齋》校讀表格奉上，歷時五天，超過原來的預計。蓋原來以為只需要看過一遍文字，校正繁簡轉換過程中導致的錯別字，文從字順即可。誰知讀到第二天，卻發現秀威和上海兩版之間原信圖版的排版也存在出入（上海版中的若干圖版秀威沒有收錄，是不是他們特意壓縮了圖版的數量？）。為了保險起見，全書讀完後，保陽又把所有涉及到的書影圖版全部和文字核對了一遍。所以超出了預估時間。

另外一個費時間的原因是：我太太是個極愛做菜的人，她最近在山中發現了一處廢棄的日本園林，那裡自然生長了好些適合做中國菜的植物，因為天氣比較好，她要我載她去挖野菜。又自學校關閉以來，孩子們天天在家上網課，缺乏運動。我也趁此帶他們到附近爬爬山，增加運動量。

另外，這本書中凡施先生寫到的英文單詞，您最好抽時間再核對一遍，因為施先生的連筆英文，保陽不敢臆斷。這本書保陽兩個月之內，已讀過三遍了，想起您十七號那天傍晚電話中跟保陽談起新批評主義注重的「closereading」，果然有不一樣的收穫。特別能夠理解您那時候和施先生的通信，因為我們現在的書信往來，大有紹續從北山樓到潛學齋故事的意味。

後面的〈校讀後記〉是今晚開夜車趕出來的，一方面談最近校書心得，另一方面談我們的新書，有給《避疫》做廣告的意思。還是草稿，比較草率，先分享給您，請您提出意見，再行修訂。

明天處理《文集》中的批註筆跡。大約兩三天可以完成。

保陽　敬上

5/24/2020

註：此信有部分刪節。

李保陽致孫康宜

孫老師，

　　現將《文集》卷五校讀稿奉上。實在有趣，保陽第一次給您呈交的校訂稿恰是此第五卷，時間是上個月的今天。

　　除去了所有批校的筆跡。並遵照您的意見，留下頁206兩處批校，是給出版社的編輯描述兩個生僻字寫法的。

　　很開心，把兩天的任務壓在一天完成了。明天開始完善《文集》校讀記，下週三左右交給您。

保陽　敬上

5/24/2020

Line訊息

李： 謝謝孫老師！現在處理文集，還是會偶爾發現一兩個錯字。真是沒辦法，先交給出版社的編輯看吧。完全消除錯誤是不可能的。

孫： Yes! We should not be perfectionists! The press editor is going to go over all the volumes anyway!

李： 是的。現在留餘的一些小瑕疵，出版社的編輯都可以處理的。孫老師，突然想起來一件有趣的事情：秀威版的《北山樓》卷尾附錄的最後兩篇文字的作者，竟然都是西安人，哈哈～～

孫： Yes! I thought about that too! My meeting with Kang back in the early 1990s was also very miraculous too! It's all due to his book 《風騷與豔情》！

李： 保陽認識您是因為《陳柳情緣》，哈哈～～

李保陽致Martin Heijdra（何義壯）

Martin館長，

您好！

實在不好意思！您可不可以幫助我？

我現在給《孫康宜文集》寫一篇評論文章。您知道，在上個世紀，Princeton的明代研究非常有成就，我的這篇評論文章裡會提到這一點。我記得您曾經告訴我，您研究領域是明代財政。我想把您和浦安迪（Andrew H. Plaks）教授，作為牟復禮教授之後Princeton明代研究的兩位代表進行論述。但是我不瞭解您研究明代的著作名稱，您能介紹一下自己的研究情況嗎？

P.S.如果您能簡單介紹一下上世紀Princeton的學者研究明代的情況，對我會非常的有幫助！您可以寫中文，也可以寫英文，都可以的。不勝感激！謝謝！

Best for you!

保陽　敬上

5/25/2020

Line訊息

李：孫老師，牟先生的書齋名稱是「學而不？齋」。那個字我看不清楚。

孫：No, we were just joking!開玩笑說的！是我們當天把牟先生取名為「樂而不淫齋主人」的！

李：哦～～了解，哈哈

孫：Hahaha!

李：牟先生真是個有趣的人～～

孫：Yes!

李保陽致孫康宜

孫老師，

　　謝謝您分享的這張施先生的照片。這張照片是施先生在杭州行素女中教書時的照片，收入上海版《北山樓》頁216中。

保陽　敬上
5/26/2020

孫康宜致李保陽

Dear BAOYANG,

　　Yes, the 秀威 editor neglected to include it! Now let's put it back!

　　Now, I'll ask 秀威 to add 16 圖版 to the book. It took me a long time to find the 16 圖版 though!

Kang-i
5/26/2020

註：此信有部分刪節。

李保陽致孫康宜

孫老師，

　　非常抱歉，遲至今日保陽才回覆您的這封信，因為上週一直在校讀秀威版《從北山樓到潛學齋》、撰寫〈校讀後記〉，並處理《文集》五卷的批註，這些工作大概費時整整一周時間。這些工作結束之後，又馬上著手續寫《文集》的

〈校讀後記〉，以便趕在文集交稿之前附入卷尾，所以最近幾乎沒有時間處理郵件和《避疫》書稿的事情。

　　謝謝您給保陽分享這麼奇妙的贈書故事。保陽也非常榮幸能夠得到高先生這本書的舊藏紀念本。不過您不用著急郵寄，等您方便時再說。

　　保陽原來計畫這個週三可以交給您《文集》校讀記，現在看來恐要延期呈交了，因為寫的過程中又有一些想法，就順便加進去了。當初讀《文集》時，順手記下來的一些筆記，如今再整理時，發現還有進一步發揮的空間，就順著思路寫下去。保陽爭取這個月底交給您草稿。

　　今天一直沒有收到您的來信，不知道秀威版《北山》您校讀如何了？感冒可好些？甚念！

保陽　敬上

5/26/2020

李保陽致孫康宜

孫老師，

　　剛剛把上週積壓到今天的郵件全部處理完了，又完成一件事情，可以稍微鬆一口氣了。

　　因為Gmail郵箱特殊的系統設置之故，有些來信是很早之前寫的第一封，後來我們如果在那第一封信的基礎上往返，我就得重新一一確認最新的來信下面那些歷史來信是否都已經編入其對應的日期中了，不得不用關鍵字一封封在編好的書稿中比對確認，所以比較耗時費事。也因為如此，我更喜歡每次給您寫信時，重新建立一個新郵件往返文件。

　　剛才在重新梳理郵件時，才發現險些把高先生一家1932年在瀋陽拍攝的這幅全家福老照片給遺漏了。這張照片效果非常好。早期氯化銀洗曬的照片，有一種立體的手工感和歷史的凝重痕跡，您用在《走出白色恐怖》中高雄鄉下洋裁班學員合影那張照片就有這樣的感覺。保陽很喜歡這種照片，這兩年在費城的Flea

Market零星收集了一些，雖然是西洋人物照，但那種可觸摸的質感，與欣賞傳統的中國舊照片是一樣的。謝謝您分享的這張照片，保陽已把它加到書稿中去了。

保陽　敬上
5/26/2020

李保陽致孫康宜

孫老師，

　　今天再次細細摩挲高先生那張全家福，乘興為這張照片寫了一段文字。在寫這段文字時，想起了去年五月，在家等待政府批准工作許可，閒來無事，整理了一本1947年的日記稿本，整理完成之後，也順手寫了一段跋語。這兩篇跋文意思可通，一併分享給您。您也可以把這兩篇文字分享給合適的朋友。

保陽　敬上
5/27/2020

5月28日Line

李：孫老師，昨天下午保陽載內子去費城一家華人超市買東西，在停車場繼續讀陳國球教授論高先生的文章。今早在網上找到去年陳教授在政治大學做的一個講座。因為陳先生的文章而延伸到讀高先生的興趣，這樣的閱讀對進一步了解您的文字，也很有助益。最近這一連串的閱讀，對瞭解海外中國文學研究很有幫助，擴大了視野，受益不淺。謝謝您的熱情推薦！！這樣的閱讀對於最近寫《文集》校讀記也很有幫助。

李：謝謝孫老師的解釋。我現在調整思路，打算在明天之前將校讀記交給您。保陽也在努力跟上您的節奏。您的這種訓練方式對於完成一件事情是非常有必

要的，您不用客氣哈。您這樣的做事方式也是給當事人自己留有緩衝餘地，非常棒的。如果我現在調整思路，不做那種全景式的評論嘗試，而是就作品論作品，只在原來筆記的基礎上做一些編輯加工工作，那麼效率就會高許多。

孫：Try to simplify things, and don't get it too complicated! Most people today like it simple and clear!

李：是的。瞭解。孫老師，您的校改意見保陽已收悉，晚上就著手改到校對單中，並分享給您。孫老師，PDF文件就那麼多嗎？還有沒有？

孫：That's all! 6 PDFs! A total of roughly 82 pages!

李：孫老師，那我就不用再更新秀威的那個校對表單了？

孫：Okay I will tell them! No worries!

李：好的。我明天中午之前把校讀記分享給您。

5月29日Line

孫：I just sent you the PDF for the suggested changes and corrections! Please see my email! Can you please delete the sentence "竊以為不可作為後世研究的可效之法"? I think it's okay to say "有一定風險". But we can only do our best according to the available sources; there is always a risk factor. Isn't that what scholars are supposed to do? Also, the *Cambridge History of Chinese Literature* gives us very strict word-limits. So, mercy on us please! Hahaha! Baoyang, I'm sorry to make you work so hard! Are you all right? 對不起，把你累壞了！

李：孫老師，您太客氣了。能有機會跟您一對一的學習，保陽真的三生有幸，您不必這麼客氣。剛剛保陽已把修訂稿奉上，請您查閱郵件。當時保陽對於小說那一節的保留意見，現在想來也是夠大膽，夠唐突，希望孫老師不要介意。

孫：Wow, your revised version is perfect! Thank you so much! Actually I like your calling me 孫老師. So please don't make more changes! I only found one English typo 英文錯字。The name should be "Auerbach" on page 9. You left out "r". (Sorry, my marking was not clear!) By the way, on page 14, should the word be 少?

李：好的。謝謝孫老師，這就再改。尟有涉及，就是鮮有涉及的意思

孫：I see, thank you! For "Auerbach" and "學術報告文學的創作", I can make the corrections here. So there is no need for you to send another version!不必寄更正稿了！謝謝！

Haninah Levine致孫康宜

Dear Professor Chang,

I am sorry it has taken me so long to respond to your kind email. I remember that day so well, and I know that seeing you meant so much to my mother that day, too. I hope you will be able to join us on Sunday for the memorial. Some day, I hope to share with you the "quatrains of the day" I wrote during the period of her final decline, in her honor.

All my love

Haninah
5/29/2020

林順夫致孫康宜

Dear Kang-i,

Thank you so much for sharing Guoqiu's article with us. I've read it with interest and admiration! And I wholeheartedly agree with you that Guoqiu is "the most amazing literary detective." I have not read that much by Stephen Soong. When I was still teaching at U of M long time ago I once read his review of David Hawkes' translation of the first 80 chapters of the Hongloumeng. It was a very positive review. But I still remember his criticism of some details of Hawkes' translation including his rendering of "怡紅院" as "House of Green Delight."

All the best,

Shuen-fu

5/29/2020

李保陽致孫康宜

孫老師

　　謝謝您的分享。郵件保陽都收到了。感謝主，五月中把兩本書稿都交清了，沒有耽誤日期。接下來可以著手《避疫》的推進工作了。

保陽　敬上

5/30/2020

孫康宜致李保陽

Dear Baoyang,

　　As you can see from the Wechat reply of 張杰 of 廣西師大出版社, this is a great day to celebrate the completion of the 簡體 version of the《孫康宜文集》五卷.（Please see attached）.

　　Again I want to thank you for your great help to my *wenji* project! Without you, I would have trouble completing such a big task in such a short time! God definitely has sent you to help me during this trying time of the COVID19 Pandemic! It's truly an amazing grace!

Kang-i

5/31/2020

孫康宜致李保陽

Dear Baoyang,

I forgot to tell you that my old teacher Lan Shun-shih 藍順仕老師, one of the most unforgettable benefactors（恩人）who gave us great help during the White Terror Era, died almost three months ago on March 4th.

As you can see, there is a special chapter about him in my book, *Journey Through the White Terror.*（見《走出白色恐佈》，第4章〈雪中送炭恩難忘〉。）

I attach here my diary entry on March 4, 2020, for your reference.

Kang-i

5/31/2002

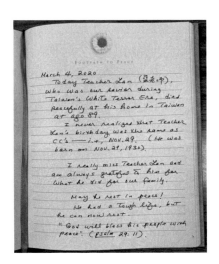

孫康宜致李保陽

Dear Baoyang,

One day I must introduce you to Prof Anna Shields of Princeton University! She teaches Classical Chinese Literature. She likes Chinese scholars very much!

I think she can be viewed as a successor of Prof Kao Yu-kung! Anna's office is in Jones Hall, not far from the Gest Library!

My friend Bian Dongbo has just completed a Chinese translation of Anna's book, *One Who Knows Me: Friendship and Literary Culture in Mid-Tang China* (2015).

Kang-i

5/31/2020

李保陽致孫康宜

孫老師，

謝謝您！保陽也希望有機會能認識一些美國漢學研究者，尤其是中國文學研究的學者，如果能在普林斯頓有這樣的朋友，那就再好不過了。我們家去普林斯頓不是很遠，將來有個可以聊天的去處。

卞東波是南京大學的教授，保陽知道他是我們這一輩學人裡非常優秀的學者，藝事多能，治學勤勉，有很多研究成果出版。現在他又要出版翻譯作品，真是打心裡為他感到高興。雖然我們沒有見過面，但保陽和南京大學的很多朋友比較熟悉，真為南京大學有這樣優秀的學者感到由衷的開心！

保陽　敬上

5/31/2020

孫康宜致李保陽

Dear Baoyang,

I'm glad you like the idea of my introducing you to my Princeton friend Anna Shields. Please see attached a picture of Anna Shields and me, taken during Prof. Kao's Memorial service in March, 2017.

Also, Bian Dongbo was supposed to visit me at Yale next month (he had even booked the airline ticket!), but the Yale conference was postponed due to COVID-19. I don't know when the conference would eventually be held at Yale, but Bian Dongbo will definitely come for the conference.

In recent times Bian Dongbo came to visit me at Yale almost every year!

Best,
Kang-i
5/31/2020

孫康宜致 Haninah Levine

Dear Haninah,

What a lovely memorial service you have organized for your mother Shula! So I hasten to give you my feedback here.

First of all, I am deeply touched by the stories of your mother and feel honored to be present at her memorial service!

I'm especially moved by what you said: "My mother never did anything by half measures." I think you have inherited that quality from her.

I'm also very happy to hear your father speak at the memorial service. His story about their experience at Yale's Branford College decades ago is so wonderful.

I really enjoyed your two sisters Tiferet and Hephzibah's accounts of your mother's life. I love your mother's paintings which Hephzibah has shown during the service. The painting called "The perfect imperfect" is truly amazing. I also like the one called "Objectivisation."

Here I attach a few pictures which I took during the service. Interestingly, in my picture for the "Perfect Imperfect" painting, somehow part of my backyard scenery has entered into your mother's painting!

By the way, It's great that Naama Nebenzahl played such great music in remembrance of your mother. She even played another song at the closing of the memorial service. It's all so beautiful!

Best,
Kang-i
5/31/2020

孫康宜致李保陽

Dear Baoyang,

Sorry for replying so late to your email of April 22, which was about your reader's response on my article regarding Prof. Mote's concept of architecture.

First of all, I want to thank you for your perceptive comments regarding buildings in general.

But I also want to let you know how much I enjoyed reading your short essay on the autumn of Philadelphia, 〈費城的秋天〉。You are indeed an excellent essayist, and I'm greatly moved by you sense of "history": "默行其中，才真的感覺到原來我們離歷史是如此之近，近到能感受到她的呼吸……"!

Kang-i
5/31/2020

孫康宜致李保陽

Dear Baoyang,

When I first read the subject line of your 4/19 email (「解構主義，您的學術路徑？」) I was truly surprised! This is because I'm never a Deconstructionist.

Actually I don't appreciate people's using any "ism"（任何主義）to describe my scholarly approach. I studied New Criticism in the 1960's, Structuralism in the 1970s, and Deconstructionism is the 1980's, as well as many other schools of criticism that were available to me along the way. But I have never followed strictly on the agenda of any particular school. I think it's more correct to say that every scholar is a product of all the learning he/she has acquired, plus his/her own judgment.

In my next email response to your 4/20 letter, I'll elaborate on this topic a bit more.

Best,
Kang-i
5/31/2020

孫康宜致李保陽

Dear Baoyang,

I'm so pleased to receive this email from you, which is very interesting.

You are right about the Deconstructionist tendency to emphasize the role of the readers.（讀者至上）。But it's more correct to say that it's due to the problems of the "author's intent" that the role of the readers have become important for the Deconstructionists. First of all, the Deconstructionists believe that authors cannot possibly know all the "meanings" of their works. This is because language itself embodies endless "meanings," and authors themselves simply cannot know them all.（語言本身帶有無限的「意義」，那不是作者本人可以全部知道的。）Since the so-called "author's intent" is so limited in terms of meaning, some Western scholars even claimed that authors are dead.（作者死亡）。

However, when we apply such a Deconstructive approach to the study of Chinese literature, we sometimes run into trouble. Please read my recent article titled "Chinese Authorship," in which I talked about this point in greater detail.

Best,
Kang-i
5/31/2020

註：此信回覆李保陽4月20日信。

孫康宜致李保陽

Dear Baoyang,

I am sorry that I forgot to reply to your excellent message dated April 25th, which was sent to me as a follow-up note. First of all, I agree that the concept of "夫妻之間除了情（Love）之外，必須有義" is admirable--especially when it's demonstrated by the action of traditional Chinese women.

By the way, the word "義" is often translated as "justice." But I think "義" in this context should be translated as "moral commitment."

Best,
Kang-i
5/31/2020

孫康宜致李保陽

Dear Baoyang,

I really appreciate your sharing with me this private episode regarding your first baby.

I am also deeply touched by your journey of finding strength from God. Indeed, with God's constant guidance, you will be in good hands all the time.

Best,
Kang-i
5/31/2020

註：此函回覆李保陽4月26日信。

孫康宜致李保陽

Dear Baoyang,

　　This is such an interesting email from you! I appreciate your analysis of the problems often found in Chinese families, where people are urged to behave in a certain way. If someone does not follow the normal way of behavior, friends and relatives would then label the person as "abnormal." And you have used your niece as an example: "後來年齡漸漸大了，除了我姨媽，親族都認為她腦子有問題，便以「不正常」人視之"。）

　　I think you are absolutely right about this Chinese phenomenon, which even exists in the Chinese communities in the US. I believe, however, people of the younger generation (the so-called "Chinese Americans") will change all of that.

Best,
Kang-i
5/31/2020

註：此函回覆李保陽4月29日信。

孫康宜致李保陽

Dear Baoyang,

　　Thank you for sharing your poem on Mr. Zhao Fusan 趙復三, which is really great!

　　Regarding Zhao Fusan, I should mention that in his old age (in 2001) he married Ms Chen Hsiao-chiang（陳曉薔）, who used to be my Chinese teacher at Tunghai University in 1963. (Remember that Chen Hsiao-chiang was the one who published the article "葬禮" about the death of Alexander's two sons back in 1965?)

　　Well, Chen Hsiao-chiang came to the US during the late 1960s and got a degree in MLS (Master of Library Science).

　　She finally worked at the Yale University Library as a cataloger. She retired from the Yale University Library in 2003.

　　When she married Zhao Fusan in 2001, Chen Hsiao-chiang was already 71 years old. Their marriage was truly a union of "last love"（末戀）。

　　After Zhao Fusan died a few years ago, Chen Hsiao-chiang got a gravesite for Zhao Fusan at Hartford's Cedar Hill Cemetery, the same graveyard where Yung Wing（容閎）was buried.

　　Chen Hsiao-chiang is still living near Hartford, Connecticut. She is 89 years old now.

　　Hope this information is helpful to you.

Kang-i

5/31/2020

註：此信回覆李保陽4月30日信。

孫康宜致李保陽

Dear Baoyang,

    Indeed, the Chinese way of viewing the Western missionary work as a kind of cultural invasion（文化侵略）is very unfortunate! As you may know, the Yale Divinity School Library is the place where most of the American missionaries' archives are kept. Next time when you visit Yale again, I'll definitely bring you to visit the Yale Divinity School.

    I feel so grateful that the "Sun Family Papers" are also preserved at the Yale Divinity School Library--in the Special Collections Department.

Best,
Kang-i
5/31/2020

註：此信回覆李保陽4月30日信。

孫康宜致李保陽

Dear Baoyang,

    Thank you for looking into the history of epidemics during the early history of the US. I really appreciate your going out of your way to collect the data!

    This information is especially helpful during this difficult time of the COVID-19 pandemic.

Best,
Kang-i
5/31/2020

註：此信回覆李保陽5月1日來信。

孫康宜致李保陽

Dear Baoyang,

From your comment regarding the Humanities（「保陽不大同意今天人文教育衰落這個說法。在保陽看來，人文教育從來就沒有繁榮過」）, I feel that you have misunderstood what I meant by "人文教育" in the U.S.！I think there is a problem of the cultural gap here. It would be difficult for me to answer your question in a few words, and so I am sending you this short article of mine that appeared in the *Yale Daily News* on January 16, 2014:

Is There Hope for the Humanities?

Kang-i Sun Chang
Translated by Victoria Wu

Time passes so quickly; in the blink of an eye, I have already been teaching at Yale for nearly 32 years. I remember when I first came to work at Yale in the eighties, I was the youngest of the professors in the East Asia Languages and Literatures Department, but now I am the oldest professor in the department.

Perhaps someone would ask me: in these past thirty years, how has college-level education in America changed in general?

In my opinion, since the turn of the twenty-first century, the greatest change in American education is the gradual decline of the humanities. Most obviously, the number of college students majoring in humanities has long since halved: during the sixties, humanities majors consisted of 14% of all students, but by 2010, the number had decreased to 7%. In other words, in this general environment that values money above all else, those students who might have entered the humanities have long since one by one entered financial fields or other advantageous science and technological professions. Thus, a question that concerned many was, would the younger generation's neglect of the humanities lead to an overall loss of cultural and ideological progress? Regarding this question, American academia has long since conducted a comprehensive self-examination; moreover, newspapers, magazines, and internet news articles have repeatedly disseminated discussions regarding this topic—among them, the recent *New York Times* article (30 November 2013) "The Real Humanities Crisis" (written by contemporary philosopher Gary Gutting) received the most attention.

The reason Gutting's argument resonated so strongly with readers was because he used a new angle to analyze the problem. He believes that the crux of the matter does not lie with the younger generation, and nor is it the fault of the humanists themselves, but in our profit-driven society. Today's society emphasizes sky-high salaries for certain professions (such as athletes), but completely neglects the salaries and benefits for those who enter fields within the humanities; teachers' salaries are low and schools naturally lose the cultural influence they would otherwise have.

Gutting's essay greatly inspired me, making me think of the problem of cultural legacy. I worry that under the influence of a profit-driven society, the younger generation will gradually forget that deep-rooted cultural tradition.

Ironically, the architecture of Yale's campus is a constant reminder of the precious heritage of "cultural tradition." This university was established in 1701 when ten Congregationalist ministers donated forty volumes in hopes of establishing a new learning institution that emphasizes scholarship and the pursuit of knowledge. In the past three hundred years, the origin story of the "book donation" was repeatedly retold, constantly reminding Yalies of this long history. To use that majestic university library (i.e. Sterling Memorial Library) as an example, when the library was first constructed in 1930, the university celebrated this humanities tradition of "establishing a university with books" in an unprecedentedly grand and festive ceremony. Apparently, many faculty, students, and alumni attended the proceedings that day, and at their head, leading the procession were the library staff members, bearing ancient texts and following the example of those early clergymen-with a spirit of respecting and loving books, they walked step by step to the great doors of Sterling Memorial Library, personally offering up the volumes they carried. They wanted to express to all that books were the treasure stored within this great hall of learning.

But what makes people worry is that many young people can perhaps no longer understand the true value of this kind of cultural spirit. To them, profit is more important than books, and monthly income is far more real to them than abstract cultural resources. However, whose fault is it that the younger generation has become so absorbed with practical gains, and so much less concerned with the value of the humanities?

I think that professors who teach the humanities ought to take on much of the responsibility. To a large degree, the decline of the humanities and the widespread abandonment of the literary canon curriculums (including in primary and secondary education) have direct correlation. If we don't teach the traditional literary canon to students, if we don't nurture habits of passionate scholarship, if we don't teach students to understand the value of the long tradition of the humanities, then it is no wonder that they don't decide to specialize in the humanities. Because to them, the contents of what is now called "the humanities" seem to appear weak and empty; depth must be added and the quality enriched. My Yale Colleague Harold Bloom once complained to me that this generation of young people is the victim of the decline in the literary canon, only reading such popular literature as Harry Potter and not studying traditional classical works. For this reason, he wrote *The Western Canon*, hoping to help young people who passionately adore literature and art to seek out the roots of the humanities.

I very much agree with Bloom's point of view. Actually, in my own classes, I have already observed some differences between the students of today and the students of thirty years ago. Once, the students in my Yale classes (many were freshmen who had only just graduated from high school) were already familiar with such canonical works as Plato, Chaucer, Shakespeare, Milton, and Yeats, because they had already read such works in high school. But few of my students have now studied this kind of literature. Of course, my classes mostly introduce classical Chinese literature-such as the *Book of Songs* (Shijing) and the works of such people as Tao Yuanming, Li Bai, and Du Fu—but I still hope students have attained a certain proficiency in the Western canon, allowing them to establish a more comparative perspective in literary and cultural studies. Fortunately, Yale has the Directed Studies Program (a seminar program that presents the Western canon), directed many years by Dr. Jane A. Levin, developed specifically for freshmen, and which manages to make up for the deficiencies in this area.

In short, regarding the education of this younger generation, we cannot blindly blame them for their deficiencies, and thus absolving our responsibilities as instructors and teachers. If we hope the young can inherit the humanities spirit, then we must make changes in education, teaching more classes that attract students and revitalize passion for the humanities.

In addition, the times have changed, and perhaps we ought to change the traditional binary distinction between "the arts and the sciences." The present trend for "interdisciplinary studies" can let us learn a method of learning that "interacts between arts and sciences", perhaps we can also take this chance to develop a new kind of humanities tradition. Actually, this was also the definition of "liberal education" set forth by the 1828 Yale faculty: "By a liberal education, it is believed, has been generally understood, such a course of discipline in the arts and sciences, as is best calculated, at the same time, both to strengthen and enlarge the faculties of the mind, and to familiarize it with the leading principles of the great objects of human investigation and knowledge."

Anyway, I do hope that the above article of mine clarifies things.

Best,

Kang-i

5/31/2020

註：此函回覆李保陽5月2日信。

Line訊息

孫：Dear Zhang Jie, 我已經交稿了！請看我的六封電子函！第一封是說明，再加上一些附件，其他五封是五卷書稿的Word files！再一次感謝你的幫助。

張杰：都收到了，一共六個郵件，最好的兒童節禮物！

李：孫老師，您的Email收到了。您太客氣了。我們是靠　神的帶領走在一起，祂在您出版文集的事情上再一次見證奇蹟！祂帶領保陽避疫期間拜讀您的文章。我們一起感謝　神！

孫：Thank you! Do you know卞東波of南京大學？

李：謝謝孫老師分享的資訊。知道卞東波，但是沒有見過面。

孫：I see! Also, I just sent you an email about the death of my benefactor恩人Teacher Lan. For the rest of today, I'll try to catch up with the email replies which I owed you since April.

孫：Also, please see my email about the Princeton Professor Anna Shields!

李：謝謝孫老師，剛剛收到您的郵件。看到了Anna教授和您的合照。

孫：Dear Baoyang, I just want to remind you that your preface 序 to the 避疫 book should be short! 要短，不要長！Remember that this book is aimed for general readers, and in this case "less is more"! As David Pawson once said: "The best historian is one who knows what to leave out." Just a reminder!

孫康宜致李保陽

Dear Baoyang,

I'm sorry it has taken such a long time for me to reply to this very important email from you! First of all, I'm grateful to you for recommending Yu Jiaxi's（余嘉錫）book,《古書通例》, which I will try to a get a copy for myself as soon as possible.

As for Prof. Martin Kern's "蟋蟀" article, in fact I am already familiar with it. But, as you know, the *Cambridge Handout of Literary Authorship* only allows 7,000 words for each article, and so I was not able to include all the sources I used for my article. But, you are right, I could have mentioned Martin's "蟋蟀" article in my Academia Sinica talk in 2018.

I should also mention that Martin Kern is teaching ancient Chinese literature and civilization at Princeton University. He is also Chair（系主任）of the Department of East Asian Studies. He is a good friend of mine, and his office is in Jone's Hall. I can also introduce you to him, if you like.

By the way, I am not going to respond to your questions regarding my connections with Deconstructionism here. This is because I have already replied to your similar questions in a previous email.

Best,

Kang-i

6/1/2020

註：孫康宜教授有關中國文學的作者問題演講影片連結（本影片由臺灣中央研究

院中國文哲研究所授權）：https://m.youtube.com/watch?v=9xA_jV85SSE
&feature=youtu.be&from=singlemessage&isappinstalled=0

孫康宜致李保陽

Dear Baoyang,

This is a follow-up message to my email yesterday regarding the Grove Street Cemetery, which I have translated as 若無街墓園. As you can see, I have also shared with you via LINE the Law School student Wu Jingjian's 吳景鍵's article, "耶魯法學院門口的亡靈". I think your 5/1 email to me and Wu Jingjian's article can serve as two interesting accounts of the history of the Grove Street Cemetery, especially about how the yellow fever pandemic in 1795 led to the origin of the cemetery. And that was 225 years ago! As we are in the midst of the COVID-19 pandemic today, we would naturally look back to the history of the Grove Street Cemetery.

However, although I'm impressed with Wu Jingjian's article and feel flattered that my name appears in the article, I must clarify something important here! The 毛骨悚然 comment at the beginning of Wu's article does not represent the general view of the Yale community. For me as a Christian 作為一個基督徒, " the dead shall be risen" signifies the eternal victory of Christ—that is, the power of resurrection , the meaning of overcoming death! Thus, we should not be 毛骨悚然 , but instead we should celebrate the joy of eternal life（永生的盼望）！

Also, I wish to mention that my husband C. C. Chang and I also own a gravesite at the Grove Street Cemetery. And the location of our gravesite happens to be on the same street as Noah Webster's 韋伯斯特 (1758-1843) burial ground—i.e.,on Cedar Avenue.

As you know, Noah Webster is known for his legendary Webster's Dictionary《韋伯斯特詞典》.

By the way, Wu Jingjian has translated Cedar Avenue as "雪松道," which I like very much.

Best,

Kang-i

6/1/2020

孫康宜致李保陽

Dear Baoyang,

　　You are absolutely right! The interdisciplinary approach is very important. Now that you are living in the U.S., I hope you will eventually pursue a degree in a different discipline. It will be immensely helpful to you.

Best,

Kang-i

6/1/2020

註：此函回覆李保陽5月2日信。

孫康宜致李保陽

Dear Baoyang,

　　I am so pleased to know that you have learned something from my essays on American culture. I am so thrilled to get such a wonderful reader's response from you:

> 現在從您的文章中，更加從一個縱闊的層面和視角瞻仰、解讀這片土地，
> 那種收穫的愉悦，是如此的真切！如此的感動！尤其是透過您的文字，給
> 那些物化的東西都賦予了一層人文精神的溫情，一下子把那些冷峻的距離

柔化了。它們不再是另一個種族的陌生，不再是另一片土地的遙遠，而是
刻下真真切切的生活……

　　Also, regarding American culture and education, I would like to mention two books
by my dear friend Richard H. Brodhead, who was Dean of the Yale College before he
became President of Duke University. (Please see also my article,〈我所認識的Dick〉,
in vol. 1（卷一）of the *Collected Works of Kang-i Sun Chang*（《孫康宜文集》）。
　　Here is the information for the two books by Dick Brodhead:
（1）Richard H. Brodhead, *The Good of This Place: Values and Challenges in
　　College Education* (New Haven: Yale University Press, 2004).
（2）Richard H. Brodhead, *Speaking of Duke: Leading the 21st-Century
　　University* (Durham: Duke University Press, 2017).
　　I have learned so much from Brodhead's books that I highly recommend them to you.

Best,
Kang-i
6/1/2020

註：此函回覆李保陽5月3日信。

孫康宜致李保陽

Dear Baoyang,
　　Regarding your May 4th email（with the subject line「保陽：馬悅然先
生？」）, I thought I had already responded to the first part of your queries regarding
Goran Malmquvist（馬悅然）. I remember that I did send you a copy of my diary
entry on Nov. 19, 2019, which was about the death of Goran. I hope that my diary entry
has been useful to you.

As for Shen Congwen, there are simply too many stories about him that I can't sum them up here. I will wait until we meet in person, so that I can tell you more in detail.

Best,
Kang-i
6/1/2020

註：**此函為回覆李保陽5月4日信，內容有刪節及修訂。**

附沈從文寫給孫康宜的信，1980年6月17日

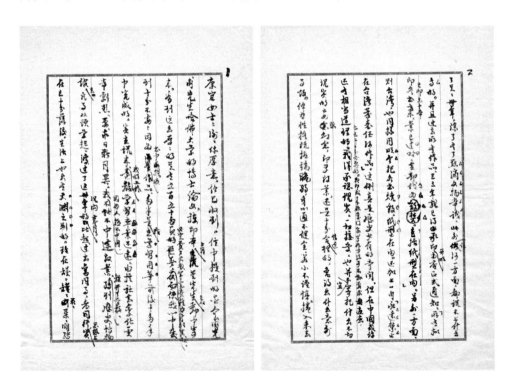

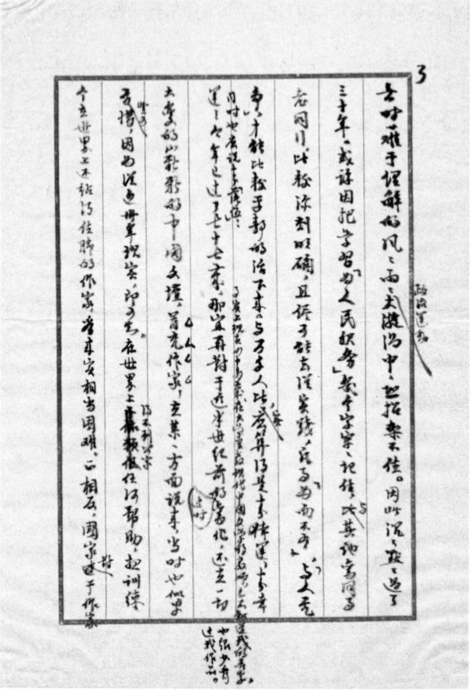

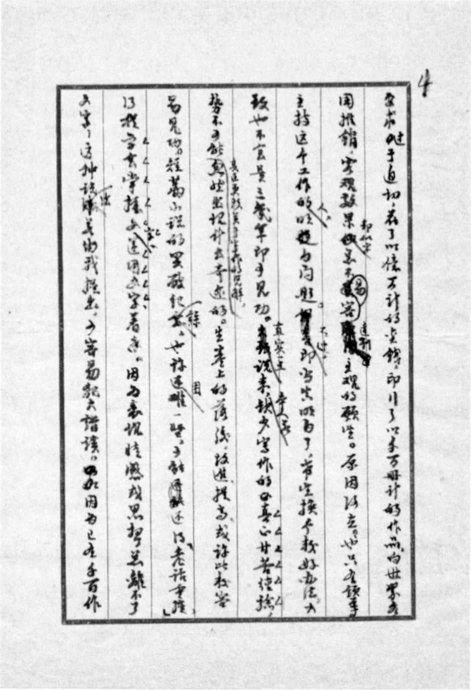

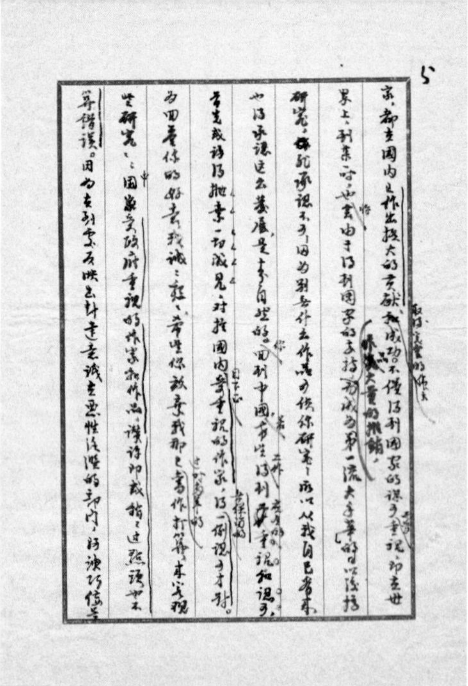

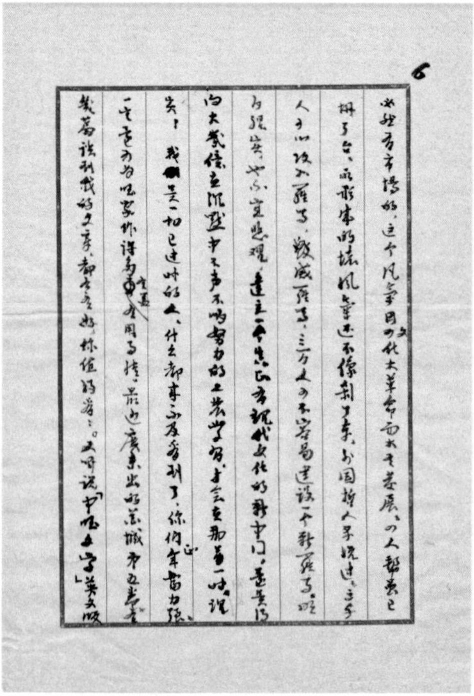

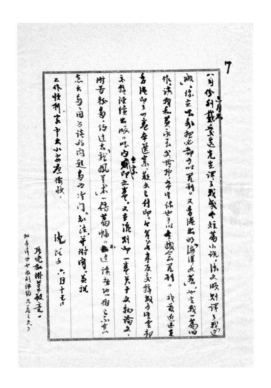

註：淩超為「沈從文致孫康宜」的長信所作的摘要：

頁一：收到轉寄的哈佛大學博士論文，其中提到的文章都是十多年前斷斷續續練
　　　筆之作。現已轉入歷史博物館，中斷寫作。

頁二：三十年來，只瞭解了一些文物常識。中國大陸和臺灣都禁止出版舊作，書
　　　版也已經銷毀。改做文物研究也不錯。

頁三：因為本人體力性格脆弱，經不住政治運動，因此努力與人無爭，才能存活。

頁四：近三十年來，政府大力贊助的作家成績寥寥，因為缺乏寫作的真正甘苦經
　　　驗，當從掌握文字運用著手。

頁五：建議研究現在受中國政府重視的作家與作品，贊許稍過也無妨。

頁六：四人幫雖倒台，政府中阿諛之風仍存。但不宜對現實絕望，未來尤有希望。

頁七：廣州出版《花城》第五卷有文章談及沈從文，值得看，並羅列其他出版情
　　　況：英文《中國文學》八月刊短篇英譯，法語《邊城》譯本，香港《海
　　　洋文藝》刊舊作，香港還出了選集，上海出了一卷文物論文。

On the whole, Shen Congwen mentioned the impact of Cultural Revolution here and there in his letter. The most important criticism he has given can be found on page 2, where he talked about how his old publications were all banned. He said that this kind of thing could only happen in China; luckily he had changed his occupation in time, so that he would not get into trouble.

孫康宜致李保陽

Dear Baoyang,

　　Thank you for letting me know that my references to Zhou Suzi周素子（as cited in my article on kunqu崑曲）has inspired you to think of a past event that seemed to mean a lot to you.

　　First of all, I appreciate your sharing the story about your reading experience of Zhou Suzi's周素子book several years ago. As you said, it was Mr. Wu Ge吳格先生 who gave you that book as a present in 2014.

　　I am particularly struck by your ability to associate your reading experiences with your life circumstances. This not only explains what "reading"（閱讀）in general means to you, but also shows that you are basically a person of constant reflection.（你是一個不斷反思的人！）

　　I'm really impressed!

Kang-i
6/1/2020

註：此函為回覆李保陽5月7日信。

Haninah Levine致孫康宜

Dear Kang-i,

Thank you so much, Professor Chang! It was a true treat to have you there, and to hear your words. I felt great love in that virtual room.

All the best,

Haninah
6/1/2020

康正果致孫康宜

墓園詠懷

紐黑文市內有一古老墓園，位於縱貫耶魯校區之格羅夫街（Grove Street）。園內埋葬耶魯大學十四任校長及當地眾多傑出人士，素有耶魯西敏寺之稱。周邊圍墻嚴實，墻外小徑清幽，其仿埃及風格之褐石門廊頂端銘刻《聖經》引文：「The Dead Shall Be Raised（死人要復活）。」園內草坪常綠，花木修整，墓地之分佈均按街區排列，儼然若民居鄰里。予課餘散步，屢入園內，愛其幽靜，欲買地卜葬焉。

　　葉落休云必落根，遠行我自善吾身。
　　試餐奶酪溫腸胃，學念英文快齒唇。
　　寄託環球仁義國，溝通網絡共情人。
　　逸民懷德不懷土，苟日新催又日新。

正果
6/2/2020

Formosa Deppman致孫康宜

Dear Professor Chang,

I am so sorry I did not reply to your message until now. This is a beautiful interview, I am also moved by Lentricchia's description of Romanticism, as well as the video of Bloom reading aloud at the end. I am currently in Taipei, Taiwan, studying Chinese and Taiwanese literature. I am taking a class called "Selected Poetry and Prose from the Ming and Qing Dynasties," and I often think of your "Classical Chinese Prose" class. In our discussion of 柳如是 your book on 陳子龍 was mentioned as well. Since my father passed away last summer, I have been pondering life and death through various literature, and I often find comfort in the 隨筆 poetry and prose of the明清文人. Particularly the pieces reflecting deep sadness. Anyways, I hope you and your family are doing well and staying healthy!

From, Formosa

6/3/2020

孫康宜致Formosa Deppman

Dear Formosa,

Here are the English translations of my two recent articles, and both touch on death and were written during the COVID-19 pandemic. Linda Chu is my translator, who moved to Taipei (from California) a few years ago. If you want, I can connect you with Linda Chu. I think the two of you will click!

I'm so pleased to know that you are currently in Taipei, Taiwan, studying Chinese and Taiwanese literature and that you are taking a class called "Selected Poetry and Prose from the Ming and Qing Dynasties."

Thank you for remembering my "Classical Chinese Prose" class and that you still recall our discussion of Liu Rushi 柳如是 and Chen Zilong 陳子龍 in the class.　You were only a sophomore then.

By the way, I can never forget your beautiful violin performance right before your graduation from Yale College in May 2019! Being able to go to your violin performance on that beautiful Monday meant all the world to me!

Best,
Kang-i Sun Chang
6/3/2020

孫康宜致李保陽

Dear Baoyang,

As you told me before, this 1932 photograph (taken while Prof. Yu-kung Kao was only 3 years old) is truly amazing. Well, I have just got Prof. Kao's nephew Andrew Wang's permission to use this picture in our book.

In his email to me, Andrew wrote: "The photograph, if in 1932, means my mother June would be four years old since she was born in 1928. She enjoyed seeing the photo again and retold the story of how back then, cameras were so rare and expensive, that families would need to go to the photo studio to have their picture taken."

Best,
Kang-i
6/4/2020

陳效蘭女士致張欽次

Hi CC,

　　A minor correction. The one labeled "Chao Rong-chi" is not T T Chen's wife Rong-chi . But the one below (first person left on the first row) is Chao Yung-long 趙榮琅, Rong-chi's brother who taught in Germany. T T Chen, Y L Chao and Fritz were classmates in the Dept of History at Jinling University.

　　The picture was taken at a dept outing near Naking in 1947 or 1948.

　　Please give my love to Kang-i.

　　Stay safe and be well.

　　All my love,

Hsiao-lan

6/4/2020

Linda Chu（朱雯琪）致孫康宜

Dear Professor Kang-i,

　　Thank you for introducing me to Formosa, and the email exchanges between you both make a wonderful addition to your new book.

　　I would love to meet Formosa!

Linda

6/5/2020

Formosa Deppman致孫康宜

Dear Professor Chang,

Your next book sounds like an amazing project, I would be very honored to have our email exchanges included in it.

Thank you for sending along the English versions of your two articles. I am so sorry to hear of your aunt's recent passing, and I am moved by Professor Alexander and his wife, as well as you and your husband's strength during times of tragedy. l remember your book "Journey Through the White Terror" well, and have been slowly exploring that history in books and places here in Taiwan. I recently went to see the gravesite of White Terror victims in六張犁，and have been studying Taiwanese literature in my "Taiwanese Novels" class.

I would love to meet Linda Chu, if she has time! And thank you for coming to my violin recital last spring, I was so happy to see my professors and friends come together to hear me play, despite being quite nervous!

Wishing the very best with this upcoming book!

Sincerely,
Formosa
6/5/2020

Linda Chu（朱雯琪）致Formosa Deppman

Dear Formosa,

It's great to hear that you're in Taipei studying Chinese and Taiwanese literature. Many years ago, I also came to Taiwan to study Chinese as well. I started as an exchange student and ended up moving here permanently after graduation.

Where are you currently studying at? Your courses sound like some of the ones I took when I studied at NTU's ICLP.

（此處刪去一段）。

Best,

Linda

6/5/2020

孫康宜致李保陽

Dear Baoyang,

I just want to let you know that it's very sweet of my two granddaughters (ages 6 and 4) to do this sketch in imitation of a 1990 picture, which is one of the most memorable pictures treasured by me. The fact that this sketch was done by my granddaughters (with some help from their father) during the COVID-19 lockdown is especially meaningful to me.

First of all, the original picture was taken in the fall of 1990, when my daughter was only 4 years old. It was right in front of the Yale Sterling Memorial Library. And it just happens that this picture has a special historical significance. This is because the location, where the picture was taken in 1990, later became the site of Yale Women's Table designed by the famous architect Maya Lin (the niece of Lin Huiyin 林徽因) in 1993.

So I hasten to share with you both the sketch by my granddaughters (done 30 years later) and the "legendary" 1990 picture.

Best,

Kang-i

6/6/2020

孫康宜致李保陽

Dear Baoyang,

　　These are indeed very precious pictures of Prof. Mote's drawing and his wife Chen Hsiao-lan's 陳效蘭 painting! Here are my descriptions of their art works:

（1）牟復禮教授於1953年的畫作。作於美國加州Los Altos城。此畫的題簽是：「給效蘭，寫洋蘭，洋人畫」。

（2）陳效蘭女士於1980初贈給孫康宜和張欽次的畫作。

　　Please see attached.

Best,
Kang-i
6/6/2020

　　牟復禮為其夫人陳效蘭畫蘭花（1953年）　　　陳效蘭女士畫蘭（1980年）

孫康宜致李保陽

Dear Baoyang,

You will be interested in seeing this old picture of Prof. Mote's class at Jinling University金陵大學in Nanking.

As you can see from the recent email exchanges between my husband C. C. and Hsiao-lan, we now know that this picture was taken near Nanking in 1947 or 1948.

Hope you enjoy this old picture. By the way, T T Chen (mentioned in Hsiao-lan's email) is 陳大端教授, who used to teach at the East Asian Studies Department in Princeton.

Best,
Kang-i
6/6/2020

牟復禮教授金陵大學就讀期間與同學合影（1947-1948年）。前排右一牟復禮，左一趙榮琅，第二
排左二陳大端。

孫康宜致李保陽

Dear Baoyang,

Again, this is a valuable picture, showing the lunch which Hsiao-lan cooked for my husband C.C. during his visit to Hsiao-lan at the Motes' estate in Denver, Colorado. The picture was taken in 2006, a year after Prof. Mote's passing. (Professor Mote died in spring 2005). C.C. went to visit Hsiao-lan while he was on a business trip to Denver. Please see a quote from C.C.'s recent email, in which he described his 2006 visit to Hsiao-lan in detail:

". . . I still remember seeing the Fortune sign hung right next to the walkway leading to Fritz's Library. For years Kang-i and I had wished to make a trip together to visit the Motes at their Colorado house, but in 2006 I alone drove from the Stapleton International Airport all the way to the Continental Divide where the Motes' estate is located. Hsiao-Lan made a luncheon for me in celebrating the occasion; it was so elaborate, with 6 dishes plus lager beer."

I should mention that this picture reminds me of the *Jinpingmei* dinner（金瓶梅大餐）which Hsiao-lan cooked for us in Princeton way back in May 1975. That was of course 45 years ago.

Best,

Kang-i

6/6/2020

張欽次和陳效蘭，2006，Granby, Colorado

李保陽致孫康宜

孫老師，

　　感謝主！感謝Andrew Wang先生的慨允，讓我們可以用高先生那張珍貴的1932年全家福照片。說來也是奇怪，當第一眼看到這張照片時，保陽就非常喜歡，次日還專門為這張照片寫了一段題跋。後來您說由於種種原因，這張照片不方便給我們拿來出版，但是保陽一直沒有在草稿中刪去。保陽想，神大概會讓我們用這張照片的。所以收到您三號的來信，說Andrew先生授權我們用這張照片，真是意外之喜又在預料之中！感謝　主！

保陽　敬上
6/7/2020

孫康宜致李保陽

Dear Baoyang,

　　C. C. just sent us a map (copied from Wikipedia) showing where the Motes' Estate is. (Please see C.C.'s letter).

　　I should also explain that, during Prof. Mote's lifetime, Mote and Hsiao-lan always stayed half a year (usually from June to December) in their family estate in Granby, Colorado, and then went down to Princeton to teach for the spring semester (i.e., January through May). In other words, for many decades, they had two houses--one in Granby and one in Princeton. They were truly a couple who knew how to live!

　　In my view, Mote was someone who knew how to enjoy the pleasures of being a hermit, while knowing how to act as an intellectual leader too. Being the founder of the East Asian Studies Program at Princeton, he was also fortunate to be granted a special privilege by the University to teach only 6 months every year, while receiving a full faculty salary. That's indeed quite unusual.

Anyway, I hope this information about Professor Mote's family estate in Colorado gives you a new perspective on his life.

Best,

Kang-i

6/7/2020

C. C. Chang（張欽次）致孫康宜、李保陽

The Motes' Estate is right on the Rocky Mountains, known as the Continental Divide which is the main hydrological divide of the Americas. Thus, it overlooks the Eastern Continent from the Rocky Mountains. As you can see from the map below, the Motes' Estate is along the winding red line following the top of the Rocky Mountains. That's why Hsiao-lan uses RKY as part of her email address.

C.C.

6/7/2020

Haninah Levine致孫康宜

Dear Professor Chang,

Thank you so much for your email, and I am deeply honored at your request. I would be more than happy for you to use our correspondence in your book, including the poems, so long as I will retain the copyright to the poems so that I can use them myself in the future as I choose. Aside from that, my one other request is that you not use the pictures from the service, since they are very personal to my family. If you would like to include pictures of my mother's artwork, though, I would again be deeply honored, and can send you better photographs.

Incidentally, I was just getting ready to send you some more quatrains, written during the "plague year" itself - the spring.

Will the book be published in the US as well?

All the best,

Haninah

6/7/2020

孫康宜致Haninah Levine

Dear Haninah,

I am so happy to receive your positive response. First of all, would you send me a photograph of your mother's painting, titled "The Perfect Imperfect" as soon as possible?

And, yes, I promise that pictures from your mother's memorial service will not be used in the book.

By the way, in my previous email, I forgot to tell you that the English title of the book, "Letters Written During the COVID-19 Pandemic," will appear along with the

Chinese title on the book cover. I should also mention that, although the book is not published in the U.S. , English readers will still be able to enjoy reading the book. This is because 99% of my letters (as well as most of the select letters from friends) are in English, although my collaborator Dr. Li's letters are mainly in Chinese. I'm sure the readers will appreciate the "quatrains " you have shared with me. Of course, you will retain the copyright to your poems. Your quatrains will appear in the book in the context of our letters, and we are extremely grateful to you for giving us the permission to do so.

    All the best.

Kang-i

6/7/2020

註：此信有部分刪節和更正。

李保陽致孫康宜

孫老師，

    真是奇妙得讓人難以置信！您1975年在牟先生家參加「金瓶梅大宴」，當時的主廚就是牟夫人陳效蘭女士。時隔四十五年，您轉來牟夫人的信和這張照片，又把近半個世紀前的故事串接起來。真是一件奇妙的事情。謝謝！

保陽　敬上

6/7/2020

李保陽致C. C. Chang（張欽次）、孫康宜

親愛的C.C.先生、孫老師，

　　謝謝你們轉來PECO公司的實時供電查詢網頁！

　　三號那天，大費城西北地區遭遇了一場強烈的雷雨風暴，受損嚴重，電力中斷數日。我們村地處Schuylkill河谷淺山平原地帶，植被茂密，當日大風毀壞樹木無算。我們這裡的居民生活用電的供給線路，全部架設在木質電線桿上。大風暴雨引起的樹木傾倒壓斷電線，電線桿被風雨刮倒，所以造成大片的居民區停電。

　　昨天保陽進山，山區受災程度較我們平原地帶尤為嚴重，觸目一片狼藉。數圍粗的大樹被連根拔起甩到路上，許多路段都豎起單行道限行牌，到處是工人在清理傾倒的樹木路障。路上跑的也大多是工程車和電力公司的維修車。疫情期間，電力公司的維修人手本來就少於平時，這次維修被損毀的電力設施，也只好優先考慮偏僻山地一帶居民區，我們社區被留在最後維修，所以整整停了五天電。所幸我們的天然氣尚未受損，可以正常洗澡燒飯。山區人家沒有電，生活就成了大問題。

　　昨天下午供電公司派員來檢修，很快就恢復了供電。孩子們看到燈亮了，就像過節一般開心雀躍。感謝主，雖然停了五天電，但大家現在都可以正常生活工作了。

　　所以遲至現在才把孫老師上週的所有來信處理完畢。真是抱歉！

　　炎夏來臨，你們保重身體！

保陽　敬上
6/8/凌晨

李保陽致孫康宜

孫老師，

　　已經把網址附錄在了您4月24日給保陽的回信後了。影片文件轉換二維碼

（QR code）需要一款專用的電腦軟體，待明早保陽試一下，如果不能解決，屆時就請出版社幫忙。

保陽
6/8/2020

孫康宜致陳效蘭（Hsiao-lan Chen Mote）

Dear Hsiao-lan（效蘭），

I'm writing to ask if I have your permission to include these 3 pictures and 2 drawings (see attached) in the forthcoming book, titled：避疫書信選：從抱月樓到潛學齋 (co-edited with Dr Baoyang Li). The book will be published by the Showwe publishing House in Taiwan（臺北：秀威資訊）。The English title for the book is: *Letters Written During the COVID-19 Pandemic.* Yale University provides a generous amount of publication subsidy for this book.

The book is mainly about my scholarly correspondence with Dr. Li, as well as my personal letters exchanged with friends during this unusual period of the COVID-19 pandemic. The book includes both Chinese and English letters.

One of the subjects my collaborator Dr. Li and I often talked about in our letters (including letters from other related scholars) is about my former Princeton professors. It just happens that my collaborator Baoyang Li, who lives near Philadelphia, often visits Princeton's Gest Library and is very interested in knowing more about Princeton. Needless to say, a topic that often comes up in our correspondence concerns Fritz. Your ingenious creation of the 金瓶梅大餐 in 1975 remains in my vivid memory even to this day, and so it has also become an interesting topic for us as well!

With your permission, I hope to add 3 pictures and 2 drawings to the Mote related subjects covered by the 《避疫書信選》. They are:（1）Fritz's class picture in Nanjing (ca. 1947),（2）Fritz and Hsiao-lan "just married" in the U.S. Embassy,

Nanjing, 1950. （3）a six course luncheon prepared by Hsiao-lan for C.C. Chang, in Granby, Colorado, August 20, 2006; （4）Drawing by F.W. Mote, 1953 Los Altos, CA. （5）Hsiao-lan's orchid painting for C.C. and Kang-i in the 1980s. (We have the original painting here in our Woodbridge home.)

　　Please let me know if we have the permission to use the above pictures and drawings in the book. Also, is it all right to include your email explaining the background of Fritz's old class picture the other day?

　　Anyway, thank you for your consideration. The book is ready to be submitted to the publisher any day now, so I hope to get your reply as soon as possible. I know you are very busy right now (as usual), so a simple YES or No from you would be sufficient.

Love,

Kang-i

6/8/2020

The 22 dishes which Hsiao-lan Chen Mote prepared for the *Jinpingmei* dinner" on May 4, 1975. Calligraphy by Kang-i Sun Chang.

Haninah Levine致孫康宜

Dear Professor Chang,

Please let me know whether the attached file will work. Please credit the picture as "*The Perfect Imperfect Circle*, Shulamith Nebenzahl Levine, 2006 (used with permission of the artist's estate)." My family and I are deeply honored by your request.

Thank you,
Haninah
6/8/2020

The Perfect Imperfect Circle, Shulamith Nebenzahl Levine, 2006 (used with permission of the artist's estate). Shulamith Nebenzahl Levine 是著名畫家，曾經任教於耶魯大學。

孫康宜致李保陽

Dear Baoyang,

As you may remember, in my 4/17 letter to the Tunghai people I already mentioned that my husband C. C. had given a copy of his *Collected Works* (2020) to his alma mater, the Chung-yuan Christian University（中原大學）. It was 57 years ago that C.C. graduated from Chung-yuan, before he went to National Taiwan University

（臺大）later for his M.S. degree. Please see attached a picture of C.C.'s *Collected Works*, which contain his notable works published during the last 50 years in the U.S.

I should also mention, however, that originally there was going to be a "Book Presentation Ceremony"（贈書典禮）on April 15, 2020, for which both C. C. and I were expected to attend in person. But due to the COVID-19 pandemic, we had to cancel our Taiwan trip, and that's why we finally had C.C.'s *Collected Works* sent to Chung-yuan University via UPS Global express.

Also, as was mentioned in the following link to the Chung-yuan website, I myself had contributed a copy of my father's book,《孫保羅書法：附書信日記》（孫保羅著，孫康宜編註），to Chung-yuan Univesity as well.

https://www1.cycu.edu.tw/news/detail?type=%E7%84%A6%E9%BB%9E%E6%96%B0%E8%81%9E&id=2300&from=singlemessage&isappinstalled=0

Anyway, it is such a coincidence that both my Exhibition （「陽光穿透的歲月」書展）at Tunghai University and CC's "Book Presentation Ceremony"（贈書典禮）at Chung-yuan University were scheduled in mid-April (i.e., on 4/13 and 4/15, respectively).

It's too bad that both of us had to cancel our trip to Taiwan due to the COVID-19 pandemic. But we are most grateful to our alma maters for giving us such great honors.

Best,
Kang-i
6/9/2020

張欽次文集

李保陽致孫康宜

孫老師，

謝謝您分享的C.C.先生捐贈給母校的文集照片。這是作為一個學者，能給自己母校最珍貴、最有意義的回饋。今年四月，世界範圍內疫情肆虐，在這樣的背景下，你們回饋母校的方式，更具特殊的歷史意義，所以不必在乎是否曾經親臨現場。

保陽非常好奇，C.C.先生文集中收錄的都是些什麼內容的文章呢？

保陽　敬上
6/9/2020

孫康宜致 Haninah Levine

Dear Haninah,

This photograph of your mother's painting is just wonderful! We will certainly include the credit line in the book. It is indeed a great honor for us to include this great work by your mother.

I often thought of your mother's art exhibition at Yale's Joseph Slifka Center. To this day I can still recall our lunch converastion at Mory's, where you and I and your mother had such a wonderful time together.

Your mother Shula will always be remembered.

Best,
Kang-i
6/9/2020

李保陽致孫康宜

孫老師，

謝謝您分享的葉國威〈十分冷淡存知己——記陶光與張充和〉。陶先生的個性，讓保陽想起昨晚和您聊起的人的個性中的「直」。人如果不能在生活中權變，真的是很糟糕的事情。陶先生大概就是這樣的例子。後世人往往只看光怪陸離的歷史表象，如果真的以讀者之「我」代入到歷史現場，作為歷史當事人來現身說法，就會發現歷史並不是後人想像的那般加了柔光的絢爛。生活和現實加諸於每一個人的不易，是一樣的。

保陽對陶先生詩集《獨往集》和詞集《西窗》尤感興趣，真想有機會拜讀一番。不知道充老身後遺物聚散於何處？還能尋得她這兩本舊藏否？

這篇文章末尾引用了董橋對充老書法的評論：「張充和的工楷小字我向來喜愛，秀慧的筆勢孕育溫存的學養，集字成篇，流露的又是烏衣巷口三分寂寥的芳菲。多年前初賞她寫給施蟄存先生的一片詞箋，驚豔不必說，傳統品味棲遲金粉空梁太久了，她的款款墨痕正好揭開一齣文化的驚夢，夢醒處，悠然招展的竟是西風老樹下一簑一笠的無恙！她那手工楷天生是她筆下詩詞的佳偶，一配就配出了《納蘭詞》裡『鴛鴦小字，猶記手生疏』的矜持，也配出了梅影悄悄掠過紅橋的江南消息，撩人低徊。」董橋無疑是讀懂了充老的書法，所以他的這段話評論得讓人驚豔不已。記得四月二十五日那天，收到您從木橋鄉寄來的《古色今香》那本書（保陽尤其喜歡那書的封面設計！），當天在日記中寫了下面一段話：

> 我尤其喜歡充和先生的字，以隸法入楷，閒逸娟淨，真率秀拙，沒有絲毫的煙火氣，能看出她晚年平靜的心境和生活狀態。楊絳先生的字，雖亦有文人的逸趣，但字裡行間始終透出一個「急」字。這大約和她晚年所處環境有關。楊先生和錢鍾書先生都是有生命智慧的人，觀錢先生的《圍城》即可知。但這種智慧一旦融入藝術，就變成桎梏。唐篔先生的書法最明顯的特徵是「硬」，這從她字的結體——尤其是豎、撇的收筆之勢——特徵上表現得尤為明顯。每一個字都飽含著一股鬱怒之氣。其字高瘦頎長，和義寧先生的體貌差似。與充和先生的肥而秀很不一樣。義寧先生的「寒」

「瘦」，在唐先生的書法中表現很明顯。（《避疫日記》四月二十五日）

董橋說充老的字「流露的又是烏衣巷口三分寂寥的芳菲」，充老自己說「十分冷淡存知己，一曲微茫度此生」，這兩句話真有一種相知於生命深處的共鳴！

保陽　敬上
6/10/2020

孫康宜致李保陽

Dear Baoyang,

Unfortunately, when Ch'ung-ho Chang（張充和）was 95 years old (in 2008), she could no longer find her copies of Tao Guang's（陶光）two collections, 《讀往集》and《西窗》。

I remember that was in the fall of 2008. At that time I was working on two books on Ch'ung-ho（namely《古色今香——張充和題字選集》and《曲人鴻爪本事》）, and so Ch'ung-ho and her house keeper Mr. Wu Liliu started to search for Tao Guang's two poetry collections. This is because I needed more information in order to finish writing the entry on Tao Guang for the the book,《曲人鴻爪本事》. (Later, the section on Tao Guang appeared in Chapter 5 of Part One of the book.)

But alas, even though Ch'ung-ho and Mr. Wu looked at every corner of the house, there was no sight of Tao Guang's two books. Finally Ch'ung-ho came to the conclusion that perhaps someone had borrowed those two poetry collections from her and had forgotten to return them to her.

I think it's a shame that the so-called "存世的孤本" of Tao Guang's《讀往集》and《西窗》could not be located now.

You also asked: Where did Ch'ung-ho's collections of books go after her death? Well, after Ch'ung-ho died in 2015, people in her family sold all her remaining items (mostly books) to a private collector（私人藏書家）。I don't know who that private collector was.

　　But by that time, there were few valuable items left in Ch'ung-ho's collection. This is because, a few years prior to 2015, one of her students already helped her ship her numerous valuable items to China for sale（拍賣）。

　　I hope the above information helps.

　　Thank you for sharing your wonderful diary entry on Ch'ung-ho's caligraphy, which I have enjoyed reading.

Best,

Kang-i

6/10/2020

陳效蘭致孫康宜

Dear Kang-i,

　　You are very kind, please use whatever photo you want. I am sure that Fritz would have felt like I do; whatever you choose is fine with me, it would be just fine with us. Thank you for your thoughtfulness.

Love, Hsiao-lan

6/10/2020

C. C. Chang（張欽次）致李保陽

Dear Baoyang,

　　Thank you for inquiring about my book which actually is a collection of published articles on my works during my professional career as an engineer. Engineering is a complicated subject and each engineering project involoves several different disciplines. The "Preface" to my book mentions not only my own engineering background but also some general information about hydrotechnical and geotechnical engineering. I attach the Preface to my book here for your reference.

Best, C.C.

6/10/2020

Mary Ellen Friends致孫康宜

Dear Kang-i,

How interesting that you wrote to me yesterday--I was just talking about you with a friend!

Of course you may use any notes or letters I have written to you. Please feel free anytime.

The book sounds wonderful! How exciting that the book will be published and that Yale is honoring you by providing a publication subsidy! I will certainly look for the book when it is out.

I hope you and C.C. are well. Today is my and John's 26th wedding anniversary, and we got in from a morning walk just as the rain started. Here in Deerfield, the hay is curing in the fields, the trees by the river and on the edge of the meadows are full of song birds, and all sorts of creatures are starting families or sending young ones out to explore. In such a beautiful, peaceful setting, I sometimes forget for a moment that my daughter and I donned masks last week and participated in a protest, or that my brother lost a dear friend to COVID-19. I feel as though I am simultaneously three or four or even five different people, some of whom are grateful and fundamentally happy, and others who feel hopeless or profoundly sad. It's exhausting. But if these times are emotionally draining for me, what are they like for those who don't live in a beautiful setting and who don't have a loving family and who don't have a secure job or excellent health care?

Yesterday I received a thank-you note from one of my 9th graders whose parents work at my school. In part of her note she wrote: "I have learned so much about the continent, research skills, and analytical writing. You never failed to make everyone laugh and feel comfortable in your classroom. On the first day of your class, I had just come from crying in my dad's office and you gave me a wonderful smile and wink. That made me feel better and reassured me. Thank you for always making my days better."

We each have our own places in this world, and I am ever grateful I answered my calling to teach at the high school level. You, too, found your place, and you made countless days better for your students by both reassuring them and holding them to high standards.

Happy Day,

Mary Ellen

6/11/2020

孫康宜致Mary Ellen Friends

Dear Mary Ellen,

Wow, happy anniversary to you and John. Indeed, today is an auspicious day! I remember that you two got married 26 years ago; it was like yesterday!

Thank you for giving me the permission to use any notes or letters from you! This really means a lot to me!

Best,

Kang-i

6/11/2020

孫康宜致李保陽

Dear Baoyang,

I was so happy to receive your package today, in which I was delighted to find an offprint of your article on the poet Wang Pengyun（〈王鵬運藏書及遺物……〉）published in the Japanese journal,《立命館文學》, Dec. , 2019.

Apart from your wonderful narration of the story of Wang Pengyun's collection, I was especially pleased to read in the "afterword"（附記）about how you got to know the great Japanese scholar芳村弘道in person. Your descriptions of how you first met with芳村先生and toured the old bookstores together in Kyoto, as well as other details, are simply fascinating!

It happens that just yesterday you had forwarded me an email from芳村先生, in which he mentioned an article by me which I wrote in 1981. (The article was titled, 〈日本文學懷古〉). I'm very grateful to芳村先生for his praises, as well as his pointing out a few errors in my article:「『柏舟私生子薰之君與光源氏的孫子匂宮』之『柏舟』當作『柏木』，『匂宮』當作『匂宮』。『匂』是日本製作的漢字之一。」

I'm especially interested in learning from 芳村先生 that the漢字character「匂」was an invention by the Japanese! After doing some research (with the help of Ling Chao凌超) on this, I also noticed that the character「匂」is not a common word in modern Chinese. Also, according to Ling Chao, the character「匈」(pronounced as "xiong") did appear in Chinese handwriting but usually not in print. So it is true that the Japanese finally made the character「匂」as a standard word in the Japanese 漢字.

Since my article was written almost 40 years ago, I don't remember if「柏舟」and「匂宮」were just typos on my part or if I merely copied the names directly from the old edition of Lin Wen-yueh's林文月Chinese translation of the *Tale of Genji*（《源氏物語》）.

In any case, I'm very thankful to芳村先生for singling out these errors. When the page proofs of the *jianti* edition of my Collected Works（簡體《孫康宜文集》5卷

本）become available, I'll definitely ask the editor to make corrections for the article, 〈日本文學懷古〉,which appears in vol. 2 of the set.

As to your article on Wang Pengyun, I have truly learned a lot from it. The story about the loss of Wang's collection during the Cultural Revolution is so sad! Looking through your catalogue of the valuable items in Wang's collection, I cannot help but think about the tragic circumstances in modern China.

Best,

Kang-i

6/12/2020

孫康宜致李保陽

Dear Baoyang,

I want to share with you this correspondence between me and Peng Shu-chen彭淑珍, who is on the staff of Chung-yuan University Library. As you know, Chung-yuan Christian University is C.C.'s alma mater. I have to say that during this COVID-19 lock-down, it is quite amazing that both Chung-yuan University and Tunghai University (i.e., my alma mater) have done similar things to glorify us, which have made us feel deeply grateful and greatly humbled.

Since April we had numerous email exchanges with Peng Shu-chen, all regarding C.C. 's donation of his Collected Works (including a copy of my father's book edited by me)to Chung-yuan University.

And then on May 7th, Peng shu-chen told us that they wanted to publish an article about C.C. and me in their university journal, *Tiandi zhongyuan*（《天地中原》）, and that's why they needed me to send pictures for the article. That explains the context of the following correspondence, which I have selected from a series of related email exchanges.

Hope you find this correspondence interesting.

Best,

Kang-i

李保陽致孫康宜

孫老師，

　　保陽剛剛收到Gest的Martin館長寫來的電子郵件，郵件中提到他曾經發表過三篇文章，都和Mote先生有關。Mote先生是您在Princeton所最尊敬的師長之一，其中兩篇文章的題目和出處如下：

（1）Martin Heijdra, "*Review of Mote's scholarly works*," in: Wang Chengmian, ed., Xinhuo xichuan-Mou Fuli yu hanxue yanjiu/ Perpetual torch of learning in the west-F.W. Mote and sinology (Taibei: Liming wenhua, 2007), pp. 91-108

（2）Martin Heijdra, "*Publications of Frederick W. Mote*," in: Wang Chengmian, ed., Xinhuo xichuan-Mou Fuli yu hanxue yanjiu/ Perpetual torch of learning in the west-F.W. Mote and sinology(Taibei: Liming wenhua, 2007), pp. 109-129

　　Martin館長還有一篇關於Mote先生的文章，收錄在Perry Link編的*The scholar's mind: essays in honor of F.W. Mote*一書中，由Chinese University Press (Hong Kong) 2009年出版，Martin館長沒有給具體的文章名稱，這本書在Yale的圖書館應該可以找得到。

保陽　敬上

6/12/2020

芳村弘道致李保陽

李保陽老兄台鑑：

　　前月捧讀尊翰及孫康宜先生〈日本文學懷古〉一文，未克裁覆鳴謝，前日又奉來示，感愧交並。

　　高編《避疫書信選》中，擬收賤翰，過蒙垂青，不勝感荷。

　　孫教授清遊日本古典文學故地，撰寫雅文，詩趣橫溢，感動無量。

　　（「柏舟私生子薰之君與光源氏的孫子匂宮」之「柏舟」當作「柏木」，「句宮」當作「匂宮」。「匂」是日本製作的漢字之一。）

　　敝國疫情小差，漸次回復日常，請勿掛念。專此肅覆，即頌

　　夏安

芳村弘道　敬上
2020/06/12

孫康宜致Martin Heijdra

Dear Martin,

　　Hope you and family are staying safe and well during this challenging time of the COVID-19 pandemic.

　　I want to use this opportunity to thank you for participating in the book,《避疫書信選：從抱月樓到潛學齋》, which is compiled and edited by Dr BAOYANG LI李保陽and myself. Please see attached a copy of my preface to this book. In fact, Baoyang will also contribute a separate preface. By the way, I was so happy to know that you and Baoyang had already met in Princeton. Actually I have never met Baoyang in person yet!

　　I am also grateful to you for sending us your articles on your mentor Prof. Fritz Mote. As you may know, one of the topics covered in this book is about Prof. Mote's life and scholarship.

On another matter, I want to make sure that I mention this to you. In the fall of 2018, I helped Prof. Kao Yu-kung's 高友工 family to donate Prof. Kao's last remaining 300 books to Wesleyan University. Before the books were shipped to Wesleyan, I specifically reserved one of the copies of Prof. Kao's legendary book, 《美典：中國文學研究論集》（北京三聯，2008）, for your East Asian Library at Princeton. The book is stamped with the inscription, "Memory of Prof. Kao Yu-kung." (I can never forget the tremendous effort you put into organizing Prof. Kao's memorial service in March 2017!)

But did I already send Prof. Kao's book to you? Just today I found 3 copies of the book (with the memorial stamp) sitting on my bookshelf. But I simply can't remember if I have sent one of the copies to you!

If I indeed forgot to send the book to you, please let me know. I can then mail it to you after the COVID-19 crisis is over.

Best,
Kang-i（康宜）
6/13/2020

林玫儀致孫康宜

康宜姊：

明天要參加中央大學一個學生的博士口考，最近忙著閱讀論文及查找資料，好久沒有與妳聯絡了。我的身體早就沒事了，勞妳惦念，真不好意思。

妳的工作效率真是驚人，一般人在疫情期間都心煩氣躁，妳潛心做學問，論學不輟，這段時間因為雜事減少，反而收穫更多，真好。保陽的功底不錯，相信你們的討論必定很精采，我也很想看看呢！

妳這本書是論學書信，參觀東海的展覽，我個人獲益良多，給妳的信中所

言，只是我衷心的體會，可談不到學術；不過確是疫情期間一件值得紀念的盛事，如果妳認為可以收入，我也很樂意藉此留下一點美好回憶。

　　今天是主日，我們教會原本都改為線上崇拜，因為疫情趨緩，從上星期開始，已經恢復實體崇拜了。我等一下要去教會，就此擱筆。順祝

　　平安喜樂

玫儀

6/13/2020

康宜姊：

　　拜讀序文，發現這本書中涉及的內容遠超過妳早上信息中所言，除了討論學術，其實還是妳這段時間的經歷、心境甚至信仰的紀錄，真是太豐富了。期待早日出版，能先睹為快。順祝

　　平安喜樂

玫儀

6/14/2020

康正果致孫康宜避疫詩一首

隔離期間在家理髮詠

疫情肆虐久，白髮漸瘋長。人人自閉症，戶戶斷交往。舉國禁行日，事事靠上網。購物送上門，髮廊盡打烊。搔首悲明鏡，潘鬢三千丈。皓首如飛蓬，坐臥時撓癢。兒媳巧試手，操剪初上場。淺薄清積雪，細密除草莽。削盡煩惱絲，豁然得開朗。

康正果

6/17/2020

李保陽致孫康宜

孫老師，

　　謝謝您分享BBC製作的杜甫一生詩旅視頻，當時我剛剛穿戴整齊，循例往後院的菜園去練習聽力，這個《杜甫：中國最偉大的詩人》影片，正成為練習聽力的好材料。我聽完之後，立即就轉給了我曾經的學生們（遺憾的是，我不知道他們在中國大陸是否可以打開YouTube）。

　　這個節目中的畫面，是如此的熟悉，這大概是在過去的二十年裡，我的足跡和杜甫大部份是重合的，所以尤其能引起共鳴，不僅僅是您預先告訴我的這檔節目取景於我的家鄉西安。

　　我想杜甫詩歌的生命力是在他常年漂泊不定的人生顛簸中凝定的，他寫出的是一種人類共同的生命體驗。這種生命體驗在不同的人群之間，是如此的普遍，以至於能穿越時空，遠在一千多年後的歐美世界激盪起人們的共鳴，還能被解讀得如此細膩真切。我特別認同主持人引用佛洛伊德在1916年說的那段話：人是有可能為某種文化的衰落而深感哀痛的。這句話應和了節目尾聲中的那個問答，即中國人為什麼喜歡杜甫？杜甫在中國詩歌乃至中國文化史上的地位究竟是怎樣的？他給出了發人深省的回答：因為杜甫用獨具魅力的中文所結撰的詩歌，塑造了中國人獨特而源遠流長的精神、審美和價值，這是中國歷史上多如牛毛的任何一個皇帝都做不到的。在我有限的閱讀經驗中，對於杜甫，再沒有比這更高的評價了。時至今日，中國文字和詩歌那誘人的魅力，仍是多少失意的人在無盡暗夜中聊以慰藉靈魂的救贖。儘管杜甫在政治上失敗得一塌糊塗，但他塑造的這種精神、審美和價值，至今仍具穿越時空的普世意義，而不單單拘限於文學。杜甫一生大半在家國多變的行役旅途中，這種羈旅不定，消磨了詩人俗世中的有限生命，卻讓詩人對生命的意義和價值有了更加深刻的體悟和昇華。後來的蘇軾，也是在黃州、惠州、儋州的一生貶謫中，逐漸體悟到有限的生命之於一個人的無限價值與意義。中國詩歌史上那些膾炙人口的篇什，多結撰於長途羈旅的寂寞中。那些震鑠古今的詩壇巨人，總是在流離的路上達到其生命與詩歌的雙重高峰。

　　Ian McKellen用西方的深情，朗誦杜詩的沉鬱頓挫，這種東西文化的異樣特質竟然可以在詩歌的名下，臻於完美一體，這正是杜甫用他的詩歌所塑造的那種

審美、精神和價值，穿越時空生命力的表徵。

　　奇妙的是，我昨晚在撰寫《避疫》前言時，正好寫到杜甫和李白：「李白總是引起杜甫的追思，柳宗元在貶謫途中不忘對劉禹錫寫信噓寒問暖……。」星期二的時候，有位朋友讓我評論另一位朋友的詩，我寫了下面的話：「如果生活閱歷與人生思考都欠火候的話，加上把寫詩作為一種炫才或謀生手段（王國維所謂『羔雁之具』），往往容易意格卑下。詩歌詞藻、平仄、用韻，都是次要的。真感情是基礎。」這裡所謂「感情」，就是指廣義的閱歷、學識、思考，不單單是指狹義的個人情感。我想把這個「感情」用來概括杜詩那種沉甸甸的內容，應該庶幾近之。

　　孫老師，欣賞完您分享的《杜甫：中國最偉大的詩人》影片，中心耿耿，久不能復，我將自己這十多來年塗抹的《抱月樓詩詞稿》呈奉給您，算是中國詩歌在我這裡的一個迴響。請您批評指正！再次感謝您的分享！專此，並頌

　　夏祺！

保陽　敬上
6/18/2020

孫康宜致李保陽

Dear Baoyang,

　　I am so happy to know that you like the BBC documentary, "Du Fu: China's Greatest Poet"（《杜甫，最偉大的中國詩人》）. First of all, I want to let you know that it was my brother K.C. Sun（孫康成）who first sent me the video for the documentary via LINE last night. And then I forwarded it to you afterwards.

　　In fact, a few months ago I was informed that, on April 6, at 9:00 p.m., my friend Steve [Stephen] Owen宇文所安 was going to show up in the BBC TV documentary of the poet Du Fu. I heard that it would feature the British actor Sir Ian McKellen, and the documentary was done by the English historian and broadcaster Michael Wood.

Unfortunately I did not have a chance to watch the BBC program on April 6 due to an important timing conflict. Several days later, however, I was glad to see a few scenes from Ian McKellen's excellent reading of Tu Fu's poems (in translation).

Needless to say, I have been waiting anxiously for the completion of a video, which I heard would soon be available. So you can imagine how elated I was when my brother K.C. forwarded the You Tube to me yesterday!

I think Du Fu would have been thrilled to know that his poetry had become the subject of such a first-rate documentary, not to mention the fact that it was written and presented by the famous Michael Wood, a person known for his love of history as well as his numerous documentaries and Television series. I can never forget his T.V. presentation called "The Story of England, " which was a 6-part documentary series in 2010. And two years after that, another documentary by Michael Wood, titled "The Great British Story: A People's History" (in 8 parts), was again shown on BBC. Thus, for someone like Michael Wood to do such a splendid project in honoring Du Fu, China's greatest poet, is indeed an important milestone in human history!

What is most amazing is that Michael Wood has invited the legendary actor Ian McKellen to be the reader of Du Fu's poems. Ian McKellen is of course well-known for his leading roles in playing Shakespeare's plays, such as Richard II,Richard III, Macbeth, and King Lear. His contribution to the theater in UK was so great that he was honored as a "knight" (KBE)for his distinguished service almost 30 years ago. That's why he is also known as "Sir Ian."

I'm also very happy that my friend Steve Own has a chance to participate in the Du Fu documentary this time. As you know, Owen has single-handedly translated the "Complete Du Fu Poems," which is quite an amazing task! I really like what he says in the documentary— "There is Dante, there is Shakespeare, and there is Du Fu."

I also found your comments on the Du Fu documentary very inspiring, especially the following:

杜甫一生大半在家國多變的行役旅途中，這種羈旅不定，消磨了詩人俗世

中的有限生命，卻讓詩人對生命的意義和價值有了更加深刻的體悟和昇華。後來的蘇軾，也是在黃州、惠州、儋州為代表的一生貶謫中，逐漸體悟到有限的生命之於一個人的無限價值與意義。中國詩歌史上那些膾炙人口的篇什，多結撰於長途羈旅的寂寞中。那些震鑠古今的詩壇巨人，總是在流離的路上達到其生命與詩歌的雙重高峰。

I could not believe that, during the last few years, you yourself have also experienced a lot of trials as a wanderer in exile--such that they remind me of Michael Wood's documentary, which describes in detail about what Du Fu had experienced during the chaotic times. In particular, I have noticed your preface to your poetry collection, called 「抱月集」, in which you described the routes of your difficult journey in July, 2013:

……二〇一三年七月二十三日零晨三點五十分寫竟於寶成鐵路秦嶺深山某小站，時由平涼乘烏魯木齊至成都夜班火車下陽平關中轉回洋州，此距第一次經此南下，恰十四年矣。

Anyway, I am greatly moved by the various wandering experiences you had in the past, as described in the many poems in your poetry collections—namely 「抱月集」、「掃葉集」、「天竺集」、「康園集」. You are only 41 years old, but you have already gone through so much!

Best,
Kang-i
6/18/2020

張宏生致孫康宜

謝謝康宜：

這本清詞的書，不久會寄上。

一口氣看完了《杜甫》，拍得很動心思，很高興在裡面看到了我們的朋友。這個題材不好拍，能夠有這樣的效果，已經很不容易。

宏生

6/18/2020

陳國球致孫康宜

Dear Kang-i Laoshi,

Many thanks for sending me the clip on Du Fu.

It is fantastic. The narration is great. I also feel the warmth when I saw Professor Owen on screen.

Best,

Guoqiu

6/18/2020

季進致孫康宜

孫老師好！

謝謝您分享《杜甫：中國最偉大的詩人》的鏈結。前不久朋友圈好多人分享，據說中央電視台都播了。我看以後覺得編導非常用心，拍得真不錯！其中還有老朋友所安的身影，倍感親切。Ian McKellen的朗誦，讓我印象深刻，雖然讀

的是杜甫詩歌的英譯，但抑揚頓挫中似乎也能感受到杜甫詩歌中人與時間、宇宙的奇妙結合。不知道西方觀眾聽了，是不是也能略略感受到杜詩的魅力。

　　祝開心！

季進
6/18/2020

林玫儀致孫康宜

康宜姊：

　　BBC製作的《杜甫，最偉大的中國詩人》這個影片，我大學同學的群組曾經傳給我，當時我正忙，沒有立即點閱。收到妳轉來的連結，今天早上出門前就先看了一部分，晚上回來，忙完諸般雜事，才再接下去看，越看越感動。像這一類介紹古代名人或是名作的影片現在並不少見，但是這一部很不一樣。這是由外國人執導、主要向外國人介紹杜甫生平的紀錄片，但對早已熟稔杜甫事蹟及作品的觀眾來說，卻也是大開眼界，頗受啟發。

　　影片的主題如片名所示，一在重現杜甫顛沛流離的一生，一在介紹他傳世不朽的詩篇。製作單位按照杜甫的傳記，回溯他的成長軌跡，由幼年開始，不計工本，跟著杜甫的足跡，一站一站實地拍攝，藉著主持人對杜甫事蹟的敘述及畫面的呈現，在歷史洪流中找尋杜甫的身影；同時選擇杜甫相關詩篇適時加以朗誦，一方面介紹杜甫的作品，一方面也因言為心聲，經由杜甫自己心靈的告白，可進一步突顯他當時的心境。這種手法甚好，雖然昔人已矣，時空環境也已有不少變化，但透過鏡頭呈現的視域，仍有助於聯想杜甫當年的生活景況。例如杜甫移居夔州那一段，影片中應用包括空拍等先進的攝錄技術拍攝三峽，隨著插天峭壁、陡峭峽谷等畫面一一出現，可以想見夔州山水之雄奇險峻，而這種山川地貌、風物景致對杜甫夔州詩的影響也就不言可喻了。再如介紹杜甫的〈閣夜〉詩：「歲暮陰陽催短景，天涯霜雪霽寒宵。五更鼓角聲悲壯，三峽星河影動搖……。」鏡頭中出現的是夜空中風雲變幻、繁星明滅的景象，伴隨娓娓的吟誦，悲壯蒼涼之感油然而生，彷

佛身歷其境般，對杜甫詩中所感，自能別有體會。此外，杜甫一生波濤起伏，撰作的詩歌又如此之多，影片卻只有一個小時，如何在有限的時間中揀選合適題材以呈現他的經歷和心境，也是極大挑戰，這令我對編劇及導演的功力極為佩服。

本片最令我感動的是製作態度的嚴謹。以上文提及的〈閣夜〉詩來說，為了配合詩情，畫面上出現的是從江面上仰視四周群山環繞的夜空景致，由一片漆黑中但見星河閃爍，漸至風起雲湧天漸發白，充滿寂寥蒼涼之感。然而江面上風譎雲詭，日夜景色瞬息萬變，要拍到合意的鏡頭，不知要付出多少代價，舉此一例，可見其他。再就語文來說，影片運用雙語，而以英語為主。說中文時標示英文字幕，說英文時則標中文字幕。主持人是英國著名的歷史學家兼紀錄片製作人邁克爾‧伍德（Michael Wood）教授，他在解說時，間中也會引用西方人熟悉的觀念如佛洛伊德、但丁等的說法來作類比；而詩歌部分則先翻譯成英文，再請英國傑出的舞台劇和電影演員伊恩‧麥克連（Ian McKellen）朗讀，凡此，均有助於西方的觀眾對杜甫其人其詩的理解。而熟稔中文卻不諳英語的觀眾，因有中文字幕，特別是引用杜詩時，除標示詩句原文外，並註明出處，因此，非但不影響對杜甫詩作的理解，且能借助影片而有更多的體會。甚至有些詩句找不到出處也會注明，如朗誦〈卜居〉時，中文字幕竟在直譯「我選擇老於此地，遠離首都，我成了一位農民」之後，附註「（這句話找不到對應的詩了）」，這雖然有點突兀，卻也可見譯者固守專業認真的一面。

這部影片向國際介紹中國詩歌，透過翻譯及字幕，中西觀眾都能瞭解詩意，既能引起大眾興趣，又能兼顧專業，可謂十分難得。中華文化博大精深，尤其古典詩歌更是精金美玉，學界一直努力想推展學術通俗化的工作，但如何拿捏其中分寸，不因太淺而流於平庸膚淺，甚至遠離專業，這在同一語文中尚且困難重重，何況向不同語文、不同文化的群眾推展？這部影片如此成功，往後我們向世界推廣中國文化，可以此作為借鏡。

走筆至此，因著「沿著詩人足跡」，腦中閃過一件舊事。想起多年前與吳熊和、嚴迪昌兩位教授合作研究，常有機會在一起聊天。有一次，嚴教授說，古代士人上京趕考，基本上都是走同一條路，我們不如按著他們的足跡，來規劃一個詩詞之旅吧。大家欣然同意，並推請嚴教授規劃路線，我說屆時我和外子可負責告知臺灣的同道，組團參與。往後再見面，也常提起此事，無奈大家都忙，遂不

了了之。如今兩位教授均已歸道山，今日欣賞這部影片，無意中觸動往事，不禁悵然良久，因附記於此。

玫儀
6/19/2020

卞東波致孫康宜

敬愛的康宜教授：

見信如晤！今天我有一個好消息分享給您，我已經拿到由我編纂的《中國古典文學與文本的新闡釋——海外漢學論文新集》的大批樣書了。本書在2019年11月已經由安徽教育出版社出版，十六開精裝，從封面設計到用紙都非常講究，也非常漂亮。您見了，一定會喜歡。更重要的是，本書是由您和蔡涵墨（Charles Hartman）教授為我作序的，這不但是我的光榮，也為本書增色很多。

本書收入包括您和蔡教授在內18位海外中國古典文學與文化研究者的二十餘篇論文，既有北美的漢學家的作品，也有歐洲和澳洲漢學家的論文，論域涉及中國古典文學、古典文獻和古代歷史，甚至還有關於中國現代文化史的題目。本書所收的漢學家既有像您和宇文所安這樣的漢學耆宿，也有剛剛博士畢業的漢學新秀，很多論文都是剛剛完成的，體現了海外中國古典文學研究的最新動態。我相信，本書的出版一定會豐富國內學界對海外漢學的進一步瞭解，促進人文思想的交流，從而推動中國古典文學研究的進步。

因為疫情的原因，要在耶魯大學召開的「第三屆中古中國人文會議」取消了，我本來也打算趁這次會議去耶魯大學拜訪您。不過，會議已經改在明年繼續召開，屆時我再去耶魯拜見您。值此非常時期，望您和欽次老師多多保重！敬頌著安！

東波叩上
2020年夏至前一日

孫康宜致李保陽

Dear Baoyang,

As you know, I have asked Prof. Jeongsoo Shin's permission to add his letters to our book.

In this email I would like to introduce Jeongsoo Shin to you. First of all, Jeongsoo is the translator for the Korean version of my book, *Six Dynasties Poetry* (1986). He translated the book in 2003, before he came to the States to work for his PhD degree at the University of Washington under the direction of Prof. David Knechtges. It's so wonderful that Jeongsoo's translation of my book was on display at the recent Tunghai exhibition. [Please see attached a picture of the Korean edition (2004) translated by Jeongsoo, as well as that of the original edition of my book published by Princeton University in 1986].

By the way, Jeongsoo and I have been in close contact since 2003, when he first visited the Yale campus. Later he even paid a personal visit to my parents' tomb at the Alta Mesa Memorial Park in Palo Alto, California.

I'm so pleased that since August 2019 Jeongsoo has been teaching at Yale as a Visiting Assistant Professor. I have enjoyed having frequent meetings with Jeongsoo during the fall semester when he was teaching the course on Korean Neo-Confucianism. But, alas, the COVID-19 pandemic suddenly came and so I could only see him via Zoom since March!

Now finally Jeongsoo will be going back to Korea next month. I'm sorry that I might not be able to see him in person before he leaves. On the safe side, I'm still practicing social distancing at this time.

Best,
Kang-i
6/20/2020

孫康宜《六朝詩歌概論》英文原著（普林斯頓大學出版社，1986年）　Jeongsoo Shin（申正秀）譯韓文版《六朝詩歌概論》（2004年）

Jeongsoo Shin致孫康宜

Thank you Professor for this great information.

I see big names there, like you, Tian Xiaofei, Knechtges, Saussy, Owen, etc. Wang Ping is also a good friend of mine.

The contents look interesting and I will soon get a copy of this book！

By the way, I have got your previous email as well. I see your dental situation. I fully understand. No worries.

The date of my flight is "just" fixed; It's July 22th. So, I still have some time here.

I will contact you again before my return to Korea.

Thank you so much for everything!

Talk to you soon.

Regards,

Jeongsoo

6/20/2020

孫康宜致凌超

Dear Ling Chao,

What a pleasant surprise to receive your 4-page letter about the Bible! And what a big treat to have this letter from you, which is written in your beautiful calligraphy!

I also found the content of your letter extremely inspiring! First of all, your comparison of the Old Testament and the New Testament is great--that God in the Old Testament was partially hidden, but in the New Testament God finally sent his only son Jesus Christ to the world so that humans could get to know Him in person. That's precisely what the term "*dao cheng rou shen*"（道成肉身）means—i.e., through Christ, God's Word (logos) has become flesh. (See the *Book of John*, 1:14).

I also found it amazing that, in your letter, you perceptively singled out the importance of the passage regarding Jesus' comparison of himself to the prophet named Jonah:

> "As crowds were gathering around Jesus, he said:
> 'You people of today are evil! You keep looking for a sign from God.
> But what happened to Jonah is the only sign you will be given.
> Just as Jonah was a sign to the people of Nineveh, the Son of Man
> will be a sign to the people of today.'" (Luke, 11:29-30).

And Jesus also said that He was greater than Jonah, and He wanted the people of his generation to repent:

"The men of Nineveh will stand up at the judgment with this generation and condemn it; for they repented at the preaching of Jonah, and now one greater than Jonah is here." (Luke, 11:32).

Interestingly, in Herman Melville's novel *Moby Dick*, Jonah was often mentioned. This is because, according to the book of Jonah in the Old Testament, the prophet Jonah was once swallowed by a huge fish. Later after Jonah's constant prayer to God, "the Lord commended the fish, and it vomited Jonah onto dry land." (Jonah, 2:10). I can see how Herman Melville would find the Biblical description of Jonah's being swallowed by a large fish inspiring, as his novel was also about the story of a big whale, Moby Dick.

As you know, my B.A.thesis was on Herman Melville's *Moby Dick*. I still remember how hard I studied the Book of Jonah from the Bible in those days so that I could understand the book *Moby Dick* better. Now your letter suddenly brings back so many fond memories I have about my life as an undergraduate student at Tunghai University. That was more than half a century ago!

By the way, I was especially happy to know that, during the recent exhibition at the Tunghai University Library, a copy of my thesis on Herman Melville was on display.

Indeed, a million thanks to you for your most inspiring letter, especially written in your own calligraphy!

Best,
Kang-i Sun Chang
6/20/2020

附凌超致孫康宜

凌超致孫康宜信第一頁　　　　　　凌超致孫康宜信第二頁

凌超致孫康宜信第三頁　　　　　　凌超致孫康宜信第四頁

Haun Saussy（蘇源熙）致孫康宜

Dear Kang-i,

This is wonderful news and a flattering collection to be in! Our friend Bian Dongbo has made quite a name for himself as a translator. He's very careful—maybe a little too careful for my style (he doesn't always try to find equivalents for the jokes), but I'm proud to work with him and I hope he gets many readers.

How are you and C.C. doing as spring slides into summer?

We try to keep the boys amused and keep on writing, for our own sanity.

Yours

Haun

6/20/2020

吳清邁致孫康宜

康宜學姊：

真不敢相信你會選中我的email! I am honored. Indeed, you have my full permission to publish whatever you would like to from our correspondence.

And, such a small world. We were visiting 曉真 this afternoon, but actually to see her husband, Curtis 龔書章, 東海28屆建築系畢業。I am forming a small advisory committee to assist Tunghai President Wang in matters relating to 東海校園規劃及美化。I invited Curtis to not only participate, which he heartily agreed, but I am hoping that he will agree to lead the group, working directly with President Wang. I invited 兆貞, two others (husband and wife team) in Curtis' class at Tunghai, and a Tunghai Landscape Dept grad of the same year to also join him. These Tunghai alumni are today active at the top of the design profession in Taiwan.

Anyway, no need to bore you further with such details. That is why we were at 曉真's home for tea this afternoon.

Warm regards,

Ching-mai

6/21/2020

註：此信有部分刪節。

林順夫致孫康宜

Dear Kang-i,

　　Yesterday afternoon when I finished watching the video "杜甫，最偉大的中國詩人" and started thinking about sending you an email to thank you for providing me on June 18 with the YouTube link, I noticed that you had already sent me an email earlier. But I did not read your latest email (and the attached preface to your new book) until this morning. It goes without saying that I feel very honored to have my name mentioned in the preface to your new book, and of course, to have a couple of brief email paragraphs included in it as well! Also, I'd like to let you know that I thoroughly enjoyed reading your quite long preface which covers not only the events associated with this forthcoming book but also so much about your work, that of your father and of CC as well. I look forward to reading this book when it appears in print!

　　I immensely enjoyed the YouTube video.　In just 59 minutes, this BBC video presented in a concise and most effective way the life, work, and times of Du Fu. It was good to see Steve Owen, now an old man, appearing several times in the video to make incisive comments on Du Fu. It brought back fond memories of my personal "encounters" with the work of this great Tang poet. Purely as an expression of my fond memory, I have taken the liberty of sending you a PDF of an old essay of mine (the first draft of which was done in 1975) in which I touched upon the friendship between Li Bai and Du Fu. (I had hoped to turn this paper into a much larger work. But embarrassingly just like in the case of a few other projects, I never got around to doing that. Back in the late 1980s when the editors of Tamkang Review turned to me to索稿, I sent them this old piece.) In any case, I was glad that the video does mention Li Bai's influence on Du Fu--I trust that Steve must have treated this aspect in detail in his work on Du Fu. One other thing that has greatly impressed me is that BBC has asked Ian McKellen to read those greatest poems by Du Fu. And McKellen has risen to the occasion to do such a superb job delivering those powerful lines! I was reminded that some years ago, I was fascinated by McKellen's analysis of Macbeth's last soliloquy (one of the Bard's greatest and memorable passages!). Although McKellen's analysis is basically from the perspective of an actor, it is done with sensitivity, insight, and critical acumen. In any event, if you are interested and can find the time, please go to the link below:

> Ian McKellen analyzes Macbeth's last soliloquy
> https://www.youtube.com/watch?v=zGbZCgHQ9m8&frags=pl%2Cwn

The last 1:40 minutes of this 12:07 minutes clip constitute a clip from the movie Macbeth in which McKellen, as Macbeth, performs the soliloquy. I've heard other readings of that great Shakespearean soliloquy done by other actors, and I like McKellen's the most.

Oh, you mention陳效蘭in your preface. How has she been? She must be in her 90s now. My attached article closes with a quote from Fritz Mote. Brief as it is, my article is sort of a tribute to Fritz in a very real sense of the word.

Best regards to you and CC!

Shuen-fu
6/21/2020

王德威致孫康宜

Dear Kang-i,

Thanks so much for sharing the preface with me. I am amazed by your collaborative work with Dr. Li Boyang who you came to know only a while ago. He is obviously a very well-trained and dedicated scholar! It is indeed a significant task during this time of pandemic, something that registers the necessity of scholarly engagement against all odds.

I just arrived in Taipei and am in quarantine right now. It is no fun to travel at this moment at all but I had to do so because my mother's health is taking a downturn. I am planning to stay till early August. Warmest wishes to you and CC. Please take care.

Best,

David

6/21/2002

盤隨雲致孫康宜

Dear康宜教授，

I hope you are having a great weekend! As planed, I road tripped to the New Haven area a couple of weeks ago and since then, have been busy selecting and assembling the furniture for my new apartment. At this time, the room is in good shape. I do enjoy the life in CT for the area's beauty, tranquility, and convenience. So, please do not worry about me.

I have been thinking of your dental surgeries and health as well. I hope the surgeries are going well so far and you are on your way to a quick and full recovery. Please enjoy the time at home and have some good rest not only to recover properly but also to offset the fatigue you might feel after being so diligent in your work throughout the years. I sincerely wish you happiness, ease, and relief! If you need any help, please feel free to let me know. I would love to do anything I am capable of to assist you both in research and in your life.

Best,
Suiyun
6/21/2020

František Reismuller致孫康宜

Dear professor,

　　In the attachment of this email I am sending you a draft of the list of characters that will be added (not in the excel form, of course) as an attachment to the Czech translation of your book. As per agreement with professor Lomová, I have tried to be as thorough as possible and at least briefly describe every character and historical figure mentioned in the book.

　　I have some questions for you there. In the excel form you will see some rows highlighted in blue and in the column E there are some questions concerning the persons mentioned there. Mostly I am missing biographical data (just year of birth and death), sometimes full names of the characters. Would you please be so kind and have a look at the highlighted rows and answer my questions?

　　(Just to explain: I am giving the biographical data in two cases only - a)when the character is a well-known public figure, b) when the character is a member of your family.)

　　I am sorry to be adding extra work to your surely busy schedule, but I would really very much appreciate your help with this. And I believe such an annex could be very helpful for Czech readers.

Thank you very much.
Best regards
František
6/21/2020

註：此信有部分刪節。

盤隨雲致孫康宜

Dear康宜教授，

　　As you are working on a new book that collects emails/letters, I took a look at (as a kind of "review") all the emails between us since our first touch. It is very interesting that from the beginning we are like故交even though we have not met each other in person yet! I also discovered in one of my emails that a promise remains unrealized. That is, to share some of my creative works with you.

　　I started to write in classical Chinese (poems, *ci,* and prose) in middle school. At that time, writing provided me with opportunities to fight against frustrations. By frustrations I mean I struggled a lot in PRC's exam-oriented education system, in which individuality seems wrong. I wanted to criticize, I wanted to express. But my oral expressions brought some troubles to myself, as I was evaluated as "morally problematic" by my teacher. Then I started to write privately. Most of those works are read only within my family. Fortunately, I figured out, in my last year of middle school, that in order to get rid of such frustrations, I must go abroad for future study. So, I decided to attend a local international senior high program that prepares students for their undergraduate studies in the U.S.. You will find in the attachment a *ci* titled Emotional Reflection升學感懷, which was written (hopefully in Xin Qiji's style) after I made that decision and was successfully accepted to the international program.

　　Besides my personal life and feelings, my reflection on Buddhist and Taoist thoughts (I believe in Vajrayana Buddhism), as well as sometimes on artistic works, is a major topic of my classical Chinese writing, as shown by my poems titled "Lingyin靈隱" and "Seated in a Piney Mountain松山靜坐".

　　In a period during my high school, I was fascinated by modern poetry. Then I did have a try. I wrote a modern poem, for a creative writing competition, to record and commemorate a poor dog who was loved by my neighbor before but at last abandoned by him. It was published in *Chinese Writers* （《中國作家》）, yet I do not like the edited version. So, I am attaching the original poem.

I hope you will have some fun reading these short works! And please feel free to give any advice to revise and improve them! I'd be willing to share more with you and discuss the interesting writing process (especially in person)!

Best,
Suiyun
6/22/2020

註：以下附盤隨雲詩一首：

賞黃賓虹《松山靜坐》
繁林坐深山，山隨雨瀑潺。
風亂青松葉，茶淡老屋安。

孫康宜致李保陽

Dear Baoyang,

I just realized that I forgot to tell you that my recent book, *The joy of Close-reading*（《細讀的樂趣》[南京：譯林出版社，2019]），was dedicated to my mentor（恩師）Prof. Yu-kung Kao（高友工教授），who died on October 29, 2016. Here I attach a word file of my "Postscript"「後記」for your information. My postscript appears at the end of the book (pp. 323-325).

Please see attached for a picture of the book cover, as well as my dedication page to Prof. Yu-kung Kao.（請見附件）。

Best,
Kang-i
6/23/2020

孫康宜著《細讀的樂趣》，南京譯林出版社，2019

孫康宜致李保陽

Dear Baoyang,

Please see the following link to an article by Octavio Paz!

I remember that Octavio Paz came to visit Yale in October 1990, the day right before he was awarded the Nobel Prize! I had the honor of attending the dinner in honor of him at the Master's house of Timothy Dwight College. I also enjoyed a long conversation with him!

And that was almost thirty years ago!

I always have fond memories of him!

https://mp.weixin.qq.com/s/WhFiwcsLS6-sJl2TgfPa5A

Best,

Kang-i

6/23/2020

孫康宜致林順夫

Dear Shuen-fu,

I was very pleased to receive your June 23rd email, informing me that you had "immensely enjoyed" the BBC documentary on Du Fu!

I was especially touched by what you said about Ian McKellen's reciting Du Fu poems: "And McKellen has risen to the occasion to do such a superb job delivering those powerful lines!. . ."

Also, I was thrilled to get from you the link to McKellen's 1979 speech in which he analyzed Macbeth's last soliloquy, "Tomorrow, and tomorrow. . ." I like that speech so much that I immediately shared your link with my Wechat friends, who all responded to it with overwhelming enthusiasm. In particular, my former student Chi-hung Yim 嚴志雄 (now a professor at the Chinese University of Hong Kong) commented: "It's a wonderful recording and lecture! We don't find people who talk about poetry that way any longer. I enjoyed it and learned a lot."

Actually I have recently been hooked by a YouTube video that features Ian McKellen's "Acting Shakespeare" dated back to 1982. Now, I'm sharing the link with you here:

https://m.youtube.com/watch?feature=youtu.be&v=25QcYpYCu4Q

By the way, thank you for sending me a copy of your old article, "Looking For Friends in History: Li Po's Friendship with Hsieh T'iao" (from *Tamkang Review*, 20, no. 2 [1989]: 131-150). Coincidentally I was just trying to find your article for my "Man and Nature" course for the coming fall. (I wanted to include your article for the session on Xie Tiao, as evidence of Xie's important influence on later poets such as Li Bai.) So you can imagine how happy I was to receive a PDF of your article, just in time for my preparation for the course syllabus.

Now, I finally recall that your article closes with a direct quote from our teacher

Prof. Mote: ". . . The only truly enduring embodiment of the eternal human memories are the literary ones." So your article is indeed a tribute to Fritz Mote!

In your email you asked about Hsiao-lan Chen Mote（陳效蘭）. I happened to correspond with her several times during the last few weeks, regarding using the Mote pictures in this book,《避疫書信選》. Well, at age 90 (she was born in 1930, the same year Yu Ying-shih 余英時 was born) she is still extremely smart and alert! As you know, she usually lives in the Mote estate in the mountains of Granby. But ever since the COVID-19 crisis came, she has been staying in Denver, so that she can be together with other members of the Mote family. Hsiao-lan is such a remarkable woman!

Please continue to stay safe and well.

Best,
Kang-i
6/23/2020

蘇精致孫康宜

孫老師：

非常謝謝您轉來中華書局關於拙書《西醫來華十記》的訊息，此書是我在印刷出版史以外的業餘副產品，能在大陸多少引起公眾的注意，我有些意外和高興。

雖然已經入夏，美國的肺炎疫情看來並沒有明顯減少，還請您和張先生千萬小心珍重！

蘇精　敬上

6/23/2020

蘇精致孫康宜

孫老師：

　　再度收到您的來信，真是高興！

　　拜讀了您的新書序文，深深覺得人間的文字因緣實在自然微妙，又承蒙您文中將我列入通信名單內，確是我的榮幸了！

　　提供一點小意見，序文第二頁，即李保陽先生第二封信，第三段：「保陽特別喜歡第二十二則馬克吐溫的話。尤記保陽曾在博士論文後記中說過：⋯」，其中「尤記」是否應為「猶記」？即繁體字「猶記」，謹供您參考。

蘇精　敬上
6/23/2020

Austin Woerner致孫康宜

Dear Kang-i,

　　I was touched to receive your message! I hope you've been well. Our experience of the pandemic has been particularly memorable because in its midst we welcomed into this strangely changed world our first child, August, who is now three months old.

　　The original plan was to give birth in Shanghai, but in early February, as news of the coronavirus spread, DKU (Duke Kunshan University, where I teach) announced that it would be moving all its classes online, and the whole country swiftly went into lockdown mode. As airlines began to suspend flights to and from China, we got a last-minute message from the school offering to book us tickets on one of the last flights out of Shanghai. And so, refugee-style, my wife already eight months pregnant, we threw our computers and a few changes of clothes into our suitcases and made for the airport.

　　When we walked off the plane in the U.S. we breathed a sigh of relief, thinking we would be able to spend the final months of her pregnancy in a place where we wouldn't have to worry about mask-wearing and social distancing and where we wouldn't have to spend most of our time shut up inside the house. How wrong we were! A few weeks later we were once again "sheltering in place," interrupted only by a trip to the hospital for August's birth. So we've had the odd experience of being in "lockdown" for almost four months running, in two separate countries.

The silver lining, though, is that we've been able to share August's first few months with my parents, with whom we've been living since our return to the U.S. It's made both being first-time parents and enduring quarantine a lot easier for us, and it's been a special time for the whole family. We feel incredibly lucky that we are safe and sound so far, and that the coronavirus pandemic has had this unexpected upside for us. And by golly will we have some interesting stories to tell August about the circumstances of his birth!

Best wishes to you and C. C., and take care!

All best, Austin

June 23, 2020

耶魯校友Austin Woerner（溫侯廷）與他三個
月大的兒子合影（2020年6月攝於波士頓）

李保陽致孫康宜

Dear Sun Laoshi,

　　Thank you for sharing Austin's letter. The couple's story is so astonishing! God bless them so that they could return to the United States in time. They got on the last flight out of Shanghai, just like Noah got on the Ark with his family.

　　I have a friend, who is a visiting scholar in your alma mater Princeton University. His visa already expired early last month. However, because of the epidemic, he can't return to China. In July, he would be repatriated by the Department of Immigration if he doesn't leave the US by then. Just the day before yesterday, he told me he booked a super expensive ticket. Since March there is only one airplane available that goes to China and returns to the U.S. every week. The fare of a one-way ticket is about ¥30,000-50,000人民幣. Even worse, tickets are very hard to get. Without the help of a travel agent, it is absolutely impossible to buy any tickets.

　　The above two stories remind me of a Taiwanese film 滾滾紅塵 and another film 太平輪. Both movies are about things that happened in 1949. A few days ago, a friend of mine said the current COVID-19 situation is somewhat similar to that of 1949. I don't know if my friend is right or not. But I have to drive my friend to the JFK airport sometime this week, and he will return to China.

All the best!
Baoyang
6/24/2020

黃文吉致李保陽

保陽賢弟：

　　覆函收到，日前去國立成功大學口考一位博士生論文，順便偕內人小遊臺

南，昨日才回到臺北。

申請基金會補助因新冠疫情而中輟，雖然不無遺憾，但看到你越挫越勇，準備申請美國學校的進修機會，熱衷學術研究的精神令人感佩！

我任教於臺灣中部的國立彰化師範大學（National Changhua University of Education），在國文學系（臺灣共有三所師範大學，因培養中學「國文」師資，故稱為「國文學系」，它的英文名稱「Department of Chinese」，仍然是中文系）擔任教授二十多年，後來本校成立臺灣文學研究所（Graduate Institute of Taiwanese Literature），因急需師資，於是我便支援為該所教授，並與國文系合聘，一直到五年前退休為止。所以我目前頭銜應該是「國立彰化師範大學臺灣文學研究所暨國文學系合聘教授（退休）」。

從你的學術著作目錄從新找出〈吳熊和先生晚年談話錄〉（《詞學》第三十二輯，2014年）一文，讀後頗有感觸，吳先生於1993年4月曾來臺參加「第一屆詞學國際研討會」（中央研究院中國文哲研究所主辦），我當時也應邀發表論文，因而與先生初次見面。1997年9月，先生應中央研究院中國文哲研究所之邀再次來臺，此行先生曾與成功大學張高評教授光臨寒舍，我陪先生到寒舍附近的蔣介石官邸參觀，並在蔣介石專屬的教堂「凱歌堂」前合影。文中提及嚴迪昌教授，我與嚴教授也是在第一屆詞學國際研討會見面，1999年嚴先生應東吳大學之邀來臺講學，12月我特別安排先生到彰化師範大學演講清詞，並留下當時演講照片。往事歷歷，兩位詞學界前輩專精學問，有讀書人風骨，而今已乘鶴歸去，令人懷念。茲將照片掃描寄上，以示不忘故人之意。

人生境遇多種，我出身農家，家境清寒，所幸以讀書、教書擺脫困境，比起中國歷經文革的學者，真是幸福多了。你目前處在艱難階段，但能到自由國度開拓視野，相信經過這一次蛻變之後，未來的學術成績必能更加開展，祝福你！如有需要協助之處，請來函告知，毋庸客氣！專此，並詢

近佳！

黃文吉覆
6/24/2020

孫康宜致李保陽

Dear Baoyang,

I was overjoyed to find this old picture of CC and Edie sitting on the famous "Giamatti Bench" at Yale's Old Campus! The picture was taken 24 years ago in June, 1996. (Please see the picture attached.)

This picture brings back so many old memories. As you may know, Yale's 19th president Bart Giamatti, whom I came to know very well in the 1980s, suddenly died of heart attack in a hot summer day in 1989. Even today I still remember the shock and sadness that the entire Yale community experienced at the time.

It was during the following year in 1990 that the Giamatti Bench (which I would call「永恆的座椅」in Chinese) was created, as a tribute to President Giamatti. The Giamatti Bench was made of granite, and it displays a quote from Bart Giamatti: "A liberal education is at the heart of a civil society, and at the heart of a liberal arts education is the act of teaching." (「大學教育乃是一個社會的心臟,教書工作乃是大學教育的關鍵中心」)。

It was around the time when Giamatti Bench was being built that I wrote a Chinese poem in commemoration of Bart Gianmatti. Many years later my student Victoria Wu (now known as Victoria Sancilio) translated the poem into English for me.

> **耶魯校長嘉馬地**
> 讓馨香的泥土把你包裹好,
> 因為你曾轟轟烈烈地活過。
> 每日清晨我走過若無街,
> 隔著墓地的高牆
> 我總是聽見
> 一陣陣琴音
> 紛紛崛起
> 在重演一個
> 美妙的故事。

今天我走在路上
我聽見有風吹來，
是時間流動的聲響，
不知從哪兒來。
我伸出右手，
將那聲音握住，
在手指間
用力捏住。

我想，
這就是嘉馬地，
是他，就是他。
我第一次和他握手時
也有同樣的感覺。

Yale President Giamatti

By Kang-i Sun Chang,
Translated by Victoria Wu

Let the fragrant earth embrace you well
Because you once lived passionately...
Each morning I walk past Grove Street
Over the high walls of the cemetery
I always hear
A swell of piano music
Crescendo suddenly
Echoing a lovely story.

Today I walk on the streets

I hear the wind blow towards me

It is the sound of time moving and flowing

I do not know from whence it comes.

I extend my right hand

To grasp that sound

Pinching it tightly

Between my fingers.

I think

This is Giamatti

If it is him, then it is him,

The first time I shook his hand

I felt this same emotion.

I can't help sharing with you this story about President Giamatti. Next time when you visit Yale again, please be sure to look at the Giamatti Bench in Old Campus--if you have not already done so.

Best,

Kang-i

6/25/2020

C.C. Chang and his daughter Edie at the
Giamatti Bench, Yale University, 1996

孫康宜致李保陽

Dear Baoyang,

Just an hour ago we heard the sad news that Dr. Jack (Jackie) Chuong , our favorite doctor in gastroenterology, suddenly died last month (on May 18th). And he was only 70 years old! Words cannot describe our sadness with his passing.

Just now I posted a memory of Dr. Chuong at the website of Guilford Funeral Home, saying:

"We have just heard the sad news about Dr. Chuong's passing on May 18th! Oh, we can never find another doctor like him. When I was staying in the Yale New-Haven Hospital due to an emergency in 2003, and then again in 2016 and 2018, he visited me at the hospital on a daily basis. I can never forget his kindness and gentle care over the years! The last time I visited him was at his Branford Office on January 28th; that was only four months ago. He will be sorely missed!"

I recall what Helen Steiner Rice once wrote in her book, *"Just for You": A special Collection of Inspirational Verse* (1967):

> It's not the things that can be bought
> that are life's richest treasure,
> It's just the little "heart gifts"
> that money cannot measure. . . .

I feel that Dr. Chuong was not just an excellent physician, but he was someone who constantly gave his patients the "little heart gifts" !

Kang-i

6/25/2020

林順夫致孫康宜

Dear Kang-i,

  Thank you ever so much for your email response (dated 6/23/2020) to my email of June 21st (not June 23rd). Thanks also for providing me with the link to 〈杜甫圈粉全世界——對話BBC《杜甫》主持人邁克爾・伍德〉in《讀品週刊》which I opened and read yesterday morning. Perhaps one reason that Michael Wood's documentary of Du Fu has appealed to so many viewers is because, as he said (on p. 6 of the interview), "我認為這部紀錄片是帶著感情來拍攝的。它讓人感覺到,這不是一個乾巴巴的事實性的學術敘述,它是一個關於人的故事;..." This remark reminded me of Harold Bloom's career-culminating book, *Shakespeare: the Invention of the Human*. Of course, I was fully aware that Wood's "人" here and Bloom's "the human" in his book do not mean exactly the same thing. In any case, I learned a lot from this interview and got so interested in Wood's works that I searched on the Internet for them. In particular, I was interested in his "In Search of Shakespeare." To my delight, I found out that I can view for free the entire four-part documentary on YouTube. I will be viewing "In Search of Shakespeare" one of these days soon.

  I am grateful to you for sharing the link to Ian McKellen's "Acting Shakespeare." Although I saw a DVD version of McKellen's "Acting Shakespeare" back in 2013 or so in Ann Arbor, I have not seen this shorter one. Yesterday morning, I only viewed the first 5 minutes of the video you mentioned just to make sure that I had not seen it before. Even in these five minutes, I was impressed by McKellen's gift in re-enacting the performances of the earliest Shakespearean actors. From 2:30 to 4:37, McKellen talked about the most famous Shakespearean actor David Garrick, and from about 3:30 to 4:37, he re-enacted Garrick's performance of Macbeth dying. I was greatly amused that from 4:15 to 4:20, McKellen acted out a posture that resembled the "Single Whip" （單鞭）posture（式）in 太極拳! Wow! Interesting! Where did McKellen get (learn?) that posture, and why did he put it in his re-enactment of one moment of Garrick's performance of Macbeth? I will be viewing the entire 30-minute video soon.

While we are on the subject of Shakespeare, allow me to relate a couple of personal experiences. In August 2012, Kathleen and I took our son and his family to visit her brother and his family who were then living in Greenstead, Essex, which is about an hour by train to London. At the time, there was the exhibition named "Shakespeare: Staging the World" at the British Museum. So, one day I took my son Andrew to the British Museum where we spent several hours viewing the fascinating objects on display. It was after that visit, I spent quite a bit of spare time in 2012-2013 viewing some DVDs of films based on Shakespeare's plays, McKellen's "Acting Shakespeare," and above all, John Barton's "Playing Shakespeare." If you have not seen the video of John Barton's "Playing Shakespeare," check it out. I had to borrow the DVD from the Film & Video Library at the University of Michigan back in 2012. But now you can view it on YouTube! For your convenience (and just in case you have not seen it), I attach a file containing the links to all nine parts of Barton's video. Barton is a legendary director and teacher for decades at Royal Shakespeare Company. In 1982, he ran a 9-session workshop that involved 21 famous and accomplished actors (McKellen, Judi Dench, et al) of RSC. At the beginning of the 9th session, Ian McKellen gave a tribute to John Barton. Even if one is not interested in acting, one can learn a lot from John Barton's video (each part lasting about 50 minutes).

By such a happy coincidence, I sent you a PDF of my old article while you had been looking for it for inclusion in your reading list for your course "Man and Nature." I am touched by your interest in this old article of mine! I also appreciate very much for keeping me posted about 嚴志雄、陳效蘭 and 余英時. I agree with you completely that our "師母" is a remarkable woman——陳效蘭 would not like us to call her "師母," actually! As for 余英時，even though I have never formally studied with him, I always consider him as one of my most important mentors (through reading his books and articles)!

I better stop now before this email runs too long!

Stay healthy and keep well!

Shuen-fu

6/25/2020

Abigail Long致孫康宜

Dear Professor Chang,

I recently returned from my semester abroad with the Light Fellowship and wanted to just send you a quick email to thank you again for the letter of recommendation that you wrote for me so long ago. I had a wonderful time in Beijing until my program was closed due to COVID19. Thankfully, there was an opening at the ICLP program at National Taiwan University and I was able to complete my semester abroad. This summer I am still taking classes through ICLP, but am taking them online instead of in-person.

While I was studying in Taiwan, one of my professors assigned a research article on 女書, one of the topics that we covered in Women and Literature in Traditional China. The prospectives and insights that I gleaned from your class have definitely been an asset to me as I have continued my studies.

Thank you again for all of your help and I hope you have been well.

Best,

Abigail Long
6/25/2020

C. C. Chang致孫康宜

Kang-i,

Bill must have died a decade ago. A few years before he died, Bill tried to cut down his asset by giving out huge tips. I remembered he gave Edie $250 one time at IHOP Pancake House in Orange. At that time Edie (still in high school) worked as a waitress at IHOP in her spare time.

C.C.

6/25/2020

註：Bill (William)Carney, known as an extremely dedicated member of the Yale community, worked for the university for 41 years, until he died on May 2, 2010. Bill served in the Human Resources department at Yale, and often "helped people overcome obstacles, and offered his experience and encouragement with grace and generosity." (Quoted from Michael Morand, May, 2010. See "In Memoriam: William Carney, Manager of Yale Homebuyers Program," May 7, 2010. https://news.yale.edu/2010/05/07/memoriam-william-carney-manager-yale-homebuyers-program).

Bill Carney spent most of his life taking care of his mother. After his mother died, Bill tried to catch up with what he had missed from life. First of all, he worked even harder on his job than before, trying to make sure that Yale would sponsor the individual faculty's retirement savings. He was aware that he had cancer and might die anytime. I remember that he often took us out for dinner and gave big tips to waiters. He must have donated money to other socially worthy initiatives too.

Bill Carney and his mother visited Kang-i and C.C. Chang's home on July 18, 1998.

Pauline Lin致孫康宜

　　Wow-what a wonderful preface, dear Kang-i Ayi. A quietly serendipitous beginning that resulted in all these modern epistolary exchanges during the pandemic. What a wonderful, wonderful piece of work. These scholarly conversations would indeed be fascinating to read. I loved that he [Li Baoyang] wrote a poem to your work, and I loved that Isaiah Shrader became a part of this conversation too!

　　Thanks again for sharing this project with me! You are amazing—so productive and so creative. You turned anything into a positive experience, including this period of isolation during the pandemic.

Yours,

Pauline

6/26/2020

諸位友人致孫康宜（悼念Dr. Jack Chuong）：

來自Pauline Lin

Dear Kang-i Ayi,

　　Thank you for this touching statement. You hit it right on the spot: he was the most kind and gentle man, with a good heart.

　　We heard about Dr. Chuang's passing a couple of weeks ago through the Med School newsletter. We were very sad, because he was both Albert and my gastroenterologist, and I agree with you that he is the most wonderful doctor, with the kindest heart. We were so sad to hear of it, because we just saw him not long ago. He was young too.

　　Thank you for letting us know about the online website.

Take good care.

Yours,
Pauline
6/26/2020

來自王郁林

　　感謝康宜來函告知！閱畢之後，幾個字立刻跳進我的腦海中──啊，他是「神所喜悅的人」！

Yu-lin
6/26/2020

來自凌超

Dear Prof. Chang,

　　I'm sorry to hear this sad news. Thank you very much for sharing your message with me.

　　Your message left at the funeral home and the quotation are very touching! Condolences to his family.

Chao
6/26/2020

來自胡曉真

　　雖然不認識這位醫師，但透過孫老師的文字就可以想見他是一位仁醫！

Siao-chen

6/26/2020

來自Linda Chu（朱雯琪）

I'm really sorry to hear this and for your loss. Dr. Chuong sounds like an amazing doctor that really made a difference in the lives of many.

Linda

6/26/2020

孫康宜（和張欽次）致王德威（David Wang）

Dear David,

Monica Yu just called us a few minutes ago, informing us of your mother's passing last night. (She said it was Josephine who told her the news.) C.C. and I would like to send our condolences to you. Also, Monica and Ying-shih wanted us to convey their condolences to you as well.

Your mother姜允中女士was truly an amazing person, and she was blessed to have a long and happy life. We can certainly say that she had a life well lived! CC and I were lucky to visit your mom on May 14, 2018, and were amazed by her intelligence and wit at such an advanced age. (Please see a picture attached here.) I'm also very honored that I had the privilege to write an article about her, titled 〈道德女子姜允中〉, in 2006. I do treasure our friendship with her over the years.

From your email to me dated June 21 (i.e., 6 days ago), I know that you might still be in quarantine right now. Please take care.

Best,

Kang-i (and C.C.)

6/27/2020

孫康宜致林順夫

Dear Shuen-fu,

　　I was thrilled to receive your June 25th email, in which you attached a file containing the links to all nine parts of John Barton's video, titled "Playing Shakespeare." This is like a library of treasures for me! As you said, Barton is a legendary director and teacher for decades at Royal Shakespeare Company. The 9-session workshop he had created in the early 1980s that involved more than 20 famous actors (including McKellen, Judi Dench, Peggy Ashcroft, etc.) was most amazing! Right after I got these videos from you, I started to watch them!

　　At this point, I have finished watching Series #1 and #2, #6,#8, #9, as well as parts of #3, #4, #5, #7. In fact, I like Series #9 so much that I watched it twice! I found the subject, "Poetry and Hidden poetry," fascinating. I admire John Barton's idea of "acting 6th sense" very much, and his discussion about the sense of ambiguity in Shakespeare's lines is most inspiring. He also pointed out that Shakespeare often used monosyllabic lines to heighten certain particular moments with thought and feeling. I found the three topics Barton focused on--i.e., time, love, and death--very interesting! Also, I very much enjoyed seeing Ian McKellen play out the lines about death from a scene of the "Merchant of Venice." I also love Peggy Ashcroft's reciting the verse lines from "All's Well that Ends Well."

　　Apart from #9, I especially enjoyed watching #2, "Using the Verse," in which Barton stressed the importance of treating Shakespeare's verse as a help (rather than a hindrance) in acting. I also like parts of Series #4 ("Set speeches & Soliloquies") and #5 ("Irony & Ambiguity"). Series #8 ("Exploring a Character") is also excellent. Shylock is indeed a very interesting and controversial character in Shakespeare! It's wonderful that Barton invited two different actors to play the parts of Shylock, so that we can get a comparative perspective.

Well, all this brings back so many fond memories to me, because during the 1980s I often indulged myself in watching the BBC playhouse on Television! That's when I was hooked by Peggy Ashcroft ; she got the British Academy Television Award for Best Actress Award. She later died in 1991. Now, because of you, I was able to see her again in Barton's series of the "Playing Shakespeare" video series. So, a million thanks to you. As you said, "even if one is not interested in acting, one can learn a lot from John Barton's videos."

By the way, I'm glad that you like the link I sent to you last time for Ian McKellen's "Acting Shakespeare." I did not realize that in the video McKellen acted out a posture that resembled the "Single Whip"（單鞭）posture（式）in太極拳! That's incredible.

As you can see, you have re-opened a gate to the world of Shakespeare for me.

Best,
Kang-i
6/27/2020

孫康宜補註：**此信第2段，第4行有誤。"Also, I very much enjoyed seeing Ian McKellen play out the lines about death from a scene of the 'Merchant of Venice'" 應作："Also, I very much enjoyed seeing Ian McKellen play out the lines about death from a scene of Henry IV, in his role as Old Justice Shallow."**

孫康宜與林順夫合影（2017年3月11日，
普林斯頓大學）

孫康宜致季進

Dear Ji Jin（季進），

I want to let you know that I really enjoyed reading your article,〈審美的普適標準與文學的大同世界——關於夏志清的博士論文及其他〉. Your article impresses me both in its depth and scope. As you have said, few readers today are familiar with Prof. C.T. Hsia's（夏志清）Ph.D. dissertation, titled "George Crabbe: A Critical Study" (1950), now preserved at the Dept of Manuscripts and Archives of Yale's Sterling Memorial Library. Thus, your article has a lot to contribute to the field.

I was delighted that in you article you did mention C.T. Hsia's dissertation adviser Prof. Frederick A. Pottle, whom I happened to know quite well during the early 1980s. In those days I often visited Prof. Pottle's Special Collection of the Boswell papers at the Sterling Library. On one occasion Prof. Pottle told me that C.T. always treated him like an intimate old friend. Once C. T. came from New York City to visit Prof. Pottle. Before Pottle had a chance to turn around and say Hi, C.T. had already put his big hands on Pottle's shoulder, shouting " Ah, you old hunchback. . . ."（你這個駝背的老頭子……）. And then both of them had a belly laugh right there, among the Boswell papers.

　　I thought you might be amused by this Hsia-and-Pottle episode which I always remember.

Kang-i
6/27/2020

李保陽致黃文吉

文吉先生尊鑒：

　　華箋奉至，正保陽瑣務纏身之日，故遲至今日始得便回覆先生。

　　十分感謝先生，實在讓保陽感慨、感激！所附吳、嚴二公舊照，猶多勾起保陽十年之思。

　　先生所見《詞學》所刊吳公與保陽對話，僅為當年日記之一部分。另有與詞無關以及今日不便刊出者尚夥。2010年，保陽服務於浙江大學圖書館，迄2012年離職，兩年之間，得仰吳公謦欬者兩載。吳公逝後，保陽於2014年承乏杭城西天竺山中某寺。保陽彼時蕭條，一日下山看望吳師母，吳師母將吳先生生前的衣物打包送給保陽，並殷殷囑云：「杭人忌諱往者衣帽，你在山寺獨睡夜冷，可墊身下保暖……。」讓保陽感激不已。但吳先生身材高大，保陽穿吳先生衣服不合身，就寄回西安老家給　先父穿。2017年6月，　先父棄養，諸姊在盡七禮當晚，將那些吳先生衣物與　先父生前存用之物一併焚化。2015年初，保陽離開山中，吳師母又送保陽吳先生舊藏舊書若干，其中《文心雕龍》與《宋詩選》中，先生藍、朱二色批註滿紙，不時展讀，仍可想見吳公當日言談神色。又嚴公1990年簽贈吳公《清詞史》一冊，可以想見二公當日風神。前年倉促去國，書物多

棄，此三書仍在身邊。茲隨信附上諸種書影，先生清賞。吳公《唐宋詞通論》，早為學界不刊之論，學界皆知公論詞眼界高、論斷確。然以保陽個人感受，吳公治學仍以傳統讀書法為宗尚，乾嘉諸老中，尤其推重章實齋。實齋能論斷，然吳公不廢吳中經師細讀批註之法，轉益多師，得傳統學術各家之長，故其詞論允當可信，邁越群倫。倘非公晚歲罹患沉痾，一定可為學界提供更多鴻論。公批註《全宋詞》垂數十年，近聞杭省將印行其手批《全宋詞》，為治詞者福音。

　　2010年秋，保陽曾專程趕往蘇州十全街拜訪嚴夫人曹林芳女士，並因之牽線，使吳、嚴二公之間的聯繫再度接續。後來保陽將嚴夫人口述諸節，載入兩年後由保陽創刊之《掌故》，取名〈憶嚴迪昌先生〉。三年後，吉林的《社會科學戰線》轉載了那篇文章（見https://mp.weixin.qq.com/s/pQRFfMLEEES0wbIBcH9kgg，這篇文章的最後一幅圖片即嚴夫人為保陽簽贈自印本《嚴迪昌作品集》）。一晃十年了，不知道嚴夫人如今怎樣。

　　專此，並頌

　　諸安！

晚　保陽　敬上

6/27/2020

Josephine Chiu-Duke（丘慧芬）致孫康宜

Dear Kang-i,

　　Thank you so much for sharing with us your photo with Dewei's mother and your moving essay about her "moral power". I think it is more than apt to use this term "moral power" to describe Dewei's mom, though I have never had the opportunity to meet her since the days we knew Dewei way back in 1980.

　　Back then, Li Hsiao-ti, Luo Jiu-jung and I were all "tongxue" and we often got together with Dewei over the weekends and we also liked to kid Dewei saying that Mrs. Wang had formidable power over her son. When looking back, it is of course through

Mrs. Wang that Dewei has developed into such a gentle gentleman.

I told Dewei that I believe Mrs. Wang departed from this world with all the happiness that a person could enjoy in this world, and that she certainly left without any regrets. I also just read Dewei's email telling us that he and his family are facing this departure with the most "zhengmian de taidu." That will be a comfort to his mom, I think.

Life in the pandemic time is strange and hard, but we know you and CC will continue your daily routine and treasure all the joy that life brings us even in this difficult time.

Our very best to both of you,

Huifen
6/27/2020

Josephine Chiu-Duke（丘慧芬）致孫康宜

Dear Kang-i,

Hearty congratulations to you and CC on both of your new books!

Yes, of course you can include my email in your new book. I only feel honored to have my email included in your new book, and I also feel greatly moved when reading Dr. Li's poem on his feelings about your work on Chen Zilong.

In this difficult time, nothing is more valuable than the kind of heartwarming feelings friends bring to us. I do appreciate it very much.

Take care！
Huifen
6/27/2020

張宏生致孫康宜

再次恭喜康宜！

　　文集的設計很見心思，令人興起閱讀的衝動。如果問我一見之下的感受，儘管我作為朋友，不可避免地會有感情的成分，但客觀地說，幾個主題既各自獨立，又互相勾連，既傳統，又現代，我想，可以覆蓋不同的讀者層面，一定會引起很多讀者的興趣。

宏生
6/27/2020

註：「文集」指的是簡體增訂版的《孫康宜文集》五卷本（將由廣西師範大學出版社出版）。

李保陽致孫康宜

孫老師：

　　昨天接到您Line傳來的消息，告訴保陽王德威先生的母親以一百零五歲高齡仙逝。我就又把《文集》卷三收錄的那篇您寫的〈道德女子典范姜允中〉重溫了一遍。剛才看到您轉來德威先生和季進老師的郵件，王先生說他將來會寫一寫他的媽媽，並明確要寫「Ethical Society down the road」。季老師說：「您把王媽媽放到現代西方的『道德權威』的背景下來認識，真是別具隻眼。」由這兩位的話，保陽想起您在研究明清女性時，曾經有一個很重要的觀點，即十七、十八世紀的女性雖然在儒家正統社會統序中是邊緣化的一個群體，但是她們在家庭或者社會角色中，以重塑其道德的完美來贏得不管是家庭還是其他男性的尊重。

　　我在移居美國之前，對美國人的「道德」觀念很隔膜。現在對此有了一點體會。我們住在思故客河畔一個有著一百四十多年歷史的傳統德裔美國人社區，一到週末，村裡的停車場上就停滿了車，大家都是待在家裡，享受和家人在一起的

那份溫馨與快樂。另外一個有趣的現象是，村裡絕大多數的婦女都是在家裡全職帶孩子。我曾經在工作日去過幾次村圖書館，所有活動區域都是全職媽媽們和孩子的天下。這兩個有趣的現象，讓我生發出一個直觀的認識：今日美國雖然是世界上最為發達和強大的國家之一，不管是經濟、政治、文化、科技、教育等等，都在領導著這個世界的前進方向。但是美國人的價值觀尤其是家庭觀念，還是非常保守的。也許是這份保守傳統的厚重，生發出推進社會的巨大力量。據我觀察，美國社會生活中，女性的地位是很高的。這種以女性為核心的家庭觀念非常重要。價值觀上的這種保守，我覺得比多數後發國家聲嘶力竭地將婦女驅趕到職場上，要更加有利於促進社會的進步。

　　所以我就想，德威先生之所以能有今天的成就，大概和他有這麼一位具有典範道德觀念和勇氣的媽媽有很大的關係。我想這可能就是「道德的力量」。

保陽　敬上
6/28

李保陽致孫康宜

孫老師，

　　不知道這位丘教授是否即十年前在費城召開的亞洲年會上，和汪暉有過一場精彩辯論的那位丘慧芬教授？

　　謝謝丘教授欣賞保陽呈給您的那首詠《陳柳》的小詩。如果和汪暉辯論的正是這位丘教授，那麼她的那份浸潤在學術中的人文關懷，尤其讓人肅然起敬。學者的人文關懷，是防止其成為精緻的利己主義者的最佳防護。中國歷朝歷代都不乏這樣的利己主義學者，實在讓人感慨！

保陽　敬上
6/28/2020

王德威致孫康宜和張欽次（C. C. Chang）

Dear Kang-i and C.C.,

Thanks so much for your heartwarming messages.

My mother passed away in sleep; fortunately I've made it back in a timely manner and can take care of everything.

She had a great life and an illustrious career, truly a model lady of her time.

Please take care. We will stay in touch.

Best,
David
6/28/2020

王德威致孫康宜

Dear Kang-i，

Many thanks for sending me the piece, which brought back my mother's wonderful meeting with you years ago.

She has had a very dynamic life and her legacy will be remembered.

She left right on the day when I finished my quarantine, as if she were in charge of everything till the last minute.

A miracle indeed.

Best,
David
6/28/2020

註：信中第一行所提到的「the piece」乃是指孫康宜於2006年所寫有關王德威母

親姜允中女士與道德會的關係──文章題為〈道德女子典範姜允中〉。

王德威致孫康宜

Dear Kang-i,

Please help extend my thanks to Professor and Mrs. Yu. I feel humbled by their message of good will.

Hopefully I will write something about my mother and her time, as well as the story of the Ethical Society down the road.

Thanks very much for your conscientious messages which really warmed my heart!

Best,
David
6/28/2020

季進致孫康宜

親愛的孫老師：

謝謝您對拙文的肯定和鼓勵，太開心了。如果沒有您的幫忙，就不可能找到夏志清的博士論文，也就不可能有這篇文章，所以飲水思源，還得要謝謝您！

沒想到您還熟悉Pottle教授，您所講的夏志清與Pottle教授見面的細節太生動了，希望以後有機會把這個細節補充到拙文中。這再次說明了夏志清與Pottle教授深厚的情誼，讓人感動。

再次感謝！

祝安好！

季進致孫康宜

親愛的孫老師：

　　我前天獲悉消息，馬上就給王德威寫了郵件，請他節哀順變。他們好像不願意驚動大家，所以我也就沒跟您說。抱歉。

　　王媽媽我也有幸見過一面，她真是一位偉大的傳奇女性，道德楷模，一生做了無數的好事，得享高壽也是福分，但對於子女來說，還是無法承受之痛。

　　謝謝您發來照片，好珍貴。您把王媽媽放到現代西方的「道德權威」的背景下來認識，真是別具隻眼。正如您所說，王媽媽身上所體現的那種「發自內心的道德信仰和對人的包容態度」，賦予了她們強大而堅韌的生命力，令人無比欽佩。

　　祝安好！

季進
6/28/2020

Josephine Chiu-Duke（丘慧芬）致孫康宜

Dear Kang-i,

　　Thanks a lot for sharing with me Dr. Li's email. Yes, Wang Hui and I had a debate at the AAS annual meeting about ten years ago. Please give my thanks to Dr. Li for his kind words about me. I am honored to receive such comments and can only say that his words will only remind me of my responsibility as a teacher who aspires to be in the company of you and Dr. Li himself and of course all the others with same concerns about humanity.

Best to you and CC,

Huifen

6/28/2020

王雅萍致孫康宜

孫院士您好，

在臺灣已是每天攝氏三十五度上下的盛夏，聽著這音樂格外舒心。他的文字也很棒，照片中的耶魯建築真的很有文化底蘊，風景如畫！讓人想去拜訪一趟耶魯了！

雅萍

6/28/2020

註：這是指耶魯大學音樂系畢業生潘暢的一篇文章，題為〈Mini Concert／耶魯校歌，讓你在我的心中撒下一道陰影〉。（https://mp.weixin.qq.com/s/vINN_i7MLuukTiL_DbkcQg）。文章裡還包括潘暢的大提琴獨奏：Schubert, An Die Musik（〈獻給音樂〉）。那首歌也正是耶魯音樂學院的「院歌」。

孫康宜致林順夫

Dear Shuen-fu,

Oops, I just noticed that in a hurry I wrote it wrong regarding Ian McKellen in my email to you on June 27th. In Paragraph 2, line 7 of my email, I said that "I very much enjoyed seeing Ian McKellen play out the lines about death from a scene of the "Merchant of Venice." Well, I meant to say Henry IV Part Two, not Merchant of Venice. Back in 1959 Ian McKellen played the role of Old Justice Shallow in Henry IV

Part Two. In one of the most memorable scenes he was talking to an even older friend Silence about the inevitability of death.

In John Barton's "Playing Shakespeare," Series #9 (on "Poetry and Hidden Poetry"), I was especially impressed with Ian MeKellen's acting out the old role in a new way. I was deeply moved, when Ian McKellen (as Shallow) said to Silence with a new sense of energy:

> Certain, 'tis certain, very sure, very sure.
>
> Death, as the Psalmist says, is certain to all; all shall die. . .
>
> Death is certain. . . .

Indeed, Ian McKellen has captured the hidden meaning of Shakespeare's poetry.

Best,
Kang-i
6/29/2020

林順夫致孫康宜

Dear Kang-i,

Both of your emails have been received. Thank you so much for your comments on John Barton, Ian McKellen, etc. I am delighted (actually, impressed!) that you have watched so many of the Barton videos already, and with care too. It's been a few years since I watched the entire 490+ minutes of John Barton's workshop videos. So, I have no recollection of McKellen acting out a scene from Henry IV Part Two at all. I will be looking at all of the videos again when I have more time. These videos are so wonderful, and they are so accessible online now! John Barton's teaching and interpreting of Shakespeare brings back the fond memories of the Shakespeare course (taught by Dr. William Buell) that I took in my junior year at Tunghai. The way Dr. Buell taught Shakespeare was to read out loud passages from Shakespeare and then to make commentary as he went along. His voice would change as he assumed from role to role and situation to situation. I remember that I was totally amazed that he could change his voice as he assumed the roles of different characters by turn, male or female, heroic or villainous. Of course, we couldn't do too many plays in their entirety in the space of one term. But thanks to Dr. Buell's teaching, for a long time I have good "conceptions" of the characters in the Bard's plays, especially Brutus, Anthony, Romeo, Juliet, Hamlet, Macbeth, Iago, Falstaff. According to Kit Salter (our teacher in "Advanced Oral" course), Dr. Buell's method of teaching Shakespeare was quite novel and popular in the US during the 1960s!

Attached please find a brief video of "楊氏太極拳單鞭式左右練習." This is for a laugh only! And of course, for showing why I think Ian McKellen was doing the "Single Whip" posture when he acted out David Garrick's elaborate performance of Macbeth dying. From the perspective of 太極拳, McKellen's execution of the "Single Whip" posture is 不及格! But he was not demonstrating T'ai Chi Ch'uan, was he?! Since I know that you don't practice T'ai Chi Ch'uan, please delete the attached video after you play it. Though it is only 21 seconds in duration, it is more than 10 megabytes long!

With best regards,
Shuen-fu
6/29/2020

Pauline Lin致孫康宜

Thank you so much for sharing this wonderful article, dear Kang-i Ayi. I not only got to know Professor Wang's mother as a person (feel like I know her), I also got to learn about the traditional Chinese ideal of a 道德女子. This essay would read really well with Lienuzhuan, I think. Maybe I will, with your consent, have this essay read in conjunction with the Lienuzhuan when I teach Literary Chinese. Please let me know if that might be OK.

Thanks again!!

Yours,

Pauline

6/29/2020

ps. Stay safe—we seem to be getting a series of thunderstorms this week.

孫康宜致李保陽

Dear Baoyang,

Good morning! Today is June 30th, the last day of June, and I feel compelled to finish as many deadlines and responsibilities as possible--including the conclusion of my duty as the Director of Graduate Studies (DGS) for the EALL Department at Yale. This is because July 1st is considered the first day of the new academic year, 2020-2021.

Anyway, I want to use this chance to review what we have gone through during the last few months. First of all, during this unusual time of the COVID-19 pandemic, the fact that we still stay alive after so many trials and rapid changes is itself a blessing. That's why I give thanks to God everyday. Indeed every new day is a gift from God!

Just this morning, I read a very inspiring article by a Chinese student called Wenduo Cheng, posted on wechat by my former student Austin Woerner. The article appeared in the 2/25/2020 issue of the journal *The Blue Dragon*, which is one of the student publications at the Duke Kunshan University located in Kunshan, Jiangsu Province, China. (https://mp.weixin.qq.com/s/OIekfEbPEPlR1H_4vkXUqw). As you may know, Austin Woerner is currently a Lecturer in English Language at Duke Kunshan University, although he flew back to Boston a few months ago due to the rapid spread of the Coronavirus in China then. (By the way, Austin and his wife recently had a baby boy! Remember? He is also a famous writer and translator, and his work has often appeared in *Poetry*, *The New York Times Magazine,* etc. His translation of my colleague Su Wei's（蘇煒）novel, *The Invisible Valley*（迷谷）, was published in 2018.)

Well, I want to share with you the first few lines of Wenduo Cheng's article, just to show you that DKU's *The Blue Dragon* journal has put out some very thoughtful essays during the pandemic season:

> "All of a sudden, people around me began to wear masks and even gloves. All of a sudden, I heard from the news that the confirmed cases of the Wuhan coronavirus exceeded that of the SARS in 2003. All of a sudden, my mom who was in a town of Hubei Province told me her city had been put on lockdown, where almost all vehicles are banned. All of a sudden, I had to stay on campus during the winter break because the airports and train stations were determined to be extremely dangerous. All of a sudden, the common new year's wish was no longer to get rich but to stay healthy. All of a sudden, people started complaining that masks had been sold out. All of a sudden, the sophomore students were told to move into the campus, leaving the Scholar Hotel locked. . . . "

As you can see, some of the things described in Wenduo Cheng's article are still "very relevant to those of us still in lockdown in the U.S." (Here I'm quoting from Austin). This is why I said we are very fortunate just to be alive today!

Best,

Kang-i

6/30/2020

孫康宜致李保陽

Dear Baoyang,

I want to share with you the great news that my student Anne Zlatow just published an article in the *LA Review of Books* (June 28, 2020), which is her first publication and the culmination of her years of research on Mulan 木蘭. The title of the article is: "Waiting for Mulan: Reflecting on the Original Legend Before the Upcoming Disney Movie."Here is a link to the article:

https://chinachannel.org/2020/06/28/mulan/

A few years ago Anne Zlatow wrote her senior thesis on Mulan under my direction. She then got her B.A. degree in East Asian Languages & Literatures from Yale. Currently she studies for her M.S. in Laboratory Animal Science at Stanford University while waiting for Disney's Mulan to come out in theatre.

As you can see (see attached picture), I posted a message on my Wechat moments, saying: "I'm so proud of my former student Anne Zlatow for writing this great article on Mulan 木蘭!" (June 30, 2020, 9:37 p.m.)

Hope you will enjoy reading Anne's article too. I just want to call your attention to the following statement in her article:

"Mulan is a story in which gender means everything and nothing. Even since the 6th century, the ballad calls the distinctiveness of gender differences into question, as seen in its final lines: "A pair of hares sprinting side by side near the ground, how could observers distinguish male from female?" Whether it's hares sprinting or soldiers fighting in uniform, individual identity becomes mottled. For Mulan, dressing as a man appears to be the moment she defies traditional Chinese expectations. . ."

Best,

Kang-i

6/30/2020深夜

黃文吉致李保陽

保陽學棣：

　　二十七日電郵述及親炙於吳熊和先生之經過，尤其吳夫人將先生生前之衣物贈你保暖，著實令人感動！若非吳先生伉儷視汝為親人晚輩，何以至此？吳先生《唐宋詞通論》早已拜讀，全書分別以「詞源」、「詞體」、「詞調」、「詞派」、「詞論」、「詞籍」、「詞學」介紹唐宋詞，具有詞史及詞學之雙重意義，其中諸多見解，均言之有據，迄今仍有參考價值。1997年9月先生光臨寒舍，我特別出示所藏該書，請先生簽名。不久，先生回杭，特別寄來合照數幀，並告知已將《天機餘錦》複印本掛號轉寄王兆鵬先生，這是遼寧教育出版社出版校點本《天機餘錦》的由來。過兩年，《吳熊和詞學論集》（杭州大學出版社）出版，我也獲得先生親自簽名贈書，每次閱讀書中論文，皆有收穫。

　　閱讀你訪問嚴夫人之鴻文〈憶嚴迪昌先生〉，對嚴先生的道德文章與境遇有更深層之認識，可見你對學術界「掌故」之重視。嚴先生在臺灣出版《清詩史》，是一種因緣巧合，容我當「白頭宮女」略述經過。先生此書因為字數太多，大陸那邊出版社原已排版完成，但礙於經費，遲遲無法付梓，先生非常苦惱，於是向我求助，看臺灣是否有書商願意出版。

　　你在〈吳熊和先生晚年談話錄〉裡提及東坡詞近年有西安的薛瑞生先生箋注本，當年薛先生曾將此本《東坡詞編年箋證》書稿，擬向臺灣「中華發展基金管理委員會」申請協助出版，他透過王兆鵬先生之引介，請我幫忙當「臺灣代理人」，個人認為該書是繼龍沐勳《東坡樂府箋》之後，校箋及考證皆非常精詳的著作，於是我滿口答應，幫忙寫推薦理由並親自搭計程車送申請書及書稿到基金會，希望能促成美事。

　　薛先生的來函，我才知道臺灣有此協助中國大陸學者出版學術著作的管道，於是我將訊息告知嚴先生，問他是否有意願申請，先生為了著作能早日出版，便答應姑且一試，並請我當「臺灣代理人」，幫忙寫推薦書及處理送件事宜。

　　審查結果出來，嚴先生《清詩史》雖然字數多，卻備受肯定，獲得協助出版。薛教授《東坡詞編年箋證》固然有其價值，但審查者認為此書是屬於「編纂譯述性質之著作」，與協助出版所訂的「學術著作」要件不合，因此並未獲得通過。

　　我與薛先生、嚴先生為了申請協助出版，曾往來書札數通，如今重新展讀，諸多感觸，所謂人之境遇，各有不同，如此之謂也。

　　嚴先生大著由中華發展基金會委託五南圖書出版公司出版，印刷精美，裝訂成兩大冊，於1998年10月初版發行，成為研究清詩者必須參考之重要典籍。唯一美中不足者，嚴先生因眼疾無法親自校對，在簡體轉繁體過程中，產生許多錯誤，另外也有一些手民之誤，這些都讓先生後悔沒有接受我的建言親校一遍，但畢竟字數太多又罹患眼疾，這也無可奈何之事。後來為了亡羊補牢，嚴先生接受我的意見，做了勘誤表，以減少遺憾。

　　薛先生花了許多心血與郵寄書稿複印本之費用，卻無法獲得協助出版，我作為「臺灣代理人」相當為他抱不平。所幸該書在1998年9月由三秦出版社正式問世，他將贈書託去大陸開會的臺灣友人轉交，看到他所題的文字，仍然不忘我的幫忙，可見他乃是性情中人。在書後識語也提及本人，只是將我任教的學校「彰化師範大學」誤植為「彰化師專」而已。我與薛教授迄今並未謀面，所謂文字交、學術緣大概如此吧！

　　年紀愈長，經歷愈多，對於人生種種境遇，感覺似乎冥冥中註定，所以許多得得失失，唯有歸之命運而已。年輕時受家庭影響，信奉儒釋道融合的傳統宗教，稍長也了解其他宗教的可貴處，兩位女兒因到國外留學改信基督教，我都給予尊重。個人認為「宗教自由」是普世價值，不應該受到任何干涉，寄望未來的世界，每個人都能選擇認同的宗教，作為精神的依歸，而不再有恐懼、受迫害的情事發生。

　　讀了你的來函，諸多有感，不知不覺中追憶起二十多年前往事，或許可作為你與學界友人談話之助。專此，並頌

　　近祉

黃文吉覆
6/30/2020

陸葵菲致孫康宜

康宜教授：

　　非常理解！沒關係，重要的是您要健康。我們接下來安排有好幾個訪談，時間上不著急，只是我們比較期待看到您的訪談。

　　請您多保重！以馬內利！

陸葵菲（方舟）

6/30/2020

張宏生致孫康宜

　　對啊，康宜，整整二十年了，這篇文章將我帶回二十年前，記得很清楚，那是會後的第二天，我們吃完早飯，就到圓明園遊覽，在那一片廢墟前流連甚久。現在藉著微信，舊事重現，倍感親切。

宏生

6/30/2020

註：「文章」指的是孫康宜二十年前所寫的「廢墟」一文，刊於《萬象》2000年12月號。

盤隨雲致孫康宜

Dear康宜教授，

　　Thank you so much for sharing this article with me! It was, of course, beautifully written. It is not only a nice reflection on Xia Jianyong's夏堅勇book, but also an in-depth discussion of life, time, and history on its own. I especially love the way you contemplated eternity through transience and sought transcendence from "ruins." We shall never forget the sufferings and pains of our nation and our predecessors. We shall never ignore either the physical ruins or the intangible, psychological ruins that impacted and shaped certain generations. Yet the best way to remember them may not simply be the tearful lamentations. Instead, the meaning these ruins "bequeathed" to us is fully realized when we transcend those scars to enter "a new realm," where we can sympathize with people in the past and be enlightened with the eternal light of the cosmos, or of the Dao. Only then could the ruins become legacies.

Best,
Suiyun
6/30/2020

Haninah Levine致孫康宜

Dear Professor Chang,

Now that spring has officially ended, I wanted to send you a full season's selection of quatrains at once. Hoping that you and CC are well.

All my love,

Haninah
6/30/2020

March 20, 2020
Flowering cherries line the rain-slicked pavement
Today is warm, but tomorrow will welcome a cold snap
Spring's first full day on an empty street:
Open windows gasp for balmy air while they can still breathe.

March 24, 2020

Playing in the park, climbing trees,

A pink cloud settles over us:

Cherry blossoms, sterile and pure,

Like heaven's unearned mercy.

March 30, 2020

Pea shoots have sprouted already

And belatedly, I remember to enrich the soil

I bury the jade-green newborns

In two inches of rotting compost.

April 5, 2020

A pastel confusion: phlox in many colors

A gunmetal sky, pollen on the car roofs

And the blossoming trees – my favorite tree is

Redbud-or-is-that-an-ornamental-plum.

April 9, 2020

Sundown, and the clouds are racing east

Today, sun and clouds fought to a standstill

The broken oak limb Emily has worried about since we moved in

Still hangs over our neighbors' house, unnoticed.

April 15, 2020

Tree-blossom season is nearly finished

Redbuds and Kwanzen cherries melt in the rain

I plant zinnias and marigolds for the summer:

"No one's come gazing" this year.

April 16, 2020

I learned that a bush I thought was azalea was flowering quince

So I went to view it before all its blossoms fell

Already, its hips were swelling with fruit

The bees, sated, were drifting towards the redbud trees.

April 21, 2020

To My Mother, As She Begins Her Journey Home

Part 1

What do the juncos and the hermit thrushes think

When spring arrives, just as they are getting ready to leave?

Do they envy of the warblers their coming moment of glory?

Do they know something the warblers don't?

Part 2

Of all the neighborhood trees, one sycamore towers over the rest

You have to stand a block away to appreciate its height

Its paint-palette skin and handprint leaves

Are all you notice standing in its shadow.

April 22, 2020

Part 3

In the courtyard in the library at Yale, there is a tree

It is very beautiful, and serene, and hardly anyone ever visits it

And is it even more beautiful, and even more serene

Now that no one visits it at all?

April 23, 2020

Part 4

Purple irises begin to fade before I notice their arrival

I never remember how rain calms me until I hear it on the windows

Blooming and falling, the timeless gestures of spring –

Fear and delight, two deep-rooted oaks never swaying.

April 25, 2020

River unseen, oak without leaves,

Clouds holding rain, first warblers hidden:

Four hillside spirits, all quiet potential,

Waiting to spring.

April 28, 2020, Israeli Remembrance Day

You've forgotten how to talk, and how to sit up

Have you forgotten sieges, and sirens, and aching wet feet in winter?

You spent a lifetime running away from your memories,

And now you have finally escaped them.

May 17, 2020

When birds sleep, their feet grasp the branch beneath them

You have nothing left but the reflex to grasp a hand placed in yours

A holding hand, and your breath: on these last two rafting reeds

You sail through your penultimate sleep.

June 7, 2020

The zinnias never emerged

And the marigolds were devoured by squirrels

I replant them again and again

But heaven's green eye is angry this year.

June 14, 2020

I don't have much to say anymore

Confinement has made me a person of thin thoughts

I try to fatten them with the day's news

But knowledge alone leaves them flabby and confused.

June 18, 2020

A puncture in the clouds, and yellow light crashes through

An oak faces west, as though hoping to bathe its face in the light

A firefly in the garden slips through a break in the weeds

The amaranth reaches out a leaf to grasp it.

C.C. Chang（張欽次）致孫康宜、李保陽

Dear Kang-i and Baoyang,

　　This bag of flowers (see attached picture) is just to celebrate your completion of the COVID-19 book. What you have accomplished is quite a task!

　　I want to send both of you this bag of flowers as my token of appreciation, before the month of June passes! I hope that we will move into a better season soon, as the biblical verse from the Book of Ecclesiastes says:

> To everything there is a season,
>
> and a time to every purpose
>
> under the heaven. . . .
>
> (Ecclesiastes 3:1)

凡事都有定期

天下萬務

都有定時……

（《傳道書》，3:1）

Let's not take anything for granted, for whatever happens to us is part of our life's journey. The joy of living is forever found in the heart that is filled with gratitude!

C. C. Chang
6/30/2020

孫康宜致李保陽

Dear Baoyang,

I am deeply touched by your postscript編後記to our book, such that I must write this response to you! First of all, you finished writing this postscript on July 17, 2020, exactly 52 years after I came to America and started my life as an immigrant in the US!

Also, I must mention that my husband C.C. Chang came to America almost 54 years ago (in 1966)! And this is his recollection:

"I remember vividly how I had my first dinner at Princeton's Graduate College.

I had to put on a gown (like a medieval monk) and march with pipe organ music to my seat, standing there until the Master blessed the meal in Latin. I was served by waiters who actually were bursary students. There were 10 people for each table, and we shared food by passing on the trays. We could always ask for a second. I still remember the food served on that day--strip steaks, mash potatoes, carrots, mixed vegetable for salad, and lots of bread and milk. The dessert was New York Cheese Cake along with ice cream."

Please see attached a picture of C.C. wearing the dining gown, while ready to go to the Graduate College dining hall back in 1966.

Later during the 1970s, when I enrolled in Princeton University as a graduate student, I no longer needed to wear a dining gown!

We hope that after the COVID-19 pandemic is finally over, you will have a chance to eat at the Princeton Graduate College, which is not far from the Institute of Advanced Studies.

Kang-i
7/19/2020

C.C. Chang was wearing a dining gown, ready to go to dinner at the Graduate College Dining Hall. (Princeton University, 1966).

The background of this picture is the famous Graduate College of Princeton University. (Princeton, 1966)

孫康宜補註：

　　趁著我寫給李保陽的這封信，我想把普林斯頓（我的母校）和耶魯（我執教將近四十年的大學）兩校之間的緊密關聯，包括其歷史意義，簡單說明一下。首先，著名的「常春藤橄欖足球賽」乃是正式以1873年11月15日的「普林斯頓和耶魯的對賽」開始的，即所謂的「Princeton-Yale Football Rivalry」，或稱「an American college football rivalry between Princeton Tigers and the Yale Bulldogs.」從1873年開始，兩校之間不斷舉行了多次的橄欖足球對賽，直到如今。他們既是競爭對手，也是良伴好友，比賽次數之多，一直名列長春藤大學之冠。據考證，到了1949那年（11月12日），兩校之間的橄欖足球隊已有過七十二次的競賽，實令人瞠目結舌！當然，後來耶魯與哈佛之間精彩的橄欖足球賽也是有目共睹的。

　　巧合的是，幾天前我的碩士生盤隨雲贈我一副有關普林斯頓和耶魯大學於1907年11月16日舉行橄欖足球賽（即兩校之間第三十三次競賽）的海報，而且那是一副從紐黑文城裡著名的Merwin's Art Shop所買到的珍貴展品。突然收到這副極具歷史價值的海報，真令我感到驚喜！這是我在「避疫」期間所收到的最佳禮物之一，更重要的是，它已成為「潛學齋」的珍藏了。

普林斯頓和耶魯大學於1907年11月16日
舉行橄欖足球賽（即兩校之間第三十三
次競賽）的海報。左邊是普林斯頓的吉
祥物（老虎），右邊是耶魯大學的吉祥
物（牛頭犬）

陸葵菲致孫康宜

親愛的孫康宜老師：

　　這是一個美好的早晨。2020年8月21日早上九點四十七分，我收到了您對訪談問題的回覆。

　　而大約在一個小時後，您又發來第二封郵件，在這封郵件裡，您提出了三處修改意見。我核對後發現，僅僅是三處標點符號的修改：一處頓號改句號，一處去掉逗號，還有一處去掉一邊括弧。

　　這並非我第一次感受到您的細緻嚴謹。

　　就在8月7日早晨，您發簡訊給我，說您將在明年六月分退休，這意味著您只有十個月的工作時間了，而期間有很多事情需要處理，您將承受巨大的工作壓力，所以訪談還要往後推。我回覆您說沒關係，雖然三啟學會很期待您的訪談，但是您的健康更是我們關心的。

　　我非常清晰地記得，數月前當我向您發出訪談邀請時，您欣然答應說，當然

可以，您也非常樂意分享您與家人的信仰見證。

　　然而您實在太忙了。5月20日您發來簡訊，說您因為最近太勞累，全職教學並擔任研究所主任（直到6月30日），還要著手書稿的校對（共六大本），所以忙出病來了。您說您已辭退無數的訪問稿及約稿。唯一的例外是，您最終一定要完成曾經答應過我的訪談稿，但要等這學期的學校工作結束，改完所有研究生的論文，並交稿完畢之後才能開始安心地回應我的訪談。

　　其實每次看到您充滿歉意的簡訊，我心裡頗為難過，我常常為您禱告，求上帝賜給您健康。雖然我們很期盼早日見到您的訪談，但是又實在是不忍心催促您。正如我對您說過的：比起訪談，您的健康對於我們而言要重要得太多。如果訪談成為了您的負擔，我心如何能安？所以，我說，請您量力而行，等工作告一段落，在您的精力允許的情況下再作回應也無妨。

　　我想著等您明年退休了，我們再慢慢地從容地對話。您也是這麼想的。

　　不曾想，您居然回覆了，於百忙之中。

　　近一年以來，我們保持著非常勤勉和愉悅的交流。一場疫情又將我們拉得更近。非常感恩您與我分享您所經歷的一些事情。我知道了您的姑姑因感染新冠去世，令人悲傷，但當我得知她是基督徒時，又倍覺欣慰。8月3號是您五十二周年結婚紀念日，您發了當年的照片給我，看您著一襲白色婚紗，站在普林斯頓大學校園裡，猶如童話般的美好。

　　回想從約您的訪談以來我與您的交流和溝通，我們常常不約而同發出「It's amazing」的感慨。是的，我們因著三啟學會的事工而相識，這就是上帝的奇異恩典。您在〈奇妙的文字緣〉裡也談到了文字的神奇，我們素未謀面，卻能於萬里之遙心靈相通惺惺相惜。

　　十幾天前您發簡訊給我：「再過幾天，我們大概就不准用Wechat微信了！或許以後，我只好與你用email的方式聯絡了！所以到時候，請你一定要看email，要回我的email好嗎？請再給我一次你的email address郵址！」

　　您近乎懇求的語氣令我愴然泣下。頃刻間這大半年以來的種種悲涼、個人命運被時代浪潮所裹挾的無奈一齊湧上心頭。

　　您一遍又一遍地測試我是否能夠收到您的email，切切囑託我要勤看郵箱，又讓我把家庭住址和電話號碼發送給您。我回覆您：「我一定會關注email，也

一定會及時回覆您。我們不知道接下來還會發生什麼，但是我們確信都在祂的愛裡。」

從您一系列的文章裡，我瞭解到您個人以及您的家庭的坎坷經歷。當然，更有您帶給我的文學美，我從您的文字裡看到您孩童般的率真，又有學者一絲不苟的嚴謹。您給予我莫大的激勵，常常讓我感覺到自己的人生才剛剛開始。

感恩您對訪談問題的真誠作答，必將有生命因它得造就。

願上帝賜福與您和您的家人！以馬內利！

愛您的葵菲

2020年8月22日於中國廣東順德

王秋桂致孫康宜

康宜：

雖你貴為院士，想你還是會想念高先生。我最近要把所有書信文件送去廢紙場回收。留一copy給你。

Ck

9/29/2020

註：王秋桂先生是孫康宜從前在臺大外文研究所讀書時代的同學（1966-1968），後來他到英國留學，獲劍橋大學的文學博士，師從著名的Denis C. Twitchett教授。曾短期在普林斯頓大學的葛斯德東亞圖書館擔任Bibliographer（書目專家）的工作。與牟復禮、高友工、余英時諸位教授過從甚密。

高友工1990年寫給王秋桂的信

附1990年高友工致王秋桂函釋文

秋桂兄如晤：

　　在紐約鄉下避暑，收到轉來四號的信。知你代理院務一年，很為你高興。作院長雖是吃力不討好的事，但是你是有遠景、有理想的人，正可趁此機會做一點事。清華正如你說有朝氣，沒有一些臺大的舊習，做起事來也許比較容易。

　　謝謝你約我和英時回來，可惜我的休假要到九一至九二才有。英時剛拿了他的休假（九〇春季）。所以在你任期都不可能回來。除非你願意再做一年，我一定設法考慮。和Iris¹談過，她的確很欣賞清華，玩的甚為開心。選上了院士也使她很高興。

　　我倒是想到在你這（一）[2]年也許可以設法辦一個像你們今夏Post modernism的Seminar之類的聚會。Post modernism可惜已經是個過時的題目，又已經講過了，不知為何辦了又辦。想一些較有意思的題目，如Semiotics就更有建設性。而且應該找可以和中國文化配合的題目來講，這樣用中文講、討論，才能作到交流的目的。Undergraduate（s）[3]也就可以參加。這樣就可在清華辦，不必上臺北。我隨便寫下這點意見，是想到也許可以在你這一年中搞一件文學院比較有創意的事。不知你以為如何？

友工　草　八月三十日

註：

[1]　Iris指趙元任的女兒趙如蘭教授（1922-2013），其正式英文名字是Rulan Chao Pian, 哈佛大學音樂系教授。與丈夫卞學鐄同為中央研究院院士。

[2]　底稿脫「一」字，為使語意通順，補足之。

[3]　Undergraduate（s），底稿原作Undergraduate，當係筆誤，補足之。

孫康宜致王秋桂

Dear秋桂，

　　My goodness, what a pleasant surprise! This is a letter from Prof. Kao to you, dated 30 years ago in 1990! Thank you so much for thinking of me!

　　You are right! I miss Prof. Kao very much! In fact, just yesterday 9/28（which was Teacher's Day教師節）I was rereading Prof. Kao's old article on Tang poetry. I'm always grateful to Prof. Kao for his inspiration ever since I became his student in 1973.

　　By the way, In my forthcoming book (co-edited with Dr Baoyang Li) titled《避疫書信選》, Prof. Kao figures prominently! (As well as Prof. Mote and Prof. Yu). If you don't mind, I'll add your brief note along with Prof. Kao's 1990 letter to the book! This would be perfect, because you were such a good friend to all of them.

Again, thank you for sending an electronic copy of this memorable letter to me!

Best,

Kang-i

9/29/2020

附録

附錄一：我的姑姑

孫康宜

兩天半以前，住在馬利蘭州的表弟志明（Jeremy）才告訴我，說他母親（即我的姑姑孫毓嫻）不幸染上COVID-19（冠狀肺炎），已從養老院被送到當地的Shady Grove醫院。

但今日凌晨，志明就通知我關於姑姑已於午夜前（5月7日）去世的消息。據醫生診斷，姑姑死於心臟衰竭，但那是直接由冠狀肺炎引起的。

> 表姊，我媽去世了⋯⋯。
>
> May 7⋯⋯only a few minutes before 12 midnight 凌晨⋯⋯
>
> 媽很棒。典型的孫家人。媽給了我做人的 discipline⋯⋯
>
> 我媽是個內心強大的人，這和孫家的人都很相似。我小時候能去好的小學，考取好的中學，考取上海第二醫學院，這跟我媽的嚴厲管教是分不開的⋯⋯
>
> ⋯⋯我媽為了教育我，在生活上不要去追求物質享受，她給我買了一件新衣服以後，在新衣服上面打了一個布丁⋯⋯
>
> 我小時候，我媽對我要求非常非常嚴格，如果我的成績不好的話，她一定會責罵我⋯⋯
>
> 我媽自律性很強，我到現在每天能按時起床，按時吃飯，做事情按時按點，這都是被我媽訓練出來的⋯⋯

幾分鐘之間，我一連串接到了表弟志明從微信送來的這許多資訊。

我立刻發出了一聲歎息，長長的歎息。

但我同時也向神禱告，感謝　祂讓姑姑活過一段路程艱難但終於圓滿的一生。其實姑姑已是八十七歲半（生於1932年12月25日），已接近九十高齡，算是很長壽了。

　　我從小就聽家人說，姑姑最疼愛我。至今我仍十分珍惜父親於1980年寫給我的一封信，信中寫道：「康宜，今日收到你姑姑來信，看到你的著作，她興奮之情溢於言表。她是看你從小長大的……。」

孫保羅寫給女兒孫康宜的信（1980年12月3日）

　　凡讀過拙著《走出白色恐怖》的讀者大概都會記得，在〈兩岸的受害者〉那一章裡，我曾經描寫1979年6月底首次到大陸探親，從紐約飛往上海的一幕：

> 6月24日傍晚，我終於到了上海的虹橋機場。當年那個機場很冷清，旅客寥寥無幾，不像現在一般擁擠。下了飛機，我很容易就租到了一部出租汽車，約半個小時後就到了和平飯店。一進旅館，放好行李，就立刻打電話給姑姑……

　　還記得，那天我一進姑姑和姑父的家門，姑姑忍不住就抱著我痛哭。之後我們又相對無言，默默地流淚。自從我兩歲（1946年春）跟隨父母去了臺灣之後，我們與姑姑及大陸的所有親人就一直沒見過面，三十多年間大家都活在兩地隔絕的景況中。

　　就在1979年6月24日那天，我從姑姑那兒得知有關許多年前（1953年）一連串的災難如何降臨到我們家，以及爺爺如何突然失蹤的悲劇：

　　　　有一天晚上，爺爺突然失蹤了。姑姑一直等到深夜，但爺爺一直沒回來。
　　　　姑姑就向後奶奶交待一聲，自己跑了出去，走遍了城裡每個角落，一直步
　　　　行到天亮。次日清晨回家後，姑姑才在垃圾筒裡揀到了爺爺親手寫的一個
　　　　小紙條：「我去天津火車站。」於是，姑姑又到火車站去，待了幾個鐘頭
　　　　仍不見爺爺的蹤影。此後也再不見爺爺出來領糧票，所以家人斷定，爺爺
　　　　一定是自殺了，或許投入天津火車站對面的海河裡去也說不定。

姑姑一直強調，絕對不能讓我父母知道有關爺爺「自殺」的事。同時，我那天也
沒有勇氣告訴姑姑有關我父親在臺灣白色恐怖期間坐牢十年的事，因為我不願意
給她加添任何精神上的刺激。

　　說起姑姑，她當年在中國大陸的生活經驗的確十分坎坷。且說，她從小就受
極其良好的教育。她初中上天津中西女中，高中上北京潞河中學，後來全靠自學
而考取上海第一醫學院（本該去協和，但協和醫院於四九後被關閉了）。她一直
是非常傑出的學生，自幼即以居里夫人（Marie Curie）為心目中的偶像。

　　然而，以姑姑剛烈而正直的個性，後來到了文化大革命期間終於遇到了麻
煩。原來，由於「海外關係」（因為她的大哥——指我父親——在國外），再加
上她從前與教會學校的關係，幾個領導開始日夜不斷地審問她。一時姑姑被他們
惹急了，就大罵那些審問她的領導們，後來他們只好溜了。為了好下臺階，他們
就說她神經有問題，從此大家就不敢理她了。

　　在那段期間，我的叔叔孫裕恆也在南京同樣受到「海外關係」的重重壓力，
一度成為被清算的目標，真乃苦不堪言。

　　後來姑姑和她的丈夫李兆強都在上海第一醫學院裡教書，一直到文化大革命
之時被送到五七幹校的勞改農場。在姑姑正式退休的前幾年，她早已從醫學院的
教書崗位上退下來。當時姑姑在上海第一醫學院（即後來的復旦大學醫學院）擔
任附屬藥廠裡的「品質總監」，所有進來的製藥材料和出去的藥物成品都需要她
的簽名才能順利過關。在她的崗位上，她一律堅守公義的原則，後來連領導們也
暗地裡欽佩她。

　　1993年姑姑和姑父移民到了美國。當時表弟志明正在佛羅里達州（Florida）

的Kennedy Space Center工作（最初志明於1982年底到美國求學，因成績優異，於1990年入選 Kennedy Space Center的實習生——從二百三十人中選出一人——又於同年入美國籍，所以他在1993年就很順利地把父母從上海接到美國來。）

不久他們全家搬到維吉尼亞州（Virginia）。志明後來轉到馬里蘭州，一直在美國政府機構裡服務，相繼任職於NASA, US NAVY, FAA等。2009年志明終於為父母在馬利蘭州找到合適的老人住宅，最後又於2018年讓父母住進附近的養老院。志明和他的妻子李曉菲經常帶兩個小孩（Susanna和Samuel）來探望爺爺奶奶，可謂一家老少其樂融融，令人羨慕。

這些年來，我一直與姑姑他們保持密切的聯繫。去年三月間姑父李兆強去世，我特地到馬里蘭州的Gaithersburg城參加葬禮。沒想到，那次卻成了我與姑姑的最後一次相聚。

自從兩天半前得知姑姑因染上COVID-19已住進醫院之後，我每天晚上上床之前都向上帝祈禱。昨天夜裡大約十一點五十分左右，我又為姑姑獻上禱告。

後來才知道，姑姑就在昨天夜裡我向神祈禱的那一時刻離開了這世界。這真是奇妙的巧合。此外，令我感到神奇的是：今天5月8日正好是我女兒Edie的三十四歲生日，但姑姑居然在5月8日將要到來的前幾分鐘（即5月7日）去世。好像冥冥中姑姑的忌日想避開Edie的生日。

這也令我回想到，十三年前（2007年）我的父親孫保羅是在5月9日上午11:00點鐘（加州時間）去世的。當時我也曾經想過，那真是奇妙的巧合，好像父親為了避開Edie5月8日的生日，故意延遲到次日才離世。

此外，我父親正好比姑姑大十三歲（他生於1919年），而姑姑也正巧在我父親離開的十三年後去世，也以八十七點五歲高齡離世。這樣的巧合實在太神奇了。又，叔叔也已於2017年逝世，相信現在他們兄妹都在天上相會，真是奇妙的恩典。

孫康宜
寫於康州木橋鄉
2020年5月8日

My Aunt

Kang-i Sun Chang（孫康宜）

Translated by Linda Chu（朱雯琪譯）

Two and a half days ago, my cousin Jeremy (Zhiming in Chinese) who lives in Maryland, told me that his mother (my aunt Sun Yuxian) had unfortunately contracted COVID-19 and was sent to the local Shady Grove Hospital.

Then, early this morning, Jeremy told me that my aunt left us just before midnight (on May 7). According to the doctor's diagnosis, she died of heart failure caused by the novel coronavirus.

"Cousin, Mom passed away..."

"On May 7... only a few minutes before 12 midnight..."

"Mom held out to the very end. A typical Sun. Mom gave me the discipline to live with integrity..."

"My mother had a profound inner strength, a trait that runs in the Sun family. Growing up, I was able to go to a good elementary school, get in a good middle school, and attend the Shanghai Second Medical College (present-day Shanghai Jiao Tong University School of Medicine) all because of how Mom raised me..."

"To teach me there are things more important than material enjoyment in life, she bought me new clothes only to purposefully spill pudding on it right afterwards..."

"When I was a kid, she held me to strict standards and set high expectations for me. If my grades were poor, she would scold me..."

"My mother was very self-disciplined. I now get up on time every day, eat meals at set times, and keep to my schedule. All a result of my mother..."

Within the span of a few minutes, I received a flurry of messages from Jeremy on WeChat.

I immediately sighed, letting out a long sigh.

At the same time, I also prayed to God, thanking Him for giving my aunt a full, albeit difficult, life. In fact, my aunt was 87.5 years old (b. December 25, 1932) and close to 90 years old when she passed. She led a long life.

Since I was young, my family told me that my aunt loved me the most. I still cherish a letter from my father written back in 1980. The letter reads: "Kang-i, I received a letter from your aunt today. Upon seeing your publication, her excitement is beyond words. She watched you grow up..."

Readers who read my book *Journey Through the White Terror: A Daughter's Memoir* will probably remember the chapter "Victims on Both Shores" where I described my first visit to Mainland China in late June 1979. I boarded a plane in New York and headed to Shanghai:

Toward the evening on June 24, I finally arrived at Shanghai's Hong Qiao International Airport. The airport in those years seemed deserted. There were hardly any customers, not crowds as there are today. After getting off the plane, I easily hired a taxicab, and about half an hour later arrived at the Peace Hotel in downtown Shanghai. As soon as I went in the hotel and put away my luggage, I promptly called Aunt on the telephone (136).

I still remember that as soon as I entered my aunt and uncle's house, my aunt took me in her arms and wept. Moments later, we sat facing each other not saying a word, shedding tears in silence. I left for Taiwan with my parents at the age of two (in the spring of 1946), and we had not seen any of our relatives in the Mainland since. For more than three decades, we lived on opposite sides of the strait in isolation.

On June 24, 1979, my aunt told me about the events that happened in 1953. That fateful year, a series of disasters struck our family, and Grandpa suddenly disappeared:

...one evening, Grandfather suddenly disappeared. Aunt waited until the depths of night, but Grandfather didn't come back. Aunt then left word with Stepgrandmother and went out on her own to walk ever corner of the city, continuing until dawn. When she returned home early the next day Aunt collected a strip of paper with Grandfather's handwriting from the garbage bin: "I've gone to the Tianjin Railroad Station." So Aunt went again to the train station and waited several hours but still didn't see a trace of Grandfather. Afterward, Grandfather was never again seen going out to draw his food coupons, and the family concluded, although they couldn't say for sure, Grandfather must have committed suicide, perhaps by throwing himself into the maritime river across Tianjin Station... (137).

My aunt had driven home the point that my parents must never find out about Grandpa's "suicide." At the same time, I didn't have the courage to tell my aunt about Father's ten years in prison during the White Terror in Taiwan. I didn't want to add to her mental anguish.

Speaking of my aunt, her time in Mainland China was a winding and bumpy journey. She received a solid education since childhood. She went to the Tianjin Zhongxi Middle School and Luhe High School near Beijing. Later, she studied on her own and got accepted to the Shanghai First Medical College. She had always excelled in school; her idol and role model was Marie Curie.

However, my aunt's resolute and upright personality brought her trouble during the Cultural Revolution. Due to her connection with "relatives overseas" (Her elder brother-my father-lived abroad.), plus her previous connection with church schools, several leaders interrogated her day in day out. One time, after a long session of questioning, she finally had enough and yelled back at her interrogators. They had no choice but to leave the room. In order to not look bad, those leaders said she was mentally unstable. Since then, no one dared to bother my aunt.

During that period, Father's younger brother Sun Yuheng who lived in Nanjing was also under much pressure. As a person with "overseas connections," he was once the government's target and suffered unspeakable misery.

My aunt and her husband Li Zhaoqiang both taught at the Shanghai First Medical College until the Cultural Revolution when they were sent to a *laogai* (re-education through labor) farm at the May Seventh Cadre Schools. Before her official retirement, my aunt had already retired from her teaching position at the medical school. At that time, she served as "Quality Director" of the affiliated pharmaceutical factory at the Shanghai First Medical College (later the Shanghai Medical College of Fudan University). She was responsible for approving all incoming raw materials and finished pharmaceutical products. While serving in her post, my aunt always adhered to principles of justice, and the leaders at the school even secretly admired her.

In 1993, my aunt and uncle immigrated to the States. At the time, Jeremy was working at the Kennedy Space Center in Florida. (Jeremy first arrived in the States at the end of 1982 to study. Because of his excellent grades, he was selected as an intern for the Kennedy Space Center in 1990-one out of 230 candidates-and also became a U.S. citizen that same year. In 1993, he had successfully brought his parents over from Shanghai to the States.)

Very soon, my aunt, uncle, and Jeremy moved to Virginia. Jeremy later transferred to Maryland; he has served various government agencies including the US Navy, NASA, and FAA. In 2009, Jeremy finally found a suitable place for his parents in Maryland, and in 2018, his parents moved to a nearby nursing home. Jeremy and his wife Li Xiaofei had often brought their two children (Susanna and Samuel) to visit their grandparents. Theirs was an enviable family.

Over the years, I have been in close contact with my aunt and her family. Uncle Li Zhaoqiang passed away in March last year. I went to Gaithersburg, Maryland to attend the funeral. Unexpectedly, that was also the last time I saw my aunt.

Since I learned that my aunt was hospitalized with COVID-19 two and a half days ago, I prayed to God before going to bed every night. At about 11:50 pm last night, I offered prayers for my aunt once again.

Later I learned that my aunt went to Heaven as I prayed to God last night. This is a wonderful coincidence. What also amazes me is that today (May 8) happens to be my daughter Edie's 34th birthday, and my aunt left us during the final remaining minutes of May 7. It seems that she didn't want the anniversary of her death to coincide with Edie's birthday.

This also reminds me that my father Paul Sun passed away 13 years ago (in 2007) at 11:00 am (California time) on May 9. I also thought about it at the time. It was a marvelous coincidence. It seemed that my father deliberately delayed his death until the following day to avoid leaving on Edie's birthday (May 8).

My father (born in 1919) was 13 years older than my aunt. Aunt happened to pass away 13 years after my father left, also at the age of 87.5 years old. What an amazing coincidence. Uncle Yuheng passed on in 2017. I believe my father and his brother and sister are having their reunion in heaven. This is amazing grace indeed.

(Written on May 8, 2020 in Woodbridge, Connecticut)

附錄二：方舟雅歌與孫康宜對話
——希望中國有更多的學者研究神學與文學的關聯

　　這是一個美好的早晨。2020年8月21日早上九點四十七分，我收到了孫康宜老師對訪談問題的回復。

　　而大約在一個小時後，她又發來了第二封郵件，在這封郵件裡，她提出了三處修改意見。我核對後發現，僅僅是三處標點符號的修改：一處頓號改句號，一處去掉逗號，還有一處去掉一邊括弧。

　　這並非我第一次感受到她的細緻嚴謹。

　　我非常清晰地記得，數月前當我向她發出訪談邀請時，她欣然答應。

　　然而她實在太忙了。七十六歲的高齡，仍然在耶魯大學全職教學，還要擔任東亞文學研究所主任（直到6月30日），並著手書稿的校對（共六大本），前不久忙出病來了。她說已辭退無數的訪問稿及約稿，而唯一的例外是，最終一定要完成曾經答應過我的訪談稿，但要等這學期的學校工作結束，改完所有研究生的論文，並交稿完畢之後才能開始安心地回應我的訪談。

　　在此期間，孫康宜老師每隔一段時間就要給我發簡訊，表示歉疚。我心裡頗為難過，實在不忍心催促她。

　　我想著等她退休了，我們再慢慢地從容地對話。她也這麼想。

　　不曾想，她回覆了。

　　回想從約她的訪談以來我與她的交流和溝通，我們常常不約而同發出「It's amazing」的感慨。是的，奇異恩典無處不在。她在即將出版的《避疫書信選》序言〈奇妙的文字緣〉裡也談到了文字的神奇，我們素未謀面，卻於萬里之遙心靈相通惺惺相惜。

　　作為西方漢學界最重要的學者之一，孫康宜同時也是散文家。讀她的作品，很難想像那是出自一位在海外生活長達半個世紀的作家。她的散文徜徉於古典與現代，體現出對古典的敬畏，對傳統的堅守，對母語（漢語）的自信與嫻熟。

一方面，她深受中國傳統文化浸潤，另一方面，基督精神貫穿於她的一些文學作品，從而形成了她作品的獨特風格。

方舟雅歌：《走出白色恐怖》是我讀到的您的第一部作品。在這本書裡，您描述了「白色恐怖」時期你們一家顛沛流離坎坷艱辛的經歷。父親入獄十年，母親憑一己之力將你和兩個弟弟養育成人。您父親後來對您母親的評價是：她獻上了生命，培植了兒女的生命，如一粒種子落地。她的生命也影響了我的生命，影響了許多人的生命。她不是為自己活。她為耶穌活，她的人生有目標，有使命。而您的父親孫保羅在走出「白色恐怖」之後（尤其在1978年抵達美國之後），度過了出死入生、完全為基督奉獻的後半生。改名保羅正是寓意他要像保羅那樣為主奔跑，為主打那美好的仗。請問您如何看待那段歷史？對於您家族的坎坷遭遇，您是否還有無法釋懷的人和事？基督信仰對您和您的家族有著怎樣的影響？

孫康宜：

　　有關臺灣白色恐怖期間的那段歷史，確實是個永遠令人難忘的時代大悲劇。記得1950年初，我當時才六歲不到，有一天夜裡軍警突然闖入家中，將父親抓走，接著父親蒙冤坐牢十年，令我們全家走投無路……。後來我們姊弟三人幸而依靠母親的堅忍不拔，很幸運地存活了下來。

　　但在我的記憶深處，尤其讓我忘不了的乃是在那段患難期間，那些為我們雪中送炭的人，包括我的二姨父和二姨母（即後來我的公婆）不但屢次伸出援手，而且引領我們全家信主，這一切都讓我無限感恩。今年（2020年）我已高齡七十六，每次回憶七十年來的人生旅程，自然感慨萬千。但令人感到慶倖的是，我早已「走出」了白色恐怖。又藉著基督信仰，我終於學會了凡事向前看，希望在剩餘的有限人生歲月中，我能繼續努力向著「標杆」跑，直到最後。所以，基督信仰無疑是扭轉我們全家命運的一大關鍵，它使我們在患難中「出死入生」，終身得到了神的奇妙恩典（amazing grace）。有關這一方面的資訊，請見我最近為家父出版的兩本書：（1）《孫保羅書法：附書信日記》（孫保羅著，孫康宜編

著，臺北：秀威資訊，2019）；（2）《一粒麥子》修訂本（孫保羅著，孫康宜編註，臺北：秀威資訊，2019）。

方舟雅歌：您1968年從臺灣到美國讀的是英美文學，而後來至今從事的卻是中國古典文學的研究與教學。請問您的教學和研究方向和您一直以來所受的文學教育是怎樣的關聯？

孫康宜：

其實我所從事的「中國古典文學的研究與教學」，說穿了就是「中西比較文學」。因為我的教學對象是美國學生，我習慣在「比較文學」的上下文中，展開對中國文學的介紹及討論。例如，每回教蘇軾詩詞的「抒情」意象時，就自然會談到義大利詩人但丁的「抒情」（lyrical）精神；講到湯顯祖的《牡丹亭》時，也一定會順便討論英京劇作家莎士比亞的作品。所以我的教學和研究方向和我一直以來所受的文學教育是前後連貫的。

但你說得很對，我當初是百分之百投入英美文學研究的。一直到1973年我念完英國文學的碩士學位之後，才決定要進普林斯頓大學東亞研究系的博士班。當時我有一股尋根的渴求，尤其意識到自己對中國古典文化知識上的不足。而且，我有自知之明，我知道自己的缺陷；除非開始埋頭鑽入中國文學研究，好好地「惡補」一番，我是絕對無法做好「中西比較文學」的研究的。所以當時在普大的博士班，我的主修（major）科目是中國古典文學，次修（minor）才是比較文學和英國文學。

我從1982年開始在耶魯大學教書。將近四十年來，我一直以「跨學科」的方式從事文學研究和教學。我不但在東亞語文系教古典文學，也同時在比較文學系和性別研究系擔任「affiliated professor」的職位。我有幾位博士生——包括目前在芝加哥大學執教的蘇源熙（Haun Saussy）——都是從比較文學系畢業的。

方舟雅歌：在您看來，古典與現代表現在您的文學作品裡是怎樣一種關係？您認為中國文化與西方基督教文化的最大差異是什麼？

孫康宜：

　　有關中國古典文學，我最景仰的乃是中國詩人（例如杜甫、蘇軾等）所表現的那種高貴而堅韌的人文關懷，加上中華文化所標榜的「憂患意識」及其特有的審美精神。從歷代詩人的作品中，我讀到他們是如何一步步腳踏實地地走過來的。

　　重要的是，中國詩歌傳統之博大精深，是全世界有目共睹的。最近由BBC所製作的 "Du Fu: China's Greatest Poet"（《杜甫：最偉大的中國詩人》）紀錄片尤其引起國際間的震撼。這部影片的主持人Michael Wood（著名的英國歷史學家）以一種嚴謹而欣慕的態度來重現杜甫的一生。為了介紹這位一千多年前的偉大中國詩人，Michael Wood特別請舉世聞名的英國戲劇家Ian McKellen來朗讀杜詩的英譯，其「沈鬱頓挫」的朗讀聲調，加上其深情的投入，特別引起人們的共鳴。不用說，中國文明那種源遠流長的精神，早已得到極高的評價了。

　　但另一方面，人們也經常意識到中國傳統文化的不足之處。就如著名的章力生先生（Lit-Sen Chang）在他的《人文主義批判》（A Christian Criticism of Humanism）一書中所說：「中國固有的『天』和『道』的觀念，和聖經中基督教的上帝，三一真神，不可等量齊觀，……唯知有上帝為一事，真正認識上帝……為又一事。」（香港：基道書樓，1963，頁127-120）。傳統中國一般較重「今生今世」（人的世界），並不強調「認識上帝」的屬靈世界（靈界之事），那是中國文化與西方基督教文化的最大差異。其實有關這一點，你在你那篇〈從魯迅到方方：啟蒙的殘燈何以照亮黑屋〉的文章裡，也已經提到了。

方舟雅歌：有一種說法是，中國文學缺少罪感，因而沒有懺悔，沒有靈魂的叩問，因而沒有出現陀思妥耶夫斯基這樣的作家。中國學者劉再復先生評價《紅樓夢》是中國古代小說唯一具有深刻懺悔意識的作品，甚至稱它為中國的《懺悔錄》，是中國文學史上破天荒的奇蹟，也是世界文學史的奇跡，請問您怎麼看？您研究《紅樓夢》是從哪個角度？

孫康宜：

　　我特別喜歡你提出的這個具有啟發性的問題。首先，我覺得劉再復先生所提出的「懺悔意識」比較接近英文裡「remorse」的意思，並非陀思妥耶夫斯基

小說中那種帶有基督信仰的「repentance」。前者（remorse）指的是一種因為反省過去而產生的自我悔恨感，但repentance卻是指一個人不但為自己所犯的「罪孽」（sin）深深感到懺悔，而且更重要的是，必須向神祈求赦免，故與贖罪（redemption）的概念息息相關。

我也同意中國文學裡缺少罪惡感，這或與中國傳統的「人本」主義有關（順便一提，家父孫保羅以為章力生先生在《人文主義》一書中所探討的主題是「人本主義」，而不是指廣義的「人文主義」，雖然二者譯成英文都是「humanism」）。「人本主義」乃是以人為主，以「自我」為中心，認為只要完全靠自己的努力修養就能成道。但基督教卻指向人的「原罪」（original sin）——因為人是「被造者」，生來就有罪性，自己無法拯救自己，所以需要上帝（創造者）的拯救。因為人是「有限」的，無法看見上帝的「無限」，所以上帝才差遣祂的愛子基督到世上來（「道成肉身」），又通過在十字架上流出的寶血，彰顯了神的大愛，全為了拯救世人的靈魂。這就是為什麼「贖罪」（redemption）的信念一直與基督徒的生命觀有著密切的關聯。

我想最好的「贖罪」故事莫過於使徒保羅的生命見證。根據《新約聖經》，保羅（原名掃羅）本是個極力逼迫基督教會的人；當耶穌的門徒司提反（Stephen）被眾人用石頭活活打死時，保羅正好在場，他對這場迫害也是欣然同意的。（當時保羅還誤以為，作為一個頂尖的猶太人，他的任務之一就是努力迫害「基督徒」，不但為眾人除害，也是為上帝作工）。但沒想到，有一天當保羅正走在大馬士革的途中時，忽然有光向他四面照射，他立刻撲倒在地，聽見有聲音對他說：「掃羅，掃羅！你為什麼逼迫我？」。之後，保羅從地上爬起來，三天三夜都看不見什麼，不能吃也不能喝。（《使徒行傳》，9:3-4，8-9）。

那次在大馬士革途中的奇異遭遇，完全改變了保羅的一生。他原來是以捉拿殘害基督徒聞名，現在他卻突然開始在會堂裡為耶穌基督證道，傳講耶穌就是舊約中所預言的彌賽亞（即神的兒子）。保羅的「反常」行動後來引起了猶太人的反感，因此大家集體揚言要殺他，最後他只好逃之夭夭。在這同時，保羅的行動也引起了耶穌門徒們的懷疑：「他們都怕他，不信他是門徒。」（《使徒行傳》，9:26.）

然而，保羅從此甘心情願地「冒險犯難，不辱使命，至死忠心」（《提摩太

後書》4:7）。這就是真心懺悔和贖罪的表現。

　　總之，我以為基督教的「贖罪」精神與《紅樓夢》中的「懺悔意識」有著根本的不同。

方舟雅歌：您用西方學界的主流研究範式來研究中國的古典文學，更注重從現代性的視野下凝視中國古典文學的傳統性變革，這和傳統的考據研究有什麼根本性的不同？

孫康宜：

　　前頭已經說過，我的研究和教學的方法一直是從「中西比較」和「跨學科」的觀點出發的，這當然和傳統所謂的「考據研究」有很大的不同。這並不是說，我對「考據」沒有興趣。其實我每次做研究，都先從考據開始，否則無法產生令人信服的理論和結論。俗語說「慢工細活」，那是我一直以來的信念。其實我並不喜歡隨便套用西方理論，我只是一個「細讀」文本的人。就如我在最近出版的《細讀的樂趣》（南京：譯林出版社，2019）一書的〈後記〉中所說，我的「細讀」教育來自從前博士班導師高友工教授的諄諄教誨：

> 我……把這本集子取名為《細讀的樂趣》。在將近半個世紀以前，如果不是高友工教授不斷教導我如何「細讀」文學（包括中西文學、藝術、電影等），並鼓勵我不懈地努力朝那方向走去，我也不會養成今日凡事細讀的習慣。

方舟雅歌：請談談在您的學術研究中，神給與了您怎樣的啟示？您平時的信仰生活如何？您認為基督徒過教會生活有什麼重要性？

孫康宜：

　　有關我個人的信仰生活，說來慚愧！我早在十二歲時（1956年）就已「受洗」歸主了，但數十年來我的屬靈生活一直沒有進步，有時反而退步。就如王文鋒先生最近在他的〈一場靈命深處的對話：讀經、禱告與靈修〉一文中所說：

「我們需要明白，有時缺乏靈命的磨練，人總是會忽視讀經和禱告，什麼意思呢？因為感覺不到重要性。」

　　我想就因為「感覺不到」靈命磨練的「重要性」，使我大半生（尤其在繁忙的教書和研究的生涯中）經常把日常的讀經和禱告忽略了。突然間，2009年2月，女兒的一場大車禍，立即改變了我的人生方向。四個月後，我的丈夫又因腦震盪而瀕臨生死關頭，使我在絕望中真正學會了仰望上帝，從而在屬神的世界裡得到了意外的平安。〔「我留下平安給你們，我將我的平安賜給你們。我所賜的，不像世人所賜的；你們心裡不要憂愁，也不要膽怯。」（《約翰福音》14:27）〕從此，我的靈命生活獲得了徹底的改變，目前我不但每日讀經禱告，而且還經常寫靈修日記。

　　誠然，王文鋒先生在他的文章裡說得很對：「有時上帝就會安排一些苦難讓人去經歷，其目的就是要通過一種絕望或絕境來催逼人來親近祂、仰望祂。因為人本能喜歡依靠自己的經驗或思維，因此上帝就設計一些環境來逼使人依靠祂。」

方舟雅歌：您曾經談到過：「在中國知識分子的圈子裡，還普遍流行著一種普通
**　　　　　人的過敏症──即對凡與宗教有關的東西均加以拒斥。」您認為這是**
**　　　　　為什麼呢？**

孫康宜：

　　其實我所謂的「宗教」是指的基督教。中國知識份子一般不會排斥佛教（佛教也是外來的宗教），但卻經常對有關基督教的東西「加以拒斥」。這是為什麼呢？我以為這是國人對有關基督教入華歷史的誤解。例如，十九世紀期間許多英美傳教士進入中國，他們冒險投身於宣教工作，經常還因此殉道，其偉大的犧牲精神實在令人欽佩。然而，今日有不少中國人卻誤以為當時傳教士的宣教活動是一種文化侵略，誤將他們所謂的「文化侵略」與當時西方列強對中國的「政治侵略」畫成等號。這是一件很令人惋惜的事情。

　　事實上，這些傳教士不只在傳教方面做出了莫大的貢獻，他們還從事了許多醫療和慈善方面的工作，並在中國普遍設置學校，給國人的教育起了深遠的影

響。此外，就如蘇精先生在其代表作《鑄以代刻：傳教士與中文印刷變局》一書所示，基督教傳教士自1807年來華至1873年為止，六十餘年間引進了「西方活字版」終於取代了木刻印刷中文的技術，其功實不可滅。然而令人不解的是，今日中國學者每談及十九世紀的文化史時，經常略去西方傳教士對中國文化的一連串貢獻，這是對歷史本身的曲解。

方舟雅歌：在西方，懂文學的人不能不精研宗教、哲學，研究哲學、神學也不能對文學陌生。對於神學和文學的相互影響，您的感受是怎樣的？

孫康宜：

從今日「跨學科」的立場看來，神學與文學的關聯會愈來愈重要。有關這一點，我特別欽佩我的耶魯同事Chloë Starr，她是著名的近代中國（尤其是十九世紀）文學史學者。在她的近作《Chinese Theology: Text and Context》（Yale University Press, 2016）一書中，她充分地表現了中國神學與文學的密切關係。

作為一個「開荒」的學者，Chloë Starr這本書獲得了國際間學者們的一致好評。例如，比利時University of Leuven的Nicolas Standaert教授評道：

This is the most inspiring book on Chinese theology that I have read. In a captivating literary style, Chloë Starr guides the reader through the history of Chinese theological texts, examining their ties to Chinese literary forms.

在這方面，我衷心希望中國將來會有更多的學者研究神學與文學的關聯。

方舟雅歌：在全球性的信仰危機之下，您對教育有怎樣的憂慮？您見證了美國高等教育半個世紀以來的變化，您認為它和半個世紀前有什麼不同？您如何看待現在的西方文化？

孫康宜與Chloë Starr合影（2019年耶魯畢業典禮）

孫康宜：

你說得很對，目前我們正面臨著「全球性的信仰危機」。有關下一代的教育，我們確實應當感到憂慮。首先，以美國為例，我親自目睹了半世紀以來在美國的許多變化，其中的變化多端真令我難以置信。據我看來，最大的變化之一就是中小學裡相繼取消了每日「晨禱」（school prayer）的固有傳統，以及後來有關《聖經》課程的取締。難怪今日美國的大學生們大多對《聖經》的內容感到陌生。

另外，你問我目前美國的高等教育和半世紀前有什麼不同。其實早在2014年，我已經發表了一篇有關這一方面的文章，題為〈人文教育還有希望嗎？〉。後來該文的英文版登在《耶魯日報》（Yale Daily News），還引起了耶魯師生們的熱烈反響。

記得在那篇文章裡，我曾經提到，美國教育最大的變化就是人文教育的逐漸衰落。最明顯的就是，專攻人文學科的大學生數目早已減半：六十年代期間專攻人文學科者占學生總數的百分之十四，2010年已減為百分之七，到了今年（2020年）可能變得更少了。我想，那些可能專攻人文學科的學生們，處於目前這種金錢至上的大環境中，早已紛紛轉入了金融專業或其他更有利的科技專業了。

　　其實在我自己的課堂上，早已覺察到目前的耶魯學生和三十多年前的耶魯學生有很大的不同。從前我班上的學生（有許多是剛從中學畢業的大一學生）早已熟悉柏拉圖、喬塞、莎士比亞、彌爾頓、葉慈等人的經典著作，因為他們在中學裡就已經讀過。但目前的學生卻很少讀過這類文學作品。

　　不過，換一個角度來看，今日的時代已經不同了，我們似乎應當改變「文科與理科」的傳統二分法。而目前的「跨學科」傾向正好讓我們學習「文理互動」的思考方式，或許我們也可以趁機發展出一種新的人文傳統。其實那也就是當初1828年耶魯教授們對「通才教育」一詞所下的定義：「所謂通才教育，就是在文科和理科之中，利用最有效的方法，制定一套共同學習的方式，從而增強學生思考的能力。」

　　所以，真正令我感到不安的，還是以上所提到的「全球性的信仰危機」。有關下一代精神教育的何去何從，我確實感到憂慮。

附錄三：《孫康宜文集》校讀後記

李保陽

一、緣起

　　世間事，往往奇妙得不可以言喻！我為孫老師校讀《孫康宜文集》書稿，就是一個奇妙的見證！

　　今年三月，當新冠病毒席捲新大陸的前夜，我正在休假，那段時間每天開車跨過德拉瓦河，到普林斯頓大學葛思德東亞圖書館看書，有一天傍晚，借了幾本書準備回家，走出書庫的一瞬間，瞥見書架一角有一冊《耶魯潛學集》，因為「耶魯」兩個字，心想作者不會是孫康宜教授吧。於是就多看了一眼書脊，發現作者赫然就是「孫康宜」。二十多年前，我在陝南讀大學的時候，曾經讀過孫老師《情與忠：陳子龍柳如是詩詞因緣》。但是對孫老師印象最深的，是傳說中她那一百平方米大的書房潛學齋，以及齋中那足足五張的書桌，這對直到現在尚無一個像樣書房和完整書桌的我來講，是怎樣的一種誘惑呢？於是想都沒想，順手就從書架上抽出那本《耶魯潛學集》一起借出。我要看看孫老師的書房究竟長的是什麼樣子。

　　讀了書中〈在美國聽明朝時代曲——記紐約明軒《金瓶梅》唱曲大會〉那篇文章之後，燈下無言，感慨久久。溯自2016年秋，我到紐約訪書十多天，有一天走出哥倫比亞大學東亞圖書館，信步閒走，竟然走到了中央公園旁的大都會博物館，就進去匆匆忙忙地「到此一遊」。說來也是奇妙，在那迷宮樣的博物館裡，我竟然上了二樓，歪打正著地闖進了一座精雕細琢、美輪美奐的江南園林。在大洋彼岸的曼哈頓鬧市區大都會博物館二樓，竟然藏著這麼一個完全傳統中國風的江南園林！我在江南生活過十多年，走過的江南明清時代遺留下來的山水園林，不下什百，但還是被眼前的這座原汁原味的藝術品給驚呆了！那時候我還不知道這座園子叫「明軒」，也不知道在三十五年前，這裡曾發生過一批當時蜚聲海外漢學界的漢學家們的絲竹雅集。是次雅集，以耶魯大學傅漢思先生的夫人張充和

女士演唱《金瓶梅》小曲為中心，參加的人計有：張充和、傅漢思、夏志清、王洞、浦安迪、高友工、江青、孫康宜、芮大衛、陳安娜、唐海濤、袁乃瑛、高勝勇等數十人，多是當年北美漢學研究界一時之選，極中國傳統流風餘韻之雅。

上世紀七八十年代，普林斯頓大學的明代研究很是興盛（我猜那個「明軒」的名字，很可能和當時普林斯頓大學的明代研究之繁榮有某種關聯），高友工、牟復禮（Frederick W. Mote）兩先生勤耕教壇，培植出一眾研究明代的高足，如浦安迪（Andrew H. Plaks）之明代敘事文學研究、何義壯（Martin Heijdra）之明代財政研究等等，都是傑出代表。關於普大的明代研究，有兩個有趣的故事值得一提。

第一個故事是，1975年前後，當時任教於耶魯大學的張光直教授，要寫一本有關中國人飲食文化的書，他找到牟復禮教授，請牟先生寫有關明代一章。牟先生思來想去，關於明代飲食最直觀的材料就是《金瓶梅》中大量關於宴會細節的描寫，於是他發揮了西方學者一貫的實證學風，專門請了浦安迪、孫康宜、高天香等當時普大一眾師生到他府上聚餐，讓擅長中國廚藝的牟夫人陳效蘭女士掌勺，按照《金瓶梅》全書中描寫的二十二道不同菜品譜式，燒製了一席「金瓶梅大宴」。當天還請孫康宜用毛筆把那二十二到菜譜抄錄了下來，一直流傳到今天（見本書6月8日孫康宜致陳效蘭信函附圖）。

第二個有趣的故事發生在「金瓶梅大宴」後六年，即1981年4月。一次偶然的機會，時任普林斯頓大學葛思德東亞圖書館館長的孫康宜和東亞系浦安迪教授兩人建議張充和女士組織一次《金瓶梅》唱曲雅集。充和女士是有名的「合肥四姐姊妹」中的么妹，被譽為中國「最後一位閨秀」。她最為人稱道的故事之一是當年以數學零分、國文第一的成績被胡適校長破格錄取，進入北大中文系讀書。張家世代書香，子弟們自動浸淫於傳統文藝環境中。充和女士少女時代就在蘇州接受傳統的崑曲訓練。1949年，她與夫婿傅漢思（Hans Hermann Frankel）教授移居新大陸，一直沒有放棄她的書法和崑曲愛好。數十年來，她以這種根植於傳統中國的藝術，涵養其高雅的生命氣質，並且以耶魯大學為基地，培植弟子，讓英語世界瞭解這種精緻典雅的中國藝術精髓。在孫、浦兩人提議之後不久，當時尚未完工的紐約大都會博物館明軒，就為他們的雅集提供了活動場地。於是就有了1981年4月13日紐約明軒的「《金瓶梅》唱曲雅集」。

　　上述的兩個故事可以作為本書卷一〈一九四九年以來的海外崑曲——從著名曲家張充和說起〉、卷三〈在美國聽明朝時代曲——記紐約明軒《金瓶梅》唱曲大會〉的背景來讀，也可以當作《金瓶梅》海外傳播的史料來看。那兩個故事，也反映了上世紀七八十年代，中國古典研究在美國的一個繁榮時代的側影。後來的中國文學研究重心，逐漸向現代研究轉型了。對於古代文學專業的我來說，讀了孫老師的那篇文章後，遂對那段美國漢學研究，產生了一種「勝朝」的「東京夢華」式想像和感慨。尤其是孫老師在〈在美國聽明朝時代曲——記紐約明軒《金瓶梅》唱曲大會〉一文中，詳細記載了明軒的建造過程：明軒是參照蘇州網師園的殿春簃異地仿造，肇造於1977年，由當時普林斯頓大學教授藝術史的方聞先生，奔走於紐約和蘇州之間協調，最後由蘇州園林管理處派工二十七人建造。「那五十根楠木巨幹是由四川、雲南等僻遠之處直接運來，那些一寸一寸的鋪地磚則全為蘇州『陸墓御窯』的特製精品。此外像那參差錯落的太湖石也輾轉自虎丘附近一廢園搬運來的。」原來我當日所見的那精緻的園子，是一磚一瓦地由中國萬里跨海而來，於是不由得讓人那對一磚一石，頓生一種「我亦飄零久」的跨時空共情。

　　讀完那篇文章後，我在耶魯東亞文學系的網頁上找到孫老師的Email地址，給她寫了一封長長的讀後感。當時也沒有奢望孫老師會回信給我，她那麼忙，我僅是她千萬讀者中默默無名的一個而已（孫老師後來告訴我，當時七十六歲高齡的她，仍擔任東亞語文系研究所的負責人，每天要處理近百封來自世界各地的郵件），我的目的只是把自己當年讀她書，和二十多年後在海外再讀她書的巧合告訴她而已。沒想到過了三個星期，我都快要忘記這事了，突然收到孫老師一封長長的回信（不是一般作者敷衍讀者的三言兩語式的那種客套）。她除了向我抱歉遲覆郵件的原因外，在信中還附贈了2018年在臺灣出版的《孫康宜文集》五卷電子本全帙。這完全出乎我的意料。於是我有了機會，更加集中地系統閱讀孫老師的著作，並有機會就閱讀過程中的一些感想，直接和她Email分享，她也會及時回應我。大約一週後，當我剛剛拜讀完《走出白色恐怖》時，收到孫老師的一封郵件，在那封郵件中，她告訴我，她正在廣西師大出版社出版中文簡體字版《孫康宜文集》，因為她的文章非常專業，她本人一直在海外從事教學和研究工作，希望能夠找一位「特約編輯」，為書稿的編輯工作提供必要的學術和技術支持。

孫老師告訴我，她經過認真考慮之後，打算請我幫她承擔這個工作。我是古典文學專業畢業，又做過編輯，能得孫老師信任，自感不勝榮幸。同時我還有一點小私心：即我一直在中國上學，沒有機會接受歐美現代學術訓練，對海外的中國學研究甚感隔膜，通過這次系統「細讀」孫老師半個世紀以來的學術結晶，可以幫助我瞭解歐美漢學研究的方法、歷史和現狀，彌補我這方面的缺憾。經過大約一週的相互磨合、調整，以及工作試樣，但最後卻因為一點點的技術障礙，沒有了那個「特約編輯」的名分，但仍由我為孫老師擔任proof-reading工作。[1]

通過校讀《文集》全稿，我當初的那個「私心」之願實現了。我以孫老師的文章為起點，對海外漢學研究──尤其是新大陸漢學研究──有了一個鳥瞰式的瞭解。現在就我的校讀感想，對孫老師的這部大型的作品集，做一粗略的解讀。我的解讀是在校讀過程中隨機而發，故沒有宏觀的系統性，對孫老師的研究也沒有存全面式解讀的宏願，只是作為一個「細讀」者的隨感，純粹是我自己的感想，也許對讀者有他山之石的作用。

二、孫康宜教授的古典文學研究

孫老師的研究領域非常之廣。1966年，她畢業於東海大學外文系，本科論文是《The Importance of Herman Melville to Chinese Students with a Comparison between the Ideas of Melville and Prominent Chinese Thinkers》。畢業後，旋考入臺大外文研究所，但碩士學位還未念完，就到美國來了。1969年1月，入讀美國新澤西州立羅格斯大學（Rutgers the State University of New Jersey），1971年，獲得圖書館學碩士學位。當時她已進入南達科他州立大學英語系攻讀英國文學，1972年，以《Carlyle's Literature of Heroism and Its Contmporary Model—Mao》一文獲得文學碩士學位。1973年，她進入普林斯頓大學東亞系，師從高友工教授攻讀中國古典文學，1978年，以《The Evolution of Chinese Tzú Poetry：From Late Tang to Northern Sung》（《晚唐迄北宋詞體演進與詞人風格》）一文獲得文學博士學位，從此奠定了她此後半個世紀的學術研究大方向。

---

[1] 關於我和孫老師一起合作的詳細經過，可以參見秀威版《從北山樓到潛學齋》卷末附錄拙作〈校讀後記〉（臺北秀威資訊科技股份有限公司，2020年版）。

　　孫老師是一個高產學者，其文學世界[2]很難用傳統的分類法來描述。我在通讀其全部五卷《文集》和其他一些作品之後，將她所涉及的文學世界粗線條地概括如下：（一）中國古典文學研究，包括六朝詩歌研究、唐宋詞研究、明清文學研究、中國古典詩歌譯介、中國古典文學史編纂；（二）西方文學批評，包括現代歐美作家介紹、書評、電影評論；（三）文學創作，包括傳記散文的創作、中西文詩歌創作、學術報告文學創作[3]、書信創作。（四）橫跨古今中外的女性文學研究；（五）多面向的理論嘗試與創新，比如「影響的焦慮」、文學的經典化、「面具」理論等等。因為學術背景的限制，我無法對孫老師的全部文學世界進行全景式的探索，本文著重就校讀其《文集》過程中，對其中國文學研究成就，略談一談自己的感想。

（一）有關鮑照和謝朓對律詩的貢獻

　　在《六朝詩概論》這本書中，作者論述鮑照詩歌的「社會現實主義」（social realism）特色時云：「鮑照的革新，在於把常規的『閨怨』改造成了男性的口吻。現在，是丈夫而不是妻子在抒發強烈的懷人之情。通過男性主人公的詳細描述，詩中的女性成為關心的焦點。」（頁99）也只有女性的敏感，才能從這個角度來探討鮑詩的個性特色。

　　我對這本書的興趣點在於，作者以鮑照的參照系，從技術層面論述律詩結構的內在邏輯云：「1.從非平行的、以時間為主導的不完美世界（第一聯），到平行的、沒有時間的完美狀態（第二聯和第三聯）；2.從平行而豐滿的世界，回到非平行和不完美的世界（第四聯）。通過這樣一種圓周運動的形式化結構，唐代詩人們或許會感到他們的詩歌從形式和內容兩方面，都抓住了一個自我滿足之宇宙的基本特質。」（卷五，頁121）這正是律詩創作過程中，創作者完整的心理和技術過程的細微描述。律詩的首末兩聯，經常承擔的是一種「附屬結構」的功

---

[2]　這個名詞是筆者的一個自造詞，其內涵可參見本文第三節第一段。

[3]　這個名詞是筆者創造出來的一個不得已的名詞，它既不同於傳統的學術報告，也與傳統的報告文學有異。它包括孫老師對身邊的學人的走訪記錄，與傳統的「劇本式」訪談錄不一樣，既是當代學術史文獻的客觀真實紀錄，又有散文創作的隨興和文藝筆調。學術報告文學還包括作者對一些學術會議的紀錄，這種記錄不同於一般的學術祕書做紀錄的那種公文文體，它既有學術研究的客觀嚴謹，又有遊記散文的輕鬆與灑脫。

能，一般是首聯引起將要進入的詩境緣起，尾聯則需有對全詩收束的儀式感。這兩聯都有賴於中間兩聯的豐滿，方始能將全詩「黏」起來，形成一個完整的美學宇宙。中間兩聯要有一種承繼或者平行的關係，又不能犯複，還要講求意蘊的字面的對仗，所以是律詩中特別化花費心力的部分。因而作者將第二、三兩聯定義為「完美狀態」，洵為的論。而首尾兩聯的不平行和不完美，常常是對讀者的誘惑所在，從詩人角度來講，又是支撐中間兩聯「完美」的動力所在。

而謝朓何以能在詩歌形式上突破傳統的拘限，孫老師從謝氏取景與陶淵明筆下景物之異趣得到靈感：「謝朓與陶淵明還是有區別的。謝朓的山水風光附著於窗戶，為窗戶所框定。在謝朓那裡，有某種內向與退縮，這使他炮製出等值於自然的人造物。」「他用八句詩形式寫作的山水詩，可能就是這種欲望──使山水風光附著於結構之框架──的產物。」「他的詩似乎達到不同類別的另一種存在──一個相當於窗戶所框定之風景的自我封閉世界。其中有一種新的節制，一種節約的意識，一種退向形式主義的美學。」（卷五，頁130-131）這種細膩入理的文本細讀和聯想體味，在學理上能自圓其說。有關詩體演變的事實，這是一個角度非常新穎的解釋。

（二）《詞與文類研究》的「細讀」貢獻

撰寫《詞與文類研究》的起因，孫老師如是說：「一九七〇年代初期乃風格與文體批評盛行之際，我正巧在普林斯頓大學研究，有幸向許多專家求教，高友工教授所賜者尤多。他以研究中國古典文學知名學界，精深廣博，循循善誘，啟發我對文學批評與詩詞的興趣匪淺。我對傳統詞家的風格特有所好，始於此時，進而有撰寫專書以闡明詞體演進之念頭，希望藉此把主觀之欣賞化為客觀之鑒賞。拙作《晚唐迄北宋詞體演進與詞人風格》（The Evolution of Chinese Tzú Poetry：From Late Tang to Northern Sung, Princeton, 1980），就是在這種機緣與心態下撰成。」（〈北美二十年來詞學研究──兼記緬因州國際詞學會議〉）

對唐詞肇興的原因分析，孫老師指出唐玄宗的梨園」設置，功不可沒，而其作用卻並非是皇室本身以詞為娛樂形式的正面催化刺激，乃在於安史之亂後，梨園子弟星散民間，使得「伎館」在原有基礎上，補充大量高素質的專業樂工與歌伎。「中唐以後，教坊頹圮，訓練有素的樂伎四出奔亡，直接影響到往後曲詞的

發展。」（頁33）

　　此外，這本書以西元850年（唐宣宗大中四年）為研究的上限時間點，是因為這一年是《花間集》收錄的作品可考知的最早年限。除此而外，從文體演進本身的發展進程著眼，：「八五○年以前的詞，大受絕句掣肘，其後的詞體才慢慢有獨特的結構原則，不再受絕句的影響。」（頁41）「八五○年以後的新詞，結構與長度都不為絕句所限，反而含括兩『片』等長的單元，雖則其加起來的總字數不超過五十八字。」（頁43-44）「八五○年前後，確為詞史重要分水嶺。原因無他：『雙調』小令適於此時出現，而其美學體式也於此時確立。八五○年以前，『詞』還不是獨立文體，其後則進入一個嶄新的時代，逐漸發展出特有的傳統。我們常說溫庭筠和韋莊是詞史開疆拓土的功臣，原因概如上述。」（頁44）

　　孫老師在文本細讀方面的一個顯著的特徵是，尤其注重詞體的本體特徵，比如「換頭」和「領字」以及「襯字」這些詞體特有的文體結構特徵。「詞體演變史上最重要的新現象乃『換頭』的形成。」「『換頭』一旦出現，詞的讀法也有新的轉變，較之曩昔體式，可謂角度全非。」（俱見頁44）「慢詞最大的特徵，或許是『領字』這種手法。其功能在為詞句引路，抒情性甚重。柳永提升此一技巧的地位，使之成為詞史的重要分界點……。『領字』是慢詞的獨特技巧，有助於詞句連成一體。」（頁86）「這些詩人詞客（保陽按：指柳永之前少數創作慢詞的唐五代作家）都沒有施展『領字』的手法，而『領字』正是宋人的慢詞所以為慢詞的一種語言技巧。」「柳永首開『領字』風氣，在慢詞裡大量使用，往後的詞人又加以沿用，使之蔚為慢詞的傳統技巧。」（俱見頁92）「『領字』可使句構富於彈性，這是慢詞的另一基本特徵，也是柳永的革新何以在詞史上深具意義之故。」（頁94）此外，孫老師用襯字來解釋柳永詞集中同調作品沒有一首相同體式的原因，從而對前代詞學家語焉不詳的這一現象，予以讓人信服的解釋：「詞學的另一重要關目是詞律的體式。柳詞讓詞話家深感困惑者，乃為同詞牌的慢詞居然沒有一首是按同樣的詞律填的……。同詞牌而有不同律式，並非因許多詞學家所謂的『體調』變異有以致之，而是由於『襯字』使然。」（頁114）而襯字的熟練使用，乃在柳永高人一等的音樂素養。基於此，作者對歷代墨守成規的詞家大不以為然：「他視自己的每首詞為獨立的個體，即使同詞牌者亦然。這

表示他極思解放傳統，不願再受制化結構的捆綁。遺憾的是，後世詞家仍沿襲一脈相傳的『傳統』，以致自縛手腳，發展出『填詞』與『正體』的觀念，以別於所謂『變體』者。他們步步為營，對正統詞家立下的字數與律式的注意，遠超過於對詞樂的正視。這種發展也為詞樂分家種下難以拔除的根苗。」（頁114）學術界目前公認慢詞成熟並大興於柳永之手，但多從詞學接受史視角進行歸納式論證。作為受過新批評理論影響的孫老師，她通過細讀文本，從柳詞作品本身出發，以詞體有別於其他文體的個性特徵來論證柳永對詞史的貢獻，這個論證策略無疑是相當具有說服力的。另一方面也表現出作者立排眾說，不為前人成說所囿的理論勇氣。這一點在四十年前的海外詞學研究領域中，尤其難能可貴。該章第三節「柳永的慢詞詩學」前半篇把領字和換頭分析得淋漓盡致，後半篇以劉若愚的「連續鏡頭」和佛里曼（Ralph Freedman）的「鑒照」理論為工具分析〈夜半樂〉和〈戚氏〉，行文真可謂「峰巒疊嶂，翠墨層綿」，層層遞進，如破竹剝筍，讓本來紛繁雜杳的意象「紛至沓來，幾無止境」，「行文環勾扣結而連場若江河直下」。這些話語雖是作者用來評騭柳詞的，但移以表彰該章行文的綿密酣暢，亦恰當合適。

　　孫老師論述蘇軾在詞史上貢獻，集中在「最卓越的成就則在拓展詞的詩意」、「蘇軾卻是為詞特撰長序的第一人」、「蘇軾另一詞技是使用史典」這三個方面。孫老師對蘇詞的這三個方面的總結，直到今天的一些蘇詞論著中，仍被採納。孫老師對蘇軾詞中小序的論述尤其別見手眼。她稱蘇軾〈江城子〉（夢中了了醉中醒）一詞的小序是「自我體現的抒情動作的寫實性對應體」，這句讀起來有點拗口的中文結論，可以看作是她對詞序這個獨立存在的文體下的定義。她對此定義有下面一段解釋：「如果詞本身所體現的抒情經驗是一種『凍結的』、『非時間』的『美感瞬間』——因為詞的形式本身即象徵這種經驗，那麼『詞序』所指必然是外在的人生現實，而此一現實又恆在時間的律動裡前進。事實上，『詞序』亦具『傳記』向度——這是詞本身所難以洩露者，因為詞乃一自發而且自成一格的結構體，僅可反映出抒情心靈超越時空的部分。詞家尤可藉詞序與詞的結合，縮絞事實與想像為一和諧有序的整體，使得詩、文合璧，再不分離。」（頁121-122）這段文字流轉如彈丸，似鹽入水，可以看作是以西方文論解釋傳統詩詞的範本，為華語世界本土學者提供了一個思考問題的向度。

另外，孫老師將宋詩傾向於理學哲思的整體風格的形成，與蘇軾開拓詞的功能聯繫起來，這個觀點亦頗具新意。蓋蘇軾在詞壇的開拓革新，使得早年屬於「豔科」、「小道」的「末技」，一躍而成具備了與傳統詩歌並駕齊驅的文學體裁，成為「抒情的最佳工具」，於是宋詩只好別尋蹊徑，開壇張幟：「近體詩在唐代抬頭，變成抒情詠頌的工具，『詞』在宋代也成為純抒情最佳的媒介。所謂的『詩』呢？『詩』開始跑野馬，慢慢從純抒情的範疇轉到其他領域去。宋詩和唐詩有所不同，對哲思慧見興趣較大。宋人又競以理性相標榜，養成唯理是尚的作風。因此，隨著時間的流逝，『詞』反倒成為『抒情的最佳工具』，以別於已經轉向的『詩』。這種轉變誠然有趣，但若無蘇詞推波助瀾，絕不可能在短時間內成就。」（頁123）

（三）回歸文本的文學研究

從上文對蘇詞小序功能的論述，讓我想起另外兩篇文章，這些都在在彰顯出孫老師對文體的敏感。

如果我們把詩詞看作是作者內在情緒的一種抒情文本，那麼不管是詩詞外的序跋，還是夾雜在詩詞字句之間的注釋，都是一種外化的說明。孫老師將這種「內在」和「外化」稱之為private和public，並認為這是龔自珍之所以被稱為是近代文學開山之祖的文體證明：「龔的自注賦予其詩歌強烈的近代氣息。對龔自珍而言，情詩的意義正在於其承擔雙重功能：一方面是私人情感交流的媒介，另一方面又將這種私密體驗公之於眾。事實上，《己亥雜詩》最令人注目的特徵之一，就是作者本人的注釋散見於行與行之間、詩與詩之間，在閱讀龔詩時，讀者的注意力經常被導向韻文與散文、內在情感與外在事件之間的交互作用。如果說詩歌本文以情感的濃烈與自我耽溺取勝，詩人的自注則將讀者的注意力引向創作這些詩歌的本事，兩者合璧，所致意的對象不僅僅是情人本身，也包括廣大的讀者公眾。這些詩歌之所以能深深打動現代讀者，奧妙就在於詩人刻意將情愛這一私人（private）體驗與表白這一公眾（public）行為融為一體。在古典文學中很少會見到這樣的作品，因為中國的豔情詩有著悠久的托喻象徵傳統，而這種特定文化文本的『編碼』與『解碼』有賴於一種模糊的美感，任何指向具體個人或是具體時空的資訊都被刻意避免。郁達夫曾指出，蘇曼殊等近代作家作品中的『近

代性』（modernity）在很大程度上得益於龔自珍詩歌的啟發，或許與此不無相
關。」（〈寫作的焦慮：龔自珍豔情詩中的自注〉）

　　後來當孫老師撰寫施蟄存的〈浮生雜詠〉時，她認為施蟄存的這種自敘傳式
的詩體創作，有著對龔自珍《己亥雜詩》——尤其是後者文本中的自注這種文體
特徵——的自覺繼承。這種繼承在文學史上相互表現為各自的「近代性」與「現
代性」的創新：為了表達施蟄存與龔自珍在這方面的相似性，孫老師幾乎一字不
改地援引了上引〈寫作的焦慮：龔自珍艷情詩中的自註〉中的原話。

　　孫老師認為，施蟄存〈浮生雜詠〉中每首詩採用的註釋自有其個性，即龔
註本事，讓讀者穿梭於內在的抒情文本與外在本事之間，彰顯出一種文學的「近
代性」。而施注則有一點隨筆的性質，充滿一種趣味或者生活的智慧，這是一種
文學的「現代性」：「施蟄存在〈引言〉中已經說明，他在寫〈浮生雜詠〉詩歌
時，『興致蓬勃，卮言日出』，因而使他聯想到龔定庵的《己亥雜詩》……我想
就是這個『趣』的特質使得施先生的〈浮生雜詠〉從當初模仿龔自珍，走到超越
前人典範的『自我』文學風格，最明顯的一點就是施的詩歌『自注』已大大不同
於龔那種『散見』於行與行之間、詩與詩之間的注釋。施老的『自注』，與其說
是注釋，還不如說是一種充滿情趣的隨筆，而且八十首詩每首都有『自注』，與
詩歌並排，不像龔詩中那種『偶爾』才出現的本事注解。值得注意的是，施先生
的『自注』經常帶給讀者一種驚奇感，有時詩中所給的意象會讓讀者先聯想到某
些『古典』的本事，但『自注』卻將讀者引向一個特殊的『現代』情境。（〈施
蟄存的詩體回憶：〈浮生雜詠〉八十首〉）

　　從上文所引蘇軾詞的小序，到龔自珍《己亥雜詩》註釋，再到施蟄存〈浮
生雜詠〉的註釋，在在表現出孫老師對文體的敏感。上世紀七十年代末，她撰作
《晚唐迄北宋詞體演進與詞人風格》時，關注的重心即在「genre」（文體，文
類），故此書後來中譯本乾脆名之為《詞與文類研究》。迨近年來她以學術之筆
敘寫施蟄存〈浮生雜詠〉時[4]，仍以文體的不同功能彰顯施蟄存的創作特色。孫
老師關注的始終是文本自身的特色及其繼承性。通過細讀，展現文體特徵在文學
史發展進程中的意義。尤其是龔自珍和施蟄存，他們韻文體詩詞和散文體註釋的

---

[4]　〈施蟄存的詩體回憶：《浮生雜詠八十首》〉發表於《溫故》2013年9月號。

相互出入所形成的美感和張力，是奠定他們文學創作之近代性和現代性的一個不可忽視因素[5]。以文體互動的角度解釋文學史的發展，這種研究向度，給近年愈來愈「歷史化」的文學研究，提供了一個成功的範例。這樣的研究告訴我們：文學研究，還得回歸文學本身。

（四）《樂府補題》研究的創新試探

　　〈《樂府補題》中的象徵與托喻〉。全文有一個強烈的符號：作者在盡全力嘗試一種新理論對《樂府補題》進行解讀。這種努力的一個明顯的表現是：作者不斷在分析詠物詞的意象時，楔入對解構框架下理論名詞的解釋。這是中西文學比較研究無法回避的一個技術問題。因為《樂府補題》自從清初被發現以來，傳統的批評家一直在對其進行政治解讀，萬斯同編纂《南宋六陵遺事》、朱彝尊重刊《樂府補題》都是這一努力的佐證。但是如何避免附會式閱讀（allegoresis），就得尋求一種大而化之的理論高度來進行解說，這樣可以避免只見一城一池的零碎與不合理。當作者肯定遺民詞人「理想的間接表意形式」是詠物詞時，她自己也找到了解剖詠物詞的理論手段——象徵（symbol）和托喻（allegory）。但是這兩種方法在西方批評語境中是完全不同的兩個事物，「西方批評家在閱讀作品時，一般不把這兩種手法結合起來」。而作者認為：「象徵與托喻在中國詩歌中不是互相區別而是互為補充的，而且兩者可以並存於同一文本。」這是作者在結合中西文本與批評的操作過程中遇到的第一個挑戰。她的處理策略是「專注於討論《樂府補題》中的象徵與托喻是如何與西方概念相似而又（更重要地）相區別的」，為了證明這一策略的「吾道不孤」，作者引用葉嘉瑩（Chia-ying Yeh Chao）在其〈Wang I-sun and His Yung-Wu Tzú〉中對「托喻」符合中國傳統的解釋為自己佐證。這是中西比較文學實踐中的權宜辦法，也是作者折中中西文學研究的高明之處：「西方批評僅在開始比較概念時起作用，但在使用它的時候，我們不能為它的獨特『西方』涵義所限制。」這還不是西方理論和中國古典詩詞結合時的第一次扞格。

---

[5]　當然，龔自珍的「近代性」還和他所處的十九世紀中國政治及社會變遷有關，施蟄存的現代性與他所處的二十世紀中國社會、文化背景，以及他的現代派小說創作有很大關係。這是值得另外深入研究的主題。

　　另一個表現是，在分析的過程中創造性地綜括出一些術語，以方便論述，比如「樞紐意象」、「意向型托喻」、「托喻詞集」等等。這些可以視作是作者在彌合東西方文學批評的技術性貢獻。

（五）《情與忠：陳子龍與柳如是詩詞情緣》

　　孫老師對明末清初文學的描述，從她的這本書章、節題目中即可窺其一斑，如她所謂「情與忠」，這裡的情特指的是「豔情」，尤其是男女之間那種無關乎政治托喻的豔情，甚至是和歌伎之間的豔情。作者以西方術語「譬喻（figura）」來宏觀視角地綜觀陳子龍前後兩期創作中的「情」與「忠」，實在是一個非常獨特的視角。蓋「『譬喻』主要用於《聖經》的詮釋，讓《舊約》人、事預示《新約》出現的人、事。」「『情』與『忠』都是陳子龍切身的經驗，故可視為喻詞的兩極，彼此互相關涉也互相『實現』（fulfilling）。此外，就像譬喻詮釋中的兩個條件一樣，『情』與『忠』由於皆具『時間性』，對陳子龍而言就更加重要：一個代表過去的時間，一個代表目前的生活。『愛』與『忠』一旦形成譬喻上的結合，詞人目前的生活就會摧拉人心似地展現過去的意義——這個『意義』過去的陳子龍並不知道——而在此同時，目前的生活也會回首從前，從而又擴大目前的意義。從更寬的角度來看，『情』與『忠』根本就包容在某『超越時間』（supratemporal）的整體裡：不為時間所羈的真情世界。」「陳子龍另有貢獻：他把文化現象轉化為新的詞學，故而在美學傳統裡樹立起一種重寫式的詮釋方法。」

　　孫老師以席沃（Richard Sewall）的「悲劇靈視」（tragic vision）來審視陳子龍的詩作，並解釋道：「『悲劇靈視』（tragic vision）有別於亞里斯多德（Aristotle）所謂的『悲劇性』（the tragic）。此書所指乃賢者遇逢的悲劇性苦難，至於亞氏所指，則需有基本的『悲劇缺憾』（tragic flaw）才能成立——至少典型的亞氏『悲劇』必須如此。Sewall以約伯的苦難為例來定義『悲劇缺憾』。他說：『[約伯]受苦受難並非他犯有死罪。他一再遭受打擊……，也不是因為過去[作惡多端所致]。』（頁12）」而陳子龍正是具此「悲劇靈視」的人。「我們在臥子詩中所看到的，是苦難與高貴情操的如影隨形。在他的詩中，詩人的悲劇英雄形象重新定位：悲劇英雄主義已經轉化成為美學原則。本章擬舉若干

陳詩為例，藉以檢討詩人的悲劇形象。」（頁273）

（六）明清文學研究

明代文學。關於明代文學研究，2008年孫老師在接受寧一中、段江麗伉儷採訪時坦言：「到了八〇年代末，我回憶自己在普林斯頓所受的明代歷史的教育，聯想到明代以及清代文學，發現當時在北美，除了《紅樓夢》等少數幾部小說之外，明清文學幾乎被忽略了，尤其是詩歌，1368年以後的詩幾乎無人論及。於是我準備關注這一領域，在我的知識儲備中只有一些歷史知識，於是自己想方設法彌補文學方面的知識。」作者在本世紀前期，先後發表了五篇和明代文學相關的長篇論文[6]，這些論文之間有內在的學理聯繫，可以視為作者對明代文學研究的一個著作系列。

孫老師對於撰述明代前中期文學史，雖言「填補空白」，但其視角之宏大和實際操作之成功，比之《詞與文類研究》，雖在系統性上稍遜，但其撰述視角的獨特和理論勇氣，都超過了《詞與文類研究》。若能展開章節，增加篇幅，與《陳柳情緣》合璧，可稱一部視角新穎立論別出的明代文學史。

〈重寫明初文學：從高壓到盛世〉寫明初文學。本文最特出之處乃在於為明初、中文學發展史做出三段劃分。〈臺閣體、復古派和蘇州文學的關係與比較〉，是最精彩的明代文學研究篇章。〈中晚明之交文學新探〉探討貶謫文學、婦女形象（文學）重建，尤其是對婦女文學復興原因的分析，認為是男性文人的邊緣化社會趨勢，導致他們對一直處於社會邊緣的婦女地位的認同，這個論點很有見地。本文中論及的小說改編。文言之「剪燈」系列；三大白話小說的改編，其中對《三國演義》在嘉靖年間的改編特色總結非常有新意。

明清易代之際文學研究。這一時期的研究實際上可以看作是上承明代文學研究而來的自然結果。我之所以將這短時期的文學研究單獨列出，乃是鑒於近年來，學術界在文學歷史分段方面有一種趨勢，即將「明清易代之際」作為一個特

---

[6] 這五篇文章分別是〈重寫明初文學：從高壓到盛世〉（2006）、〈台閣體、復古派和蘇州文學的關係與比較〉（2005）、〈中晚明之交文學新探〉（2007）、〈文章憎命達：再議瞿佑及其《剪燈新話》的遭遇〉（2007）、〈走向邊緣的「通變」：楊慎的文學思想初探〉（2010）。這五篇文章都已收入《孫康宜文集》卷一第二輯《由傳統到現代》。

殊的文學時間段單列出來[7]，這段時期既屬於明代文學史，也可含括進清代文學史。這一時期獨特的社會歷史背景，造就了獨特的文學面貌，並形成了一種有別於此前文學傳統的精神，影響頗及於後世。這種獨特的文學風貌與大時代變局的激蕩、新的社會思潮以及社會生活形態的新變息息相關。孫老師的《情與忠：陳子龍與柳如是詩詞情緣》一書中，有精彩的論述。我之所以說孫老師的這一段文學史的研究是承其明代文學研究之續餘而來，仍見於上引她回答甯一中、段江麗的採訪：「正是在這一『補課』（筆者按：指填補明代文學研究之缺失）的過程中，我接觸到了陳寅恪先生的《柳如是別傳》，這本書對我影響很大。我覺得柳如是很有意思，對她產生了濃厚興趣，這就是我第三本書《陳子龍柳如是詩詞情緣》的寫作背景和因緣。」除此而外，屬於這段時間範圍內的文學研究還有幾篇代表性的單篇論文，如〈隱情與「面具」——吳梅村詩試說〉（1994）、〈錢謙益及其歷史定位〉（2006）等。

　　清代文學研究。孫老師的清代文學研究代表性篇章有〈典範詩人王士禛〉（2001）、〈寫作的焦慮：龔自珍豔情詩中的自注〉（2005）、〈金天翮與蘇州的詩史傳統〉（2006）。在清代文學研究中，我印象比較深的是孫老師對「蘇州」這個超脫的文學意象描述。蓋蘇州一詞，在中國文學世界裡，早已超越了地理和歷史概念，成為一個十分複雜蘊涵的意象。如果實在要借用一個不很貼切的意象來進行類比，我想「一九四九」可以勉強當之。但前者遠比後者的文學積累和歷史厚重感強得多。孫老師在〈金天翮與蘇州的詩史傳統〉開篇，給出了一個文學定義的蘇州，即：「蘇州在世人心目中還代表了一種以詩證史的強烈抒情聲音，即以詩歌見證人間苦難和當代重大歷史事件。」實際上在我看來，蘇州的這個定義不僅僅是蘇州的，更可以視作是近六百年文學史中的一種「江南精神」。元末的顧阿英的自我放逐，明初蘇州人高啟被朱元璋殘殺、明朝中後期的「後七子」、清初金聖歎的哭廟，這些彪炳於文學史上的個體蘇州事件周圍，還有席捲明末江南地區的東林黨人活動，「十郡大社」在蘇州附近的嘉興的雅集，清初江南三大案，甚至越過所謂的「康乾盛世」二百年之後，以蘇州為中心而影響及於

---

[7]　十多年前，筆者在杭州，曾不止一次地聽沈松勤教授談論這段時期文學的特殊性及其研究構想。2018年，沈松勤教授出版《明清之際詞壇中興史論》，是其對這段時期文學特殊性（以詞這種特殊文體為代表）研究心得的總結。

全國乃至海外的南社，都在蘇州的文學書寫之外，平添了一股糾結於士大夫立身處世和道德操守面向的崇高和凝重。孫老師將之總結為：「蘇州精神：將個人自由看得重於一切。」（〈臺閣體、復古派和蘇州文學的關係與比較‧蘇州的復興〉）。這個總結，在我有限的閱讀視界中，尚未見如此精準的總結。如果讀者參考本書中收錄的另一篇文章〈一位美國漢學家的中西建築史觀〉，會對孫老師筆下的文學蘇州有更加了立體的瞭解。

三、學術報告文學的創作

文學創作是孫老師文學世界不可忽視的一個部分，其作品大多收入《孫康宜文集》卷一和卷二。其中傳記散文的創作、中西文詩歌創作、書信創作等等，這些作品要麼已經有前人進行過研究和評論，比如《走出白色恐怖》；要麼因為筆者的學術背景所限無法客觀論述，比如西文詩歌創作等等。但在孫老師的所有創作當中，有一類特別的作品，引起了我特別的關注，我姑且為之命名為學術報告文學。這個名詞是我創造出來的一個不得已的名詞，它既不同於傳統的學術報告，也與傳統的報告文學有異。它包括作者對一些學術會議的即時紀錄，這種紀錄不同於一般的學術祕書做的會場紀錄的那種公文文體，它既有學術研究的客觀嚴謹，又有遊記散文的輕鬆與灑脫。另外還包括孫老師對她身邊的學人的走訪紀錄，與傳統的「劇本式」訪談錄不一樣，它既是當代學術史文獻的客觀真實紀錄，又有散文創作的隨興和文藝筆調。

孫老師創作的學術報告文學如〈跨學科的對話——關於瑞典「文化詮釋」國際會議〉報導的是2000年5月在瑞典斯德哥爾摩召開的「文化詮釋」國際會議；〈二十年後說巴特〉報導的是2001年初，耶魯大學惠特尼人文中心（Whitney Humanities Center）特別為紀念巴特而召開了一個盛大的國際會議；〈「無何有之鄉」：六朝美學會之旅〉記錄的是2000年秋在伊利諾州召開為期兩天的六朝美學大會。這些文章都是作者以與會學者的身份分，對這些學術會議的討論主題，每位學者的學術論點，進行了詳細的記錄，並且及時刊發在中文媒體上，一方面向當時的中文學術界及時傳達了國際學術發展的動態，以今日眼光視之，則是一個時代學術史的紀錄。它既是當事人的即時紀錄，其客觀真實性自然無疑。加之

作者本身又是這一領域的專家，其記錄和思考的向度可以為學術史研究提供第一手文獻。有趣的是，作者在記錄學術資訊的同時，不忘對中外學風進行比較，比如〈跨學科的對話──關於瑞典「文化詮釋」國際會議〉記錄了那次討論會：「共邀請了四十多位學者，但為了促進深刻而豐富的討論，大會只安排了十四個與會者發表論文，其餘皆為評論者、發問者或是幾場討論會的主持人。會議連續開了四天，專心討論了十四篇論文，其討論的深度與持續性實與今日流行於美國和臺海兩岸的『速食』式討論會相去甚遠……。」這樣的紀錄，以中國傳統的「董狐」筆法來看，一定會給後人提供一個當代學術史的切面。

除此而外，孫老師對西方文學的研究也傾注了不少精力，如現代西方文學（苫哈、賀蘭德、柯慈、希尼等等（參看《孫康宜文集》卷一、卷二部分文章）。其中有好幾位研究對象都是其耶魯的同事，這一類文章有一個非常鮮明的寫作結構：以某一小事件為緣起──引入要介紹的學者──對該學者的研究主題進入學理層面的描述分析──中間甚至會穿插一些學者的成長背景等故事性較強的內容（如卷一的亞歷山大・洛夫等），這些靈活跳躍的內容是調節枯燥專業論述的有效手段。比如寫研究俄國形式主義文學研究專家維克多・艾里克（Victor Erlich）教授的那篇文〈俄國形式主義專家：艾里克和他的詩學研究〉，開篇以輕鬆明快的筆調，描寫了作者沿途所見風光和異樣的心理感受，並將這情感投射到艾里克所住房屋：「令人如置身古代隱者的住宅區」，就為下文鋪設了一個非常自然合宜的敘述環境和心理暗示。這種結構安排的好處是，讓讀者可以像讀龔自珍的《己亥雜詩》那樣，不時出入於敘事和學理兩個世界，即便面對完全隔行的讀者，也不會產生閱讀的疲倦和畏懼心理。（龔自珍的詩和註釋讓讀者不時出入於隱晦抒情和詩歌本事之間。這種寫作安排層層剝筍，也有點類似於傳統中國話本小說的特殊結構[8]。這種寫作藝術得益於孫老師的中國古典文學學養）作為學者撰寫學術文化散文的一種範式，孫老師的這種學術訪談散文模式的創新，有別於刻下流行的「劇本對話」式訪談錄文體，為同類型寫作提供了一個多樣嘗試的可能。除了文體上的創新意義外，筆者以為，孫老師撰寫的這類學術訪談散文，在一定範圍內保留了二十世紀最後幾十年美國文學研究界的學術史。比如

---

[8]　比如「楔子」、開場和收束時的說話人套語。讓讀者不時出入於故事情節與閱讀現實的兩個世界。

〈俄國形式主義專家：艾里克和他的詩學研究〉介紹了上世紀二十年代前後流行於俄羅斯學術界的「形式主義」批評理論、〈掩蓋與揭示——克里斯特娃論普魯斯特的心理問題〉介紹了上世紀九十年代流行於法國的「演進批評」（genetic criticism）和流行於美國的「新批評」（New Criticism）的關係等等。這類文章尤其呈現了西方文學研究理論策源地的耶魯大學此一時期文學研究的現狀，給中文世界的讀者解讀二十世紀後半段日新月異的文學批評新理論，提供了一個比較宏觀的學術背景。

四、孫康宜教授的「偶然」

孫老師最慣常的一個用語就是「coincidence」（偶然，巧合）。

孫老師對「偶然」情有獨鍾。她「每年教『詩學』的那門課，其中有一個專題叫做『偶然』，專門欣賞和討論詩與偶然的關係」（〈我最難忘的耶魯學生〉）。這表現出她對陌生世界那種不期而遇的嚮往和衝動。正是這種對於擴大自己世界的衝動，支撐著她幾十年來一路奮鬥，取得意想不到的成績。

如2004年在耶魯慶祝男女合校二十五週年的會上，建築設計師耶魯校友Maya Lin設計了一張「女人桌」獻給了母校，並安置在大學圖書館（Sterling Library）的面前。對那個安置地點，作者就充滿了一種懷舊式的偶然情懷，故這篇文章十七年後收入其文集時，還專門在文末做了一個注註解：「1990年有一天，我那四歲的女兒Edie突然在耶魯大學圖書館面前瞥見我，立刻興奮地跑來和我擁抱，就在那一瞬間，我的先生拍下了一張照片。沒想到後來1993年Maya Lin所建的『女人桌』就在我和女兒曾經『擁抱』的地方，因此這個巧合頓時成為與『女人桌』有關的一段佳話。後來我們為了紀念這個冥冥中的巧合，就把那相片取名為『母與女』。」（〈從零開始的「女人桌」〉）、1968年婚後在耶魯度蜜月與後半生定居耶魯的重合（〈難忘的耶魯老校園〉）、張永安第一次訪問其辦公室與其好友David次年逝世日期的重合（〈耶魯上海生死交〉）、二十年前她的外套穿在現在學生身上的偶然（〈我最難忘的耶魯學生〉）。「在編造的故事背後，其實蘊藏著中國人對『偶然』的重視。」（〈我最難忘的耶魯學生〉）「生命本來充滿了偶然的色彩，可以說最寶貴的人生經驗莫過於某種偶然經驗的

啟發。」（〈極短篇七則・六〉）「生命中所謂的『偶然』，似乎充滿了一種神祕的『必然』。」（〈耶魯上海生死交〉）孫老師在與耶魯同事大衛斯的一次聊天中，她很同意大衛斯的經驗：「其實人生永遠充滿了偶然性（contingency），唯其富有偶然性，生命才有繼續開拓、繼續闡釋的可能。我告訴他，我就一直用這樣的態度來研究歷史：歷史是一連串的偶然因素的組合，而我們的責任就是要從這些偶然之中設法找到生命的意義。」她在這段話後面有一段發揮：「大衛斯這段有關『偶然』的話很富啟發性。我想起唐代詩人杜牧那首〈赤壁〉詩的末尾兩句：『東風不與周郎便，銅雀春深鎖二喬。』意思是說，如果當年的東風不給吳國的周瑜方便，東吳就會被魏軍所敗，二喬也就會被曹操擄去，整個三國的命運自然改觀，歷史也必須重寫了。據杜牧看來，歷史中有很大程度的偶然性，而東風也就成了這種偶然性的象徵了。我想大衛斯所謂的『偶然性』大概就是這個意思。」（〈人權的維護者：大衛斯和他的西方奴隸史〉）「這世界充滿了偶然，卻又十分真實。」（〈我被掛在耶魯的牆上〉）「我很珍惜自己與施先生之間的忘年之交，覺得如此可貴的神交，看來雖似偶然，實非偶然。」（〈施蟄存對付災難的人生態度〉）「就如許多人間的事情一樣，『偶然』常會帶來好運，但刻意去求常會適得其反。」（〈狗的「人文化」〉）「這個巧合，不是一般的巧合，它象徵著一種人生哲學。」（〈重新發掘施蟄存的世紀人生──《施蟄存先生編年事錄》序言〉）。在亞馬遜上買到十多年前簽贈給友人《陳柳情緣》，「我相信這是一個冥冥中的奇妙安排」，「這種『如往而復』的回應立刻令我聯想到《易經》裡的『復』卦。我也同時想起美國詩人朗費羅（Henry Wadsworth Longfellow）所寫的一首題為〈The Arrow and the Song〉（〈箭與歌〉）的詩。該詩的大意是：詩人向空中射出一支箭，不知那支箭最終落於何處。接著，詩人又向空中高唱一曲，不知那歌曲有誰會聽見。但許久之後，有一天詩人偶然發現那支箭原來附在一棵橡樹上，仍完好無缺。至於那首歌，從頭到尾都一直存在一個友人的心中。總之，我感到自己的經驗也呼應了這種反轉復歸的人生意蘊。」（〈永恆的緣份──記耶魯同事Mc Clellan〉、《陳柳情緣》北大版自序）「確實這世界充滿了偶然，卻又十分真實。」（〈我被掛在耶魯的牆上〉）

　　這種對「偶然」和「巧合」所滲透出來的好奇心，表現在她的生活中，就是對所有身邊的人和事，保持一種旺盛的求知欲。比如她嘗試去瞭解不同專業的

人的背景，希望從他們各自獨特的經歷和專業方面，得到新知識。這種新知識，可以是純粹滿足其好奇心，也可以是建立在學科交叉的專業基礎上的背景豐富。她寫過的人物背景，真可謂五花八門，有耶魯歷史系同事、有兒童節目主持人、她的家庭醫生Gary Price等等，但她的採訪大致都會圍繞一個中心：即人文精神或者文學話題。而她往往能「慧眼識英雄」，所採訪的人，不管其職業多麼天差地別，卻都具有一顆沉潛內心深處的文學之靈。這大概就是文學讓人著迷的地方罷。Gary Price醫生說過一句話：「美國可以說是世界上最能容忍和接受diversity的國家了。其實，就是這個文化意義上的diversity使我特別喜歡我的職業。我喜歡努力瞭解不同的文化，也喜歡通過瞭解來幫助別人。」孫老師自己從這些「跨學科」跨領域的拓展中，得到了靈感的激發和靈性的滋養「這次我真正體驗到，希臘神話不僅反應映了西方人自古以來對人性本質深切的瞭解，而其情節之戲劇化也預設了後來西方科學與醫學研究多層方面的發展……。作為一個文學研究的專業者，我對希臘神話的重新領會卻得自於一個外科手術醫師的啟示。那種啟示是極其偶然的，但也是最寶貴的。」（〈一個外科醫生的人文精神〉）這句話如果挪用來形容孫老師，如不十分恰當，當亦庶幾近之。甚至和人文精神相去甚遠的太空科學，她也能津津有味地瞭解其過程，體味其中的人文意義：「在逐漸複雜的今日世界裡，真正的成功乃是團體力量的成功，而非少數個人的榮耀。」（〈在休士頓「遊」太空〉）我們就能理解為什麼她會在中國古典文學、西方文藝理論、電影批評甚至人物傳記寫作等跨領域甚至完全不搭界的領域有諸如文集中所呈現出來的多元化成就。

孫老師的這種「巧合」與俄國小說家納博科夫宿命論下「對富有預言性的日期的巧合」（fatidic dates）有某種近似之處。納博科夫的這種「日期的巧合」，可以看作是通往他所認知的「彼岸世界」的一種管道。當人類還無法解釋一些宿命論中的現象，這是一個人拓展未知世界的動力。有「納博科夫專家」之稱的弗拉基米爾·亞歷山大洛夫（Vladimir Alexandrov）解釋說：「在納博科夫的世界裡，這一類的巧合確實具有非常的重要性。這就是為什麼我要在書中屢次強調彼岸世界的原因。我認為納博科夫一向對形而上和精神界的事情特別感到興趣，每當他處於時空交錯的情況下，他總會把現世和彼岸世界連在一起。」孫老師說她對「納博科夫的宿命觀，我格外感到興趣」。所以如此，是因為「巧合對納博

科夫來說，都是命運的啟示。至於命運，那個來自彼岸世界的神祕動力，也正是他所謂的『繆斯』（Muse）」。至此，我們就不難明白，孫老師對於「巧合」這種帶有宿命論的信仰般癡迷，蓋來自其生命深處對於文學那種宗教般赤誠的熱愛。如果再往深一點引申，就是孫老師是欣賞納博科夫的那種建立在宿命論基礎上的彼岸世界，而這樣的世界，在當代的美國學術界是不為大多數人所接受的，比如美國著名哲學家Richard Rorty曾在一篇評論裡勸導讀者：「還是不要去深究神祕主義方面的事情，因為這種考慮是不重要的。」也許正是歐美思維的嚴謹和實證主義傳統，讓西方世界對於接近於東方文化的這類模糊世界和模糊文化不能接受，孫老師對納博科夫的好奇心，可證明她雖然身在美國逾半個世紀，接受西方學術訓練，但她身上仍然葆有一種東方文化的底色，這也是她在西方漢學研究界能夠出入遊刃的個性與特色（以上引文見〈納博科夫專家——亞歷山大洛夫和他的新發現〉）。

五、結尾

我無意——也沒有那樣的學術能力——對孫老師的研究做全景式描述，以上僅是通讀其《文集》中文簡體字版書稿的一些個人體會。有些體會比較深，就多說幾句，有些體會不明顯但卻很重要，比如孫老師文學研究中關於經典化的問題、女性文學研究、電影批評等等，牽扯的中外理論和作品非常複雜，為了避免說外行話，姑且存而不論。另外孫老師先後主持的中國女性詩人作品的翻譯工程以及《劍橋中國文學史》，雖然在其學術生涯中佔有非常重要的地位，但《文集》中既然甚有涉及，加之我本人對翻譯文學沒有任何研究經驗，亦避而不談[9]。類此情形尚多，不能枚舉。即便是上面談到的面向，也僅是個人一得之見，有些地方說了外行話，在所難免，希望孫老師和方家不要見笑是感。

猶記八、九年前，我在杭州和朋友編輯同人刊物《掌故》，那幾年，幾乎每年要校讀兩三本書稿，六年前的冬天，我在杭州城西的山寺校完最後一輯，我們那本刊物就歇止了。此次校讀孫老師的書稿，讓我再一次回到那幾年的校稿情境

---

[9] 李懷宇採訪孫老師的〈重寫中國文學史〉（2009）和孫老師的〈《劍橋中國文學史》簡介〉對《劍橋中國文學史》的內容、特色、撰寫過程皆有詳盡的描述。

當中，實在是一種美好的回憶！

　　　　2020年5月28日，關中李保陽初稿於思故客河上之抱月樓

附錄四：抱月樓詩詞選

蝶戀花　端午。用章衣萍韻。

卅載紅塵無定處。流落江南，看徧江南樹。歲歲端陽頻指顧。端陽總被勞生誤。

　　淒涼心思誰可語。獨上西泠，怕與俗人住。夜夜問儂欲何去。玉泉山下夕陽暮。

近事

十年蹤跡十年心，患難萍飄有此人（謂內子）。

贏有篋中三萬卷，漁樵山水共為鄰。

（以上《掃葉集》）

壬辰冬十既望，洋縣醫院涸中見簷頭青霜，越四時，小兒出生

寒月昨宵冷到明，剝簷凍雀曉聲清。

曉來紅日知應是，啼破人間第一聲。

早起送小女上學，見校門外電線桿上張貼公開信，為某鄉村教師致信縣政協主席，揭發某校當局侵吞學生膳食津貼事。憤悶出離，成此紀事

一封朝奏沐朝暾，方寸庖廚勺水渾。

漏屋著書何處補，悲歌請劍更無門。

徘徊斗室星天外，俯仰人間我斷魂。

百載樹人高論計，羞言教育為兒孫。

癸巳春三月，應浙大博士試。試畢返陝，便道探望父母。與家兄聯床夜話。家兄近年生計吃重，我亦如之。深宵共話，多激勵共勉語。事已隔月，吟此寄懷。

天涯兄弟歎留離，話雨分甘數別期。
四海子由真健者，窗前棠棣正紛披。
挑燈三復常無語，沙漏二驚對酒卮。
南北明朝契闊路，天涯各自慰調飢

（以上《抱月集》）

內子外祖高齡九十，十年前別我於漢中，旋賃居湖北利川。今夏，輾轉千里來浙依我。相見之下，哽咽數度。相對無語，三復淚下。中夜無寐，抑鬱感歎。聊吟四韻，不計辭之工拙與否也

山南一別久無家，萍聚十年苦作涯。
此刻抱頭全失語，相逢揮淚唯聲嗟。
中年子女多歧路，少壯兒孫似剖瓜。
伴我寄身鴛渚上，床前尚可奉粗茶。

晨起上竺

山中忽見桂，天氣已秋涼。
同種生高處，骨寒晚更香。

江城子

卅五生朝，內子為烹梅菜扣肉，小女滿斟紹興老酒為壽。小兒跳踉繞膝，呀呀語笑。醉眼朦朧，輕撫兒髮，不知人間何世矣。

曾經詞筆水般柔。上高樓。逐浮漚。一縷閑愁，恁處可勾留。若問今昔孰可記，應看者，醉雙眸。　　十年江左汗漫遊。少年愁。委渠溝。三十五年，不料鬢邊秋。何事眼前聊可慰，為兒女，作馬牛。

（以上《天竺集》）

乙未春仲，赴中山大學博士試，歸過贛南，旅次口占。

棘闈九戰始成功，凡鳥仰天破網籠。

三稔春秋時易變，一身蕭瑟氣猶虹。

天涯輾轉常獨客，湖海去來又飄蓬。

從此笙歌絃誦罷，康園煮酒雨聲中。

金縷曲　先父棄養匝月，哭於靈前。用彈指詞韻。

老父平安否。便魂歸、泉臺路遠，莫頻回首。黃葉彫零人間世，四十孤子尚幼。

賸淚和、杯中椒酒。九轉熱腸欺酸眼，認依稀、閒了回春手。陰陽隔，一月久。

　　　三旬悲慟穿腸透。念阿爺、九原無兒，牽衣誰夠。形影堂前依舊在，只恨音

聲烏有。強忍者，餘生苦受。生育恩，來世謀贖救。獻此曲，淚盈袖。

丁酉中元節洛杉磯爾灣望月

鐵翼逐長庚，長庚復洛城。

洛城今夜月，夜月照歸程。

重九前一日與內子偕游京都大學百萬遍左近書肆，得舊籍一篋，時已萬家燈火。

過葵橋，一彎冷月，照徹鴨川，口誦白石道人「淮南皓月冷千山」，久不忍去。

是日百萬遍得京都詩人芹水逸人《醒心齋詩集》殘本一卷，集中有《嵐山看櫻

花》，詩風搖曳，即用其韻

東游猶作衙書鼠，秋到洛城澹似煙。

凝佇葵橋山影裡，一河月碎滿鴨川。

薄暮陰霾中返抵廣州車中讀寒柳堂集和義寧六十二歲生日原韻

其一

燈火羊城漸黃昏，暗雷驚淚詩中存。

低微螻蟻南州飯，風雨難鳴去國門。

其二

亂愁如水去還休，銀火千江萬樹樓。
康樂園中惜瞽叟，強留嶺表又何求。

（以上《康園集》）

登從化門樓關絕頂憶東坡

倚仗南天草木深，群山寂寞出凡塵。
一為海外飄零去，從此天涯落拓身。
最恨多情累紙筆，可憐無益費精神。
青山幸可常為伴，萬里崎嶇一欠伸。

丁酉冬月游從化獅象巖見嶺上梅花盛開

萬里投荒不自哀，嶺南山色久徘徊。
江山信美真吾土，雲水不居我遲來。
人物百年俱草草，川原今日復哀哀。
寒梅嶺上今猶艷，冷眼人間車倒開。

過寒柳堂

百鳥來朝亂紛紛，康園柳色舞腰裙。
長留白眼獨遺世，徒剩熱腸空著文。
舉世狂飇千里馬，萬方勸進趙家軍。
戊戌偏又逢雙甲，萬歲耳邊再度聞。

題《笑傲江湖》之東方不敗

江山如畫人心寒，
蒼狗白雲冷眼看。
空有鐵琴操舊曲，
不知哀樂對誰彈。

去國

廿四字前再造神，百年賽德又蒙塵。

河山意氣悲寂寞，華夏蕭條久沈淪。

鐵筆誰言天下事，書生我斥虎狼秦。

銅仙辭漢秋風去，白馬西風且待春。

（以上《流溪集》）

夜飛鵲　日暮過曼哈頓大橋。用彊村香港暮眺韻

　　建男兄步彊邨香港秋眺韻柬我。亂紅荒臺，丹厓燕雀，深寓感慨。日暮過曼哈頓大橋。憑闌極目，落日融金，水雲渺渺。紐約灣頭，自由女神像獨立自由島。天涯咫尺，悵觸百端。彊村飄零香海，半塘浪跡吳中，百年而後，俱作古人。皆詞人之不幸者。余自蓬轉萬里，中心耿耿。舉目遠天，中心何極。聊藉彊村之杯，澆我塊壘也。

　　灣環白雲處，津渡縈迴。心事暗映弓杯。長橋極目夕陽裡，黯然迷霧難開。西河水波裡，有亭亭阿姊，獨立層臺。高擎火炬，向人間、照徹萬萊。　　流水不分南北，山色俱明寒，咫尺天涯。俗世浮沉榮辱，風潮未定，無語低徊。別枝落葉，盼西風、再熱殘灰。問何來家國，鄉關甚處，是我從來。

　　客歲今日，余啟遠竄之旅，四日後抵思故客河畔。日昨驟冷，薪水始到。攜兩兒往村中沽歐西各國洋酒五罌。小兒為我解釋西班牙酒牌文字，小女為我付鈔翻譯。抵家，老妻笑我衣食不周，仍作酒國饕餮。余生平四友：窮、書、酒、友。唯窮最堅貞，不離不棄。自客河上，藏書散盡，舊友割席，獨村肆洋酒易得。今夏，筠珺女兄自臺北寄舊籍一篋，星鳳拱璧，可資賙飢。昨與筠珺閒話，不盡天涯知己之感。因成數韻，不知所云為何耳。

天涯已冷畏秋颸，倦鳥飛飛辭舊枝。

薪水橫流酒國去，醉鄉高臥愁城移。

兩兒爭譯鬼方字，內子笑嗔饕餮飢。

除卻平生窮字伴，硯田雖薄可耕詩。

廣南地氣早暖，嶺梅先發。從化流溪一帶，村人多藝梅為業。丁酉冬，予執教從
化山中，課餘輒入山探梅。花下路旁，時有村人兜售蜜橘、臘味、米酒、醬菜
等物。登高攬勝，流溪水庫，星島點點。山路如帶，縈迴盤曲。虹橋橫跨，連接
水涯。日昨寒夜清夢，又見流溪香雪。追憶年時梅下清賞，不勝感懷。今萬里挨
隔，又到流溪梅開時矣。
太平洋水隔芳塵，萬里清香夢比鄰。
調鼎吳鹽終勝雪，冷香滿地醉如菌。
天邊月寫暗香態，橋下波吞疏影鱗。
別後憐君誰可賞，漫山寂寞少幽人。

拉法耶特侯爵鐵炮
法蘭西拉法耶特侯爵崇尚自由，年方二十，新大陸獨立戰爭爆發，侯爵自備戰
艦，橫渡大西洋，為華盛頓羽翼。戰無不勝，所向披靡。戰後，留贈此炮與美利
堅聯邦。今藏華盛頓渡河紀念館。

他鄉殊死建奇勳
黑字斑花鑄鐵筋
百戰不關榮辱計
自由是賴重千斤

讀李炎全《康樂園》
四十一年慣飄零
人間冷暖幾曾經
來時不改書生氣
歸去康園草色青

黃龍帶楊梅

黃龍帶在從化城北五十里九連山中，盛產楊梅。初夏梅熟季節，枝頭累累，色味俱佳，土人爭以竹籃承載，沿途販售。戊戌初夏，余執教山中，課餘入山採梅，與諸生分食，其事至今為諸生樂道。

山色九連最可親
流溪逝水逐香塵
春風老去枝頭色
猶似蟾宮逐夢人

附記

　　保陽三十以後，始近聲律。抑鬱窮愁，輒發吟詠。壬辰甲午，陝南杭州，行吟所得，裒為《掃葉》、《抱月》、《天竺》諸集。乙未七月，負笈康園，時有所作，成《康園》一集。丁酉戊戌，執教從化山中，遙想嶺表東坡，詩興益發不可收拾。課餘行吟山水，常至物我兩忘，途窮輒大哭而返，遂有《流溪》一集。茲懸海外，山川舊影，時或入夢，又成《思故》一集。今夏避疫家居，康宜老師分享BBC攝製杜甫紀錄片，一時感慨，遂將諸集寄奉康州。旋得康宜師勗勉，稍加刪汰，權作續尾，並記因緣如右。庚子新大陸獨立日關中李保陽記於美東思故客河畔。時客河上，兩閱春秋矣。

後記[1]

李保陽

一

　　十年前，齊邦媛教授的《巨流河》在中國大陸甫一印行，即洛陽紙貴。我當時正服務於浙江大學圖書館，中研院的林玫儀老師向我推薦了這部書，當時我正在讀夏志清的《中國現代小說史》。這兩位同時代的學者，都在風起雲湧的時代變局下離開中國大陸，面對各種艱困環境，為華文文學在海外的研究、傳播不遺餘力。那個初冬的下午，我從杭州北郊的三墩鎮家中，趕去錢塘江南岸的杭州郵政局倉庫，領取岳母從陝南山中郵寄的乾菜。在公車中，我手握《巨流河》，抬頭遠望一片茫茫迷霧的錢塘江面，那裡是蘇軾筆下的「錢塘江上，西興浦口」。一時間，那種思接千古的惆悵與感慨，竟讓我無來由地想到齊邦媛教授筆下的啞鼻灣。夏志清小說史之所以具有穿越時空的生命力，經久不衰，我以為是他在新大陸接受的西方學術訓練有以使之。我不知道蘇軾、夏志清和齊邦媛，是以一種什麼樣的邏輯，在我腦海裡糾合成了一種對海外中國文學的意象。也許，是蘇軾在最後一位知己王朝雲死於惠州後，他登上一葉扁舟，沿西江繼續南行往荒草煙瘴的瓊崖海島，夏志清在風雨飄搖中漂洋過海遠赴新大陸，齊邦媛筆下的巨流河與啞鼻灣，以及十年前那一刻的錢塘江，都以水為圖騰，將文學與人生扭合成一個遙遠印象，載沉載浮，飄搖在我的腦海裡罷。

二

　　能夠有幸和孫老師一起編撰這本書，實在是一個完全意料之外的巧合。這個巧合，在本書孫老師的〈序言〉和附錄三中，都講得很詳細，在此不再贅述。[2]

---

[1]　本文得到孫康宜教授、國立彰化師範大學榮休教授黃文吉、東海大學林香伶教授的寶貴建議，謹此致謝。

[2]　關於本書緣起，有興趣的讀者請參看《從北山樓到潛學齋》卷末附錄拙作〈校讀後記〉，臺北秀威資

當孫老師提出要把我和她之間的通信編印出來這個設想後，我心想，孫老師怎麼和我想到一起了。我有掌故癖，幾年前在杭州和友人編印《掌故》，就是這個癖好的直接外化。後來在杭州又和友人籌編一本閒談掌故的《夜航船》，第一輯書稿已竣，惜功敗垂成。近兩年，我一直想收集海外漢學界掌故，編成小書。孫老師的這個提議，讓我可以進一步直觀地了解海外中國文學研究的歷史、現狀，且能向她請教更多的漢學界掌故。過程中，我經常會有意把話題引向她的師長輩，聽她談論這些學者們的治學和生活，比如高友工、牟復禮，以及施蟄存、沈從文、張充和、馬悅然、夏志清等孫老師的友朋故交。有時候孫老師會覺得文字表達不夠清楚明瞭時，就直接打電話向我講學界舊事。孫老師思維活躍，在學術界人緣好，當我們談到某些專業的學術問題時，她當下能就這個話題，把專門研究這方面問題的學者介紹進我們的討論之中，這樣一來，我們的討論就不再是我們兩人之間封閉的書信往來，而形成一個「書信圈」。我很喜歡孫老師用「書信圈」這個詞，來形容我們這段時間的討論。事實上，古人很早就這麼「玩」了，讀者如果留意，就會發現，李白、杜甫、蘇軾、王安石那些人，他們總是高頻率地出現在對方的筆下。李白經常引起杜甫的追思，柳宗元在貶謫途中也不忘給劉禹錫寫信噓寒問暖，在我們現代讀者的眼中，唐宋文壇的「朋友圈」似乎就是這樣子的。孫老師建構起來的這個「書信圈」，實際上也為日後的讀者，構建出屬於「我們」這個時代海外漢學研究的一個歷史想像的縮影。

①李保陽與友人在杭州編印的《掌故》（2012-2015年）
②101歲的江南文化老人柯大庸先生為李保陽編撰的《掌故》題簽（2015年）

訊科技股份有限公司2020年7月版。

　　孫老師在海外從事學術工作逾半個世紀，她不僅熟知新大陸漢學研究界掌故史事，並且她本人就是一座海外漢學研究的豐富寶庫。比如6月1日孫老師回覆我的信中，附錄了1980年沈從文先生寫給她的長信，篇幅幾近兩千字，是用毛筆寫在朱絲欄八行箋上，足足七頁，上面塗乙滿紙。可見蜚聲中國現代文學史的沈從文先生，以及他們那一代文人的風雅傳統和仔細認真。沈先生當時已經七十八歲高齡，這封信應該不是在一天之內完成的。我想他寫給孫老師的這封信，應該是老人晚年創作的長篇文字之一。在信中，他除了談及為他作傳記的金介甫（Jeffrey C. Kinkley）哈佛大學博士論文之外，還談了八十年代初的中國文學界現狀及他個人的感受。中國文學在二十世紀的後半頁，非正常地走過了數十年，即使被公認的比較開放的八十年代初，其病態仍可隱隱約約見諸沈先生的筆端。他雖然沒有流露出那時流行的「階級性」、「人民性」等時代審美術語，但言必稱國家，且時時不忘將文學創作與「國家」、「政府」等聯繫起來，這實在讓人無法把一位要在「沙灘上建築人性神廟」的理想主義作家，和這些瘦硬可笑的術語聯繫起來。從這個側面，我們也可約略窺見那個非正常時代，對文學和人性的壓抑扭曲，是達到了何等地步。沈先生的筆下，我們能看到，這位三十年代文壇的「鄉土文學」健將，雖然四九之後被貶謫到博物館的「罈罈罐罐花花朵朵」間，但他並沒有被放廢三十年的「沉淪」時光消蝕掉文學的理想。沈從文特別重視文字的簡淨，這使他的作品既有現代文學的鄉土情調，又有中國傳統文學的抒情色彩。在這封信中，沈先生一再強調文字的重要性：「得從學會掌握文字、運用文字著手。因為表現情感或思想，總離不了文字。」他特意在「學會掌握文字、運用文字著手」旁加了三角符號，以示強調。他寫給孫老師的這封信的底稿，顯然是改了又改，思忖再四後方始落墨，其中有些地方的增刪不止一次。至於有些他需要強調的地方，則加上強調符號，以示重視。所以這封信本身，就是沈從文先生一生敬重和愛惜文字的縮影。晚年的沈從文始終堅持文學的獨立審美品位，他在信中一再強調文學創作的「世界性」，這樣的眼光在八十年代初期，實在讓人肅然起敬。這位沒有被四九之後的洪流裹挾著走的「邊城獨行者」，以其「赤子之心」，在晚年的這封信中，給中國文學史，再度留下了一份真實且珍貴的紀錄。沈先生是中國現代文學史上一個相當獨特的存在，他在這封信中說，人民政府早在1953年，就將他那些「過時」的作品「全部代為焚毀」，播遷海外

的國民政府則明令他「永遠禁止在臺灣發表任何作品」。沈先生一再在信中強調他的人和作品皆已「過時」，在其他不同的語境中，他也一直以「過時」這個字眼來作為自己的敘述基調。在我看來，在沈從文的內心深處，他一方面對作品的「被過時」中心耿耿，不能釋懷，另一方面，也以此自豪。在他看來，作品被禁，嘲弄的是整個時代。沈先生在信中說到：「因為已有千百作家，都在國內已做出極大的貢獻，取得完全的偉大和成功，不僅得到國家的認可而蒙重視，即在世界上，到某一時，也將會由於得到國家的支持，作品大量的推銷，而成為『第一流大手筆』的。以後搞研究，非承認不可，因為別無什麼作品可供你研究。」在我看來，這句話皮裡陽秋，是一句充滿智慧的春秋筆法。他用這種隱晦曲折的言說措詞，來堅持其純粹的文學理想，他相信歷史會還他一個清白。有意思的是，他的作品被焚八年之後，孫老師任教的耶魯大學出版社，出版了孫老師的好友夏志清先生的《中國現代小說史》英文本。在這部文學史中，夏先生以其獨到的文學敏感與超群的學術眼光，發掘出錢鍾書、張愛玲、沈從文等一眾在四九後被邊緣化甚至「打倒」了的作家。雖然這部小說史在它問世之後半個多世紀，才出版了簡體字節本，但仍一時洛陽紙貴。早在八十年代，錢、張、沈等作品的不斷翻印，已無須證明沈從文湘西人的那份執拗和穿透歷史的眼光是否高遠。1977年，就讀哈佛大學的金介甫，以〈沈從文筆下的中國〉一文獲得博士學位，八十年代，他多次赴北京採訪沈從文，撰寫了《沈從文傳》，在中國文壇奠定了沈從文堅實不移的地位。沈先生寫給孫老師的這封長信，是他那份近乎宗教般篤誠的文學理想的表達。關於這封信還有一個故事外的故事：孫老師1982年從普林斯頓搬家到耶魯，中間丟失了一些東西，其中就包括沈先生的這封信。現在我們看到的沈先生手跡影本，實際上是這封信存在沈先生家的底稿。後來收入北嶽文藝出版社2002年出版的《沈從文全集》卷二十六[3]。但我相信，今天我們把這封信公佈出來，絕對會是現代中國文學史極為真實且重要的一份紀錄。

3　此信最初發表在《沈從文別集‧丈夫集》中（嶽麓書社1992年12月出版），發表時增加了標題〈給一個圖書館中朋友〉。《沈從文全集》據《丈夫集》收錄此信。發表的版本除全信已另行分段外，信末的「談的問題多為冷門」一句，揆諸句意，似未完結。今考底稿原文，作「談的問題多為冷門知識」，應是前面兩個整理本遺漏了這兩個字。另底稿中張兆和落款後有「和本月廿七收到紐約只差三天了」十四字，不詳所指，茲予錄出，以俟沈從文研究專家解決此一懸疑。《沈從文全集》收錄該信的資料，承蒙臺灣大學佘筠珺博士惠示，謹此致謝。

　　關於沈從文的故事在本書中還有繼續，今年5月7日，孫老師的姑姑孫毓嫻女士因感染新冠病毒病逝，去世前，孫女士曾住在馬里蘭州靠近華府的一家老人康復中心，與她比鄰而居的是一位名叫劉緣子的老太太，她曾就讀於西南聯合大學，沈從文先生是她的大一國文老師。同時，這位劉緣子老太太竟是著名文學批評家劉大白先生的女兒（見本書5月10日收錄的相關通信）。同住在華府附近的老人康復中心，因感染新冠病毒而逝的，還有旅美的華裔著名作家於梨華老人（見本書5月2日、5月8日通信）。

　　夏志清和余英時兩先生，是孫老師風誼兼師友的好朋友。我們的這個書信圈中涉及到夏先生的內容，尤以孫老師寫給蘇州大學季進教授6月27日的通信最為有趣。季進教授是研究夏志清的專家，孫老師和季教授兩人從學術研究與日常生活間兩個向度，描述出一個立體的夏志清，孫老師講述了1980年代初，夏志清和Frederick A. Pottle教授之間的一個故事："In those days I often visited Prof. Pottle's Special Collection of the Boswell papers at the Sterling Library. On one occasion Prof. Pottle told me that C.T. always treated him like an intimate old friend. Once C. T. came from New York City to visit Prof. Pottle. Before Pottle had a chance to turn around and say Hi, C.T. had already put his big hands on Pottle's shoulder, shouting " Ah, you old hunchback...."（你這個駝背的老頭子……）. And then both of them had a belly laugh right there, among the Boswell papers."這個生動的故事場景，大概可以和孫老師的那篇〈「快人」夏志清〉，同時作為這位中國現代小說研究巨擘的生活花絮來閱讀。

　　余英時先生和孫老師曾在耶魯大學有過五年的同事交集，雖然余先生後來移席普林斯頓，但是他們的交往卻一日未減，我們的書信中也十數次涉及余先生。我向來對能作近體詩的當代學人多所留意，對海外能作舊體詩者更是好感有加。有一次，我問孫老師海外能作舊詩者誰何？孫老師向我歷數海外諸家，其中余先生之名豁然在焉（見5月17日孫老師寫給我的信）。我記得以前曾經在某處看到過余先生的夫子自道，他說自己向來不甚措意為詩，其主要精力沉潛於中國學術的研究。讀了孫老師的這封信，聯想到余先生為數不少的詩作墨跡，讓我深感余先生的不甚措意為詩的自陳，借用孫老師的理論來說，只是一副「面具」，下面實際隱含著他一顆熾熱的詩心。余先生雖然主攻中國古代思想史，但他把對

現世的關懷和文學的理想，一總揉進了詩的世界。2017年春，我專注地閱讀余先生的著作，當時網上正廣泛傳播他為顏純鈎箋注的《雙照樓詩詞稿》作的長序，那時候我深深地被他深入沉潛於汪精衛的詩心所感動。八年前的春天，我也曾一度沉浸於汪氏《雙照樓詩詞稿》而不能釋卷，當時南京有一家小書店影印了陳群澤存文庫舊藏本《雙照樓詩詞稿》，我第一時間在網上訂購了一本。每每讀過，便禁不住遙想那站在日本海船頭孤獨寂寞的汪兆銘先生，身處風雨飄搖的時代劇變下，面對波濤翻滾的巨浪，慨然將其詩集首卷命名為《掃葉集》，一定是世事時勢劇變的無奈，與不能忘情於詩心的痛苦相互激蕩磨礪後所凝結之作。當現實不得不將他掃入歷史的悖逆中去時，他只能像無奈的黃葉一樣，凋落飄零於苦寒蕭瑟的詩詞世界裡去。那股力透肺肝的孤獨無奈與寂寞失落，也只有詩心方能舒緩。這種微妙的詩心，被余先生在他的長序中敏銳地捕捉到，給當時的我以強烈的閱讀震撼。余先生早就為陳寅恪先生的詩歌「發皇心曲，代下注腳」，成《陳寅恪晚年詩文釋證》一書。遺憾的是，我至今無緣拜讀此書，但今春我讀過余先生1958年寫的〈陳寅恪《論再生緣》書後〉，對余先生在此文中所持論斷，佩服得無以復加。我當時稱讚文中論及俞平伯、胡風一段為該篇之「文眼」，並在讀完全篇後，在書頁空白處草草地寫了一段後記：

> 余先生此文，真義寧先生解人也。惜同時異地，萬里暌隔，義寧不知有海外後學能揣其文心如此。六十年後再度捧讀，仍有力透紙背之感。戊戌春夏間，課餘每讀《寒柳堂集》若干頁，義寧詩中，多風雷暗驚之語。中外文人，於時勢變局之下，出處選擇，大不相同。然其反映於歷史人心，激蕩起深沉感慨，一例相同。不管借助於何種言語陳說，其悲愴色彩，絲毫不減於歷史本身之厚重。

我注意到，在余先生的詩歌世界裡，他尤對變局中的歷史人物三致慨焉。如此說來，《陳寅恪晚年詩文釋證》雖然我沒有拜讀，但作為康樂子弟，我想余先生的鄭箋，一定也是得我先聲的。由此我再進一步「大膽假設」：余先生藏在詩歌「面具」後的詩心，一定和歷史上的長吟短唱者一樣。他除了作為一個史家飲譽當世，若果有心人能深入解讀其詩心，收穫當亦不讓前者。這確是我們在通信中

談及余先生之外，讓我最感意外的一個收穫。

在我們的書信圈中，還涉及當代中國文學研究的其他話題。本書4月24日前後，選錄了一組關於哈佛大學王德威教授研究理論的通信。是由我引起這個話題，孫老師邀請了季進教授加入我們的討論，因為季進教授的研究方向和王先生比較接近，他的解釋比我直觀的印象更富學理。孫老師4月24日當天寫給我的一封長信中，詳細評價了王德威教授的學術研究特色和成就。我相信再過若干年，孫老師的這封信一定是研究海外中國文學學術史不可多得的詳實資料。5月分的時候，陳國球教授撰就一篇研究高友工先生的新作〈「美典」內外：高友工的學思之旅臆解〉（見5月12日孫老師和我的通信）。謙虛的陳教授將文章初稿給孫老師，孫老師又將之在書信圈分享開來，先後引起了多位學者的閱讀興趣。密西根大學林順夫教授更因此回憶起1970年前後，在葛思德東亞圖書館他和高友工先生父母見面的細節，以及高先生父母在葛思德圖書館辦公室拜訪牟復禮先生的往事（見5月18日林順夫致孫康宜函）。另外孫老師和林順夫先生、吳清邁先生等同時友人，或談論學界舊事，或追憶半個世紀前東海大學的往事，常常會讓人對那些遠隔時空的歷史有一種奇妙的熟悉和親近。這本通信集還有很多有意思的篇章，比如1975年在牟復禮先生家舉辦的那一席「金瓶梅大宴」、1981年在紐約大都會博物館舉行的「金瓶梅唱曲」雅集，這兩次發生在上世紀新大陸漢學界的故事，都是《金瓶梅》海外傳播史上生動的寫照。在本書中收錄了孫老師寫給我的一系列信中，有這些活動的背景介紹。尤其6月8日孫老師的來信中，竟然附有她四十五年前那次宴會後，手抄的二十二道菜譜的名單，在這個毛筆抄錄的菜單中，當時與會者給牟先生取了一個別號「樂而不淫齋主人」。透過小小的一份菜單的落款，牟先生在生活中幽默大度、不拘小節的生動形象躍然紙上。

關於陳寅恪的「恪」字的讀音，多年前曾經在中國大陸的文化圈引發過一場聲勢不小的辯論，至今軒輊兩途，莫衷一是。哈佛燕京學社的李若虹博士找出陳寅恪先生1936年發表於《Harvard Journal of Asiatic Studies》上的〈Han Yü and The T'ang Novel〉一文，署名為「Tschen Yin Koh」，則「恪」應該讀若「客」（kè）（見李若虹博士5月3日致孫康宜函）。中國人身上經常會體現出很強的鄉土文化特色，很多人的名字不協國音，而以方音為準，比如施蟄存先生晚年寫給孫老師的信封上，其名字一律拼寫為「Shi Zhicun」，我猜這應該是吳語中

「蟄」的拼法就是「Zhi」而非「Zhe」使然。另外，大部分中國人的生日都是按照舊曆而非西元紀年（見本書5月9日我與孫老師的討論）。這些林林總總的現象，是一種多元的文化存在。多年前那場關於「恪」字讀音的辯論，未得定論。今日我們繼續討論這個問題，也不必一錘定音。探究這種多元化現象本身，就是一件有趣的事情。那些定於一尊的文化學術，也未必能行之長遠。值得一提的是，我們的書信中，還有許多珍貴的照片，比如高友工先生全家1932年在瀋陽拍的全家福（見5月20日孫老師致林順夫、陳國球兩教授的信之後），1948年左右牟復禮先生在金陵大學求學期間的班級合影（6月6日孫老師給我的信之後），高友工先生1973年在普林斯頓大學授課的照片（4月6日孫老師給我的信之後），牟先生和牟夫人陳效蘭1950年在南京美國駐華領事館前的合影（5月7日孫老師寫給我的信之後），牟復禮先生夫婦畫的蘭花（見6月6日孫老師寫給我的信後），孫老師1964年在東海大學就讀期間的照片（見附錄二〈言猶未盡：且從「陽光穿透的歲月」書展說起〉），高友工先生退休前的最後一節課後與余英時先生的合影（見4月6日孫老師寫給我的信之後）、余英時先生的諸多墨跡（4月6日、5月7日等）、孫老師與夏志清先生夫婦合影（5月7日）等照片，這些老照片大多數是第一次公開發表，具有珍貴的史料和紀念意義，不言自明。

除了郵件往來之外，我們在社交平臺Line上聊天的內容比較隨意，有時候非常生活化。這次也將其中一些內容選錄進來。主要涉及一些我在校讀《孫康宜文集》簡體版書稿過程中的讀後感，此外還有一些和學術、人生有關的話題。後者有時是我有意提出聊天話題，以便引出孫老師對學界舊事的回憶，作為學術界——尤其是新大陸中國學研究界——的掌故。談這些話題的時候，我也不怕自己的幼稚和無知，因為我知道，在孫老師這樣一個年長我三十五歲的前輩面前，我的狂妄也好，膚淺也罷，都是她能夠包容的。而我則在孫老師的包容中，學習到前賢的很多寶貴的經驗。在編輯這本書的過程中，不斷涉及美國學術表達的規範，大到行文習慣，小到標點符號使用規範。這些對於初來乍到的我，無疑是一張白紙，但孫老師不棄我的老大愚鈍，手把手地教我如何學習和適應新規範。甚至推薦她的中國學生在美國訓練英文寫作的《The Holy Bible：Contemporary English Version》和《The Chicago Manual of Style》供我學習參考。孫老師的耐心，實在讓我既覺慚愧，又深感榮幸！

三

　　截止六月，美國第一波新冠病毒疫情基本結束。這波疫情已在美國導致近二百七十萬人感染，死亡十二萬多人，全國各工商業全面停擺近三個月。七月前後，疫情進入第二波，這波疫情感染人數之多，超乎所有人的想像，僅7月16日一天，全國感染人數即接近破天荒的七萬八千人。第二波疫情並未造成如第一波那麼高的死亡率，但截至今天，已經導致超過三百六十六萬人感染，死亡超過十四萬，這是新大陸乃至世界上前所未有的人類災難。每天晚上，當我在日記中記錄下當天的感染和死亡數字時，總感覺到每一個冰冷的數字背後，都是一個鮮活生命消逝的悲劇。摩西帶領以色列族人，先後經歷大大小小的災難，最後走出埃及，到了應許之地。我們渺小的人類，在上帝面前，何嘗不是九死一生的以色列族眾？我們在災難中生恐懼心，也應在恐懼中生敬畏心。有敬畏心，才能得到完全的救贖！

李保陽在教堂（RUMC），疫情期間坐席已分隔出六英呎法定社交距離（social distancing），攝於2020年7月。

　　我3月11日凌晨給孫老師寫第一封信，3月29日孫老師回我第一封信。在近四個月中，孫老師和我的通信有數百封之多，我們將本書收錄書信的截止日期選在6月30日[4]，這是美國第一波疫情大致結束，第二波疫情捲土重來之際。我們選錄的標準是，以關涉學術文化為主，同時也關注了和疫情有關的話題。書中書信大體按照每封的撰寫時間為序排列。來信中凡涉及一些個人隱私等信息，我們都做了技術處理，這種情況，我們都在相應的位置作註解加以說明。所有書信的落款日期，我們在編校初稿時，為了編稿方便，統一改作美國紀年格式。

　　全書附錄中的《抱月樓詩詞選》，是6月18日孫老師分享了BBC製作的《杜甫》電視片，影片用一個小時的時間，濃縮了杜甫顛沛流離的詩旅一生，看完後讓人心情久久不能平靜。我在回覆孫老師的信末，附上這十多年來東塗西抹的習作草稿百數十首。沒想到引起孫老師很高的閱讀興致，不時致信問訊，並建議我刪選一部分作為本書附錄。我是三十以後才漸次學詩，無人指導，全憑直覺落筆，故此一直不敢示人。今次榮幸得孫老師嘉勉，心實喜之卻又惶恐不已。惴惴不安中選錄若干首，多是近十年來樸被南北的生活紀錄，方諸中國傳統詩歌的精緻高雅，實在粗陋不堪。但詩心所在，並無虛飾。故從孫老師建議，選出二十五首附後。昔譚復堂選《篋中詞》，末附己作《復堂詞》一卷。今我亦效顰東施，還望讀者諸君不要見笑是感。

　　除了感謝孫老師提攜後進的熱忱之外，還要感謝疫情期間和我們一起書信討論的各位朋友，他們的名字都已在孫老師的序言中列出，我不在此一一贅述。但是有三個不在本書中的人，我要特別感謝，他們是我們教會的吉姆·麥金泰爾牧師（The Reverend James F. McIntire, MDiv, JD.）[5]、聯合衛理公會聖喬治紀念教堂（Historic St. George's St United Methodist Church）的馬克·薩爾瓦西翁牧師（Rev. Mark I. Salvacion）和我們教會祕書黛碧·潘特李奇（Debbie Pantelich）女

---

[4] 最後五封信是個例外。孫老師寫於7月19日，原因是信中談到普林斯頓大學六十年代中期仍然延續的研究生就餐儀式，這一儀式未久即廢除，具有紀念意義；另外一封信與本書附錄二有關；最後三封信涉及上世紀初高友工先生的一封舊函，關於臺灣清華大學和普林斯頓大學學者之間的學術交往，故破例收錄。

[5] 麥金泰爾牧師（James F. McIntire, 1959.9.21-2020.9.23））不幸於2020年9月23日病逝於費城賓夕法尼亞大學醫院。麥金泰爾家族來自愛爾蘭，他們移居新大陸已有300年歷史。他從高中時加入美國聯合衛理公會教會，大學畢業後放棄作律師的職業，專職事奉教會，並取得神學碩士學位，在衛理公會教會服事、牧會長達四十餘年，是一位和藹仁厚的牧者和長者。2020年，他曾為其女兒Lindsay出版*Lindsay's Gift*一書。我在此要特別表達對他的感激之情。希望他在天家安息！

士。他們無論是在屬靈世界，還是在現實生活中，都給我了數不清的幫助，我無法用言語來表達對他們的感激之情！

走筆至此，十年前在錢塘江上讀《巨流河》的那份感慨與惆悵，又莫名其妙地奔湧而來。載浮載沉的流水，從巨流河到啞鼻灣，到錢塘江，最後一起匯入太平洋。十年後，我站在抱月樓頭，看著思故客河水湯湯東去，流入大西洋。人往往會高估一年能做的事，卻低估十年能做的事。今日去我初讀《巨流河》，恰好十年。那時候，我萬萬沒有想到，有朝一日會和孫老師記錄一段艱困時期的海外中國文學。

截止今日，美國疫情已經得到了有效的控制。我也在今天接受了第二劑疫苗的接種。從去年至今，全美累計逾三千三百萬人感染，死亡人數接近六十萬。全球感染人數逾一點七億，死亡人數超過三百七十萬。此刻，病毒仍在全球肆虐。但疫苗已然投入使用。人們用不懈努力給了自己希望。本書因著普林斯頓的一個巧合而起，今日殺青，我特地又回到學校，雖然校園各處依然閉門謝客，但坐在葛思德圖書館樓下校畢書稿中最後一個字，仰望藍天下古老斑駁的石頭外牆，初夏季節明媚的陽光和清爽乾淨的涼風，讓人心曠神怡。這本小書在去年艱困下動議，今年希望中收束。本月孫老師從她任教三十九年的耶魯任上榮休，這本小書正好可以作為獻給她的一份禮物！

2020年7月17日傍晚關中李保陽記於美東思故客河上
2021年6月5日校定於普林斯頓大學葛思德東亞圖書館樓下

語言文學類　PG2509　秀文學41

避疫書信選：從抱月樓到潛學齋

作　　者 / 李保陽、孫康宜
責任編輯 / 許乃文
圖文排版 / 楊家齊
封面設計 / 蔡瑋筠

發 行 人 / 宋政坤
法律顧問 / 毛國樑　律師
出版發行 / 秀威資訊科技股份有限公司
　　　　　114台北市內湖區瑞光路76巷65號1樓
　　　　　電話：+886-2-2796-3638　傳真：+886-2-2796-1377
　　　　　http://www.showwe.com.tw
劃撥帳號 / 19563868　戶名：秀威資訊科技股份有限公司
　　　　　讀者服務信箱：service@showwe.com.tw
展售門市 / 國家書店（松江門市）
　　　　　104台北市中山區松江路209號1樓
　　　　　電話：+886-2-2518-0207　傳真：+886-2-2518-0778
網路訂購 / 秀威網路書店：https://store.showwe.tw
　　　　　國家網路書店：https://www.govbooks.com.tw

2021年7月　BOD一版
定價：850元
版權所有　翻印必究
本書如有缺頁、破損或裝訂錯誤，請寄回更換

國家圖書館出版品預行編目

避疫書信選：從抱月樓到潛學齋 / 李保陽, 孫康
宜著. -- 一版. -- 臺北市：秀威資訊科技股份
有限公司, 2021.07
面；　公分. -- (語言文學類；PG2509) (秀
文學；41)
BOD版
ISBN 978-986-326-903-8(平裝)

856.286   110005598

讀 者 回 函 卡

感謝您購買本書，為提升服務品質，請填妥以下資料，將讀者回函卡直接寄回或傳真本公司，收到您的寶貴意見後，我們會收藏記錄及檢討，謝謝！
如您需要了解本公司最新出版書目、購書優惠或企劃活動，歡迎您上網查詢或下載相關資料：http:// www.showwe.com.tw

您購買的書名：_____

出生日期：_____年_____月_____日

學歷：□高中 (含) 以下　　□大專　　□研究所 (含) 以上

職業：□製造業　□金融業　□資訊業　□軍警　□傳播業　□自由業
　　　□服務業　□公務員　□教職　　□學生　□家管　□其它____

購書地點：□網路書店　□實體書店　□書展　□郵購　□贈閱　□其他

您從何得知本書的消息？

　□網路書店　□實體書店　□網路搜尋　□電子報　□書訊　□雜誌

　□傳播媒體　□親友推薦　□網站推薦　□部落格　□其他_____

您對本書的評價：(請填代號　1.非常滿意　2.滿意　3.尚可　4.再改進)

　封面設計____　版面編排____　內容____　文／譯筆____　價格____

讀完書後您覺得：

　□很有收穫　□有收穫　□收穫不多　□沒收穫

對我們的建議：_____

_____

_____

_____

11466
台北市內湖區瑞光路 76 巷 65 號 1 樓
秀威資訊科技股份有限公司　　　收
BOD 數位出版事業部

┄┄

（請沿線對折寄回，謝謝！）

姓　　名：＿＿＿＿＿＿＿＿＿　年齡：＿＿＿＿　性別：□女　□男

郵遞區號：□□□□□

地　　址：＿＿＿＿＿＿＿＿＿＿＿＿＿＿＿＿＿＿＿＿＿＿＿

聯絡電話：(日) ＿＿＿＿＿＿＿＿＿＿　(夜) ＿＿＿＿＿＿＿＿＿＿

E-mail：＿＿＿＿＿＿＿＿＿＿＿＿＿＿＿＿＿＿＿＿＿